GATEWAY TO THE NOTHING

JOYCE SERRANO

GATEWAY TO THE NOTHING

Introduction

Gateway to The Nothing, book three in The Turned Gods series, takes place approximately two hundred years after the end of book two, *Immortals in the Everything*.

CHAPTER ONE

Grace always got homesick long before Ivan did. He had lived in isolation for most of his life but understood Grace had always been among people. While she needed more social stimulation, he didn't feel the urge to be with anyone except for her. He did like the few friends he had, and since they were all immortal, the time away didn't bother him much. He was, however, looking forward to savoring a fine bottle of scotch when they got home.

The first thing I want to do when we get back is to submerge myself in a long, hot bath. Grace passed the thought to Ivan.

Grace relished the idea of soaking for hours until her shell was waterlogged with shriveled fingertips and red-hot skin. The tactile sense of touch didn't exist in her energy state, and she yearned for it. Steaming hot water enveloping her skin with scents of eucalyptus and mint, a glass of rich red coating her tongue and throat, and something decadent to read was her version of having a perfect evening to herself.

The first thing? Ivan joked.

Well, the second, she replied salaciously.

Before heading back to their individual ideas of heavenly bliss, they had one last stop to make. There had been something unusual a few sectors back that they wanted another look at. They shifted within sight of a black hole that had formed on the border between The Everything and The Nothing. There was a certain peculiarity about this one that made Grace uneasy. It faced outward toward The Nothing. It took them a few seconds to notice that there appeared to be a thin stream seeping in from the border that separated The Everything from The Nothing.

As they approached the stream, they could sense it was made of molecules of matter, energy, and waves of light. Maybe the matter was only coming close to the border, curving over the event horizon, and only appeared to be coming across from The Nothing. The closer they came to the origin, the more they realized their initial thought had been correct. Particles were streaming out of The Nothing, feeding through the black hole into a lower dimension. They never imagined something like this could happen. From everything they understood about The Nothing, it should have been impossible for the membrane to be open in this way. Their perception seemed unreliable. Were they seeing what they thought they were?

Grace asked, *Is your sense of the situation the same as mine?*

If you mean the impossible particle stream coming through an impervious border? Then, yeah. We've either both become dazed or we are witnessing an unprecedented occurrence. Ivan wasn't certain they could rely on their senses when it came to The Nothing. No one knew anything about what it contained.

The event that followed made them wonder even more. A small entity came through with the stream. It was the elusive eternal child they had been seeing for centuries. The silent, empty vacuum of space burst to life with the sound of his laughter, a unique blend of a soft whisper and a resounding echo, as he joyfully chased after a small asteroid. Due to the lack of sound transmission in their environment, they could only detect auditory stimuli through telepathy. He must have seen them in the same way that they saw him. He came to an abrupt halt, and for a moment he seemed to waver, turning away from them before finally turning toward them. In his hesitation, Grace sensed uncertainty and confusion.

He appeared as a luminous swirling mist with an opaque core, the same as they did, only dimmer. With lightning speed, he dashed toward them, took an unexpected sharp turn, and squeaked out a high-pitched giggle as he resumed his pursuit of the asteroid heading toward the center of the black hole.

Ivan and Grace were taken aback, needing a moment to catch up to the event they were witnessing. A hole in the membrane, a black hole, and now the appearance of the child. Were the events related somehow?

I think that was an invitation. Grace was almost certain at this point they were experiencing some maddening disorientation. Could their proximity to The Nothing be causing it?

Ivan remained unresponsive to her assumption, pulling her into the chase. They followed the child over the event horizon, speeding deep into the anomaly of the black hole.

The surrounding space seemed to have frozen in place, and the progression of time ground down to a near standstill. Everything around them was being pulled in. They seemed to move so fast compared to their surroundings that they couldn't discern planets and asteroids from stars. The scene before them was a chaotic blur of color and light. Gravity didn't affect Grace and Ivan when they were in their risen state. They had no physical form. No mass, only energy and consciousness. All the surrounding matter became deformed, stretching and pulling into thinner, sinewy strands. The deeper they went, the more they sensed the strands surrounding them being ripped apart, stripped down to their most microscopic particles.

They focused on the child ahead, who was descending rapidly into the vortex. He was giggling as if this was the best game of tag he had ever played. The asteroid had long since broken down to dust. Should they stop? Should they follow him? Grace wondered what would happen when they got to the bottom. She felt Ivan wanting to press on. This may be their only chance to capture him, to find out what had happened to him. How had he managed to be out here alone for so long, surrounded by nothing but the vast expanse of cold, dark space? They felt compelled to follow the child.

The closer they came to the core, the slower things around them moved. They, however, remained unaffected, as if they weren't really there at all, except for the electrical sensation of passing through particles. Even light was grinding forward inch by painstaking inch into the deep abyss. Particles compressed themselves into a dense mass as they approached the core, like grains of sand under pressure at the bottom of the oceans.

The child began moving in random patterns, zigzagging back and forth. A thought occurred to Grace that he was playing. They were experiencing his emotion.

With a suddenness that matched his arrival, the child promptly disappeared, leaving behind only bewilderment. Despite their heightened senses, Grace and Ivan couldn't pick up any trace of him through the tightly compressed matter. Had he shifted or taken another direction? Grace tried to connect with the child, but she couldn't. Through the compacted opaqueness, something manifested in front of them. The tiniest aperture was at the exact center of the constriction, barely large enough for a single quark to fit through. The contents of the black hole had compressed so tightly that particles were being forced through the fissure. If they wanted to catch up to the child, they would have to go through. It was their only way to the other side. They couldn't shift to the other side, since they did not know where it led.

Do you think this is a smart idea? Grace asked.

She was typically the impulsive one and this time even she wasn't convinced they should go through. She wasn't certain if they even could go through. The anomaly hadn't affected them so far, but that didn't mean it wouldn't scatter them into oblivion if they tried to pass through.

We've come this far. May as well see what's on the other side. Ivan's thought returned to her.

As they moved forward, Grace's apprehension grew. The concept of particles on such a microscopic scale was foreign to her, making the experience entirely new. The speed at which the quarks were pushing through was akin to funneling a raging river through a keyhole. Grace wasn't claustrophobic, but even with no form, she felt compressed. Grace and Ivan squeezed through and were immediately hit with an intense, combustive sensation.

The other side was a mass of pulsating explosions. Particles were crashing together, forming combinations of elements and creating new masses, which were hurled into existence all around them at speeds that left them feeling they were the ones standing still. It took Grace a few seconds to realize the other side of the black hole was a white hole in a brand-new, blossoming universe. In this fresh-forming canvas, all they could identify was the white hole and deep ebony space. The dimensional bridge was a single quark-sized opening between the two sides. One draining, the other exploding outward.

They already understood the process of how dimensions drained and formed. Knowing was one thing, experiencing it was quite another. They felt flushed with excitement, able to appreciate why the child liked this game. Space was his amusement park. They sped up, passing through newly forming galaxies being propelled outward on their way to other places in this other universe.

Ivan noticed the child first. He had stopped to peer back at them. Negative energy waves curved their routes around him, repelled by his own negative energy. His polarization was like a magnet for positive streams, and they changed in their paths as he increased or decreased their electrons. That action must have been why Gaia and the others thought the child was seizing bits of the dimensions. He didn't seem able to prevent it. It happened because of what he was. He wasn't doing it on purpose. He couldn't control it like Nyx could. Compared to Grace and Ivan, he seemed to have very little positive energy. But they possessed enough of a balance from Ivan's creation to enable them to manipulate either type. Ivan wondered if there was a way for them to help transform the child's energy the way Ben had changed Nyx when she encased him.

Ivan experienced the child's sheer delight and his warm innocence. As he watched the child shift away, Ivan equally felt the child's underlying sadness. He emanated a yearning to stay and play with them, but something unseen was pulling him away. Ivan noticed the child's apprehension and concluded he was hoping for their help. There was no doubt he had captured their attention.

Unable to follow his shift, they changed their focus. Realizing the importance of the fracture in The Nothing's membrane, they doubled back to the border to examine it. They did not take the path back through the white and black holes, opting to shift instead.

It was a bizarre sight. The fracture in the dividing border between The Everything and The Nothing wasn't a fracture at all. It had a flawless, spherical shape, as if someone had taken a puncture and blown it up to the size of a small shuttle. Grace wondered if the matter that was pouring through was what had disintegrated back into Chaos from The Everything, or if The Nothing had never been empty at all. If it had been desolate at the beginning, how could The Everything have emerged from it?

We need to go in, Grace said.

Her statement disturbed Ivan. *I don't think that's a good idea at all.*

Someone has to. We may be the only ones who could survive The Nothing.

Ivan considered her statement. *Surviving isn't the only goal. We need to learn about it. Nyx and Ben would have a better chance of entering without disrupting anything. They're neutral when they rise together. We're not.*

Grace couldn't resist her curiosity and pulled him closer to the edge.

Grace. His tone was a warning. This was by far the dumbest idea she had ever conceived. *NO!*

Fine! We won't go in. Can we at least move a little closer? I mean, everything is streaming out. And it's not like we can get dragged in. Even the black hole couldn't drag us in.

Grace couldn't explain why she felt more comfortable with the idea of passing through this barrier than she had been with the black hole. An inexplicable force was luring her in, beckoning her forward. A powerful urge surged within her, persuading her to break away from Ivan and bolt through the opening. If she had been in her physical form, she knew she would have succumbed to the temptation and Ivan wouldn't have been able to stop her.

Ivan was open to compromising, but only to a limited extent. He could feel her urge, her need, but he couldn't let her go headlong into an unknown chasm. *If you try to take us inside, I am splitting off from you.*

That's the meanest thing you've ever said to me! She had had the idea herself, but hearing the words from him hurt her. What could be so frightening that he would leave her behind without a second thought?

This is the worst idea you've ever had! I mean it, Grace. Do NOT try to drag us in.

I know you're scared, Ivan, so am—

He cut her off. *Don't try that BS line with me. I know you better than you know yourself.*

Fine. She pouted. *Two hundred yards then.*

Two hundred yards closer or two hundred yards from the edge? He wasn't about to let her get away with anything at this point. He tapped into her thoughts, unsure of what was captivating her into such a reckless act, and grew anxious that it might be a trap.

She sighed. *Two hundred yards closer.*

Not that I don't trust you with my life, but I want full control. Relinquish it, Ivan demanded, feeling her anxiety increase.

Sometimes I wonder what happened to your sense of adventure.

Sometimes I wonder what happened to your sense.

Ouch! That hurts. Deeply. Her tone feigned profound injury. She had no argument she could win here. Deep down, she knew he was right. She needed to let him hold her back. She acquiesced and transferred power to him, handing over full control, including her ability to break off. It was almost a relief knowing she couldn't give in to her urge.

Thank you.

Ivan moved them forward with a significant amount of caution. They didn't feel any difference in the material coming out of the puncture at this close distance. It was identical to what was present in The Everything. Perplexity consumed Ivan, leaving him at a loss for words. It prompted so many questions in his mind.

They made a wide circle around the perimeter of the hole. Nothing changed. Nothing felt altered. The material comprised a nearly balanced mixture, equivalent to every other dimension they had visited. Several hours had passed from what they could estimate.

They went forward in time a little and backward a little, always returning to the exact moment they had left. They witnessed the child come through the barrier into The Everything, watched him look at them in their current, time-altered position, then saw him turn to look in the other direction where they had been when they first encountered him. It was odd they didn't see themselves when the child clearly could. Could that have been why he had paused? Was the sensation of having them simultaneously on either side of him the thing that gave him so much delight before he chased after the asteroid? Did they themselves look in his direction because they sensed their own energy? They had no memory of detecting any energy, aside from the child's. Ivan's mind had wandered. Those were altogether different questions and not ones that were likely to be answered soon, if at all.

I think we should head home. Brighter minds than ours need to work this out.

I agree. We may possess unique skills, but analyzing the physics of deep space isn't one of them. Grace knew full well she was out of her depth.

As Ivan pulled her away from the opening, Grace felt a pang of longing to stay behind. The pull she felt gradually diminished when their distance from the anomaly increased.

CHAPTER TWO

The child had been toying with them for well over a century, popping up here and there long enough to be seen, but never long enough for them to get close to him. Grace and Ivan were still as puzzled by him as they had been the day they first learned about him. Today had been their first significant interaction, and it had produced more questions than answers.

Chaos was the sole individual capable of furnishing them with explanations, yet she appeared to be avoiding them. It would be so much easier if they could receive some guidance from her. They had gone to her conscious space many times. Ivan especially enjoyed spending time with the children she protected in that place. They had become surrogates for the ones he and Grace didn't have. Each visit was brief, so as not to give in to the temptation of staying forever. They could only remain for a day at most.

Within the space Chaos had created, everyone had physical form. Grace's and Ivan's bodies were obviously virtual, but having physical form allowed them to interact and play with the children. The fields came alive with the sound of the children's little hearts racing as they squealed and ran with excitement, filling the air with joy. They would pick sweet-scented bouquets of wild flowers to place throughout the bright farmhouse. Grace and Ivan could hug them and tuck little ones off to sleep before returning home. If only they could bring the children safely back to Rasa, they could be quite content. The children could grow up and have lives of their own instead of being trapped as children for eternity. For now, Ivan and Grace cherished the moments they could steal with them.

Grace and Ivan returned from their latest adventure in The Everything to their shells. Since they had realized their purpose, Grace and Ivan had dedicated most of their time to it, working hard to establish balance. When they woke, only Leo was there to greet them. Their bodies ached as they came out of stasis, although not as much as they had in the past.

"How long this time?" Grace asked.

"Seventy-four days," Leo said.

"Rasan or Universal?" Ivan asked.

"Universal."

That was two days shy of six months in Rasan time. Leo cast a disapproving glance in their direction. "How are the shells?"

Grace twisted her back and cracked her neck. Her fingers brushed over the warm skin on her face, noting the dryness of it. "Not bad. We're recovering quicker this time. Did you do something different with them?"

"I increased the stimulation levels for the muscles. The organs and other tissues maintain themselves at this level of stasis. Sadie keeps the brain functions stimulated. You've both learned how the water reclamation system works this time." Leo smiled at them before continuing.

"I'm working on something to manipulate the joints inside the pods. Full stasis would be best since partial stasis doesn't work long term with your shells like it does with other turned. It suppresses some of your natural healing functions the same way it slows your hair and nail growth.

I'm just not quite certain you could come out of full stasis on your own if no one was here when you returned."

"Can't you program Sadie to bring us out when she senses us coming back through?" Ivan asked.

"What if something happens to Sadie while you're up there?" Leo asked, pointing up.

"What if something happens to you while we're up there? You can't save everyone all the time, Leo." Ivan gestured toward the ceiling, mocking him cheerfully.

Leo smirked, shaking his head at him. "Bringing someone out of full stasis is a complex process. Unlike a biological process like turning, which only involves accelerating the natural state, it requires more skill and presents greater challenges. Losing one of you would be far worse than some unknown person dying from a botched turn."

"All loss is painful, Leo, even if we don't know the individual personally," Ivan said.

"I didn't mean it like that." Leo realized the statement sounded callous regarding the loss of any life. He stroked his chin. "I could program the pods to come out of stasis if they lose contact with Sadie. I guess if you can't rouse them up, you can always rise again."

"True. And we can always get to the ones in cryo-freeze if we need to. It'll require a few additional hours, but they're already set up to thaw when activity is detected." Ivan shrugged like it was no big deal. He was taunting Leo just a little. He had a reason to be in a good mood. Despite their inability to communicate with the child, he felt optimistic about the day, thanks to the brief moments of interaction they had.

"That's supposed to be more of a fail-safe than an option. The shells are in full cryo, anyway. It's a radically unique process. It's more like bringing a newborn into the world than bringing someone back from the dead." Leo shook his head at Ivan.

Frigg had developed new shells for them a few decades ago and placed them in cryo-pods inside an asteroid in the newest dimension. Only Ivan and Grace could locate them because of the manner in which they were cloaked and blocked. Using a device combining the two techniques, one of

Sadie's developers, Harmon, had come up with a method to align the rock so it would repel passing space debris and be undetectable by other vessels. In the event of any damage to their present shells, they would be attracted to the new ones. In the last centuries, their community had developed an abundance of new technologies.

"We bring people back from the dead all the time," Ivan said, flashing him a broad grin. He thought Leo could be far too serious sometimes.

Leo massaged his temples in frustration. It was like explaining fire to a Dryopithecus.

"Stop provoking him, Ivan," Grace intervened, grasping Ivan's rough hand. She made a mental note to ask Leo to add a bit of moisture to the air inside the sealed pods.

"See you at the briefing tonight, Leo. We have some news." Ivan smirked, not waiting for Leo's questions, and shifted himself and Grace back to their apartment.

Leo was in awe of Grace and Ivan's remarkable talent for returning to their surroundings as if they had never left, even after long periods of absence. They slipped back in effortlessly, as though they had only been gone for a few hours instead of several months. He envied that about them. They always had each other and didn't need anyone else. Coming back remained a choice for the pair, not a necessity. Seeing that kind of ease had been part of what made taking the turn a simple choice for Leo. The possibility of finding a connection like that was too alluring to pass up.

He had a family eons ago, but his children had grown and made families of their own. Throughout most of his life, adventures in The Everything had occupied a vast majority of his time. It was no surprise to anyone that his wife abandoned him. Least of all to him. She wasn't the adventurous type, never once choosing to come along with him, although he often begged her to.

His work was the only thing remaining when he made his final decision to turn. He was glad he had done it. The connection to the community was something he hadn't possessed in his life before. It was something he hadn't recognized he missed. He belonged here. He didn't need to seek adventures anymore. Adventures made their way to him.

"Sadie, inform all Rasans of Grace and Ivan's safe return," Leo spoke into the empty room.

~~~~

While Viv and Galin were in the terraforming lab, engrossed in a deep discussion on the intricate details of preparing Rasa's second moon, Betis, for habitation, Sadie's holographic form appeared. "Grace and Ivan have descended."

Viv and Galin had already felt them come through. The unturned on the planet couldn't feel them, so they set Sadie to notify everyone as a courtesy, so no one felt excluded.

"That couldn't have been better timing." Viv winked at Galin, extending her hand toward the hologram.

"Thank you, Sadie," Galin replied as the image disappeared. He turned back to Viv. "I guess that means we can get started in the next few days."

Viv nodded as they returned to complete their notes for the briefing.

Betis was large for a moon, with a mass about a third the size of Rasa itself. Rasa had grown to hold a dense population without becoming overcrowded, with hundreds of cities scattered throughout the planet's central, climate-controlled band. Their goal was to keep it that way. The planet was the hub of the community, with a massive social club and cultural center hosting hundreds of events throughout the year. After Grace had stepped down, the community elected Galin as the new Administrator, and his primary goal was to ensure adequate living conditions and resources were available to everyone. The administration had also considered floating a few cities in the lower atmosphere but decided against it. Given the proximity of various choices for expansion, there was no justification for
~~~~

overcrowding one planet. The moon was also close enough to be included in their current defense array, as well as being a logical choice for the first extension of their home world.

Betis would be a full form effort. It had reduced atmosphere and gravity, but what made it most attractive was it had plenty of liquid water. They would need to speed up the rotation to match Rasa's gravity and calendar. Grace and Ivan could complete that segment with little effort, allowing the forming team to take care of the rest of the arduous tasks. They were conservatively estimating having the first five cities complete within four months. Effects on Rasa would be minimal since they artificially controlled the weather along the most habitable band of the planet. The primary effect would be that the tidal flows would change, but even that would remain manageable.

~~~~

Meanwhile, Ben sat in his office above the Council chambers, reviewing yet another dispute over who possessed rights to an inhabited planet. He hated this part of his job with the Council, constantly quelling one ego or another. He knew they had assigned him this task because other Council members were unwilling to risk their political standing by making the wrong person angry. There were uncountable habitable planets and moons throughout The Everything. Yet, as always, these pompous narcissists would rather bicker over one planet than seek another. Compromise was outside the vocabulary of these unenlightened, self-proclaimed gods. Looking back, he found it difficult to fathom he had once been exactly like them. They had an inane habit of seeking conflict, frequently going out of their way to create it where it hadn't already existed.

As Ben stared at his data screen, he could see neither party had claim to the world. A lower-level mortal species inhabited the planet. Neither
~~~~

pantheon staking a claim represented the predominant religion practiced by the people of the disputed planet. Most of the populace was agnostic, worshiping no specific gods. Many appeared to covet nature as their higher power, which gave Gaia rightful claim. Ben denied both claims and tossed his screen on his desk. Their pettiness as they vied to improve their positions on the Council irritated him. The sole focus of both leaderships was to acquire power and control, with no consideration for other factors.

Council meetings had become almost intolerable for him. The disdain Ben smelled oozing from the others was suffocating. The turned were decimating the Council's constraint of The Everything. In response, Council members were becoming desperate. They had resorted to unscrupulous measures, including utilizing methods that were haphazard and unreliable, in their desperate attempt to regain control. Ben had always been wary of their intentions. Now he could see they were close to becoming dangerous to themselves and mortals throughout The Everything.

Ben pulled his vibrating TAC from his pocket. It had received an upgrade a few days prior. The new systems worked on telepathic waves. Sadie, their species' artificial intelligence, read the user's intentions or questions and allowed them appropriate access depending on the user level. He wanted to check the source of the notification from Rasa. Sadie recognized what the most significant news would be for him.

Greetings, Ben. Grace and Ivan have descended. There will be a briefing in one hour. Shall I respond with your intention to attend? Her communication had been inaudible to anyone except him.

"Affirmative, Sadie. That will be all." Ben voiced his reply, folded his TAC, and returned it to his pocket.

He leaned back in his chair, breathing a deep sigh of relief. The news of their return had made his outlook somewhat brighter. It also provided him with a reason to leave.

CHAPTER THREE

Grace and Ivan shifted into The Six. There had been a few minor changes over time and one major recent addition to the command headquarters since they had been away on this last undertaking. An enormous display of the dimension stack hung overhead. Each dimension showed every planet, space station, and ship containing turned members, who were identified with a dot. Every individual in the community had their own dot representation. Thoth had altered the device they had first seen in their cabin so long ago, on a grand scale.

As they were looking up at the display, Viv was the first to approach them. She gave them each a hug. Physical contact was essential for the turned. Their bond almost demanded it. Before Grace and Ivan had merged, Viv would have never hugged a stranger and had seldom displayed any emotion with those outside of her family. Now, she needed contact almost as much as she required the blood that flowed through her veins. They all did. The original community had always been closely bonded, but Ivan and Grace's merge had created something deeper, reverberating through the entire species. Something that spread their connection outside the clans to knit them all into the same fabric.

"You like it?" Viv asked, pointing toward the ceiling. "The display screens were becoming so cluttered. We had to do something. I think Thoth outdid himself on this one."

"It's amazing." Grace unconsciously touched her chest as she inspected it, brushing her fingers over the ghost of the amulet that had once held a position there.

"Isn't it cumbersome looking up at it all the time? When you need to use it, that is." Ivan considered it a curious place for the stack to be displayed. It was a proficient use of space, but how did they present it when they required it for a briefing?

A smile played across Viv's lips. "That's only where we store it. We can examine any portion on the table or pull it down in front of any space in The Six. Alerts display on the screens." She paused, pointing to the wall of screens at the head of the conference table. "We can drill all the way down into a specific individual if we want to. There's another one in the grand hall, minus the individual markers. We simply couldn't keep something as magnificent as this to ourselves."

Grace squinted upward, twisting her mouth as if she had a question she couldn't form. Viv answered before she could ask.

"How do we do it since almost no one wears the uniforms anymore? Well, except for Ben and Vaeweth. They apparently sleep in theirs." Viv's tone was chiding with a hint of snideness.

"Yeah. I thought they tied the display markers to the uniform, not the person," Ivan added.

"Sadie possesses all of their genetic codes. We don't receive much information if they're not wearing a uniform or one of the new adornments, but we get their basic location information." Viv extended her right hand, displaying a silver band.

"And that little ring displays everything the uniform did?" Grace asked.

"This little ring is the uniform." Viv tapped it twice. The ring opened, spreading over her entire body, covering her in a modernized uniform including the headpiece and visor.

Surprised by the movement, Ivan pulled back. "That's slick. Everyone get one of those?"

Viv tapped the uniform off. "Security units, so they're protected when they are off duty. Leadership officials, species liaisons, blah blah blah. Pretty much anyone else who may have a need and asks for one. And Ma'at is the only unturned we've issued one to. Wouldn't want to leave her unprotected behind enemy lines. Hers doesn't include all the bells and whistles, though. She won't be capable of fully controlling all the features until she takes the turn. It's got enough to keep her safe until Ben can get to her if he needs to."

"I am amazed they haven't discovered her duplicity," Grace said.

"After they demanded we release her, she couldn't exactly tell them she had only been there to spy on them, could she? Our truce was too precarious. Besides, she's privy to a lot of information that Ben isn't, with them as suspicious of him as we are of Kali and Ares," Viv answered.

"She's definitely going above and beyond. I'll just be glad when she can come home for good, and I'm sure Thoth will."

"She gets to come back occasionally, and she meets Thoth off-world from time to time."

"I couldn't imagine being away from Ivan for that long."

Viv chuckled. "I'm sure a century isn't the longest they've been apart."

"Being as stubborn as she is, probably not," Grace said, agreeing by shaking her head.

Ivan stroked his chin, scrutinizing the display, deep in thought and oblivious to Grace and Viv's conversation. "You said adornments. They're not all rings?"

Viv glanced back at Grace before answering him. "No. We can package the uniform into just about any piece of jewelry. Anything that looks like metal, really. Rings, necklaces, bracelets, piercings, subdermal implants. We even have one placed in a tooth implant. We leave it up to the individual."

"Tooth implant? How do they eat?" Ivan grimaced.

"Oh, that one uses telepathic activation only. The manual sensor is inactive," Viv said, shuddering and outstretching her hand in front of her, curling her lip as if she were attempting to push the vision away. The thought of a uniform growing out of someone's mouth was sickening to her. Especially knowing it had to go back in after it was used. She could only hope that individual had access to a clean one, or at least a sanitizer, before returning it to its inactive state.

"That sounds disgusting." Grace nearly gagged at the thought.

Ivan glanced around the room, determined to push the conversation in a new direction. He landed on a few unfamiliar faces among them before he caught sight of Thoth.

"Is Ma'at able to join us tonight?"

Viv looked over at Thoth with a forlorn expression. Then she sneered as she inclined her head in Kali's direction. "No. She can't as long as the treaty dictates they're still allowed to be here for our briefings."

Ma'at had returned to her seat on the Council, never revealing her allegiance to the turned. Osiris, discovering her duplicity early on, had maintained her confidence, and they discussed taking the turn themselves in private. She knew the direction the Council had taken unsettled him, but she also knew to keep a healthy suspicion of everyone around her. Ma'at had set a time limit for herself of two centuries after she had returned to the Council. By that time, she thought either the issue with the child would be resolved or the Council would be obsolete, relegated as a relic of the past.

Thoth had pledged to wait for her so they could take the turn together. Despite the difficulty of being apart, they found creative ways to connect and spend time with each other. Every fiber of his being yearned for the turn, making his desperation palpable. He longed to experience the connection the turned had with each other. The community did everything they could to make him feel accepted. Often, he still felt isolated living among them on Rasa. There was just something missing he couldn't quite grasp, like he had walked into a room and missed the first half of a joke. Briefings had become difficult. He didn't attend them often anymore since Jack had taken over R&D. The connection was considerably deeper when

Grace and Ivan were around, making him feel much more uncomfortable. Today he was sticking close to Frigg. Aside from Kali and Ares, she was the only other unturned in the room, and he certainly wasn't inclined to hang around with the other two.

With the brief delayed by half an hour, people mingled and engaged in small talk. The research team was finishing final assessments on Betis, and the project had run over the expected time. They had placed Ty Lawrence in charge of the terraforming project. His background in archeology had allowed him to extend with little difficulty into ecological sciences. Well, that and half a century of nonstop education accompanied by a lifetime of strict organizational acuity. He had assembled an excellent team from several newly turned species adept at terraforming other planets.

Galin and his assistant entered the room, joining Viv, Grace, and Ivan. Galin leaned in, giving Grace a hug.

"Good to see you back safe." He kissed her on the cheek before moving to Ivan.

Galin gripped Ivan's hand in a maneuver closer to arm wrestling than a handshake. Ivan leaned in with a brotherly hug as they slapped each other on the back with their free hands. This had become the conventional greeting for their species, although the more traditional style of hugging was still a common sight in public between close friends and family. Galin and Ivan had been closer in their original timeline. Since Galin didn't remember they had been friends, Ivan didn't take it as a personal affront that Galin hadn't given him a hug as he had with Grace.

"Grace, Ivan, this is my new assistant, Finna. She's from Etheria."

Finna was a svelte, graceful creature. She was a little shorter than Grace, with a slim torso and long legs. Her skin was pale blue with a metallic sheen. Her striking appearance caught everyone's attention, from her deep blue lips to her large, mesmerizing silver-blue eyes and cascading pale pink hair that faded to white at the tips. Illuminated beads were woven into an intricate pattern on the back of her head, allowing the remainder of her hair to flow in loose waves down her back. She was quite becoming, leaving Grace to feel like a troll in comparison. Even her scent was perfection, giving off hints of lilac, vanilla, and the slightest tinge of ginger.

Viv lowered her head, passing Grace a thought while concealing a smile. *She makes us all feel like that. The worst part is she's just as gorgeous on the inside. Sweet, compassionate, absolutely the most perfect thing you would ever wish for.*

Great, Grace passed back sarcastically.

Don't worry, she only has eyes for Lukkas. Viv gave Grace an empathetic glance.

Oh. That makes it better. My ex, who doesn't remember he's my ex, and his perfect new girlfriend. That's every girl's dream. Grace's tone was again sarcastic, with an uncharacteristically harsh edge to it.

Well, I guess it won't improve your mood if I tell you she's his mate, then?

Grace's eyes grew enormous, locking with Viv's. She grabbed Viv subtly by the arm, stepping back ever so slightly.

"I apologize for being rude. It was lovely to meet you, Finna. I need to speak with Viv for a moment before the brief starts. Please excuse us." Grace didn't wait for a response. She shifted Viv to the SCIF, slamming the button to seal the room so no one could see or hear them.

"WHAT?!" Grace exclaimed with an unexpected wave of jealousy.

Viv squirmed, dropping into a chair.

"Come on, Grace. Whether he knew it or not, he compared everyone he met to you. You've got to admit, she's freaking perfect. Aren't you at least a little happy for him?"

"Yes," Grace said with a groan. She exhaled deeply with disappointment at her reaction. "Of course I am." She plopped down into the chair next to Viv. "It was just so … unexpected. It shocked me a little, I guess."

"Shocked you? Or made you jealous? Don't lie to me either. You know I felt it."

"Shut up, Viv."

"To be fair, we were all a little shocked. It happened over a very brief span of time."

"I can see how he could be attracted to her," Grace said.

"She *is* Etherian."

That statement perplexed Grace. "What do you mean by that?"

"Well, Etherians are, I don't know … ethereal?"

Grace shook her head. "I still don't know what you're saying."

"The species is hypnotic. They take every desirable thing you ever wished you were and reflect it back at you. They're beautiful, kind, compassionate, considerate, and they create a serene, calming atmosphere wherever they go. Being around them is like being on the best high of your life without the coming down part. She makes Galin a much less uptight person. And our sex life …"

Grace cut her off, waving her hands. "Okay. I get it. She's phenomenal to have around. How many of them do we have in the community?"

"A couple thousand. Mikkel and Lilly employ most of them in the social clubs. It's like having magical calming entrancements for everyone. They no longer have disputes from unturned jerks at the clubs anymore. And they're making bank from the expanded business."

"Really?"

"Yup. The credit pool has never been so unimaginably huge. Lukkas is happy. Mikkel and Lilly are set, and Ben has even taken on two Etherians for his Council scribes. We're fortunate to have them. They've made an enormous impact on the entire community. We're much less restless having them around when you and Ivan aren't here."

"*Ben* feels their effects?" Grace thought Ben was immune to any external emotional stimulus.

"Not like everyone else. You know, he's different. But they enchant everyone on the Council when they come to his offices. It makes his life a little more tolerable when he's over there."

"And they don't mind menial tasks like that?" Grace wondered if they were happy about their choice to join the community.

"Not at all. Their emotional intelligence is remarkably high, even though not all of them have conventional intelligence like Finna. Mostly, they're content with spreading peace and calmness. A lot of them have become educators, too. They believe the purpose of their existence is to establish emotional stability. Even their unturned population likes to interact with us. I think they can feel our connection and urge to serve each other." Viv splayed her hands toward Grace.

"We need to make sure we protect them from outsiders, so they're not taken advantage of."

"Oh, we do. Especially the ones who work in the clubs. We're fiercely protective of them. Mikkel has set extremely stringent policies in the clubs regarding their interactions. They are discouraged from engaging in any type of intimate work. And if they do consent to physical comfort with any patrons, a Jur member supervises their interactions, since they are the only ones who have consistently been capable of blocking the Etherians' emotional effects for short periods. And Mikkel. Mikkel has, for some inexplicable reason, exhibited the capability to obstruct their effects entirely. Leo has been vainly trying to investigate that."

Grace thought about the last part. "We know Ivan and I don't affect Ben in the same way as the others, so I understand how that might be possible for Mikkel. And he rose when he was turned, so he's different from Alex and Erik already. Maybe he inherited it from Ben?"

Viv was stunned. "Mikkel rose when he was turned? Are you sure he didn't just flee? It doesn't seem possible for anyone to rise during a turn."

"Erik said he rose. Ami had to catch him, and she said it was difficult pushing him back into his shell. I don't know if he can't do it again or if it unnerved him and he hasn't tried, but he rose when he turned and his unessenced shell nearly killed Lilly."

"Well, that's something we should report to Leo. It may alter the direction of his research."

"It could, but I don't see how he couldn't know it happened. The entire event was pretty dramatic. Don't you remember when Lilly snapped at Ben during that briefing?"

"I think I was pretty angry with Ben at that point in time myself. That briefing was so long ago, I can't say I remember anything from it."

Grace performed a mental check-in with Ivan, feeling his irritation with her. "We should probably get back in there."

"Agreed," Viv said. "But don't make an ass of yourself when Lukkas shows up."

"I promise," Grace said, wondering if she hadn't already made an ass of herself. The initial shock had worn off, and she hoped Finna hadn't noticed her reaction.

Grace took the SCIF out of private mode, allowing them to walk out into the group.

You okay? Ivan asked. Grace's response to the news about Lukkas did not surprise him. It had, however, affected him more than he liked.

Grace raised her eyes timidly. *I'm sorry about that. I didn't think it would bother me as much as it did. We've been together for so long, I don't have any right to feel that way. I'm especially sorry it hurt you.*

Ivan wouldn't deny it had wounded him. She would know he was lying if he did. He squeezed her hand, averting his eyes from her.

I know you are. I remember you had to rip your own mind open to avoid facing losing him when it happened. You're entitled to your feelings. I also know it doesn't take away from what you feel for me.

She squeezed his hand back, lowering her head so no one would detect her contemplative expression. *No, it doesn't.*

Ivan straightened his posture, releasing her hand. He saw Ben come through the doorway and head toward the bar. His appearance was a welcome distraction. Ivan jiggled his empty glass, holding it in the air for all to see.

"I believe I'm in need of a refill. Excuse me." He walked toward Ben, leaving Galin, Viv, Finna, and Grace to languish in an awkwardness he didn't want to engage in. If he and Ben could become friends after everything they had gone through, certainly Grace and Finna could at the very least figure out how to be cordial. He rethought that last sentence. Grace could figure out how to be cordial since neither Finna nor Lukkas knew the depths of his original relationship with Grace.

Ivan slapped Ben on the back. "You can't imagine how glad I am to see you right now."

Ben turned, peering over Ivan's shoulder, and grimaced. "Yeah. I'm gonna say I do. Refill?" Ben held up the scotch bottle he had used to replenish his own glass.

Ivan held out his glass, which Ben filled four fingers deep. Ivan slugged it back, then presented the glass for a second fill. Ben did the same before refilling both.

"Add a splash of water. I want to sip this one," Ivan said.

"Water? Why?" Ben was curious.

"Just do it. You'll see."

Ben splashed a few drops of water into his and Ivan's drinks. He took a sip. "Wow. I wondered how it always seemed to taste better when you were here."

"I add a little when I decant it from the cask. Makes a world of difference as long as it's only a splash. Opens up the flavors."

"You could have shared that info years ago."

"I could have." Ivan grinned with a mischievous glint in his eye.

Ivan surveyed the area as he spoke with Ben. Alex and Erik were on the other side of the room with Paneth, who had taken Mikkel's command spot after he had left the service. Vaeweth was also with the brothers, along with a few others Ivan didn't recognize, of which two were Jur and another appeared to have flattened gills on the sides of their nose. Throughout The Everything, most intelligent life seemed to be organized according to a bilateral template, with only a few superficial differences to distinguish them. The number of extremities could vary, but the colors and thicknesses of the skin, eyes, hair, et cetera were more similar than not. More importantly, they all had a highly evolved, independent sentience attached to their genetic forms. For the first time, Ivan fully realized how incredibly diverse their community had become.

CHAPTER FOUR

The briefing had many moving parts to it these days. With Sadie keeping the population informed, fewer briefings were necessary. The entire administration only met once each universal year. Briefings like today's happened quarterly. The gatherings were mainly a formality to introduce new species' representatives and make sure each department had properly disclosed its activities. Even with the advances in transportation for the turned, particularly with porting, some representatives attended by holographic projection.

In order to accommodate thirty-six seats, they had enlarged the briefing table as the community had expanded. In front of the screens, they had built an elevated row where six representatives attended by projection, filling the meeting space.

Grace was pleased to see that Lilly had slipped in at some point. She assumed Mikkel would not be attending, since normally one of them would be tending to business. Leo had entered the room without attracting attention, and Nyx had come in soon after Ben's arrival. Morgud and Violet sat together near the center of the table across from Jack and Thoth. Galin stood, bringing the meeting to order before yielding the floor to Ty.

"Grace, Ivan, it's splendid to have you back," Ty said, nodding toward the head of the table.

Grace and Ivan returned the gesture.

"I apologize for the delay this evening. While we were performing the final determination of Betis, we discovered a multi-celled life form deep in an underground ocean. We have removed, secured, and placed them in stasis so that we may return them to their habitat once the terraforming is complete."

Galin drew attention to himself by asking a question. "Are they compatible with the ocean life we will introduce once the terraforming has finished?"

"Yes. They are a species we already have here on Rasa. They will thrive in the new ecosystem we are introducing."

"Do we expect any additional complications with the process?" Thoth asked.

"No. Everything else was as expected," Ty answered.

"Thank you, Ty. You may continue," Galin said.

Ty explained the process and timeline for the project, including a request for Grace and Ivan to speed up the moon's rotation. He assured them he had already done all the calculations. Grace was relieved she wouldn't be required to do any math in order to complete the procedure.

Each representative took turns providing updates on their sector's activities and requirements for support. Leo briefed them on the turned populations and species requesting to be added to the community. Jack provided updates on new technologies being implemented, including the issuing of adornments and completion of the dispersal of new uniforms.

Violet had taken over as the head of the committee for Grace's education plan. She presented the updated status of the educational and socialization goals for pure-born children. With the growth of the turned population, there was an increase in the number of children born to the turned. Programs ensured that the existing children of recently turned parents could make an informed decision about taking the turn, as their parents had, when they reached the age of consent.

Grace's attention peaked, and she felt a flush of pride at what Violet had accomplished regarding the program. She leaned forward, enthralled by the way the systems had developed.

In the first few years the plan was formulated, families were provided with tutors or monitored self-education programs, giving a choice to the individual families based on their personal needs. Once the child reached an age that would benefit from socialization, they attended sector-specific facilities. They could either port to the schools each day or board at the schools if the parents were in situations that didn't allow for daily porting. A few families had requested remote learning by holographic projection. This was the least desirable option, as schools were also a child's first experience with group interactions with peers. The education criteria covered culture-specific topics as well as basic common languages, math, science, and the arts. If a child excelled in an area, the education system provided them with advanced education tailored to each individual.

Once Violet's presentation was over, Grace's attention waned as each subsequent speaker droned on. Her fingers played with loose tendrils of her hair, sending an obvious message to anyone who knew her that she had lost all interest. She and Ivan had absorbed the information from Sadie when they came back through. Her thoughts had wandered for quite a while before they landed back on something Ivan had said to Leo that morning. She felt a sense of unease, as if something important was missing, but she couldn't quite put her finger on it. It had been gnawing at her since then.

Ow! What was that for? Grace winced as the sting from Ivan kicking her under the table shot through her shin.

Ivan continued, addressing the assembly seamlessly. "It was a short encounter. It made us think he was seeking our attention."

"And he didn't appear malevolent at all?" Nyx studied Grace and Ivan with a suspicious eye.

"It felt like he was playing. Not toying with us." Grace shook her head rapidly. "Trying to get us to play with him. Or follow him. Or something like that." The corners of her mouth turned down, and she squinted when her own thoughts perplexed her.

Ivan displayed a slight scowl in response to her lack of confidence. "No. He seemed like a child. The interesting part was where he came through. It was an opening in the border," Ivan said, pausing for gasps and whispers to cease. "And more interesting was what was coming through with him."

"What was coming through with him?" Thoth perked up, finally interested in something fascinating happening in the room.

"Elements, light, energy waves. Exactly like what we have on this side of the border. Negative and positive energy, particles, masses, all of it," Ivan answered.

"We should launch a sensor array immediately," Thoth said with an eager edge to his voice.

"I agree. We need to learn as much as we can while we have the chance. The opening seems stable for the moment, but if it grows, we may need to figure out a way to seal it up. We don't understand what will happen if there is no barrier between The Everything and The Nothing," Ivan stated pragmatically.

Jack was fervently shaking his head, whispering in a discussion with Thoth.

"Jack?" Galin said. "Do you have something to add?"

"Yes, sir. We need to look for other openings. This may not be the only one. Sadie doesn't have full reach into every dimension or even every sector of the ones we populate. Thoth and I are assessing if we have the resources available to launch a project of that size," Jack said.

Ares stood, presenting a smug demeanor. He cleared his throat before speaking. "I am certain the Council would be open to the prospect of providing assistance in a joint venture, seeing as we have access to dimensions your people may not be aware of. Of course, a partnership in something of that magnitude would require a full sharing of information, as well as an announcement to the inhabitants of The Everything." He paused, attempting to appear concerned, but his body language lacked any genuine emotion and the display appeared insincere. "Only to ensure they are aware we are working together, of course. Oh, and it may also require some financial assistance, seeing as the Council's assets are somewhat meager at present. Wouldn't you agree, Ben?"

Ares was as versed in politics as he was in war. Teaming up with the turned on this endeavor would give the Council some positive PR and credibility they had been lacking. Not to mention the opportunity to load their account with credits.

Ben flashed a wry grin. "Yes, Ares. Thank you for your support. If the community vote is in favor, I will introduce the motion for the Council's consideration at the next session."

"No offense, Ben, but that seems inappropriate and self-serving, doesn't it? I mean, it could appear as a conflict of interest by those who don't share our view of cooperation, couldn't it? If I may suggest, the optics will appear better if I presented the idea of a joint venture," Ares said with obviously false contrition.

Galin could feel Ben beginning to seethe and he intervened. "That is quite the magnanimous gesture, Ares. Given that the resources needed to involve the Council in our project are expected to surpass our allocated expenditure limit, it will be necessary to submit the proposal to a community vote. Would you be willing to accept the responsibility of drafting the ballot proposal?"

Ares puffed out his chest, nodding to Galin. "Thank you, Galin. I would be honored to draft the proposal. When will the vote take place? Tomorrow? The day after?" Ares appeared proud of himself, pressing out his chest with his chin high.

"Ares, you've been attending these briefs long enough to know that once a vote is proposed, it must take place before the meeting adjourns or be held over until the next assembly." Galin opened his arms, gesturing to the others around the table. "We understand that this is the first time you have contributed to the community, but we simply can't change the rules. Are you prepared to have the proposal completed by the time we adjourn? Say, thirty minutes? We understand if that's not enough time for you." Galin peered at Ares with an overly animated expression of concern.

"It can always be presented at the next quarterly meeting if the task is too overwhelming for you."

"No, no. Of course." Ares sank into his seat with bitterness projecting from his squinted eyes and pursed lips. "The proposal will be ready for a vote prior to adjournment, as required by *your* rules."

Kali lowered her head, struggling to maintain her composure, and resorted to biting her lip to keep from laughing. Ares's arrogance and bloviating had irritated her the entire time she had known him. Her amusement heightened as she watched Ares frantically typing into his device from the corner of her eye.

At the end of the briefing, the vote went in favor of utilizing the Council's support. Barely. Many suspected their self-serving intentions. Most wanted to set a funding limit, and no one wanted to give the Council access to Sadie. After careful consideration, the administration decided that if the Council accepted the partnership, they would have a restricted role in launching sensor arrays.

The turned community had grown to encompass a sizable portion of many advanced immortal species in The Everything. Their population exceeded the numbers under the Council's reign. The turned came from many dimensions, embracing a peaceful way of life. Their people were content and engaged in bringing harmony to everyone they encountered. Their outlook was a marked contrast to that of the unturned communities, whose conflicts seemed motivated solely by the desire to prove their own righteousness and their opponents' wrongness.

Following the briefing, the Council decided their image would benefit from the light of cooperation if they accepted the request for partnership in the project. Maintaining the illusion of their relevance in The Everything could be achieved by the mere appearance that the turned had requested support from them. The turned community viewed its gesture of partnership as a means to quell a few egos by extending a proverbial olive branch. The Council's participation wasn't required for the project, but it could speed up the venture and ease fears of sabotage by the Council for political gain. Cooperation was in the best interest of both groups.

Grace didn't like the thought at all. The Council had manipulated and lied to her far too often for her to think sharing anything with them was sensible. But despite her concerns, the vote had already happened. It was done, and she needed to let it go. The process of organizing the arrangements and allocating the required resources would take a few days. In the meantime, Grace and Ivan would set Betis's rotation. Afterward, she would have time to wind down and visit her sons.

~~~~

Once the Council vote was done, the specifics were negotiated and settled. Galin asked Finna to have a meeting with Lukkas concerning the initial payment requested by the Council.

"So, I'm not sure I understand how the funding is supposed to work. Don't we have a different financial system?" Finna asked Lukkas.

"We have a community credit pool, so payment for the Council's participation will need to be funded from that, which was why the vote was required," Lukkas answered.

The community facilities of the turned were unmonetized. All of the turned shared basic resources. This type of living situation would never be possible in other communities that were based on greed for the acquisition of power and resources. Only a community in which all its members had equal status and levels of contribution could make an unmonetized community successful.

Those who lived among the unturned civilizations did, however, require use of the credit system prevalent throughout The Everything. For financial transactions outside of the community, every turned member had access to the community credit pool. If one of the turned required funds over one million credits, the community would need to vote on the purchase. No one had made use of the approval process until now.
~~~~

"But that's the part I don't understand. Where do the credits come from if we don't use the same credit system?" Finna asked, tilting her head as if looking for answers from above.

"Right. The age-old question of where the money came from." Lukkas smiled at her. If he really thought about it, he guessed most of the citizens wouldn't know how a species that started from a planet without access to The Everything would get credits.

"Exactly. Where did the money come from?" Finna asked, eying him with a questioning expression. She had never been interested in money or credits before, as her species hadn't used them either. Etherians used a barter system to provide for their needs. Other species always just seemed to want to give them things, which they were more than happy to accept.

"Well, the Æsir provided the initial funding for the pool through credits of the deceased as well as the credits from the monarchy claimed by Ben when he took over Tyr's seat on the Council—before we moved to Rasa. Asgard was an excessively rich realm before its end."

"That had to have been quite a lot of credits to last this long." Finna's eyes widened.

"It was a lot, but as expected, the Council took a hefty twenty-five percent from the total, which was cited as an inheritance tax. They graciously waved the administrative fee for transferring the credits," Lukkas said sarcastically. "Ben considered it extortion and had to make a conscious effort to control himself until the credits were transferred. It was a genuine struggle for him, since he wasn't turned back then. A while afterward, when we joined the Æsir and came to Rasa, he turned over the accounting and investment of the funds to me. Once I understood the credit system and made some contacts, I think I made some pretty smart investments, making several times the original sum."

"We're lucky to have someone as smart and handsome as you," Finna said, smiling at him while running her finger down his shoulder. "But seriously, why do we need all those credits if we don't need to use them?"

"We do need to use them," Lukkas said. "Sometimes we need things that aren't available in the community facilities. We also have citizens who don't live close to any of our resources. For those situations, pool credits are available. But pool credits can't be used for gambling or pleasure services at the social clubs or any outside facilities, so some members find other ways to earn personal credits. Any community member can still hold personal credits if they want to. To take part in certain activities and earn personal credits, some people engage in contract work with populations outside the community. Does that make sense?"

"I never really thought about that. It makes sense that some people would need credits. I don't gamble though, and I have you for pleasure, so I can't see why I would ever need credits."

She spoke her statement with such innocence that Lukkas's cheeks blushed and he smiled broadly.

"That is very true, Finna," Lukkas said, trying to hide his amusement. "Since security service in our community is now voluntary, because there are so many turned across the dimensions, we also lease out security services to the unturned. Our turned security units have earned a reputation for resolving disputes for the unturned without incident. They are fair, honest, and don't take sides. Their telepathic abilities also made them extremely skilled negotiators. Figuring out what each side needs or would settle for versus what they say they want is key to their success. We also provide security during negotiations or mediations that we aren't actively taking part in. It's easier for leaders to pay us a small sum than it is to take their dispute before the Council and possibly wait years for it to be addressed. Individuals are even hiring the services of turned contractors rather than presenting disputes to their own governments. It's a profitable business to be in."

"I can understand how that makes sense." She nodded. "I guess we should send the credits then, shouldn't we?"

"How much of the agreed-upon sum are we sending?" Lukkas asked.

"Galin said to send thirty percent and if they protest, they can talk directly to him."

"I'll definitely pass on the last part of that message," Lukkas answered while entering the transfer information into his TAC. Although he had become used to seeing deities walk around like any normal person would, they still made him nervous.

Finna admired the security forces, although she could never see herself in a unit. Every turned member received initial defensive training to instruct them on how to harness their newly acquired abilities, but once that was completed, they were free to pursue any endeavor they wished. She thought she would do well with the negotiating part but wouldn't be able to deal with what might happen if things didn't go well. She understood why negotiators needed to be careful.

It didn't sit well with the Council that pantheon citizens had access to an alternative justice system, though. They saw it as another way the turned were undermining their power. What they wouldn't admit was their citizens didn't trust them and they likely never had. The Council had no grounds to challenge the services provided by the turned. They were treading a delicate balance. They couldn't make third-party negotiations illegal without losing their own power altogether. None of them could afford for the Council to be viewed as totalitarian rulers. Their citizens would no longer tolerate it. The Jur were no longer on the Council's side to enforce their laws. Controlling their people had to be done by coercive means, or they had to subvert their people with violence themselves. Their tactics were only pushing more of their people to turn away from Council rule even if they weren't considering taking the turn. The Council was losing its grip on The Everything, and the Council members knew it.

The ancient ways were ending. The relevant question was, what could they do about it? There were plenty of war-ridden mortal species they could reveal themselves to. Some Council members entertained the idea of seeding habitable planets with their own mortals away from the other pantheons. Isolate populations and expose themselves as those populations' only choice in gods. If the Council were to collapse, there would be no universal laws in place throughout The Everything. No rules, no negotiating, no politics. A small group within the Council had already formed, supporting the idea to burn it all down. However, the turned recognized that the Council must stay united, even if it was solely to regulate human populations, which did not concern the turned.

Hades longed for the days before the Council formed, when there was little oversight outside of individual pantheon leaders. He encouraged dissension wherever possible. His recruitment efforts extended to several species, including a contingent of D'rixxok known for their sly, observant ways. Much of the Pesmox pantheon had also been verbal about leaving the Council, but not necessarily about joining with the likes of Hades. They were a species out for themselves and had felt forced into accepting Council rule in the past in exchange for protection. Now that the Council could no longer provide protection, and there was no threat from the turned, the Pesmox felt no obligation to provide funding or loyalty. They had been the first civilization to resign their seats. They could rule themselves and provide their own protection from the weakened rulers.

CHAPTER FIVE

"**C**ome on, Frigg. It's not at all what you imagine," Grace pleaded. "It all seems so improper. A social club is a place for the single and immature. I prefer to spend my time at the community center where I can appreciate music, philosophy, and art," Frigg said, dismissing Grace's words with a wave.

"It's a place to have fun. Nothing inappropriate goes on there. Well, not in the public spaces, anyway. Besides, I'm hardly home anymore. You should come out with us."

"Why are you so excited? You don't enjoy crowds," Frigg asked.

"I can be social sometimes. It's so seldom I have a chance, and Ivan is looking forward to it. Besides, everyone will be there. Ami's even coming in for it," she continued.

"I thought you were trying to convince me to come," Frigg said, cocking her eyebrow at Grace.

"Pleeeease!" Grace put on her best wounded child expression, making her already huge green eyes even larger. No matter how old she was, she would not hesitate to engage in childish tactics with Frigg. Frigg was the closest thing Grace had to a mother.

Frigg sighed. "Fine, I'll go," she said, holding up a finger. Her spine stiffened and her shoulders pulled up as she gave in. If she was going into that torrid place, she would go with dignity. "But I simply must leave before one."

With a hint of suspicion, Grace examined her intently. "Why? Is something going to happen after one?"

Frigg had long ago told Grace that she frequently knew what was going to happen before it did. She had learned early on that telling others had little effect on the outcome, nor did it ever go well for her. She eventually figured out it was better to keep things to herself. With that history, Grace learned to become cautious when Frigg didn't give her an explanation.

"No," Frigg said, waving her off again. "Nothing is going to happen other than I have an early morning and I'll need a minimum of thirty minutes in my sleep pod and two hours to transform myself into a presentable state after a raucous night of drinking. I'm not as young as I used to be," she said as she flashed an impish grin.

Grace wasn't sure whether to believe her. Frigg had a way of skirting the truth without actually lying, and since she had no guilt associated with lying, she didn't give off the bitter scent of one. "Excellent. I'll send Ivan by to round you up at eight."

"I am not an untamed creature, Grace—I can see myself to the club."

"I wasn't implying you were. Only that the clubs have port blockers inside. Unescorted, they would charge you credits at the door. You're unturned." Grace hadn't needed to remind her of that. She also hadn't meant it to be hurtful.

"That is unacceptable. I'm the proprietor's grandmother. No one is going to charge me anything. I don't even plan on paying for drinks," Frigg said, posturing herself with an air of importance.

"Drinks are free," Grace replied with a hint of a smug smile.

Frigg leveled her eyes.

"Seriously, Grace, I'll meet you there at eight. No reason to bother Ivan to escort me. I'll be fine." Frigg patted Grace on her upper arm.

There was no use arguing with her. Grace knew she would never win. Frigg was likely the only person in this dimension or any other who was more stubborn than she was.

"All right. See you then," Grace agreed as she left. She would be sure to get to the club a few minutes early to ensure the door attendant knew who Frigg was. There wasn't any real reason to charge her. She was as much a part of the community as any of the turned. They never charged Thoth, but then again, he was a regular since Ma'at left.

Grace shifted back to her apartment, feeling accomplished. The moment she became solid, a piercing squeal reached her ears and an intense wave of energy barreled toward her. She phased, allowing her would-be attacker to pass through her, then turned toward a crash followed by a thud to see the most childlike archangel, Amitiel, sprawled out on the floor. Her heart swelled with excitement when she saw Ami pulling herself to her feet and rubbing her head. It had been years since she had been back on Rasa. Grace rushed to gather her friend from the ground.

"Ami! I'm so glad you're here!" Grace said, hugging her tightly. "Are you okay? You really shouldn't surprise me like that."

Ami hugged her back. "I can't help it. I was happy to see you. One day, I *am* going to catch you."

"Not if you squeal like that. Come, tell me all about where you've been." Grace dragged Ami toward the stools at the end of the counter, making a mental note to let Ami catch her next time. "Coffee or wine?"

"Ooh, coffee, please. I miss your coffee. When I'm not here, I don't always eat very much. The food in some places is disgusting. Except for Etheria. They have the best food in the whole Everything. It's like eating happiness," Ami said, practically swooning at the memory.

"Is that where you've been? Etheria?"

"Mostly. I really like it there. They are very welcoming and I have so many friends. It's the happiest place I think I've ever been," Ami said, grinning broadly.

"So, Etheria is The Everything's Disneyland," Grace quipped.

"The … huh?"

"Never mind. Caramel, mocha, or vanilla?" Grace asked, turning toward the food station, grinning. Ami always exuded pure joy, and Grace hadn't realized how much she had missed her.

"Caramel, please."

Grace and Ami talked for hours, eventually moving onto the sofa with wine. Ivan shifted in behind them with another very welcome surprise.

"Ma'at!" Grace squealed nearly as childishly as Ami had earlier. She wasted no time in giving Ma'at a tight embrace. "I'm so glad you're here. How? What if someone sees you? Ivan, how do we keep her visit secret? Ma'at, does Thoth know you're here? Does Thoth know she's here?" Grace peppered both Ma'at and Ivan with questions in rapid succession, without taking a breath.

Ivan placed his hand on Grace's shoulder. "Grace, calm down."

Grace released Ma'at, seizing Ivan around the neck. "Thank you, Ivan. This is the best surprise ever," she said, planting a sloppy, wet kiss on Ivan's cheek.

Ami stepped sideways to face Ma'at. They had become close over the years. Ami's innocent demeanor allowed her to pass without suspicion into the Council's dimension, as well as anywhere else she wanted to go. Despite being half as old as Nyx, Ami had a different outlook. While Nyx had developed a tougher exterior, Ami embraced a more optimistic perspective, always focusing on the best qualities of those she met. Her accepting nature allowed her to observe things others thought her oblivious to. She was far more intelligent than anyone credited her with. She was incessantly questioning to the point of irritation at times, which caused those who didn't know her to think even less about her intelligence.

"Don't worry, Grace. It's all taken care of. I'll stay hidden," Ma'at said, her face beaming.

Grace released Ivan, briefly looking between them. "But what about the party? She can't go to the club. What if someone sees her?"

Ivan eased Grace's apprehension. "It's all taken care of. Mikkel is closing the club to outsiders. Community only tonight. He's diverting the unturned to another club, enticing them with a generous number of personal credits. She'll be safe. Oh, and no, Thoth doesn't know she's here. It's a surprise."

"Where does the Council think she is?" Grace said, flicking her attention to Ma'at. "Where do they think you are?"

Ami answered. "They think she's there. Why wouldn't they?"

"She doesn't know, Ami. Sadie has that information stored in Frigg's personal dataset." Ma'at winked at Ami, and they exchanged an amused glance.

"*She* doesn't know what? And what does it have to do with Frigg?" Grace asked, narrowing her eyes and tightening her lips to show her displeasure at not being included in the secret.

Grace heard Ivan snort behind her. It was apparent he was in on it, too. Grace was mildly irked at being left out.

"Frigg created a shell for me, and Sadie programmed it with my neural waves. We're connected through my adornment," Ma'at said, holding up a large ruby ring.

"She looks and acts exactly like the real Ma'at. It was Ivan's idea," Ami said.

"Ivan's been with me. How was it his idea?"

"Not so much my idea as it was a question. Last time we were home, I took Frigg to perform a maintenance scan on our shells. I asked if it would be possible to create a backup for Ma'at in case she got caught out. Frigg took it from there," Ivan said with a shrug.

"I wish I could be mad at all of you for keeping me in the dark, but this is the best surprise. I can't believe Frigg made me beg her to come to the party tonight," Grace said with a chuckle. "That old woman is cunning as they come."

"You better not let her hear you say that," Ma'at said.

"She's heard me say worse. So, what happens to the other you when you go back? Will you send her back here to go into stasis until you need her again?" Grace asked.

"Grace, she's not going back." Ivan stunned her with the statement.

"Oh? OH! You're staying. That's brilliant, but how are we going to keep you secret?" Grace asked, concerned for her friend's safety.

"Thoth and I are going to live in Hel. Since the Jur all took the turn and moved back home, it's been virtually empty for decades," Ma'at said, eager to come back to her friends.

"Won't it be lonely there?" Grace asked.

Ivan shook his head. "They've been busy since we've been gone on this last trip. The special projects facility has moved to Hel. It's always been unlocatable and secure. They've upgraded security even further so no unturned can get in. You have to provide a bio scan and a venom match."

"That had to piss Nyx off. She loves that place." The entirety of what Ivan had said eluded Grace.

"It absolutely was the final straw for her. No one keeps my sister out of anywhere she wants to go without paying a hefty price," Ivan said.

Grace winced. "How's Ben?"

"He's great," Ivan answered.

"Great? How is he not devastated? He worships her." Grace twisted her face up to him with her mouth agape in confusion.

"You're denser than I am sometimes," Ami said, capturing Grace's attention. "Ben turned Nyx three months ago."

Grace spun around, punching Ivan in the chest as he laughed. "You are such an asshole! No wonder you spent the whole afternoon with Ben. You were avoiding me! What else are you three keeping secret?"

She wasn't angry; she was genuinely enjoying all the little surprises. It was a startling revelation for her to realize that she had failed to sense Nyx's presence in the turned community. They already had a such a close connection through Ivan, she hadn't detected a difference. Grace had gotten used to having a strong bond with her. Maybe that was what had been nagging at her since their return. How had she become so oblivious?

Ma'at's laugh diverted Grace's attention from her thoughts.

"I'm astounded you didn't catch on to the fact that Thoth and I need to turn to live in Hel. Thoth doesn't know that either. Well, I mean, he's aware, but he's unaware that it's happening tonight," Ma'at said, looking at Grace.

"Holy hells, I am such a fucking idiot! When are … wait, that's why Frigg has to leave the party by one, isn't it? For your turning, right?" Grace had been off her game all day. Some tiny little fragment of memory sat like a knotted string she had been tugging at since their return, refusing to come undone. Hopefully, the revelation about Nyx's turn would set her thoughts back on track. She walked around the couch and refilled her wineglass.

"Give the lady a prize!" Ivan exclaimed, extending his hands in a cheesy gesture that was very uncharacteristic for him.

Grace flung a chilling stone at him over her shoulder. "Anything else you want to tell me?"

Ivan caught it, then tossed it back at her. "Nope. I have a few more things I need to take care of, though, so I'll leave you ladies to catch up. I'll meet you at the club. Ami, make sure she's not late."

Ivan immediately shifted out before anyone could respond.

Right, Grace thought to herself. Like Ami was the person to put in charge of making sure someone wasn't late for something.

The hours slipped away as the old friends laughed and conversed. Suddenly, Grace sprung from the sofa, realizing they needed to change into more appropriate attire for their night out. So much for putting Ami in charge of the time, she thought to herself.

CHAPTER SIX

The three women ported to the outside of the club's entrance fifteen minutes early. Ami wore pants, as she almost always preferred. The fabric was weightless, shimmering in silver, projecting the illusion of transparency in a certain light. In direct contrast to her unique personality, the only decorations on her sophisticated outfit were a silver metal collar and a thin matching chain at her waist.

Ma'at dressed in gold, as was her usual choice. The crystals on her shimmering top were in deep Egyptian colors—blood red, cobalt blue, and emerald green—which looked striking against her golden-brown skin.

Grace had chosen a deep-green iridescent jumpsuit, which she found both practical and comfortable. The solitary thing on these women's agenda tonight was to celebrate.

Upon their approach to the door, they were greeted by the sight of four unturned males engaged in a heated dispute with the attendant.

"C'mon man. We're taking the turn tomorrow. We don't want to go to the club in the next sector." One man was pleading the group's case.

"I've already explained to you that this club is closed for a private party. No canis, no entry. There's a port station right across the street. Either take the credits and go to one of the other clubs or go somewhere else. Sorry guys, there's nothing I can do for you. You are not getting in here tonight," the attendant explained, remaining staunch while holding out his TAC to transfer credits to the men's devices.

Grace smiled and nodded at the attendant from behind the prospects. With a wave, the attendant motioned for the three women to come forward, nudging the men aside to open the barrier.

The speaker for the prospects moved forward. "So, the ladies don't have to show teeth? It's that kind of private party, huh?" He rubbed his chest, sliding his hand down to his waistband in a lewd gesture.

Grace and Ma'at ignored the comment and gesture. They had both seen and heard far worse remarks from primitive, unturned males. Ami looked over her shoulder at the young man curiously as she walked past him. She wasn't sure what to make of the comment. The man took the look as an invitation to give Ami a rough slap on the ass. Ami did not appreciate the uninvited touch. She quickly spun, unfurling her wings to their full breadth in a swift, angry motion. The sound of the slap accompanied by Ami's intense, unexpected movement prompted Ma'at to do the same. Whereas Ami's wings opened with a silent flutter, Ma'at's polished gold ones dispersed with the sound of a thousand razor-thin knife blades scouring against each other. The luminescent glow from Ami's wings reflected off the mirror finish of Ma'at's glimmering expanse, rendering the arrogant little group nearly blind.

Grace walked through her two friends, positioning herself between the two women and the prospects, giving the young men an additional level of intimidation by adding in a set of glowing green eyes. The men cowered in place, frozen.

In that exact moment, Erik and Asta ported in behind the prospects, who Erik recognized from his prep class that afternoon. Erik conducted a quick assessment of the situation, believing the young men had been sufficiently admonished and traumatized for whatever affront they had caused, and moved forward to speak. The prospects snapped back the moment they saw Erik approach them. Their faces were a canvas of fear and confusion, with fear being the predominant emotion.

"Mother? Is there anything I can help you with?" Erik asked cautiously.

The prospects recoiled into themselves upon hearing Erik's question. This wasn't just three random women they had insulted or technically assaulted. One of them was the most revered of the entire race. The one who had laid his hands on Ami groaned, certain he would be, at the very least, terminated from the list, if not terminated altogether.

"Well, Erik, that depends on your definition of help. One of your prospects mistakenly thought he had the right to lay his hands on Ami in an uninvited, improper manner. We believe, at the very least, Ami is owed an apology. I personally find it necessary to ensure that all persons requesting to join our community fully grasp what our society deems is appropriate touch and consent." Grace's eyes were still blazing, although her tone was cold.

Erik addressed the men. "Gentlemen, you have placed me in a difficult and embarrassing situation. It is with great remorse that I acknowledge my apparent disregard for a significant aspect of your preparation, which has resulted in your unwise engagement with three of the most formidable beings you may ever come across. I have assuredly placed your safety in peril. Adding to the embarrassment, one of those beings happens to be my mother, who must now be wondering if I am effective in my job. So now, not only have you embarrassed yourselves, you have embarrassed me in front of four people I have a close personal relationship with." Erik paused, opening his arms to designate Grace, Ami, Ma'at, and Asta. "What would you consider to be the first step in resolving this situation?" Erik asked as he stepped forward, standing toe-to-toe with the man who had laid his hands on Ami.

The man went pale. Erik smelled an acrid odor of fear pouring off him, along with an excessive amount of sweat for an evening as cool as this one.

"An apology?" the man asked. His voice cracked before he swallowed noticeably hard, both signs his mouth and throat had gone dry.

"Yes, an apology." Erik nodded.

"I'm sorry, sir. My actions were inappropriate."

Erik clenched his jaw, speaking through gritted teeth. "Not. To. Me."

The man swallowed again, turning toward Ami. "Please accept my sincere apology. I did not intend to offend you," he said with a quivering voice.

Ami's expression was stoic. "What *was* your intention of striking me without provocation? Did I do something to offend you or make you believe I was an impending threat?"

The young man's posture relaxed as his face twisted with confusion. "No, not at all. Just the opposite, in fact. I thought you were attractive. I wanted to get your attention."

Ami closed her wings as silently as she had opened them. She placed her hand on her hip, turning to face Grace and Ma'at. "Grace, I don't understand. I know males used to accost those they saw as potential partners on some planets. Is that abhorrent behavior still a typical practice among humanoids? Should I be upset? I'm unsure what an appropriate response should be."

Ma'at pulled in her wings slowly, accompanied by the melodic sound of wind chimes fluttering lightly in a breeze, then by a round of eye rolling.

Grace let the glow from her eyes fade. "Ami, if the contact caused you to feel uncomfortable, then he needs to understand that was inappropriate behavior. You can be upset if that is how you feel. He didn't only touch you; he struck you with force in a place that is inappropriate for him to touch in your current form. As I see it, you can tell him how you feel. Let him know it was inappropriate, and Erik can ensure he is instructed on our community's view of consent. Your second option is to have him detained and punished for assault. But if you do that, he will be withdrawn from the list and not allowed to take the turn tomorrow." Grace wasn't certain Ami had a full grasp of what she was saying about what an appropriate touch was. Ami herself had habitually had an issue with inappropriate behaviors and personal boundaries, like watching people sleep.

The young man in front of Erik gasped, stiffening his body. His eyes darted with fear at Grace's words.

Ami studied him. She approached him and placed her hand on Erik's shoulder. Erik took a single step to the side.

"It has taken me a very long time to learn each culture has different views on what is appropriate and what is not. In this community, I can touch Erik's arm like this because we are familiar with each other, but it is inappropriate to touch someone I am unfamiliar with in the same manner. It is never appropriate to strike someone without provocation," she said, hesitating momentarily to add as an afterthought, "and not always even with provocation." Ami conveyed no emotion. Grace's mouth gaped open. She was astonished Ami had finally grasped the concept of a personal boundary.

"I'm sorry. I didn't know you were an angel," the young man responded.

Asta stepped to the other side of Erik. "It wouldn't matter if she was a sex worker. That type of behavior is not acceptable in our community, period."

The prospect lowered his head. "Yes, ma'am," he said remorsefully.

Ami continued. "I have always preferred helping others become better than they think themselves capable of. I will not have you detained, but I am going to strike you inappropriately as you struck me. Is that acceptable, Erik?" Ami released her grip on Erik's shoulder, looking at him for approval.

"Yes, Ami. I think that is quite reasonable. But not too hard. He's not as strong as we are," Erik replied, turning back to the man. "Is the suggestion acceptable to you, or do you prefer to be detained on charges?"

"Yes, sir. It is acceptable. I prefer not to be detained." He diverted his eyes to the ground, shaking his head.

"Do you see the lesson there? The verbal exchange we just had. That was consent," Erik stated, motioning between himself and the man.

"Yes, sir. I understand." He nodded.

"Go ahead, Ami," Erik said, giving her permission to proceed.

The young man winced as Ami walked behind him. She smacked his buttocks with both hands hard enough to lift him off the ground, turned on her heel, and went straight back to where Grace and Ma'at stood.

Erik instructed all four of the young men to go back to their quarters to receive instruction from Sadie on appropriate touch and consent. It quickly became apparent that their night was taking an entirely different course than the one they had initially anticipated.

Ami looked at the group. "His haunches were very firm. I understand why he wanted to touch mine."

Grace rolled her eyes. "Ami, please stop saying things like that."

Ami shrugged. "Okay."

"Well, that was energizing. I haven't had my wings out in a while," Ma'at said as she rolled her shoulders to stretch.

"Great job keeping yourself hidden," Grace said.

"They have no idea who I am," Ma'at replied.

"Are you an angel too?" Asta asked Ma'at.

"See?" Ma'at said, pointing at Asta.

Erik snorted as he unsuccessfully tried to restrain his laughter. "Asta, this is Ma'at. You know, the weigher of souls? You met her at Violet's wedding."

"Ahh," Asta exclaimed in recognition. Then she furrowed her eyebrows, taking on a puzzled expression. "Oh."

"Oh? Oh what?" Ma'at questioned Asta.

"I thought your wings were supposed to be, well, feathers." Asta splayed her hands as she shrunk in unease.

"No," Ma'at replied, her eyes crinkling with amusement. "Every heart carries weight, child. How would it be justice to weigh an entire life against a single weightless bird's feather? Even the most gracious among us has a regret or two, wouldn't you think?" Ma'at peered wisely up at the taller Asta.

Asta's cheeks flushed with embarrassment. She seemed to shrink several inches in stature. Ma'at grasped her hand. "No reason to be embarrassed. At least you didn't slap me on the ass," Ma'at said as she walked forward, smirking, and pulled Asta with her through the door toward their tables at the head of the bar.

After an hour or so, the club was packed. It seemed every turned member in the entire sector was in the place. The noise level on the main floor was loud, and the energy was percussive to Grace, reverberating through her chest and head. The smell of sweat and alcohol added to the assault on her senses.

Grace scanned the bar area, her eyes landing on Mikkel, surrounded by a flock of women vying for his attention. As popular as he was, he wasn't one that would be tied down anytime soon. Women in Mikkel's life fell into two categories: ones he loved and wanted to protect and ones he wanted to screw. Until now, only one had crossed that boundary and Grace wasn't supposed to know about her since the woman had died with their world.

She saw him glance up at the office where Lilly sat laughing at him through the transparent wall overlooking the club floor. The pair shared a closer bond than most sires with their sired. She was the little sister he would never have while he was the older, more immature brother she didn't think she wanted. Even though she was his sire, they had a uniquely equal dynamic. They shared everything, protecting each other from the outside world. Sometimes, their bond seemed even closer than the one he shared with his brothers, if that could be possible. He brought out a different side of her, one that was open, sweet, and unguarded, unlike her usual sarcastic and flippant display.

To others, Lilly was closed off, somewhat cold and acerbic. She enjoyed being at the club, but not in the club. Being around people without being among them. Watching, though seldom interacting. She was introverted, not antisocial, never caring what anyone thought about her, except for Mikkel and maybe Viv. This was the first place that seemed to fit her. The way the thought slipped into her mind was odd to Grace, but it made sense. Lilly could fit into any group when she wanted to, any social situation. She read others well, sliding in with little effort. She was bright and amiable when she wanted, and an excellent conversationalist, if you could get more than a few words out of her. For her, though, past groups had been like oversized clothes. She could make adjustments, so they would look appropriate to an observer, but they never really fit her well.

Grace felt the urge to go up and sit with her away from the overcrowded club floor. She excused herself from the table, grabbing a bottle of vodka, Lilly's drink of choice, and two glasses from behind the bar. When she got to the top floor, the door at the back of the viewing deck was open. Lilly's look had changed since the last time Grace had seen her. Her shoulder-length hair was wavy black with almost white blond tips. Most of her piercings were gone, with only a single nose stud remaining. It was much more of a refined look than her previous neon colors and multiple piercings. Grace tapped on the door frame. The desk Lilly was sitting at had a low bank of viewing holograms rolling through corridors and angles that could be difficult to see on a crowded night. She had seen Grace coming. Not that seeing her mattered much. She had felt Grace's approach.

"Hey, Grace, come on in. Sorry I didn't come to see you. It gets a little stuffy down there with so many people. And everyone came to see you and Ivan tonight, not me," Lilly said. She spun her chair around, motioning Grace to a second chair at the desk to her left.

"More like overwhelming. Ivan and I occupy months at a time in The Everything, and even though I love coming home, being around so many people at once is difficult. I hope you don't mind me invading your space. I didn't want to leave the party—I just couldn't stay down there another second," Grace said. She apologized by holding up the vodka bottle as she took the seat.

Grace filled the glasses about halfway, slid one to Lilly, and kicked off her shoes.

"*Skål*," Grace said, leaning over and clinking glasses with Lilly. Grace drank and then slid the glass back into her left hand, resting it against the edge of the console.

Lilly took down about an inch of the liquid. "I can only imagine what you must be experiencing. I probably only have half your sensitivities, and I can't take it for long. He's the total opposite." Lilly motioned with her glass down toward Mikkel. "He seems to thrive on it. I think it's because he can block it out. When he's one-on-one with someone, he can focus with laser precision into their emotions, and when he's in a group, it's like an iron curtain drops and he doesn't feel any of it. I wish I was more like that."

"Work with what ya got, kid. I think you're perfect," Grace said, gripping Lilly's left hand, which was resting on her chair arm.

It was the first time she and Lilly had touched bare skin. The knot that she had been working at all day came undone, and along with it, the entire blanket fell loose. Grace's eyes snapped up, suddenly locking with Lilly's surprised ones. They both saw all of it. They both felt all of it. The panic sweeping over Lilly resulted in uncontrolled trembling as she relived the horrifying ordeal.

The not-quite-seventeen-year-old girl staked in the middle of a field, pressed with hundreds of pounds of stone. A loud, angry mob surrounding her as she suffered a lingering, horrific death. The combination of Lilly's memories and ones Grace shared with Ivan slammed together, completing Lilly's story.

Ivan raged through the mob, killing them all. In a torrent of unprecedented violence, he ripped them to pieces, except for one standing over the girl, commanding her to die. With calculated precision, he pursued the despicable woman who had accused Lilly, reveling in her suffering, until she finally succumbed to exhaustion and fell to the ground. He dragged her by the hair over to where Lilly's crushed body lay and held her face close to the blood-soaked ground. Ivan forcefully tore the board off Lilly, causing stones to be flung over the evil woman's head. He eased the girl off the ground and bound the woman in her place.

He tried desperately to save Lilly, giving her his blood, but her wounds wouldn't heal. When that didn't work, he tried to turn her. For three full days, he sat clinging to her, his heart heavy with the weight of his prayer to any deity that would listen to let her turn. He only left after three days because he didn't think the turn had taken. He sensed nothing but death inside of her tiny, crushed body. He had never seen a turn take longer than two days, even in the most desperate circumstances. Abandoning her there, under a tree, surrounded by a field of wildflowers, was the most difficult thing he had done aside from burying his own children.

The guilt that consumed him from abandoning her had directed the rest of his life. One more child he couldn't save. One more who didn't deserve to die on the receiving end of unearned torment and hatred from humans. He didn't know it would take so long to heal that extensive amount of damage in her body. There was no way for him to realize there was still a chance for her to recover. It had taken her four days to transition and another day to heal completely by the end.

The regret at not being able to save her had sent Ivan into a spiraling depression that lasted almost two centuries.

Lilly thought her sire had abandoned her because they didn't want her. Why should they? No one else had. In Lilly's mind, she hadn't even been worthy enough for her own father to keep. He had sold her at the first chance, chained like a common animal.

Lilly couldn't have recognized Ivan because she had never seen him, and he couldn't recognize her because of how badly deformed her face had been. Even her scent had changed after the turn, as they all did. Since she hadn't awoken before he left her, they never established a sire bond. They had never been alone in a room together. They had never been face-to-face. Though they had been in the same room numerous times, they had never truly seen each other. Never within arm's reach. Neither had heard the other's story. Neither Lilly nor Ivan would have recognized that connection if Grace hadn't taken her hand.

A single tear slid down Lilly's cheek as she again relived the event that had so often tormented her in her nightmares. Grace's eyes welled as they stared in silent, motionless, surreal realization. Both were stunned with pain and anguish that neither could readily process. The combined force of Lilly's and Ivan's thousand years of suffering, shared with Grace through her bond with Ivan, suffocated them.

Mikkel glanced up toward the office, expecting to see Lilly laughing at him as she regularly did. What he saw instead shrouded him with dread. He instructed the club's AI system to turn the clear glass wall opaque. He caught Ivan's eyes scrutinizing him with a concerned focus and signaled him toward the back. Ivan met Mikkel in the hallway at the top of the stairs, sensing something was horrifically wrong with Grace. Within three seconds, they stood together in the open doorway of the room.

"Mother?" Mikkel whispered nervously.

Grace's gaze never wavered as she slowly lifted her free hand a few inches, all while clasping Lilly's overly warm hand tightly. She forced into them all the memories, the physical pain from Lilly's pressing, the unanswered agony of Ivan begging for her life. The emotional pain both suffered from abandonment and regret. Waves of it. More than anyone should suffer. She stuffed it into the two men, surpassing their capacities. Mikkel's legs gave out as he tried to push it away. It was too much, too overwhelming, so he couldn't avoid facing it, not from his mother. He knew Lilly's story well. Living it was entirely different. Grace hammered it further down into the men. Mikkel slid against the door frame onto the floor.

Ivan allowed the waves of pain to wash over him as he lowered himself down the wall beside Mikkel. Half of this pain was already his; an old friend, always present throughout the entirety of his life. Never forsaking him, never allowing him to forget his past failures. He did possess the ability to push it away, but he chose not to. He wanted to understand Lilly's pain. What wandering alone for centuries had meant to her. How it affected her perspective. What he had done to her.

Once they possessed all of it, Grace lowered her hand, pulling everything back from the three of them. She absorbed every bit of physical pain, mental anguish, guilt, and regret, and then gifted them with the comfort of realizing Ivan and Lilly had finally found each other. Neither had failed. Neither had rejected nor abandoned the other. Ivan had found the child he had always longed to save; Lilly, the sire she thought had cast her aside.

After finishing, Grace shifted out, inundated with emotion, leaving them to their long-overdue reunion. This had not been the night she had planned. She was elated for them, but she was incapable of joining in. Not yet. She went back to her apartment, changed into her running gear, and shifted high into the mountains.

Running was the way she resolved what she absorbed from others. Running was her solace. Physical pain had become easy for her to process.

The emotional trauma was hard. The emotional pain of an immortal was so much greater than the pain of mortals, and she had taken a lifetime of trauma from them both. She expected it would fuel her running through the morning, if not longer.

CHAPTER SEVEN

Grace normally ran for clarity to process the pain she had taken, but tonight she also ran because she regretted what she had done to Mikkel and Ivan. Lilly's pain and turmoil had affected her so deeply, she had disregarded the men's choice of whether they wanted to see and feel it for themselves. She had forced it on them, knowing they couldn't stop her. Ben caught up to her a few hours into her self-imposed penance. She was sure Ivan had sent him. He just ran with her in silence, and his presence helped her feel a little less like she was drowning. It was comforting having him by her side, pushing her, forcing her to her limits. She had long since worked through her feelings toward Ben regarding the way he had treated her when they were married. He had given up so much of his life to protect her. Even after she no longer needed him, he never abandoned her, even when she pushed him away. When he was in his darkest places, Ben had often proved he would do what was best for her, despite whether the choice made her despise him. Ben's capability to see what was best for her never wavered, even when he was locked away in the depths of Hel. It had taken her time to see he was right in sending her away without her memories, and longer for her to see how much she had hurt him.

If Ivan had sent anyone else, Grace would have resented it. If anyone else had come, Grace would have shaken them off. But Ben had an uncanny way of predicting which moves she would make, what path she would take. Sometimes she thought he knew her better than she knew herself. He had certainly known her the longest of anyone except for Frigg.

They ran hard and fast through the mountains, leaping wide streams, dodging trees and boulders. Grace wouldn't phase through things on this run. It was harder not to phase through objects. She needed it to be hard. She needed to become impervious to the pain stabbing at her own mind and heart. That meant incurring risks. They ran for hours before barreling forward toward the edge of a cliff. Sunrise was still hours off, but she could tell Ben could see where this was going. He glanced at her with that familiar "oh shit" look on his face. She observed him getting agitated, realizing she wasn't going to stop.

This is going to hurt, Ben thought, taking the final leap into the air beside her.

Grace twisted to face Ben as they plummeted toward the ground littered with jagged rocks and trees. Abruptly, she reached forward, seizing Ben by the forearm. He gripped hers hard as her fingers dug in below his elbow. Their identical phoenix tattoos appeared locked in battle, each chasing the other's tail. Who was going to give in first? With the abruptness of an explosion, she sharply jerked, pulling up his consciousness from its shell to rise beside hers. They watched their empty bodies smash into the cliff base, bouncing against the rocks below. The sickening sounds of empty sacks of flesh thudding and bones cracking echoed around them.

You're going to regret that when we crawl back into those. Ben wasn't happy about watching his body become mangled at the bottom of the cliff beside hers.

Their shells lay bent in directions not natural for their extremities. They were still gripping onto each other's forearms in a pool of Grace's blood. Just because his skin was impenetrable didn't mean his shell hadn't suffered the same severe internal damage as hers. If they had stayed in them, they could have phased solid and would have shattered the rocks underneath instead of shattering themselves. It still would have hurt, but they wouldn't have been injured. He was bewildered, unable to figure out what she could be up to. Grace had been so predictable to him in the past, but these days, she flipped through emotions and ideas like others inhaled air. He simply couldn't keep up with her anymore.

They'll be healed by the time we get back. Follow me. I want to show you something. Grace launched herself out into The Everything, with Ben gloomily following close behind.

Sure. Got nothing else to do for the next few hours, he lamented, glancing back at the pile of wet meat lying on the ground.

Moments later, they arrived at the puncture adjacent to the black hole.

You ever see anything like this? Grace asked. The urge she had felt when she and Ivan first saw it was significantly reduced this time. She still felt a pull toward it, but not as substantial as it had been before.

Really? You dragged me all the way out here to ask me that? Ben asked irritably.

Just take a look.

Ben encircled the opening, examining the edges. Curiosity got the best of him as he observed the material coming through. Although he wasn't an expert, he didn't find any difference in what was coming out of the puncture to what was in The Everything. He followed the stream, studying the effects the black hole was having on the substances. He spent almost an hour looking over whatever he could, seeking anything he could determine to be unusual.

Grace was getting restless with Ben's time-consuming assessment, although she had no right considering she was the one who brought him out here.

I don't know, Grace. It doesn't seem any different to me. It shouldn't be long before we can launch a probe into it.

Do you think it's safe to go in? Because I think it's safe to go in, Grace said.

No.

That's it? No? No what? You don't think it's safe to go in? Why?

Ben's answer had puzzled her. She expected after his long assessment he would have agreed with her.

No, I'm not allowing you to use me as an excuse to support your stupid decision and break your word to Ivan. Is that why you brought me out here? Because you thought if I jumped off one cliff with you, I'd jump off this one too? He paused for a second. He could tell she was pouting. *I'm not getting in the middle of the two of you.*

How could you think I was asking you to do that? I really only wanted your opinion! Grace huffed.

No, Grace, you really only wanted my permission, so you'd have someone to share the blame with. Don't pretend I can't spot your bullshit a galaxy away. Ben paused, giving his words a second thought. *On the other hand, if you really didn't want someone to stop you, you wouldn't bring me, would you? Plenty of others in the community would have agreed with anything the high and mighty Grace had to say, and let you go right on in. So, did you want me to give you permission, or did you want me to stop you?*

Grace sighed in frustration. *I don't know, Ben. I don't know if I wanted you to stop me or push me. What I absolutely know is that this opening bothers me. It bothers me a lot. If The Everything and The Nothing are exactly the same, then all we know about the creation of our world, our reality as a whole, is wrong. And if that's true, it means Chaos has been lying to everyone since the very beginning. I have a bad feeling about this, Ben. I need to get to the other side of that opening.*

Grace, you have no facts to substantiate that theory. Wouldn't it be equally plausible that The Nothing is where the problem is? What if the material coming through that opening leaked out of The Everything in the first place? Couldn't it be possible that once all that stuff drains in, The Nothing will actually be empty again? Waiting until the probe is ready isn't going to alter anything.

I hate it when you make sense, Grace said, resigning herself to Ben's reason.

Yeah, I know. Let's head back and climb into our broken meat sacks.

Fine, Grace agreed. *They should be healed by now, anyway.* Grace started moving away from the opening hesitantly, while peering back at it.

Your optimism astounds me, Ben replied. *Our shells don't heal as quickly when we're not inside them,* he groaned.

How do you know that?

Grace wouldn't know that little nuance. Leo had always contained her shell in a stasis pod when she was outside it.

Accidentally, Ben replied sarcastically. *Just, trust me, it's not going to be fun.*

As they approached their shells, Grace could see Ben had been right. They were partially healed, but nowhere near where Grace thought they should be.

Just remember, you have no one to blame except yourself. And I have no one to blame except for you, Ben said, with an edge of bitterness to his voice.

He dove into his shell, groaning as his eyes opened. He dragged himself up the incline and leaned his back against the boulder he had bounced off last. One of his legs was still pointing in an unnatural direction.

"Argh!" Ben growled loudly when he snapped the leg back into position with a sharp pain shooting up to his hip. He continued to breathe heavily, slumping back against the rock.

Grace groaned as she stumbled up to his side. She eased herself down beside him, blood running from an open gash in her head. "Sorry."

Ben raised his hand weakly between them. "Stop. Just. Stop. Talking."

They sat in a tense silence until they could stand again.

"I should probably go for a swim in the lake and get some of this blood off my clothes before I go home." Grace's outfit was soaked and sticky with partially dried, coagulated blood.

"You do what you want. I've got a hot spring waiting for me back at Tartarus." Ben couldn't think of anywhere he'd rather be than a steaming mineral spring after the night he'd had.

Grace halfheartedly smiled at him. "Bring Nyx for dinner tonight?"

"Sure. Why not?" Ben grimaced, warily limping off a few steps before he shifted out.

Grace felt terrible about the miscalculation she had made with the healing speed of their shells, but at least she felt like she had processed the bulk of the emotional trauma from the previous night. She limped down to the icy lake and dove fully clothed into the freezing water, which felt soothing to her remaining open wounds. The worst of them was the two-inch-long scabbed-over cut on the side of her head. It had been the full length of her skull with a missing chunk of bone when she had first taken the fall. At least her ear was back in place instead of flapping over the side of her face like it had when she slid back into her shell. She could feel her bones were healed, and the missing chunk of flesh from her calf was back.

By the time she got out of the lake, she was completely recovered, feeling refreshed and ready to go home. Her top and running shoes were stained pink. They would definitely end up in the recycling pile.

Grace shifted to her bathroom and began peeling off the cold, wet clothes clinging to her skin. A hot shower and an intensive hair scrub were as far as her plans for the morning had gone. Ivan wasn't home yet, and she hadn't expected he would be. He was still with Lilly and Mikkel. She knew he had become close with Mikkel over the years, and now he had gained peace of mind knowing Lilly had lived. Grace hoped that Ivan wouldn't be disappointed, as she feared that he might have unrealistic expectations for a relationship with Lilly.

~~~~

Ivan was already feeling more of a lightness about him as he sat at the kitchen counter in Mikkel and Lilly's apartment. Lilly had taken Erik's vacant room not long after she and Mikkel had opened the first social club. The apartment bore her unmistakable touch, clear in the vibrant colors and cozy atmosphere that stood in stark contrast to the impersonal communal area it had replaced. Her artwork was everywhere. The room was filled with stunning paintings and sculptures, each one capturing a sense of inner turmoil despite the bright hues.

Lilly sat cross-legged in the middle of the center island, flipping a throwing star through her fingers. Mikkel was in front of her beside Ivan, pouring another round of vodka. The sharp scent of alcohol filled the room in which they had spent hours apologizing for slights and regrets that each held. Now they were moving on to getting to know each other.
~~~~

"You know, we almost met once about a hundred years ago," Lilly said without looking up from her star.

"Lilly, we've met many times," Ivan said and leaned back in the bar chair.

She looked up, meeting his eyes. "Being in the same room and meeting are two different things. We've never had a conversation or been properly introduced."

Ivan looked toward the ceiling, searching his memory. "Huh, I guess you're right. I got so used to seeing you around, I hadn't realized we never met."

"It's not like I'm at your level. You don't typically talk to worker drones like me." Lilly shrugged flippantly.

"That's not really fair. It's not like you talk to anyone either. How many friends do you have besides Mikkel?" Ivan wasn't trying to be disparaging; he was making a point.

Lilly straightened up and scoffed. "I have friends. I have … Viv." She perked up. "And, well, there's …" She scoffed and sank, defeated. "I talk to people," she muttered, flipping her star again.

"It's nothing against you, Lilly, but that's my point. We're both introverted. The two of us meeting without an external influence is about as likely to happen as a comet making a ninety-degree turn. The only person I associate with on my own besides Grace is Ben."

Mikkel seemed offended. "What am I, then?"

"You know what I meant, Mikkel. I see you more because you're family."

"Wow, that's harsh, Ivan," Mikkel teased, trying to keep the mood light for Lilly's sake. He liked Ivan and all, but Ivan had a tendency for seriousness and Lilly had a tendency to disparage herself when things got too serious.

Ivan sighed, returning his focus to Lilly. "It's not a bad thing to be self-reliant. We both talk to people, but I don't think either of us goes looking for a conversation or camaraderie all that often."

"True enough. But that brings me to the point I was going to make," she countered.

"Which is?" Ivan let the "is" drift up.

"As nice as it is to find out you exist, and that you didn't throw me out like last night's garbage, we have no commonality. We have no reason to create a relationship. We've been in close proximity for centuries without speaking as much as a single word to each other in a personal conversation. I have no expectations of you, and I don't think you should have any of me either." Lilly tapped her star on the counter.

Mikkel's attention peaked as he sought Ivan's reaction. Lilly was being far more pragmatic and detached than he had expected. Ivan studied Lilly for a moment, considering his reply.

"I have no illusions about creating a bond with you. The time for that is well past, and I don't want to make you uncomfortable. I equally cannot unknow what I now know. I respect your boundaries and won't assume anything about your life, but I want you to know that I'm here to support you. The simple fact that you're alive is all I need to feel content."

Lilly sat up straight, flashing a satisfied smile that didn't reach her eyes. "Good."

Ivan thought the best thing he could give her was the feeling she had control. He'd be here if she needed him, but he wouldn't force her into a relationship she was uncomfortable with.

"I should get home then. Grace is back." Ivan nodded to Lilly and Mikkel, sliding the chair out and stretching his arms in front of him as he stood.

Lilly nodded in agreement and laid the star on the counter in front of her.

Ivan shifted back to his apartment. A familiar sharp, metallic scent mixed with the lighter floral scent of Grace's soap filled the apartment. He heard the shower running and made his way into the bathroom, where his foot landed on a pile of cold, wet, blood-soaked clothes that slid forward under his weight. He picked them up and tossed them into the recycler.

"Somebody had an interesting time." Ivan sat on the floor, leaning his back against the shower wall, avoiding the wet spot left by the clothes. This wasn't the first time either of them had disposed of bloody clothes and it probably wouldn't be the last either.

"How did it go with Lilly?" Grace deflected, not wanting to get into the specifics of her interaction with Ben.

"About how I had expected. She's practical. Lilly agrees there's no need to launch into a new connection, based solely on an overwhelmingly poignant moment. It would never be a substantive relationship."

Grace stuck her head out of the shower, leveling her eyes at him. She decided the comments invading her mind weren't worth a debate. She shook her head and went back to let the hot fluid stream over her back. "Great. There's two of you," she mumbled.

"What do you mean by that?"

Grace sighed, disregarding his question. "Ben and Nyx are coming for dinner. I think we should take them with us when we go back to launch the probe into The Nothing."

"I think that's an excellent idea," Ivan agreed, but probably not for the same reasons Grace wanted them to go.

"So, when do you think we can go back? Is the probe ready?" Grace asked.

"Another day or two, maybe. Not my department." Ivan shrugged. He wasn't in any rush to get to the future. There was no point in being in such a rush when it would certainly arrive either way.

"That's one way to evade an answer." Grace grabbed a towel for her hair and stepped over Ivan. The drying lights never got her long, thick hair thoroughly dried.

"Like the way you avoid living in the present? How about we just have a nice day?" Ivan got up, stripping off his shirt.

Grace smirked at him, spun on her heel, and left the room. "Fine."

"Grace, The Everything isn't going to implode because we took a couple of days off," Ivan said.

When his words had hung in the air for too long without a response, he added, "Put on something comfortable. I've got something fun planned." He stripped off his pants and climbed into the shower without waiting for a reply he already knew wouldn't come.

Thirty minutes later, Ivan was leading Grace outside, blindfolded.

"Okay. You ready?" Ivan asked with a little more excitement than was normal for him.

Grace wondered what that elevated energy meant for this morning's "fun." "Uh, yeah. Ready as I'll ever be, I guess," she answered unenthusiastically.

Ivan slipped the blindfold off. Grace's eyes got huge. "Holy hells! I can't believe she still looks so fantastic!" Grace shrieked with excitement.

"Surprise!" Erik and Asta yelled in unison. They were leaning against the alpine blue '68 Pontiac GTO he and Ivan had restored so long ago. The paint sparkled like the day it was finished, and the sun glinted off the polished chrome.

"Does she run? Where'd you get the fuel?" Grace asked.

Erik was beaming. "Well, we had to cheat. Jack and I converted her to an oxide cell. You still get the big-engine rumbling feel without the toxic discharge. That's the fun part, anyway. Now get in."

"Oh, yeah. Gimme the keys. I'm driving!" Grace reached out, expecting Erik to hand them over.

Erik snatched his hand away. "Oh, no you're not! I've seen you drive. You sucked centuries ago, and I seriously doubt you've gotten any better since." He backed away from her, chucking the keys to Ivan. "You can drive."

Asta snickered, pulling Grace by the arm. "C'mon, you're in the back with me. Let them play with their toy."

Grace glanced into the back seat. "Where's the baby?"

Asta looked at her like she was insane. "I'm not putting my son in this thing. He's with Violet."

"Probably for the best," Grace agreed.

"Yeah, probably. You can see him tomorrow," Asta said.

"We'd love that. Let us know the best time to come by."

Asta glanced at Ivan and assumed he hadn't told Grace that he and Ben had spent a few hours at their house yesterday. Ivan had played with the boy while Grace had been with Ami and Ma'at.

Grace climbed into the back seat of the car with an enormous smile on her face. The familiar scent of real leather, along with the smooth feel of the stiff upholstery, brought back pleasant memories. She couldn't remember the last time she had been in a car. Ivan always knew the exact thing she needed, even if she didn't.

They spent the better part of the day driving through the landscape. Seeing the planet from this view was an entirely different perspective. A welcome one. The air rushed over her face through the open windows, making Grace glad she had worn her hair up. It was a leisurely drive, topping out at a mere eighty miles per hour because of the road conditions. Most of their low land vehicles hovered, producing a smooth, glass-like surface over the sand and rougher areas where rocks poked through under the compacted dirt. The car's suspension was getting as much of a workout as the interior was as it caught their tousled bodies. She could have spent an entire week out here, but everyone had evening plans to get back to.

When Erik and Asta dropped Grace and Ivan off in front of their building, a wave of nostalgia mingled with sadness washed over her.

CHAPTER EIGHT

"If you don't include the excitement of riding a black hole like a Slip 'N Slide, that's the most fun I've had in years." Grace flopped down onto their bed, kicking her shoes off into the air. "How do you always know the exact thing to make me happy?"

"This time, it wasn't about you. *I* needed today. You having a good time was a bonus." Ivan pulled off his jacket, flinging it over her face.

Grace slid the jacket under her head. "You're so easygoing, Ivan. I forget sometimes you need things I don't."

"Seems like you needed today, too." Ivan took off his shoes and sat on a chair across from the bed.

"I enjoyed today. I didn't necessarily need it." Grace leaned up on her elbows and studied Ivan. "It's weird to imagine we're so close that we sometimes can't see each other."

Ivan pulled off a sock, tilting his head up to smile at her. "I see you pretty clearly. Guess you just have a little more narcissist in you than I do."

Grace gasped. "I can't believe you said that to me!"

"Are you denying it?" Ivan sat up straight, dropping his second sock onto the floor with the first.

"Everyone can be a little self-involved, even you," Grace said defensively.

Ivan's eyebrows shot up as he turned to look at her, his expression unreadable.

"Okay. Well, maybe not you. I wouldn't go so far as to say I'm narcissistic, though." Grace scowled.

"You've kind of turned this whole 'saving The Everything' into being about you."

"I don't think that's fair," she defended, shaking her head.

He leaned back, folding his arms across his chest. "No one said it was going to be fair. But you've gone overboard. You are laser-focused on saving The Everything so everyone can live happily ever after, and you aren't living at all. When you get homesick, we come back here for a few days and all you can think about is getting back out there. You make certain everyone knows how much you're doing to save them. You're barely here when we're here. I'd lay odds that going to see your only grandson hadn't crossed your mind until you saw Asta and Erik today. In the beginning, all you used to think about when we were out there was getting back home to see your family. I don't know when that changed." Ivan uncrossed his arms, splaying his hands in front of him, and continued.

"You used to be the very definition of alive. You exuded joy of life from every pore. But you haven't been like that for a while. You're burdened and you're heavy. You don't seem to notice your friends and family want to spend time with you. Do you even know why Erik and Asta wanted to take us out driving today?" Ivan raised his eyebrows, scrunching his forehead.

"No." Grace tightened her mouth. Her whole body seemed to stiffen in a defensive posture. Ivan's words were upsetting, but she acknowledged a hint of truth in them.

"Look, Grace, I know better than anyone what this is costing you. What it's costing us. But you can't disconnect. We need to pay a little more attention to being present. When we're here, I want us to be here. We can't lose who we are, to what we do." Ivan leaned forward, resting his elbows on his knees.

Grace slid down to the edge of the bed, mirroring Ivan's position. "You're right." She paused. "Irritatingly, perfectly, always right. I can't imagine doing this without you. What did I do to deserve you?" She leaned forward, sighing. She dropped her eyes to the floor, unable to look at him.

To Ivan, her statement sounded more sarcastic than heartfelt. Maybe his words were harsh, but even though her tone was brisk, she had at least acknowledged his opinion of her behavior. Ivan went to sit beside her on the bed, wrapping his arm around her shoulders.

"I have no idea," he said, jiggling her shoulder with his hand, making her entire body move.

"You're such an ass." Grace leaned her head against his shoulder.

"I know. So are you."

"It must be nice to be so certain of yourself all the time. To know you're always right," Grace said.

"I don't always think I'm right. I listen and I trust myself to see all the possibilities before I make a decision about something. You only see the outcome of my thoughts, not the struggle it takes to get to whatever comes out of my mouth. You tend to say what's on your mind before you start that elimination process. Your struggle just takes place in public." He chuckled and kissed the top of her head. "Get changed. Ben and Nyx will be here soon."

Grace got up and walked toward her closet. She turned back. "So, why did Erik and Asta want to take us out today?"

Ivan got up and walked past Grace to his own closet. "They're leaving Rasa."

"What?" Grace spun back toward him. "What do you mean, they're leaving Rasa?" She didn't know why they would ever want to leave such a paradise.

Ivan turned with a smug expression. He knew she hadn't been paying attention today. "They're going to Betis. The agriculture colony? Not ringing any bells?"

"I thought they were discussing the colony in general—not moving there."

"Well, they are. Asta has experience with growing grapes and olives from the wineries. She wants to get her hands back in the dirt. And Erik is going to be working with some new type of accelerated-growing dome. Why did you think they were talking about it?"

"Conversation? I don't know." She ran her hand through her hair and sighed. "I am an ass."

"Yup."

"Thanks for agreeing," she said, lifting her eyes up to meet his.

"Anytime." Ivan smirked, turning back to his closet. He grabbed a yellow collared shirt and strolled out to the kitchen to find something to cook for dinner.

Grace stood in the middle of the room alone. Ivan was right, as he typically was. She had become obsessed. She had no boundary when it came to her mission. Grace's attention had become focused on The Everything, to the exclusion of all else. Even when she was running with Ben, she couldn't help herself. She dragged him right into it with her. It was ironic that she and Ivan were supposed to be creating balance in The Everything, and balance had become the very thing she had lost in her own life.

The only way out was forward. She smirked to herself as the thought of time shifting came into her mind. She did have the ability to go back and change the past, but that could have some very negative repercussions. And it would be excruciating for Ivan. Nope, forward was her only option. Grace grabbed a clean shirt, fixed her disheveled hair, and walked out to the kitchen with a resolve to do better for herself and for Ivan.

Grace poured two glasses of wine and slid one toward Ivan. "I'm sorry."

"For what?" Ivan asked, taking the glass.

Grace tilted her head sideways. "For being an ass."

Ivan set his glass down and leaned his hands on the counter. "Grace, I've always appreciated who you are. You're driven and passionate, and yes, sometimes you can get obsessive. You never have to apologize to me for that. It's my fault I waited so long to tell you."

"You're apologizing to me? For my behavior? How does that make any sense at all?" Grace leaned onto her elbows, looking up at Ivan.

"Oh, I am not taking responsibility for your behavior. Let's get that straight right now. I am apologizing for enabling you to get away with it for as long as you did. I figured I'd give you enough—"

Grace finished his sentence. "—rope to let me hang myself?"

"Now you are being an ass. I was going to say 'time to realize it yourself.'" Ivan glanced across the room. "Answer the door."

Grace chuckled as she crossed the living space. She pulled open the front door, letting Nyx and Ben in. It was merely a formality to ring or knock. Everyone already knew when others were there. It was still polite to wait until the home's occupants invited you in. Rasans enjoyed keeping some level of privacy, even if it was an illusion.

Ivan was nearly finished prepping the food. He loved cooking. It was satisfying to take fresh, raw ingredients and turn them into something enjoyable.

Nyx came around the counter. "Ivan, why do you insist on toiling with something as trivial as food when we have the ability to replicate any dish your heart desires?"

"Because, dear sister, I enjoy the process of cooking," he answered, bestowing a swift kiss on the top of her head. "Twenty minutes to simmer. Wine or something a little stronger?" he asked.

"Gin and tonic," she answered, taking in the aroma of the sauce on the range.

Ben was already at the bar pouring himself a scotch. "Coming right up," he acknowledged.

The three of them sat at the kitchen counter while Grace set the table.

Nyx glanced at her. "Grace, let a service unit do that. Come join us."

"We don't have a service unit," Grace said with a smirk.

"I will never understand that," Nyx replied, sipping her drink.

"Some of us prefer doing things for ourselves," Ben said.

"And I will never understand that, either. What is the point of possessing technological advantages if you don't utilize them?" Nyx shot back.

Grace smiled, shaking her head at the comment. They continued chatting about things that had happened while she and Ivan were gone until dinner was ready, saving the heavier topic of The Nothing for full stomachs. The most significant news was that Galin would step down as Administrator after his term was up. Almost two hundred years of politics were enough for him. The consensus was leaning toward Viv to be elected as his replacement. She enjoyed a good political game, but her vacancy in operations would be difficult to fill. Alex was turning up on the short list along with Vaeweth and, more surprisingly, Violet. She was young, for sure. The one advantage she held over the others was the drive she inherited from her mother. Her leadership style was similar too and would cause the least impact on the division. Alex was more calculated, but also prone to taking risks. He was also a little too tightly wound for some people's taste. Others were concerned his views could come across as a little sexist. Vaeweth had been Viv's second almost since the division formed. All three candidates had equal chances for varied reasons. That was, if Viv took the Administrator vote.

The four moved to the table once Ivan plated the food. It was an odd group of friends. Ivan was known for his practicality and patience, while Ben had a reputation for being both cynical and charming when he wanted to be. Nyx was the oldest, having the most knowledge of The Everything. Her experience with The Nothing was the same as that of the others, relegated to secondhand knowledge. As far as anyone knew, the only beings to survive The Nothing had been Chaos and the child. Grace was the least like the others, viewing the world with optimism and a naïve sense of hope.

"What, specifically, are you hoping to find out there?" Ben posed the question they had all been thinking about.

Ivan answered first. "Not that we will probably find out on the first exploration, but my primary goal is to find out why this hole has formed and if there are any others."

"I think that may take a longer time to figure out," Ben replied.

"Well, I want to find out what's on the other side," Grace added, shoving a bite of pasta into her mouth.

"Of course you do. Why would you want to know what you're jumping into when you can simply jump in and not worry about the repercussions?" Nyx asked, with condescension dripping from her words.

Grace swallowed her food and scoffed. "I worry about repercussions. I don't see the reason for waiting if what is coming through is the same as what's on our side."

"The probe goes first, Grace. That is not up for discussion," Ivan said sternly.

"I KNOW THAT. Why does everyone think I'm stupid?" Grace snapped.

"No one thinks you're stupid, Grace. We think you're reckless. From my personal experience, I know you're reckless." Ben folded his hands and frowned across the table at her, remembering the cliff jump that morning.

"Invincibility has a way of doing that to people," Grace said, defending her actions.

"I spent nearly two thousand years in Helheim thinking that way. It's not all about you. People around you aren't so invincible. My hubris got me to Hel. If my ego hadn't gotten in the way, Mikkel wouldn't have challenged my father, getting The Three banned from Asgard when the great war came. Asgard wouldn't have fallen, and you wouldn't have been sent away without your memories before all of that started," Ben said. He had been shouldering the blame for everything negative that happened to their people. He didn't say any of that with anger. It saddened him.

"We also wouldn't be here, sitting at this table, with this community. None of this would have happened. You only see the negative side of your actions, Ben. You've done more than your share of positive things too," Grace replied empathetically.

"Not the point, Grace. The point is your actions have repercussions for those around you too," Ben said with the same heaviness in his voice.

Nyx was becoming uncomfortable with the awkwardness of these former spouses sounding like they were still married. "How do we know that hole is new? Just because we never noticed it doesn't mean it wasn't there all along, does it?"

As soon as she spoke, the other three stared at her with expressions of utter disbelief, as if she had grown a second head right before their eyes. It was a thought that none of them had even considered.

"Well?" She shrugged. "What if it has always been there? I don't know every single inch of The Everything, do any of you?"

"Hmph." Ben was thinking. "Like a drain for stuff that has seeped into The Nothing. That's a theory. We know there are black and white holes that drain from one dimension to another. What if this is the same kind of thing?"

The four of them sat with their own thoughts and theories for some time.

"When is the probe going to be ready, Ben?" Ivan finally asked.

"The probe is ready. Getting it there is what is going to take some time. The ship is already en route. Jumping it will take close to two days," Ben answered.

"Can't we shift it?" Ivan asked.

"Thoth isn't sure if shifting will throw off the calibrations. He recommends mechanical travel," Ben replied.

"It appears waiting is our only option," Nyx said, closing the topic. "Now, who wants to tell me why Ma'at and Thoth have taken over my rooms in Hel?"

~~~~

The next two days were a mixture of relaxing and miserable for Grace. Waiting was excruciating. However, it allowed her time to catch up with family and things she missed about being shell-bound. It also gave her
~~~~

time to think, which hadn't always the best thing in Grace's past. She went to see Mikkel and Lilly.

"What are you saying, mother?" Mikkel asked and leaned against the counter.

"If you think about it, Ivan sired Lilly before we merged, but he was already a Primordial. And she sired you, which means you got a more concentrated primordial line than your brothers. They have only one primordial source since I am their mother, whereas you have two. I'm wondering if either of you has some additional abilities you're not aware of," Grace theorized as she paced in front of them.

"Which could be what?" Lilly asked.

"For you, possibly shifting and only a slim chance of rising since you were previously human. For Mikkel, shifting, phasing, and rising," Grace answered. She could usually tell exactly what abilities those around her had. These two were a mixed bag, and she hadn't thought to look at them. If they had the abilities she was thinking about, she wasn't convinced they had enough potential to employ them.

"Well, wouldn't I have a greater chance? Dad can do all of that too, right?" Mikkel queried.

"It doesn't work like that. You couldn't inherit any of those things from your father because he didn't have those abilities when you were born. He received those from Ivan later. That's why Lilly wouldn't have phasing either, because Ivan didn't have it when he sired her. He got that later when we merged. Ben has it because Ivan had it when he sired him. Mikkel, you could have phasing because that was one of my abilities when you were born. Does that make sense?" Grace explained.

Mikkel and Lilly both nodded. "Yeah," they agreed.

"Okay. What do we do?" Mikkel asked.

"I'll take Lilly first." Grace motioned for Lilly to join her in the middle of the room. "Shifting is easier than opening a port, and you can go anywhere. Any planet in any dimension as long as you either have the coordinates or a clear vision of the place you want to go to," she said, reaching for Lilly's hand.

"Can you shift to a person?" Lilly knew you could port to people, but she wasn't sure if shifting had the same rules. She clasped Grace's hand.

"Yes." Grace closed her eyes. "You definitely possess a powerful ability to shift. I'm not seeing your rising ability being remarkably strong yet, but it is there. Maybe in another couple of thousand years?"

"Well, that's something to look forward to," Lilly replied sarcastically.

"Alright, smart ass. Pay attention. Can you feel me focusing on my energy?"

"Yes."

"Concentrate on that. I'm going to shift there. You are going to shift us back. Got it?" Grace opened her eyes.

"Got—" Lilly started to reply, but they were gone.

A few seconds later, they returned.

"Holy shit!" exclaimed Lilly. "That was fucking awesome!"

"Told ya. Really easy, right?" Grace was beaming.

"Way easier. It's all inside. You don't have to create anything external."

"Nobody can follow you either. Shifting isn't traceable, and port blockers don't affect it." Grace winked at her.

"Yeah, but you just said you can shift to a person," Lilly said.

"Well, a port tracker can't follow you, and if you're blocking, neither can anyone capable of shifting. Is that clearer?"

"That is going to make the club rounds so much easier. I don't need to go down to the community hall or generate port codes for a thousand places." Lilly was very excited by her newly gained skill.

"And they don't have to know you're coming," Grace added.

"Step aside, little girl. It's my turn," Mikkel said, pushing his way between Grace and Lilly.

Lilly couldn't help but scoff as she playfully shoved his shoulder, a smile tugging at the corners of her lips threatening to betray her false indignation.

Grace took Mikkel's hands. "Ahh, it appears you, my son, have hit the trifecta. I will not teach you how to rise, though."

"Why not?" Mikkel was offended.

"Because you won't want to come down and I don't have time to chase you around and drag you back," Grace said, smirking.

"Way to keep me down, old lady."

"What are mothers for if not to dash the hopes and dreams of their children?" Grace smiled with superiority.

Mikkel sighed.

"Enough playing around. Are you ready?"

"Yes."

"Can you feel—" Mikkel shifted them out before Grace finished her sentence.

A few seconds later, they were back. "I felt the way Dad did it when he took us up to Amun's chambers to rescue Ma'at. I just didn't know I could do it," Mikkel said, flashing a wicked grin.

Grace shook her head. "In the future, if you feel something like that when someone else can do it, chances are, you can too."

"I'll remember that. Ready for phasing?" Mikkel was eager to pick up that skill, if for no other reason than to dominate his brothers the next time they sparred.

Grace spent the next two hours showing Mikkel the nuances of phasing. It was subtle, something Mikkel was decidedly not. There were intricacies in feeling the surrounding particles. He would need a lot of practice before it became natural for him. As she contemplated, she could already visualize his near future, which would be riddled with episodes of him inadvertently grafting himself to unintended objects. After today's session, she had doubts it would be a skill he could master anytime soon.

Prior to her departure, she gave him a warning about the risks of attempting to phase with living things, emphasizing the possibility of being unable to separate himself from the entity he was attempting to phase through.

When she got back to the apartment, Ivan and Ben were watching a live feed of cage sparring.

"How'd it go?" Ivan asked her.

"Lilly and Mikkel both have high-level skills in shifting. Mikkel has phasing abilities, which are rough. Don't be surprised if one of you gets an emergency call from him because he's stuck in something. I'm sure he won't call me."

Ben and Ivan both laughed and placed a bet on who would get the first call. While Ben and Ivan were busy yelling at holographic images sparring in the middle of their apartment, Grace wanted to indulge in a long, hot bath and a frivolous book.

In the morning, the four of them would go back into The Everything, and she wasn't sure when she would have another chance at this much time to relax.

CHAPTER NINE

Well, that sucks, Ben thought.

I told you it wouldn't work, Grace said with a smugness to her words. *Looks like someone has to go in.*

Grace began pulling Ivan toward the opening. With Ivan alongside her in their risen form, the enticement of the opening was nearly impossible to ignore. Ivan pulled back hard enough to stop their motion.

Grace, we have already had this discussion. We aren't going in until we have more information. I don't care if it takes another millennium. You're too eager to jump headfirst into an unknown and possibly destructive situation.

Oh, please! Nyx exclaimed. *I will retrieve the sensor array.*

Ben could tell by her tone that she would have been rolling her eyes if she were in her physical form.

You mean we, Ben added.

No. I mean I. I've been zipping around out here for over thirteen billion years. The rest of you have, what, a century or two of experience? Her tone was condescending. *I'd be safer on my own. Now that we can see The Nothing isn't the empty abyss we were led to believe it was, I'm not seeing the issue with crossing into it.*

It may not be an empty abyss, but it's not the same as it is on this side. Something caused that probe to deactivate.

We don't know it stopped working. The only thing we know is we can't get the signal from it on this side.

I'm not letting you split off. If you go in, I go in, Ben said sternly.

You think you can stop me from splitting off?

Probably not. I still won't let you go alone. I'll follow you. Your choice, although I prefer we go together. Ben knew she wouldn't risk him following her in on his own.

Nyx had a tough exterior and wanted people to think she was cold and unfeeling, but the truth was, she had started them on this path and felt responsible for keeping them safe. She was the one who sought them out to save The Everything. She wouldn't put any of them at risk, especially not Ben.

As Ben and Nyx argued, Grace felt something approaching rapidly from behind. She almost hadn't detected it as they hung in the space between the mysterious opening and the black hole. There were many objects being flung toward them, only to be caught in a spiraling curvature of the gravitational force. This object was unusual. It wasn't following the path into the event horizon. It was heading directly toward her. By the time she realized what was happening, it slammed into her, ripping her away from Ivan.

Grace was confused, disoriented. It should have passed through her. She experienced an overwhelming sensation of being dragged. She couldn't get her bearings, unable to direct her motion. She was senseless, helplessly racing toward The Nothing as though being ripped from the ground by a tornado, whirling, swirling, and tumbling. The harder Grace tried to pull away, the faster they went forward. Stars were nothing but streaks she couldn't focus on.

Ivan shrunk in pain and disorientation of his own. They did not willingly choose to separate. Something had severed their connection.

Nyx and Ben's argument came to an abrupt halt. Something was dragging Grace through the opening to The Nothing. Ben's protective instincts took over as he pulled Nyx toward the opening after Grace. Even at their topmost speed, they couldn't catch up before the entity pulled Grace through to the other side. Ben didn't hesitate. Nyx didn't stop him. The two crossed over into The Nothing, but the pair they were following was gone. Ben had no sense of which direction they had taken.

Ivan regained his senses, catching up to Ben and Nyx on the other side, but they were too late. He couldn't perceive Grace's presence in any specific direction, either. He possessed no feeling of dread like he had when she shifted through time. It wasn't as though she was gone; it was more as if she was everywhere.

They moved through The Nothing as easily as they moved through The Everything. There were no planets or stars, only a thick blanket of velvety black, dotted with baseball-sized rocks and small asteroids. Waves carrying imperceptible sound and light disrupted the space around them, just as the vacuum of space in The Everything did. All the same building blocks of their world were here, only in smaller sizes and quantities.

They searched for days, then weeks, never finding anything larger than the tiniest of moons and no signs of Grace at all. Nyx and Ben had separated so she could retrieve the sensor. It hadn't been destroyed when it crossed over the boundary, and they hoped it had collected some information about the boundary. She propelled it through the opening into The Everything where the ship could retrieve it. Maybe it could give them an idea of what had happened, or where to look for Grace.

~~~~
~~~~

Grace found herself sitting on a cold, hard floor, utterly confused and aching. She was in a corporeal form that felt like hers, but in some ways was more. Different and the same. It was her hair, her hands, her clothing, her rings. Everything her shell was wearing back in the stasis pod on Rasa. Except this wasn't Rasa. She didn't know where she was.

A large, bright globe hovered above and in front of her, surrounded by a dim cage of lights coming up from the floor. The sphere and its accompanying enclosure were the only lights in a massive room that felt hollow and bleak. She could tell the ceilings were high from the way the sounds of her movement reflected back to her. The surfaces reverberated with a sharp echo, as if they were crafted from solid stone. It reminded her of a library, but sleek, without the dampening properties from loads of books. In her night range of vision, she could see floor-to-ceiling shelves on both sides of her filled with small stone or metal boxes. Millions of them sat stacked on top of each other. Pairs of rectangular stone columns, each intricately adorned with geometric shapes, bordered the central pathway for the full length of the room.

Somewhere in the distance behind her, a heavy metal door squeaked open and slammed into a hard surface. Ten pairs of boots rushed in her direction. She jumped to her feet, spinning around in a single swift motion. Dark, hooded figures surrounded her, standing stoically still, keeping a distance. They had no weapons. Grace felt their strength, and she could tell they didn't need weapons. She speculated if the purpose of the hoods was to intimidate her or if they were simply the customary attire in this place.

Two more sets of footsteps moved slowly toward her. One set was larger, striking the floor hard. The other set was small, moving at a slightly quicker pace.

What in all hells was this place, and how did she end up here? Her initial instinct was to shift out, but where would she shift to? She gathered a deep, calming breath. The figures didn't feel threatening. They smelled nervous. They seemed to be afraid of something, except for the two still walking. The larger figure exuded no feeling. The smaller figure felt pride or happiness. Grace wasn't confident about what the specific emotion was. The circle around her opened, allowing the two figures through. They halted in front of her as the circle again closed. The larger figure slipped off her hood and the lights in the room came up.

The woman standing in front of her had features similar to Grace's own. Long dark hair and large, clear green eyes. Not the same shade as Grace's, but a more common, muddier green. Her face was shaped the same. She had a similar height and build, and her skin was paler than Grace's. The woman projected a calculating, calm demeanor.

The smaller figure beside her appeared to represent an adolescent of around thirteen or fourteen. Prepubescent, at any rate, but not readily identifiable by appearance alone as any gender. Depending on the species, in Grace's experience, they could be anywhere from twelve to infinity. Appearance suggested nothing of age either. Aside from their appearance, their energy also projected neither a male nor female marker. The entity was several inches shorter than Grace, with light hair and brown eyes. They had a timid smile. Their scent was familiar, although not specific to any species she knew. Was it possible this was the child she had been chasing for so long? That child had displayed a distinct masculine energy and appeared significantly more naïve than the one in front of her.

"Grace. We weren't certain you could discover the way out." It was the woman who spoke. The tone of her voice was rich and smooth.

"It seems you have me at a disadvantage. I had little choice in the matter since I was dragged here. And what do you mean by 'out'?" How did this woman know Grace's name?

The woman nodded toward the sphere.

"Are you telling me I came out of that? Where is Ivan?" Grace narrowed her eyes skeptically at the woman and attempted to read her. Strangely, her action was being blocked. Had this woman read her? Grace wondered. Could that have been how she knew Grace's name?

"Now, now, we don't need any of that. Let's start over properly. I am Renata and this is Iniko. We should have this conversation in a more pleasant setting. Follow me," Renata said before she turned sharply and began walking away.

Grace wasn't having it. "I'm not going anyplace until you tell me where Ivan is."

Renata didn't stop walking. "I expect this Ivan person is exactly where you left them. You're the only one who came out."

The hooded figures formed lines, following Renata and Iniko out of the room. If Grace wanted any answers, her only option was to follow.

The lights dimmed behind the procession. The two-story-high metal doors closed, locking themselves as Grace stood there watching. She phased through them, catching up to Renata, who didn't seem surprised the doors hadn't stopped her. They walked for several minutes down the corridor, ending in a small sitting room. The hooded figures peeled off, lining the hall outside the room. Renata and Iniko sat in two of the three armchairs. Renata motioned Grace toward the other chair across from them.

"Tea?" Renata offered.

"I prefer coffee," Grace replied.

Coffee appeared on the side table next to Grace's chair. She picked it up, taking in the scent. It was regular coffee, with no nefarious additions. She could feel the particles swimming around inside the cup. She took a sip. It was a decent brew. If they had wanted to do something to her, she didn't think they would offer her a beverage.

Renata scrutinized her, probing her. The perplexed look on Renata's face pleased Grace when she easily used her own blocking abilities. She didn't want to push back too hard. She didn't want to reveal how strong her own ability was yet. The women sat in uncomfortable silence, bitter smiles sitting stiffly on their faces, matching their postures. They were at a standoff. Neither was giving in.

Iniko sat quietly, sipping something that smelled sweet and fruity. They leaned back in their chair beside Renata, swinging feet that didn't reach the floor. It was the first clue suggesting they were immature and not an entity of any significant age.

Renata, seeing the restlessness, placed her hand over theirs. Iniko instantaneously stopped moving, although they didn't look up at her.

"This is getting us nowhere. It would be far more beneficial if you would allow me to read you."

Grace scoffed. "No. It would be far more beneficial if you would allow me to read you."

Renata didn't appear to be someone who heard the word no very often. In response, Grace received a skeptical glare from her.

"You're in no position to demand anything. You're the one who escaped out of the confinement into our world."

"Being ripped away from minding my own business, dragged unwillingly, and then dumped onto a cold, hard floor isn't my idea of an escape," Grace said.

Her entire reality was fracturing as the idea of this place existing outside of her known world gripped her. Her understanding of The Everything slipped away. It was not at all what she had believed it was. It was a tiny world inside of another vast world. How could this be the truth? Had she been pulled into another being's consciousness, like when she and Ivan had been drawn inside of Chaos's? Grace had physical form when she was in that conscious place, but there she could tell her shell wasn't real. Was she still in a hidden part of The Everything? This place, it felt more a part of her than the one on Rasa did. Then a thought struck her as hard as any slap across the face could.

"Our entire reality is Chaos's prison?" She leaned on the arm of the chair for support, not understanding how the suggestion had entered her mind. Had Renata placed it there when she wasn't paying attention, or had it come from somewhere deep inside her?

A small smile flashed across Renata's face, followed by an overt look of confusion. "You call her Chaos? We created the confinement for Aphya. We incarcerated her for attempting to annihilate our entire species. She devoured nearly half of us before we could capture her. Her only goal is to release herself from her prison and devour the rest of us. 'Chaos' is an appropriate thing for her to have named herself."

Grace was cynical about this being the truth. She had witnessed many things in the last few years, but this was so far outside of the realm of possibility, she couldn't accept it. She had met Chaos and had felt nothing from her other than calming acceptance, admiration, and love.

"Do you take me for some kind of idiot? You're saying my entire reality, dimensions, universes, galaxies are all an illusion contained inside of that sphere at the other end of this hall? And all of it was created just to imprison one singular being? We're all her little puppets, and she's yours. What would make you think I would believe any of that nonsense?" Grace sat back hard against the chair. She placed her left boot across her right knee and folded her arms across her chest in defiance of a conclusion that she did not accept.

"All? How many others like you are in there with her?" Renata's question sounded like an interrogation to Grace instead of an answer to her question.

"I don't understand what you mean, 'like me.'" Grace understood interrogation tactics well enough to realize Renata was fishing.

"Grace, I understand your apprehension in believing what I've said to you. And no, your world is not an illusion any more than ours is. The only difference is your world is compressed into that sphere inside of ours. And yes, it was created to imprison a solitary, very dangerous, genocidal being." Renata's face was blank, not showing any emotion. Her body was motionless, offering no clue either.

"Then how? How is everything I understand about my world in that sphere? And if she's so dangerous, why would you leave anyone inside exposed to her?"

"I have no words to explain the sphere unless I know what it is you think you understand about your world. We only recently discovered that Aphya wasn't alone inside the confinement. We didn't know she could generate other beings. Illusions, yes; consciousness, no. And you are certainly not an illusion, are you?"

Grace's brow crinkled, and her mouth was tight. She was concentrating on the disconnect between Renata's words and her body language. She bit at her lip, not wanting to let Renata into her mind. "You'll need to let me pass my thoughts to you. I don't trust you to rummage around in my head."

There was something off about Renata. Grace didn't trust her at all. Her stomach seized when Renata spoke, making her uneasy. It wasn't the coffee; it was something in the tone of her voice.

"No offense, but I don't think a species generated in such a primitive place has the ability to efficiently transfer the quantity of data I need to understand your perspective. It would be far more efficient if you let me obtain what I need."

Renata was condescending. She seemed to be working a little too hard at getting inside Grace's thoughts, so it didn't seem she could have already been in them.

Grace wasn't known for her self-control. Historically, she had the most difficulty when she felt she was being underestimated. If there was any truth in what Renata had said, Grace had every right to be angry. All the people she knew and cared about were stuck in that sphere. Grace leaned forward. She forced her way into Renata's mind, transferring an enormous quantity of what she understood of how her world worked and nothing else. She pressed forward mountains of geography, the little she knew about physics, and whatever astronomy information she remembered, while giving nothing about the beings inhabiting her world or what she and Ivan had been doing in it for the past few centuries. Grace was determined not to reveal any information about the people she cared about. Had Grace done this of her own volition or had she let Renata goad her into it?

Renata squeezed her eyes shut and clenched her fists. Grace was certain Renata had been inundated by the sheer amount of information. Renata pushed back into her chair, opening her eyes wider than they had been before.

"No offense taken, but I don't think you know what species I am. I don't even know," Grace said, allowing her confidence to slink away.

Iniko's face had remained concealed by their downward gaze. Grace heard them giggle in her mind. It was the same giggle. The boy from The Everything. She snapped her head around to look at him. Her eyes focused on the child. How could she not have recognized him? How could he be the same child? For that matter, how could she not realize instantly that he was? Nothing in this place made sense to her. Some things were sharp and clear, while others remained cloudy and vague.

Renata stood up. "Niko, go to your room. Grace, walk with me." She didn't wait for an answer before moving with purpose toward the door.

Grace was stunned for a moment by Renata's movement. She stood, glanced at Niko's empty chair, then followed. She had no intention of letting this woman out of her sight. It was obvious Renata wanted something from her. Had Renata or one of her people extracted Grace out of The Everything? What reason could this woman possibly have to rip her away from her familiar surroundings and throw her into such a strange situation?

CHAPTER TEN

They were back in the main chamber, standing in front of the sphere.

"You have no reason to trust me, so I am going to explain what this sphere is, and hopefully, you will see what needs to be done to keep your world safe."

Is this why I was brought here, to this place, to protect The Everything? Grace thought to herself. She nodded, encouraging Renata to continue.

"The easiest way for me to explain the confinement is to compare it to an ovipar." Renata tilted her head, appearing unsure she had used the correct word.

"You mean 'egg'? It's like an egg?"

"Yes, an egg." Renata extended her hand toward the sphere. "The outer layer is the shell. It keeps all the other parts contained. Inside the shell is a small chamber or bubble that moves freely, allowing the remaining interior parts to stabilize." She studied Grace to see if she was keeping up.

Grace nodded, but she couldn't understand Renata's intention in sharing the details of the confinement's construction.

"Inside of that are two sections with a membrane to keep them separate. The outermost section is what you understand to be The Nothing. It isn't nothing though. It feeds the interior section through the membrane, like you saw at the hole on the border. But that's not typical. The hole in the membrane shouldn't be there." She glanced at Grace again.

Grace nodded once again.

"The center, The Everything, is where all you know has grown. That is Aphya's prison. We created the surrounding membrane with the singular purpose of keeping her inside. The Nothing is the buffer that circulates elements with The Everything, allowing it to sustain itself. The Nothing and The Everything exchange particles as necessary to keep the balance on each side of the membrane so it doesn't collapse. What drew our attention was The Nothing was draining at an increased rate because of the hole, too quickly to be refilled by particles moving organically through the membrane. When we examined the confinement, we found Niko in the doorway between The Nothing and The Outside. We pulled him out, and that's when we understood we had a problem."

Grace could see what she said made sense, but she was still having difficulty with the entirety of it. She didn't have time to let it germinate. She needed to gather more information before she could take the time to process it all.

"All the accounts of the creation of our world say Chaos created The Everything from The Nothing."

Renata scoffed. "Where do you think all those tales originated from? Aphya was never, nor will ever be, in The Nothing. We constructed The Everything to be as our world is, with a few restrictions, of course. The confinement contains similar elements but was originally void of your planets, stars, et cetera. It's more likely she created your structures inside The Everything out of a violent burst of anger. Otherwise, it should have taken much longer to develop such a vast number of diverse environments."

Grace let the information sink in. A burst of anger aligned with many theories of how the universes came into existence.

"If The Nothing is supposed to support The Everything, how could the entire confinement have gotten so far out of balance? Why are some of our dimensions collapsing before they should?"

"The Everything doesn't need to be in balance on its own. There needs to be an overall balance between The Nothing and The Everything. There must be equal motion between the two layers to keep the overall confinement from stagnating. As for the dimensions collapsing before their time, Aphya is causing the collapses to trick you into thinking there is something wrong. There shouldn't even be separate dimensions. She created those, and she is collapsing them to make you believe there is something wrong. She is tricking you into placing inverse pressure on the membrane, creating thin spots. Even with the collapsing dimensions, The Everything isn't actually losing any matter or energy. If one dimension collapses, the energy and matter flood into the others, allowing them to swell. It doesn't matter if there is one or one thousand. That's not what's affecting the balance. The membrane is supposed to allow the necessary elements to release through it slowly. She's using you to cause a weakening of the membrane, and Aphya has been trying to escape from those thin spots. It's still too strong to allow her through"

Grace shook her head as Renata spoke. It seemed like Renata had figured out that she had been creating on her own. It made her wonder how much Renata already knew before Grace had given her any information. "If the membrane is still so strong, how did I get out? How did Niko get out? And how does he destroy matter?" Grace didn't want to reveal that she understood the impact of his nature.

Renata wrung her hands in frustration. Her brow furrowed as she searched for a way to explain.

"Niko has an opposite polarization, attracting positive matter and correcting it by adjusting its polarity—by adding or removing electrons. His presence restores the balance between The Everything and The Nothing when he's in there, but it's dangerous for him. If Aphya finds him, she will eliminate him as she did the others Niko can't control what he's doing. He strengthens the confinement when he is inside of it by reducing the pressure buildup, slowing the material from being pressed in from The

Nothing. That's why Aphya tried to destroy him like she did all the others. That's why he escaped to The Nothing. She couldn't follow him through the membrane. As for how you and Niko got out, we did not create the confinement to contain you. We didn't create it to contain anything besides Aphya. He simply pulled you into the doorway."

Grace studied Renata's demeanor. She had a feeling that Renata was being at least partially truthful. But what part?

"Chaos, or um … Aphya, didn't destroy the others. I visit them regularly." Grace was certain Niko had already informed Renata about his belief of the other children's destruction.

Renata stared at Grace. "That's impossible, Grace. Aphya is a devourer. She feeds on energy. It's why we couldn't destroy her out here. We had to imprison her instead. She must have pushed into your consciousness and showed you what she wanted you to see. If she stays inside your consciousness too long, all of those illusions will dissolve. She will know you see through her. She must be using your energy to create the illusion of children and then feeding on that energy afterward to gain power."

Grace again noticed Renata's uncomfortable stillness when she answered. This interpretation didn't make sense to Grace, either. Grace thought back to Nyx and Frigg's conversation with Gaia. Other than some inconsistent ramblings on Gaia's part, the rest seemed similar to what Renata was telling her. Gaia must have figured out the imbalance because of her connection to the elements of living things. The part she couldn't have understood was the balance between the greater structures of the confinement. Grace definitely needed to process this. The stories were similar, but the interpretations seemed to have different agendas. Why would Aphya go through that incredible ruse to create beings to devour when there was more than enough energy in The Everything to sate her hunger? Why would she have created all the other beings in their world and not fed on them, if that's what she was doing? Then another thought came to her.

"Niko was already out. Did you send him back in, knowing how dangerous it was for him? Just to pull me out?" Grace was not happy that

Renata would endanger the boy if she believed that he was, in fact, in danger.

"Yes," Renata answered simply. "We needed to have contact with whoever was trying to destroy the confinement."

So Niko was a tattletale, Grace thought to herself as she continued listening to Renata.

"Since we were not aware Aphya had any abilities to create, we knew there must be another inside. How you got there, we still don't know. Niko volunteered to go in and get you. And you know as well as I do, despite his innocence, he is not a boy." Renata's expression was stoic.

"Why bring me here?" Grace asked.

"Because we need you to stop her before she gets out." Renata's expression hadn't changed.

Great, I knew there was an agenda here somewhere, Grace thought, rolling her eyes.

"What makes you think I can stop her? And even if I could, what makes you think I would?" Grace found it revolting that Renata might suggest she destroy the consciousness of another being. She had killed beings before, but she only destroyed their bodies, never their consciousness. She released it.

"You can control what you create and what you destroy. And you will need to destroy her to save your world. As soon as she realizes you know she's only using you to escape, she will devour every creature inside that confinement and start over. And it won't be a fresh start. She knows how she created you. She'll do it again, and she will get out the next time. Both of our worlds are being threatened." Renata locked eyes with Grace, standing deathly still.

Grace broke her gaze, lowering her head. She folded her hands, bringing them up to her lips in a motion that resembled prayer. She tapped her index fingers together and paced in agitation, feeling the walls closing in. Abruptly, her gaze locked onto Renata's once more.

"I need to think. I need to be somewhere less confining."

"Is this better?" Renata asked.

Grace blinked only once, and they were outside of the building in an incredibly strange city. It looked like two tremendous structures facing each other, with hundreds of meters in between. She couldn't be certain, but she thought it was constructed inside the planet; if it was a planet. They were standing on an overhang with a railing in front. She could see no sky or floor. The city extended as far as the limits of her view from side to side. And Grace could see for miles. Thousands of levels existed, making the space almost as claustrophobic as it had been inside.

The glow of colored lights highlighted the gravity-defying vehicles, saturating the entire space with silence. They were traveling in complex streams that crossed in front of the balcony. The buildings were constructed using a material she had never encountered before. It appeared to be an amalgamation of light-colored stone, glass, and metal with an opalescent sheen. The space was busy, filled with motion. The entire scene was bathed in a cool brightness reflected by the buildings themselves, which seemed to amplify the light. Grace couldn't pinpoint where the light was coming from, noticing that it seemed to surround them.

Grace had witnessed her fair share of technologically advanced cities before, but none of them compared to this one. Everything seemed to vibrate here. The level of energy unbalanced her. She held on to the railing with her left hand, reaching forward with her right to steady herself in the way a tightrope walker would. The population exuded a mixture of mortal and immortal physical signatures containing immortal essences. Their abilities ranged from the majority having none or minor abilities to a very few holding gifts close to her level. They coexisted in a harmony so perfect it seemed artificial. She wouldn't have thought that a possibility in her world. The overall feeling was a hypnotic, drone-like order. No anger, no resentment, no heightened emotion of any kind. It was also eerily quiet.

Everything seemed different here. The smells were peculiar. She caught the scents of minerals, elements, and biological signs of the living. What was missing was everything else. The absence of animals, insects, birds, plants, and dirt was noticeable. The pervasive scent was clean, raw energy. Overall, it was far from anything she was familiar with. The atmosphere was tidy, but not sanitized. It was challenging for her to handle everything coming at her at once.

"How?" Grace asked.

Renata didn't grasp what she was experiencing or what she was asking.

"How what? How did we construct the city?"

"No. How do physically mortal and immortal beings live together without hate or greed or jealousy? How is it so tranquil? It's like being in a trance." Grace dropped her hand, turning to study Renata's face.

Renata's shoulders dropped. She tilted her head away from Grace, and her eyes darted back and forth as her thoughts went into overdrive. She didn't seem to have an answer. At least, not an answer she was willing to share. She raised her head, focusing on Grace's blank expression.

Grace reached forward, urging a response. She placed her hand on Renata's forearm. A sense of foreboding overcame Grace. Reality swirled in front of her as a blanket of serenity doused her senses. She experienced an uncountable number of consciousnesses flowing bluntly over her. They were all the same kind. Their essences were connected, although somehow, oddly, simultaneously disconnected. Her own senses were declining, becoming dull. Grace jerked her hand away. Her knees buckled, and she lost her balance, flailing at the railing to regain her spatiality. The sharpness of her own mind came slamming back into her, and she felt she was going to be sick.

Renata stepped back, forcing distance between them. "You're like one of us," Renata said, eying her sharply.

"If I'm like all of you ..." Grace hesitated. "How did I get inside the confinement?"

"I can't fathom how Aphya could create others with the ability to develop into an infinite inside the confinement. You must be one she devoured before being imprisoned, but I don't understand how you could have survived that."

There was that strange, eerie stillness again that made Grace queasy. Or had it been the lingering sensation from Renata's touch that made her stomach drop?

Renata transported them back to the private room. Grace found herself once again seated in the chair with Renata seated across from her, folding her hands into her lap. Grace's thoughts focused on Renata's statement.

"What is an infinite?"

"It would be easier if you would allow me to transfer the information to you," Renata offered.

"I think that would be too overwhelming for me right now. Please, I would prefer a verbal conversation." Grace didn't want any additional thoughts being pressed in on her. She also possessed a strong aversion to trusting this woman.

When she had touched Renata, Grace had felt like she was being pulled down. The entire hour had been confusing. If it had even been an hour yet. She felt no reference for time in this place. The instantaneous bouncing back and forth without the feeling of shifting wasn't helping, either.

"As you wish." Renata nodded at her.

"I should start with how our species evolves. It should answer at least two of your questions," Renata said and leaned back in her chair, gripping the arms.

Grace nodded.

"We all start with an internal consciousness. Every living being does. It is our most basic form. When we are very young, we start with mortal manifestations. Bodies, as you would understand them. Once that manifestation cycles through its existence and dies, the consciousness transfers into its next cycle. The first few dozen cycles don't retain old memories. It would be too complicated for such immature beings to comprehend. What they do retain are abilities. Each cycle, those abilities improve as they become more connected to the whole," Renata said.

"So, will they all ultimately evolve into infinites?" Grace asked.

Renata nodded. "Yes, as long as they don't hold onto any issues from their previous lives. If that happens, they need to be contained and resolved before being reintroduced into society."

"Resolved?" Grace tilted her head. She didn't recognize the phrase.

"Resolving is when the consciousness is placed into a small container where it can process its prior existence. The boxes at the end of the hall.

Once they are resolved, they are prepared to be reborn into a new life. They can then be integrated into the swarm, as by that point, they are like the others again."

"How long does it take to evolve?" Grace wanted to understand the concept of time in this place.

"Your perception of time isn't the same as it is here." Renata swayed her head slowly as if reading Grace's thought. "I can say that in our existence, only a minimal percentage of us have become an infinite. The strength of consciousness dictates the lifespan of the manifestation."

A switch was tripped in Grace's mind. "Which is why I possess my corporeal form here."

"Your form here is a robust reflection of your consciousness," Renata said.

"And in there, my shell can be killed, and my consciousness can be moved to another." Grace was accepting the concept, if not the reality, of what she was experiencing here.

Renata added, "There's another considerable difference with your manifestation here."

Grace elevated her eyebrows. There had been so much going on around her, she hadn't noticed. She quickly rubbed her tongue over her gums.

"No canis," Renata said. The corners of her mouth momentarily turned up, hinting at a smile. "They're unnecessary here. They would be a detriment to the way we develop and stabilize our swarm. For you, inside the confinement, you need them to turn your populations. They allow for an immediate connection to your people."

The statement unnerved Grace. She hadn't given Renata information regarding the turned. She felt she needed to say something provocative to evoke a response from Renata.

"But that would mean you are vampires as well. Only you consume energy instead of blood."

"That's quite a vulgar-sounding word. We are infinites," Renata said, smiling condescendingly. "And you never needed to consume blood, either. You were always consuming energy. You simply became addicted to the disgusting process of draining your victim's life-sustaining fluids to get it."

That was the first statement Renata had made that Grace could completely agree with. Not for herself, though, but for the rest of the turned species. Grace had never needed to consume blood. She absorbed energy through the very air that surrounded her and the earth under her feet. Once her blood had been introduced to the others, they could too.

Grace leaned forward, placing her elbows on her knees. "So, what am I supposed to do now?" The experience of being in this place was like a jumbled montage, with topics and places shifting abruptly in an odd, staccato pattern.

Renata straightened herself. "You go home and make your decision."

"And then what?" Grace's expression was grave. How could they live inside, knowing what it was? Regardless of Aphya's involvement, they would always know their world was a prison.

"That's up to you. It's your world. You are free to live in it as you please." Renata splayed her hands in her lap.

"What if I decide I don't want to live in a prison?"

"How can you think of it as a prison? You never had until now. Is it a prison if you can leave anytime you want?" Renata asked, holding her hands tight in her lap.

Grace thought Renata's body language was once again asserting something different from her words.

"That doesn't seem to be entirely truthful."

Renata placed her hands on the arms of her chair. "Only your turned could leave. And they would need to evolve as we do. They would need to be resolved initially, of course, to release whatever negative trauma they have been exposed to inside the confinement. None of the other beings of that world would be capable of surviving here. They are purely manifestations of that world."

Grace studied Renata's posture again. She was rigid, stern. Grace was uneasy. Why would they want to escape one prison for another with no guarantee they could resolve and emerge free to live in this world?

"We have a sizable population." The information was something she was sure Niko had already divulged. Otherwise, how would Renata have known about the turned at all? Then the other part hit her—she had never told Renata they called themselves the turned, and she didn't see how Niko could know that either. "How could we possibly bring so many out if we had to? Where would we all go?"

"You can go anywhere you want. Our world is infinitely larger than yours. Your numbers are nothing compared to our existing population. You could establish your own city if you wish. Stay close together until you comprehend our ways."

"What happens to us if we don't destroy Aphya? It's what you're asking us to do, isn't it?"

Renata evaded the question. "That is entirely up to you. Make your decision. It's time for you to go back."

Renata stood and walked out the door. Grace took a few seconds before she followed. Why did it seem like the woman was rushing Grace to get back into the confinement? Grace had already figured out if she didn't destroy Aphya, the infinites would destroy the confinement. Renata was providing her options for the turned to survive, wasn't she? Maybe for the entire world to survive. But at what cost if none of them would know each other after being resolved? Grace thought the infinites could have destroyed the confinement without revealing themselves. So, what was the real reason she required Grace? Were they interested in saving the turned or were they only interested in having someone to do their dirty work of killing Aphya? Grace had a lot to discuss with Ivan and the rest of the community.

"But wait." Grace started to grasp Renata's arm before thinking better of it. She pulled her hand back, freezing it in midair. Renata turned to confront her.

"If you couldn't destroy her out here, what makes you think destroying the confinement would work?" Grace asked. She wanted the question to be blunt, thinking Renata hadn't expected her to put together the pieces of what they were planning.

Renata's posture stiffened. She blinked long and sighed. "We don't. All we can do is sanitize the confinement over and over every time she builds her world in there."

Grace had already speculated on the answer to her next question. She needed Renata to confirm it. "How do I have the ability to destroy her when all of your people together couldn't?"

Renata studied Grace's face. She swallowed with difficulty. Grace saw Renata didn't want to tell her. "Because. As much as you are part of us, you are also part of her. You are an infinite and a devourer. You can ..." Renata spoke slowly, searching for the precise words. "... cease Aphya's consciousness."

The air in the chamber had become heavy and thick. Renata's eyes were downcast, her tone remorseful, but she was still blocking Grace from reading her thoughts or emotions. Why would she feel regret at the thought of destroying Aphya? Was it regret she was feeling at all or something else?

"You need to go. Discuss it with whomever you need to, but whatever you do, don't let Aphya know. If she can separate you from the support of your people, we don't believe you will survive. We will be forced to sanitize the confinement, and that is the last thing we desire with so many conscious beings inside."

Grace lowered her head, moving past Renata with a troubled heart. She held her hand up, touching the confinement. Renata's guidance wasn't necessary for her to find her way back inside. She could feel all of it from here. She could feel Ivan inside and was being drawn toward him.

CHAPTER ELEVEN

"What the hell, Grace! Where have you been?" Ivan asked, yelling at her.

"Ivan, it's been an hour. I know you're upset with the way we were ripped apart, but why are you yelling at me? It wasn't my fault," Grace said, massaging her temples. Stuffing herself back in her shell was hard this time. Her essence had expanded from being on The Outside. Everything ached. Her head was splitting. Her thoughts were all swirling around.

"An hour? Are you fucking serious? ARE YOU FUCKING SERIOUS RIGHT NOW? You've been gone A YEAR! The last we saw of you, you were being dragged into The Nothing and you were gone," Ivan yelled back at her. He was furious. He had thought she was gone forever. How could she be so flippant?

"What?! What are you talking about? A year? No! It can't have been a year." Grace shook her head. She was unnerved. How could she have been gone for so long without feeling out of place?

Grace stood in the center of the group, cringing. So many had gathered, feeling her return. There were too many, too close, all in her head. Coming back to this shell was too confining for all the knowledge she had gained. She couldn't process it fast enough. Grace gathered every ounce of energy she had to block everyone out. She couldn't let them know. Not while her mind was so chaotic. How could she explain to them that their entire reality was a lie? That their world was a prison within another world? What they believed to be a limitless expanse was little more than a snow globe on a shelf in a room full of other snow globes.

Ivan saw she was overwhelmed. He understood the feeling of stuffing himself back into a tiny physical form. He stepped forward, grabbing Grace's arm, and shifted her away from the others. Although he couldn't see what she was blocking, he could see that she was blocking something big. Too big for her to work through in a short time frame. He hadn't meant to yell at her like that, but once he had seen her, his fear and frustration had spilled out.

Grace was almost as disoriented as she had been when Niko had snatched her. Her thoughts were melting together. Ivan pulled her down onto their bed. Sitting back up, she was in disbelief at how easily he had overpowered her. They were normally equally matched, but similar to the issue she was having controlling her mind, controlling her body was just as difficult.

With her thoughts racing, she closed her eyes. She had no leftover processing speed to anticipate his movements. She was more astonished when he seized her hard, embracing her, almost enveloping her from behind. He gripped her tight, giving her the same squeezing physical sensation her mind was choking her thoughts with. If she had been weaker than she was, he would have suffocated her. She felt like he was trying to meld with her, the way they did when they rose, only in physical form.

When she opened her eyes, Ivan was standing in front of her. She could feel him holding her, only he wasn't. He was in front of her, pacing and running his hands through his hair, unsure of what to do. She could see him, but it didn't make sense. She thought she was lying down, but she was still sitting on the edge of the bed.

Grace reached out to Ivan, but her arm didn't move. Her body was betraying her, unable to respond in the way she needed it to. She tried to speak, to call out to him to help her escape this hellish nightmare. Grace needed Ivan to pull her outside of herself. No matter how hard she tried, she couldn't escape from the confines of this physical prison that held her captive.

Ivan! Help me! I can't get out!

He didn't do it. Maybe he couldn't do it. Had he heard her? His stride hadn't stopped. He hadn't as much as glanced her way.

Grace stared as stoically as a malfunctioning synthetic. She couldn't get control of her mind. Her thoughts continued to jump randomly through scenarios of what could happen, what had happened, what was happening now. She needed Ivan to help her stabilize. Ivan was her other half. She wasn't complete without him. Everything she knew and felt, in any of these worlds, was wrong without him. Why couldn't he hear her? How could he not help her? All she could see was his steady, rhythmic pacing back and forth in front of her eyes, which were locked in place, fixated on the empty wall in front of her.

She had lost her will to get up, wanting to forget everything she had seen, but it was impossible to forget as all her memories raced past, jumbled out of order. She was unable to make sense of them. Her mind became a labyrinth, and Grace found herself lost in its intricate twists and turns. Her shell was shutting off, trapping her essence in a disjointed corridor filled with locked doors that burst open and then shut again before she could reach them. The distinction between reality and dreams overlapped. She couldn't even rise. It was like she was bound by the remnant of the long-discarded amulet hanging around her neck all over again.

Scenes flashed in front of her, showing her everything she had done wrong. She felt stupid and childish. She didn't want to drag Ivan into yet another one of her ridiculous dilemmas, but she needed him! Could he not see the trouble she was in, which was making her feel like a catastrophic failure? Maybe he didn't want to help her because she had caused this. The blame for everything rested on her shoulders. If she had never gone looking for Ben when he was hunting for her. If she had only been content with her life alongside Lukkas and not felt like she had to save every unfortunate soul who crossed her path. So many things she had done to bring attention to herself that she never should have.

Grace found it impossible to breathe. She was so confused. Too much information in her head. Too many thoughts, with nothing making sense. Traveling through the doorway had done something to her. It had transformed her. Renata's touch had altered her, too. She felt too big for her shell. Too big for this world. Her thoughts flashed through memories and places foreign and unrecognizable to her. She tried to steer them, but they only seemed to spin faster.

She was trying so hard to communicate with him. Grace couldn't concentrate. If he would only try to get in, he would be able to see it all. Grace didn't have the strength to get his attention. She was going to break soon, and he would never know what she had seen—what was out there. The room was swirling around her, and she felt she only had a few seconds before she would fold.

When it happened, everything came crashing down around her, like a wave of water rushing in and carrying out her thoughts. The wall around Grace's mind collapsed in on itself. It was only then that Ivan could see everything. Niko, the doorway, the confinement, Renata. All of it. The lies. It was all right in front of him—Grace and Ivan were the lie. They only existed because Chaos needed a way out.

When Grace's barrier dropped, Ivan rushed to her side, shocked by the experience she had had while she had been missing. He wrapped his arms around her, pulling her into his lap.

For Grace, the imagined arms dissolved away, replaced by those now wrapped around her. The only thing that was real for her was Ivan, gripping her tight against his chest. For others, if something could be touched, it was real. Grace didn't have the same perspective. She was capable of passing through things and allowing them to pass through her. Except for Ivan. He was the only thing that would always be real for her. He would always be able to touch her. In this moment, he was the only link she had to stay connected to this reality.

Her emotions were irrational and erratic. It felt like time was both flying by and dragging on endlessly.

Ivan thought he needed to force her to focus on one thing, anything with a strong emotion attached. He squeezed her as tight as he could, pulling her as close as his physical form would allow. He was trying to hold her there. Trying to direct her mind to sync with his, but he couldn't. Grace wasn't a feeble person, but this was the second time her physical form had encountered difficulty keeping up with her consciousness.

She wished she could manifest a shell here, like she had outside the confinement. A strong shell that didn't have a near mental breakdown when she forced herself back in, overloaded.

"Grace, please. Tell me what you want to do. I'll end her myself, if it's what you need." Ivan didn't have the objections to taking a life that Grace had. He didn't see it as an existential issue. He didn't define the difference between physical life and conscious life. Since he had killed his sire, he had never pondered over who was good or bad or who deserved to live or die.

He gently shook her but got no response. He pushed her further.

Ivan whispered to her, "Grace, you need to do the right thing. Even if it obliterates everything we believe in, our entire reality, you have to do what you think is right. I'm not equipped to make that judgment call for you. I'm not a good enough person to make that choice."

I can't make that decision. Please, don't ask me to make that decision, Grace thought. She couldn't pull herself together enough to speak. She collapsed into him, imagining it may be for the last time.

Her words were faint, but he had heard her. Ivan grabbed Grace by the arms, spinning her to face him, shaking her hard. "Look at me, Grace! Get your shit together. You need to decide. Renata gave you the choice. I'm sorry it has to be you, but this is your decision to make."

His words echoed from far away, muffled and unclear.

Don't make it me, Ivan. I don't want this to be my decision. I can't. Grace's thought was distant and weak. She curled up into a ball, pushing him away with her knees.

Ivan struggled against her, pulling her in as tightly as he could as he fell back. He wanted to pull her inside of him, although he knew it wasn't possible without rising. If she didn't get a grip on herself soon, he would need to extract her, and she wouldn't be able to come back to this shell again.

"Grace, I'm not the one who made this choice your responsibility! But now everything from this point forward *is* about you. Only you! It's not fair. It's just the way it is, and you don't have to like it. You just need to DO SOMETHING ABOUT IT!" He was screaming in her face. The air felt thick, suffocating. He felt her sliding further away.

Grace saw herself standing in a dark pit with only a small light that was becoming more and more distant. She could always justify taking physical life, with the knowledge she wasn't ending a consciousness. The energy of that being would go on.

The light was getting smaller. This decision was dragging her in instead of guiding her out. Words streamed toward her in whispers.

Take a single life to save the others. An immortal consciousness? She didn't want to be responsible for another ceasing to exist.

Escape the confinement. Take them to a reality outside of this place into something they wouldn't understand?

Leave them behind. All the essences she was condemning to the confinement's sanitizing would be on her. One or all? How could she make that decision? Why should she believe Renata's reality was the real one?

Grace wished she could be callous enough to cut all of them loose to save her own skin. If she was as smart as she told herself she was, she would have jumped ship and let Renata sanitize the confinement while she was outside of it. Only, that was all a lie, too. She could never leave Ivan. She couldn't leave any of them. In that instant, Grace hated her empathy, her humanity, her selflessness. She hated herself in this moment of weakness, more than she had ever hated anything in her entire life.

She was reeling beyond her ability to cope.

"Hey!" Ivan grabbed her face, pulling it hard into alignment with his own. "Tell me, Grace. What do you need?" he asked, shaking her again.

Grace didn't react. Her eyes were wide open and glazed over, and her body was limp. She looked through him. Ivan phased his arm into her, searching for her essence, but it wasn't where it should be. He desperately searched, trying to drag her out.

I can't do this anymore, Ivan. I don't know what's real. Grace's thoughts echoed, becoming harder for Ivan to hear. Her perspective was gone. Her existence was a lie. All of it. Her creation. Everything. Even if she believed nothing else Renata had said, she knew it was all set up as a way for Chaos to get out. She allowed her mind to collapse into its own failure. Grace was falling toward the bottom of her mind. The bottom of the pit. Alone in the dark. Her past, present, and hundreds of possible futures had crumbled and floated away.

She felt like she had plunged several stories into a vast nothing. At the moment she hit the bottom, she snapped. In that instant, she saw clearly.

What had she expected? For the universe to have a point? Everything was created for someone else's agenda. So what if she was created as a tool for someone else's use? She was here. This was her reality, prison cell or not. Controlled by someone else or not. It didn't matter. It never had. The darkness lifted as light broke through. What had lasted only a few minutes felt like it had taken days to push through. The muddled cloudiness was lifting. Her thoughts were finally her own again.

Grace relaxed. She released her breath, forcing her eyes to focus. Ivan's grip on her loosened as he slid his hand out of the back of her head. They lay together for what seemed like days, staring up at the ceiling.

"That was rough. My shell won't last another insertion," Grace said.

Ivan nodded his head in agreement. "For a moment there, I was afraid I had lost you. I was trying to yank you back out when your synapses started firing again. I know it's not funny, but it was like your body was a locked-up computer trying to reboot itself. At least you didn't hit that blue screen of death."

"It felt like I did. I guess it's time we ask Nyx for help," Grace said.

Nyx had been after them for years to ditch the genetic shells and move to a manifested genetic hybrid shell, like she had. After feeling the freedom Grace had experienced with the manifested shell on The Outside, she couldn't fathom what her objections had been. Probably having to listen to Nyx saying "I told you so" for the rest of their eternal existence.

After what she had just suffered, she could live with that. The process of manifesting a shell would be different here, but Grace had the principal understanding. They just needed Nyx to fill in the details.

Grace and Ivan lay on the bed a little longer, holding onto each other. Ivan needed it more than Grace did. From his perspective, they had been apart for an entire year, and she wanted to comfort him as much as she could. She also needed to know what had been happening while she was gone.

"Sadie is showing more thin spots. Have you been creating on your own?" Grace tried to make her voice soft, but Ivan could hear the urgency in it.

"Nyx and Ben have been helping as much as they can and I've taken Mikkel up a few times. He's not much help yet. He's a little … unfocused." Ivan thought that was the kindest way to phrase it.

"Does Chaos know I was gone?" Grace asked, hoping he hadn't revealed that piece of information.

"I don't know how she could. The others didn't feel your absence in the same way I did. For me, it felt like there was a barrier between us," he said.

"We should visit the children soon so she's not suspicious. We'll need to decide what to do about this whole thing first." Grace didn't know how much time they had.

"I want to see The Outside and speak with Renata. We need to see if there are other options," Ivan said.

"Ivan, we can't afford to both be gone for a year."

"We won't need to be this time. We can mark our departure time and come back to it. Now that we are aware there's such an enormous time gap, we can adjust for it," Ivan said, thinking about it logically.

Grace sighed. "We need to make new shells before we go."

Ivan felt a heaviness in his chest. Being responsible for the continued existence of every living thing was a dire feeling. If they made a mistake, all of it would be destroyed. He didn't want to rush into anything. They had to think. They needed help. The issue with getting help was that they would have to tell the others what was happening. This kind of information could shatter reality for anyone they told.

"We need to talk to Gaia first," he said, breaking the silence.

"Nyx and Frigg said she was totally insane."

"Insane or not, she seems to be the only one with any idea about what's going on," Ivan said, sitting up.

"You don't think it'll look suspicious? We've never been to see Gaia before."

"We can use the excuse that we want to ask her about the thin spots—see how she reacts before we find out what she might know about The Outside."

"I think we should send her a message first. I don't think surprising her like Nyx did is the best idea." Grace was pondering how best to phrase a self-invitation.

"Yeah, we should." Ivan rubbed his chin. "I think we should create the shells first, then see Gaia, then Renata. Once we've completed all of that, we should be able to construct a plan."

"I agree. I don't think we should tell Nyx about The Outside yet, though. It'll be better if we tell her my shell is failing and leave it at that for now," Grace said, deciding that keeping Nyx and her temper in the dark a little longer was best for everyone.

"What do you think we should tell everyone about why you were gone so long?" Ivan wondered.

"That's the easiest question of the entire conversation. I got knocked into The Nothing, caught in a time vortex, and couldn't figure out the math to get back to the precise time. Nobody will question that one," Grace answered, knowing everyone was aware of how bad her calculation skills were without Sadie.

"That is not entirely a lie," Ivan agreed. He would have believed it if he hadn't already uncovered the truth.

Ivan stood up. "You need to look more distraught."

"More distraught? I'm not sure that's possible," Grace said, reaching for Ivan's hand.

Ivan waved her hand away. "Stay there. I'll call Nyx to come here so we're not explaining to everyone."

"That's a good idea. I don't think I can face everyone right now anyway," Grace said, leaning back on the bed.

Seconds later, Nyx popped in with Ben in tow. "You want to explain where in all hells you've been?" Ben raised his voice, sounding perturbed.

Grace rubbed her head like she wasn't all there. "Time vortex."

"She couldn't figure out how to get back to when she was knocked into The Nothing. We're lucky it was only a year," Ivan said.

"I didn't know it was a different time. The child knocked me into The Nothing. I spun into a vortex and came out the other side. Everyone was gone, so I came home," Grace said, rubbing her temples as if she were still in pain.

"That's not why we called you here. Her shell is failing. She can't process her thoughts," Ivan conveyed urgently.

"I've been telling you for years a fully genetic shell couldn't last," Nyx said, looking smug.

"We get it, Nyx. You were right. Can you help her or not?" Ivan tried to sound irritated instead of angry.

"Of course," Nyx said, holding out her hand as she sat on the bed beside Grace. "I'll need some blood."

Grace bit into her wrist and reached forward toward Nyx's hand.

"Ew! Put it in your own hand, Grace." Nyx grimaced, pulling away.

Grace let the blood flow into her hand until her wrist healed. Nyx placed her hand under Grace's blood-filled one.

"Now, give me your other hand." Nyx extended her free hand. Grace took it.

"Concentrate on your blood."

Grace closed her eyes. She felt how Nyx was drawing up energy from her consciousness and repeated the steps. The blood in her hand began to swirl and take on a gelatinous texture, morphing into a blob-like shape, squirming and growing. Particles streamed toward the mass of pulp from the air around it and then from The Everything itself. Grace laid it on the bed beside her when it became too large to hold in her hand.

The bloody shape continued to grow, forming a cylindrical core with nubs from which the limbs and head would grow. It twisted and split, pushing out bones and muscle. It grew into the recognizable shape of a body with hair growing out of the wet red skull. Holes sunk where the eyes and mouth would form.

Ivan and Ben watched the little pool of blood pull and stretch into a replica of Grace's body. It didn't take long before a naked, empty version of Grace was lying next to her on the bed. When she finished, Grace opened her eyes to see Ivan and Ben staring at the body next to her.

"Really?" she scoffed at them and turned back to Nyx. "That was a lot more straightforward than I thought it was going to be," Grace said, letting go of Nyx's hand. It had taken some effort, unlike the one she had unconsciously created on The Outside.

"Told you so." Nyx shrugged. She couldn't help herself. "Take it for a spin. There's a lot more room in there."

Grace laid back on the bed and rose, but instead of escaping the room, she entered the new shell and sat up, stretching.

"Oh, wow!" She twisted her neck. "You were right. This is much more comfortable."

She got off the bed, reaching back to swing her arm through the mattress. Phasing still worked.

"It all works, Grace. Only difference is, this one is exponentially stronger." Nyx looked pleased with herself. "You're next, brother."

"What do we do with her old shell?" Ivan asked, looking at the vacated Grace lying on the bed.

Nyx shoved it onto the floor with her foot, absent of any hesitation or remorse. "We'll dispose of them when we're finished," she said, patting the newly vacant spot beside her.

Ivan exchanged a glance with Ben, then sat down and replicated the process with Nyx while Grace got dressed. When they finished, Nyx placed her hands over the empty shells, dissipating them back into particles that streamed into the atmosphere.

"There we go. Creation and destruction—perfectly balanced. Maybe next time you'll listen to me when I tell you something." She placed her hand on her hip. "I am always right," Nyx said with dramatic satisfaction.

Ivan and Grace shared a glance. The statement wasn't entirely true, although in this case, with their shells, it had been accurate. Neither said anything. Grace wasn't sure what it was, but something was different. It still felt like Ivan was part of her. The strength of their connection didn't diminish; it simply changed. She no longer felt as if he were equal to her. She had become something else, something more, and it wasn't only their new shells that made her feel that way.

Ivan felt it too. There was something new about her he couldn't understand or share. He felt blocked off from parts of her that had been open before. It wasn't only her essence; it was her shell, too. Her physical and conscious states had both completely evolved. Once they rose, he would know for certain whether she had outgrown him.

CHAPTER TWELVE

It had taken Gaia close to a week to reply to their request to see her. She had invited them for afternoon tea, enclosing coordinates they could shift to. When they arrived, they were outside of an unassuming earthen house that backed into a large mound. It was the type of home they would expect Gaia to live in.

The garden path stretched out before them, flanked by meticulously maintained flowerbeds, lush bushes, and cascading ivy. The landscape burst with color and sweet scents. Strewn throughout the garden were gazing globes, birdhouses, and a myriad of other trinkets. Behind the low stone walls, they saw animal sculptures woven from living branches, all surrounding a small pond.

Everything was random and wild. The space buzzed with insects, birds, frogs, and small scampering rodents. It was alive with movement.

Grace was admiring the garden when the front door of the house opened, revealing an unoccupied space. She and Ivan shared a wary glance before proceeding through the door with caution.

The dark hall was large, cool, and damp. Sunlight filtered through solarium glass at the far end of the adjacent corridor, where the other side of the mound would be on the outside.

Colored glass embedded into the ceiling created tiny flickering rainbows that danced through the hall. Chocolate daisies, raatrani, moon flowers, and four o'clocks covered the walls alongside other night bloomers she couldn't identify. They didn't encounter anyone as they proceeded down the dimly lit corridor to the solarium.

"Hello? Gaia?" Grace called out.

There was no answer. They walked to the elaborately set table near the curved solarium glass. Ivan felt the teapot, which was hot, then sniffed at the air. He detected the earthy, metallic-sweet scent of blood and flesh, assuring him someone had been in the room a short time ago. He began following the scent, with Grace trailing behind, scanning for movement.

When they turned the corner, a door flew open, nearly taking off the end of Ivan's nose. Gaia burst through with several heavily laden tiered platters of food.

"Oh lovely! You've arrived," Gaia exclaimed in a jovial voice. "I really wasn't certain what type of tea to serve. It's a bit late for high tea. I assumed low tea was a more appropriate option, anyway. When we finish, we can enjoy a long stroll through the gardens. Oh, how I miss a good old-fashioned garden promenade with company."

She blinked blankly. "Well, don't just stand there, Ivan. Be a gentleman and offer to carry some of these."

Ivan gave Gaia his most charming smile. "Certainly. I'd be delighted to take those for you. My apologies for not offering sooner. I thought it would be rude to interrupt while you were speaking," he said, taking two of the three tiered trays from her.

Gaia pushed the third tray at Grace without addressing her and then wrapped her arm through Ivan's. "Such a thoughtful boy." She looked up at him. "You've always been such a thoughtful boy," she repeated, patting his arm with her free hand. "Don't you think so, Grace?" she gushed without taking her eyes off of Ivan.

"Yes, ma'am. He's always been a real peach," Grace answered with overly animated sweetness as she followed behind.

I didn't think you'd ever met Gaia, Grace thought to Ivan.

Ivan looked down and smiled at Gaia. *I haven't*, he passed back to Grace. "Thank you for accepting us into your home. We understand you don't take many visitors."

"Don't be silly, Ivan. It's been such a long time since you've visited, but I know why you're here. It seems the only reason I receive requests from callers as of late. I simply refuse to speak about that detestable subject on an empty stomach," she said, her voice still carrying a light, uplifting tone. "We'll have a lovely tea and catch up before you force me into that conversation. Agreed?" Gaia smiled up at Ivan with wide eyes.

I think she thinks you're Ben, but I don't remember Ben ever visiting her, Grace suggested to Ivan.

You may be right, Ivan replied before saying aloud, "Certainly, Gaia. That sounds like a splendid idea."

They set the trays on the table as Gaia walked over and stood beside a chair. Ivan pulled it out for her to sit, then slid it in under her.

"Thank you, Ivan. Please be seated." Gaia waved toward the other two chairs.

Ivan moved behind the chair beside her and pulled it out, motioning Grace to sit.

"No, no, no. Place cards," Gaia said, directing his attention to the table.

Ivan looked down, seeing his name at the setting in front of him. "I hadn't noticed. My apologies," Ivan said, moving to the seat opposite Gaia, pulling it out for Grace.

"Thank you," Grace said as she sat.

Ivan took his assigned seat. Gaia picked up a set of tongs and selected two bite-sized sandwiches. "Please, serve yourselves," Gaia said.

Ivan selected one of each of the four types of sandwich bites Gaia had prepared. Grace reached over to select a tea cake from the top tier when she was stopped by the sound of Gaia clearing her throat.

"Grace, dear, savories first, then scones, then sweets. Don't you serve tea at home?"

"We haven't held court in a few hundred years. I don't think anyone does afternoon tea anymore," Grace said.

"Such a shame. I so enjoy the old civilities. How are the boys? Hopefully, they've gained some manners. I remember them running about recklessly, tearing through my grass and flowers," Gaia asked, changing the subject.

Well, that never happened. Not with Gaia's garden, anyway. Grace glanced at Ivan before replying to Gaia. "They're quite grown now. Erik has gotten himself a beautiful mate. Alex is still Alex and Mikkel is running a very successful string of social clubs with a friend of his."

Maybe she thinks of all plant life as belonging to her? Ivan asked.

Grace's face did not reveal their covert conversation. *Probably.*

"I don't remember receiving an invitation to Erik's binding ceremony," Gaia said.

"Would you have come?" Grace asked, remembering she hadn't attended Violet's mating, and that had been a monumental event.

"That's a rude question to ask," Gaia said to Grace in an admonishing tone. She turned back to Ivan, reprising her sweet lilt. "They *are* bound, aren't they?"

"They are," Ivan replied. "It was a very small ceremony, just us, the boys, and Frigg." He had intentionally not mentioned Ben, as it was apparent she thought he *was* Ben.

"Oh good. I'm glad Frigg was able to attend. I so enjoy an intimate ceremony. They're the best kind, don't you think?" Gaia gushed with an overabundance of happiness.

Ivan didn't think she would have enjoyed that particular binding. They didn't speak any special words or have a celebration. They simply decided from that point forward they would be bound. It wasn't a ceremony, as Gaia would understand, since it had resulted in Erik having his neck snapped. "I do like the limited amount of fuss," Ivan answered.

"I'm surprised Ben didn't attend. That's what you call him now, isn't it? Ben?" Gaia asked.

So, she doesn't think you're Ben? Now I'm even more confused, Grace thought to Ivan.

Gaia looked between them. "I can hear the two of you. No, I don't think he's Ben." Gaia motioned toward Ivan. "I know exactly who you are, Ivan. You're one of the little boys from the nursery. I can see you very clearly, hiding inside that grown man's body. When you were new, you would bring me sweet water and read your lessons to me while I tended my gardens. You were very good at finding me no matter how remote a place I was working in when you were allowed out. You always found me, even when the others couldn't."

Ivan couldn't fathom any of that occurring in his existence. He never learned to read as a child. There was no school for children of his low breeding. He had only learned to cypher so he could count money at the market. "I'm sorry, Gaia. I don't remember my childhood like you do."

"Naturally you don't, Ivan. It's not your fault." Gaia patted his hand. "It's *her*. The deceiver. She changes things in your mind." Gaia touched the side of her head. "She changes it until you don't know who you are anymore."

Gaia became more agitated as she spoke. She squeezed Ivan's hand hard. She was getting louder. "But not me! I didn't let her do that to me! I know! I *remember*. I remember EVERYTHING!"

She cleared her throat and leaned forward, relaxing her grip on Ivan's hand. She quieted her voice almost to a whisper, as if she had realized how unhinged she sounded. "I know what's real and what are her lies and I remember *before*. I remember when we were all together."

Gaia sat up straight, smoothing out her shirt, tucking nonexistent errant hairs in place. "This isn't an appropriate place for this conversation. Finish your tea. We can discuss it further in the garden where she can't hear us," she said, pouring herself another cup of tea and taking a scone.

Ivan tried to understand Gaia. She clearly thought her memories were real. He wondered what portion of those memories were real and what portion were invented by a broken mind trying to fill in empty spaces.

The remainder of the meal was amiable, centering on the new terraforming project on Betis. It was something Ivan had known Gaia would be exceptionally interested in. She offered assistance with any plant life of their choosing. They decided to put her in touch with Ty since they did not know what foliage requirements he had. Grace made a mental note to warn him to keep his conversations within the realm of botany.

The meal had ended with an invitation to stroll in the back garden. Stepping outside, they were greeted by a perfect day, with clear blue skies and a comfortable temperature. The air was mild, with a gentle breeze that carried the scents of fragrant flowers and greenery. The trio strolled in silence, taking in the afternoon. Ivan wanted to wait for Gaia to start the conversation when she was ready. The back garden was grand and formal, contrasting with the intimate, uncultivated one in front of the house.

Gaia leaned down to pull a misplaced weed from between two different species of iris.

"That doesn't belong here, creating a separation in this perfect row." She placed the weed in a small cloth bag she produced from her pocket, then tucked it back in with a gentle hand. "None of us really belong here though, do we? Nature has a way of letting some things thrive in places they don't belong."

Gaia noticed the perplexed looks on Grace's and Ivan's faces. She shook her head and smiled knowingly. "You understand this isn't real. None of this is real. We're diminished here, but not in the same way we were before. She controls us, you know. She reduces our abilities to keep us from being what we are intended to be. Don't you feel you aren't complete?" she asked, looking directly at Grace.

Grace knew it wasn't Chaos/Aphya—whatever her name was— affecting that. Like everything else Gaia interpreted, she was half right. It was the sphere that was suppressing their abilities. Grace had felt it when she was outside the confinement. Everything on The Outside was more intense.

"We feel complete together," Ivan answered, taking Grace's hand.

Gaia squinted her eyes, surveying them closely. "No. There's more," she said. "You can't see it yet, but there's more."

"More what?" Grace asked. "What do you see, Gaia?"

"Mmm. Just more," she answered as her expression turned wistful. She slowly turned, walking back toward the house. "You can see yourselves out. It was a lovely visit."

Continuing to push her for answers seemed fruitless, as there was no hope of making any headway. She was done. Ivan and Grace watched Gaia stroll back toward the house, seeming to have a conversation with herself, before they shifted back to their apartment.

"Well, that was …" Ivan started while pouring himself a scotch.

"Cryptic?" Grace added.

"Sad," Ivan finished. "She's in a perpetual state of paranoia, constantly attempting to merge bits of reality and fantasy to create something that makes sense. It must be incredibly difficult to live in a state where you can't trust your own mind," Ivan said before he sighed.

"What if it isn't made up?" Grace asked.

"C'mon, Grace. You saw her."

"There were so many things she was absolutely clear about. She knew The Three, she knew you weren't Ben. She was lucid on a lot of points."

"But there were so many more she wasn't lucid on. Like my childhood. How do you explain that?" Ivan scoffed and sat on the sofa.

"What makes you think that wasn't real at some point? What makes you think your memories are accurate? Frigg has already verified that Chaos … Aphya, whoever, attempted to create you multiple times. Or, that childhood could have happened in parallel timelines. We can go back and forth in different timelines. What makes you think Gaia can't? Or, what if she's right about Aphya and we've all lived our lives over and over but Gaia hasn't?"

"Or … what if we're all from The Outside and Renata lied about trapping Aphya in here alone? There are too many possibilities to narrow down," Ivan said, offering an alternative theory.

Grace groaned, flopping down on the sofa beside him. "I hate to say this. I absolutely hate to say this."

"We need Nyx."

He released an exhausted breath, sinking into the cushion while Grace got up to pour herself a drink.

"Answer the door," Ivan said.

"Did you call her? I haven't even had a drink yet?" In a state of exasperation, Grace stormed toward the door with heavy steps.

"I wouldn't do that without warning you."

Grace opened the door. Nyx brushed her aside, storming into the center of the room. Grace spun around to watch her approach Ivan.

"Why did you go to visit Gaia?" Nyx demanded, planting herself in front of Ivan.

Ben entered, closing the door behind him. He nudged Grace's arm with his elbow. She nudged him back, pointing to the bar and moving quietly toward it.

"And you!" Nyx spun on her heel, directing her ire at Grace. "You disappear for a year, then within a few weeks of returning, you go to see Gaia? What are the two of you hiding?"

"You should have a drink," Ivan said.

"I don't want a drink!" Nyx glared at him and stomped her foot.

"Trust me. You do," Ivan calmly insisted.

"Martini. Dirty." Nyx was seething. She seated herself stiffly in the chair perpendicular to Ivan's end of the sofa.

Ben handed Nyx the martini and sat on the arm of the chair, hovering over her. If all hell was going to break loose, he wanted to position himself between her and Grace. He didn't grasp what was coming, but the tension in the air made him certain it was going to enrage Nyx.

Grace positioned herself on the left side of the room, away from Nyx and Ben. She nodded to Ivan. In the space in the center of the room, she reached her hand forward in a spinning motion, creating a distortion. An image appeared in the concentration of energy, transitioning from hazy to clearly focused.

Nyx studied Grace in disbelief. This wasn't something Grace had been able to do before she disappeared. Thought transfer, sure; that was easy. Producing a full-scale visual image playback was something else entirely. The level of precision Grace used when manipulating the visualization was on an altogether different scale. It was a skill Nyx herself had taken thousands of years to perfect. Her attention was drawn back to the images coming into focus. Darkness grew, hovering over the center of the room. Nyx felt a wave of disorientation followed by a chilled feeling of lying on cold stone when the image expanded over them, encapsulating the space.

It wasn't the conversation with Gaia that she was expecting to see; it was what had happened when Grace had disappeared. Grace wasn't only showing them the images; she was giving them her feelings and thoughts. The scene was from her perspective. Her full experience. The playback drew them in, making them feel like they were her, living the experience in another location.

It took their senses over to the point that Nyx could no longer feel the chair she was sitting in or the martini glass in her hand. She felt Grace's boots on the floor. Nyx's thin linen jacket had replaced itself with Grace's heavier synthetic leather one. When Grace sipped her coffee, Nyx sipped her martini, only it wasn't the vodka concoction she had expected. The liquid had changed into a steaming cup of coffee. They weren't only watching Grace for the next hour. They were Grace. What she saw, what she felt, even what she thought. It was all there.

CHAPTER THIRTEEN

The moment Grace's feed stopped, Nyx slipped downward, back into her own consciousness. It felt like falling, making her feel small and weak compared to what she experienced inside of Grace's memory. All that unimaginable power and so little understanding of how to access or use it. If Nyx's own power was equivalent to the energy from a nuclear explosion, Grace's was equivalent to a sol going supernova. Even Chaos's power wasn't equivalent to what Grace held. Had she gotten it from being on The Outside, or had she always possessed it? It was yet another puzzle piece Nyx would need to fit in somewhere. For now, at least, she would need to tuck it away. This wasn't the time to reflect on such things. She needed to attend to the task at hand and examine what she had seen.

The event itself wasn't as difficult for Nyx to fathom. Her experiences had taught her anything was a possibility. It explained the questions that had loomed in her mind since her own creation. Where had it all begun? How had a single consciousness formed out of nothing? Now she had even more critical questions as she slipped back into herself. Her own intuition conveyed a sinking, queasy unease. There was absolutely no doubt in Nyx's mind. Renata was lying. Renata was afraid, only it wasn't Chaos she was fearful of. Nyx stood up, downed her drink, and placed the glass on the side table. Ignoring everyone, she slowly proceeded to the deck, closing the doors behind her.

Ben slid down into the space vacated by Nyx, absorbed in his own contemplation of the events. He leaned forward, elbows on his knees, staring into his glass.

The concern on Grace's face was apparent to Ivan. Had she broken them? They hadn't even gotten into the conversation with Gaia yet. Ivan went out to the deck to check on Nyx, leaving Grace to monitor Ben.

Ben entertained his own opinions, his own way of thinking. He was strategic, cynical. He wasn't processing the event as a whole. He wasn't concerned about the possibility of a world outside of everything he believed to be real. The part he was working out was why they had taken her. What was the endgame for Renata? Ben didn't connect to the emotional piece of the experience. His immunity to others' emotions protected him from that. He was grateful this experience was no exception to that protection.

There were tells in Renata's behavior when she lied: Her rigid posture and unwavering forced eye contact as she tried too hard not to blink. The intentional stillness in her extremities as she fought against gestures that would reveal her intent. Ben observed behavior in the way a scientist dissected an organism.

When people talk, they move. All species move when they communicate. A finger, a tail, a twitch of the nose or darting of an eye. The unconscious dynamic expression throughout the body animates and emphasizes thoughts and words.

Renata had displayed those unconscious movements during a substantial portion of the conversation. When she spoke about her world and when she explained the confinement, her body flowed with her words. The energy of her motion fit the energy level of her words. The times when she was completely still were the times that concerned him. It was apparent to Ben that when she was suppressing motion, she was also suppressing the truth. What Renata wasn't being truthful about were Aphya's crimes and why she wanted Aphya's essence extinguished.

He pushed himself back into a slouching position, downing his drink. Ben's sudden movement startled Grace. He held out the glass to Grace without looking at her. When she reached for it, he dropped it into her hand. She backed away cautiously, taking it for a refill, not turning her back to him until she reached the bar.

"What's the rest of it?"

The booming sound of his voice startled Grace, causing her to spill a few drops of scotch on the bar. She swiped her hand over the spilled liquid, melting it away in an unconscious motion. She was convinced he had done that on purpose. Considering what she had put him through today, as well as her lying to him for the last few weeks, she concluded it to be the least she deserved.

"What do you mean, the rest of it? I showed you everything," Grace said.

"But you came back a year later."

"Well," Grace hesitated. "We know why I came back a year later. My math skills suck and I didn't know there was a time difference."

"True, but that wouldn't explain why you couldn't tell what point in time you were in when you arrived back here. Was time merely moving differently on The Outside, or was there something unusual about time in general there, so that even in essence form, you couldn't detect it passing?" Ben cocked his head and squinted his eyes.

He pulled out his TAC, tapped it several times, and pulled up a scan table and a timeline map. "Hmm."

"Hmmmm, what?" Grace didn't recognize what she was looking at.

"Sadie scanned your essence when you came back. A year of time passed for us, but your essence had only recorded the few minutes it took you to get from the doorway back to here. Your essence didn't accumulate any time while you were missing."

"I don't understand what that means." Grace shook her head.

"I don't either," Ben replied. He tapped a few more times, then swiped the images away and slipped his TAC back into his pocket.

"Wait. What did you do that for? We need to figure it out," Grace protested.

Ben chuckled. "You think *we* can figure that out?"

"No," Grace responded sourly.

"I forwarded it over to Ruzzio. He can at least eliminate the readings representing an error on Sadie's part."

Sadie reacted upon hearing her name associated with the need for information. "Ben, there is a zero point zero zero two percent chance the reading was in error."

"Thank you, Sadie," Ben responded with an annoyed sigh.

"You're welcome, Ben. May I be of any further assistance?"

"No, Sadie. That's all."

Grace snickered at Ben triggering the AI unintentionally by using her name. He was usually more aware than that.

"Are you finished?" Ben asked.

"I am."

"What about the conversation with Gaia?"

"Here," she said, making a tossing motion toward him, although she had nothing in her hand to throw. With the motion, she passed Ben the conversation with Gaia, thrusting it unexpectedly into his mind. He winced, causing her to snicker again.

"Oh, that was low."

"Keeping you on your toes."

"I thought Ivan grew up in Pannonia?" Ben questioned.

"He did. Where Croatia is now," Grace answered.

"There could be a lot of reasons Gaia has different memories of him. It could be a separate timeline. What seems closer to the facts we already have is that his essence has been redeposited in various shells to produce an individual capable of merging with you.

"If you remember, mother did say Chaos tried dozens of times over several millennia to create Ivan. What if she just reused the same essence in different shells instead of creating a new one each time? Gaia could have memories of those times. Maybe there was a reason it had to be his essence," Ben pondered.

"What about when she said none of us belong here? I felt different outside. I felt more brilliant. More whole."

"Grace, you know I can't feel the emotions you push out. I can only extract my information from what I saw and heard. I'm not saying it's not a possibility. I just don't think it's the probable answer, and I also don't think Gaia is as insane as she allows everyone to think she is. Paranoid? Absolutely. Angry too, but not psychotic." Ben didn't like offering opinions based outside of factual evidence. He wasn't going to close himself off to any possibility with such a limited amount of information.

"I think she's a *little* insane. I mean, who wouldn't be deranged after living for over thirteen billion years?" Grace realized the moment it was out of her mouth that she shouldn't have said it.

Ben shot her a side glance and disregarded her comment. Nyx was as sharp as they came and she was only slightly younger than Gaia. "We need more information. We need to find the doorway. Unless we can uncover that, we have no proof there even *is* an outside."

"You think it's all in my head? You think somebody else is screwing with my memories?! AGAIN!" Grace was yelling at him. She was livid at the idea her mind was being manipulated. She was more livid that Ben thought it was a more reasonable explanation than something existing outside of their vast multidimensional universe that he didn't understand.

"No! That's not what I meant!" Ben yelled back at her.

"Then what in all hells did you mean?!"

<p style="text-align:center">~~~~</p>

Nyx stood on the deck above the community gardens, replaying the conversation over and over in her mind. It wasn't right. Something was off in the way Renata spoke about Aphya. There was something odd about her mannerisms. Something about the intentional way she spoke, avoiding direct answers or giving answers that only partially answered the questions.

Nyx could accept that her creator had faults, no matter what name was used for her. But she refused to believe attempted species annihilation was one of them. If anything, Nyx felt her creator was too soft, too cautious, overly caring. Everything she did was to teach her children a lesson. Nyx didn't retain even one solitary memory of any intentionally malicious act from Aphya.

Maybe she was just too close. Maybe you could never see a beloved parent the way the rest of the world saw them. Gaia certainly saw Aphya differently.

Ivan slipped unnoticed onto the balcony behind her. She was too deep into her own thoughts to feel him approach. When he placed his hand on her shoulder, she swung around, hissing at him.

"You really shouldn't sneak up on someone like that," Nyx said before she retracted her canis.

"I didn't realize I was sneaking," Ivan said, raising his hands, taking a step backward.

"Well, you were."

"Then I apologize."

Nyx eyed him up and down. "Apology accepted."

"You were pretty deep inside your head."

"The entire experience was unsettling. First, being inside of Grace's head like that was just so ..." She paused and shuddered. "Disorganized, emotional, and chaotic. It's a mystery to me how she can string together a coherent sentence when thoughts race through her mind so swiftly. It's all so emotionally debilitating as well. She can barely manage to pick one feeling before she jumps right into another, sometimes feeling several at the same time. There's no way I'll be unsticking that experience anytime soon. How do you possibly endure it?"

"Well, I guess it can get a little noisy sometimes. You get used to it." Ivan shrugged.

"No. *You* get used to it."

Ivan rolled his eyes. This was not the conversation he was looking for. It did, however, let him know that Nyx was back to normal. Well, normal for Nyx anyway.

"Now, tell me about the conversation with Gaia. And not the way Grace just did it, either. I think one hyper-realistic re-creation is enough for one day." Nyx rolled her eyes back at him and turned to lean against the deck railing. She didn't want to feel small again. If she could convince everyone around her that she was still the most powerful creature alive, she might believe it herself.

"I can't do that," Ivan replied, leaning against the railing beside her.

"And why not?" Nyx huffed, turning toward him. "You can tell us about Renata and The Outside, but you can't share your conversation with Gaia?"

Ivan faced her, shaking his head. "No, I mean, I can't do what she did. I was just as lost in it as you were."

Nyx furrowed her brow. "Ivan, that doesn't make sense. You can do everything Grace can. That's what the merge was. It *merged* you together," she said, chiding him.

"The merge bound our abilities at that specific point in time. This is new. I couldn't see how she did it. I couldn't feel what she was doing any more than you could."

"Hmph," Nyx pondered. "Maybe being outside changed her." She turned back, leaning forward on the rail again. "Did you feel like you were falling, getting smaller when she finished?"

"No." Ivan shrugged. "Did you?"

Nyx cleared her throat and smiled at Ivan, straightening her jacket lapels. "Not the point. Now, about Gaia?"

Ivan smiled back, amused at his sister's casual denial. He passed her the conversation in their typical way. Like a movie. Images and sounds. No feelings or tactile sensations involved.

Nyx raised her hand up to her mouth, focusing off into the distance. Her eyes darted side to side while she tapped her lip with her index finger. She began voicing her thoughts aloud.

"Renata said she didn't know we were in here, but I'm not so sure that could be accurate. If that were true, how would she know Grace had canis in here? Also, if Aphya is purely a devourer, like Renata says she is, how can she also be a creator? Renata saying Aphya is a pure devourer contradicts her statement that Aphya also created consciousness."

She raised her eyes upward over the landscape with a slight bewilderment. "Renata also said Grace was half creator and half devourer, but that doesn't seem to make sense, either. I'm not sure why. It just doesn't feel right."

Nyx bit at the bottom of her lip, staring far off, speaking more to herself than to Ivan. "If Aphya isn't a creator, how could she have the ability to create other creators?"

Nyx's body stiffened. "Gaia said none of us belong here and she has, what she believes to be, memories of the true timeline." Nyx snapped back toward Ivan. "But what if they're not? What if they're not from another timeline at all? What if she remembers living outside?"

"I don't know if I'd go that far. It's a pretty big jump to take over two short conversations. We need proof that this isn't all an illusion placed into Grace's head. It has happened before." Ivan's supposition was more cynical than normal for him.

"Not like this. She knew those other memories weren't real. Besides, where did she go for a year? Where did she get the new ability? I can't even do that to other immortals with the same immersive intensity. Humans, certainly. They're such simple creatures, but we're complex," she said, disagreeing with his assessment and shaking her head.

"I don't think my theory is such a significant jump. It would explain everything. Starting with why Gaia has always seemed so unhinged from this reality. If she has even a few memories of being outside as vivid as the ones we got from Grace today, they must have driven her mad," Nyx said.

Nyx and Ivan could hear Grace and Ben screaming at each other.

Ben burst out onto the deck, followed by Grace. "We need to find the doorway. If it's there, then we look for Aphya." Ben's demeanor was staunch and commanding. He wouldn't jump to conclusions based on supposition or interpretation. He required tangible proof.

"I have a theory …" Nyx began.

"I don't want to hear it," Ben cut her off, throwing up his hand in a gesture of silencing her. "No theories. We follow the facts no matter where they lead. I refuse to make the facts fit the theory, so whatever you think, keep it to yourself," he snapped tersely.

"It won't be the first secret I've kept from you," Nyx goaded smugly, irritated at being silenced.

"I'm sure it's not," Ben shot back dryly.

CHAPTER FOURTEEN

"We have to inform the others. Withholding something this important from the community would be no better than what the Council did to us." Ben's agitation was palpable as he paced the room, his furrowed brow and clenched fist revealing his increasing annoyance.

"I understand where you're coming from, Ben, but we need to be careful. We can't release this kind of information before we understand what's happening. It could incite a panic we're unequipped to handle right now," Ivan said. He was usually a staunch advocate of transparency, but this situation held the potential to become volatile if they didn't have a solution, or at least a basic understanding of how to proceed.

"We're part of the leadership of this community. It's our responsibility to tell them," Ben argued back.

Ivan sighed and massaged his temples. "How about we compromise?"

"Compromise what? Our integrity?" Ben asked.

Ivan ignored the comment. "I'm not opposed to sharing our situation with the community, but only when we have a firmer grasp of what's happening."

Ben slammed his hand down on the table. "It's a situation either way, Ivan! We either live in a prison or someone out there is powerful enough to mess with Grace's reality! Only this time without her knowing it was done!"

Ivan's demeanor and voice remained calm. "Don't you think we should figure out which situation we're in first? Before we start a panic?"

Ben turned his back to Ivan, letting out a growl. His frustration was growing by the minute.

"We could look for the door, like you suggested," Ivan said.

Ben let out a bellowing laugh. "I said a lot of things yesterday you seem to have disregarded. We spent a year looking for it. How do you plan on finding it now?"

"I can track Grace's path back from it. I couldn't do that before because when she was gone, I felt her everywhere. But now, since she's not surrounding me, I can pinpoint where she is, and I can sense her path from when she reentered The Everything."

"What if her path doesn't lead us to the doorway?" Ben asked, his tone decelerating from hostile to irritated.

"It'll lead us somewhere," Ivan responded.

"What will lead us somewhere?" Nyx asked as she shifted in.

"Grace's path in The Nothing," Ivan replied.

Nyx raised an eyebrow, noticing Ben's sour expression. She didn't want to challenge Ivan's declaration, nor Ben's skepticism about it.

"If you think you can track it now, why are you still here?" she asked, believing it was the best response to avoid an argument.

"I need to tell Grace I'm leaving, but she's not responding to me," Ivan answered.

"You're not attached at the hip, Ivan. I'll inform her where you went. And take him with you," she said, pointing at Ben.

"Why do I have to go?" Ben protested.

Nyx lifted her eyes to Ben. "None of us should be alone up there until we understand what's happening. You two go find the doorway while Grace and I search for Aphya."

"I don't think it's the best idea for all of us to be away at the same time. We're the only ones that know what's going on," Ben interjected.

Nyx chuckled. "That's adorable. You think we know what's going on?"

"You're just going to emasculate me like that in front of your brother?" Ben asked, splaying his hands in front of him.

Nyx smiled while Ivan lowered his head to avert his gaze from the uncomfortable situation.

"Go. We have work to finish," she said, ordering him off before shifting out.

~~~~

Nyx shifted back to the garden, where Grace was sitting on the crest of a small hill alongside Viv and Lilly. Billowy clouds passed overhead, creating threads of coolness against the warmth of the sun.

"What did they say?" Grace asked, straightening up with anticipation.

"I didn't tell them," Nyx answered.

"Why didn't you tell them?" Viv asked with a weary expression, reminding herself this wasn't a new theme for Nyx. It was her nature to be unreliable in direct opposition to Viv's own regimented approach to sticking with a plan.

"They're going to look for the doorway. If I had informed them we were telling others, they would have wanted to stay here. Splitting up allows us to accomplish two tasks at once."

"Killing two birds with one stone," Lilly said absently before lying back on the grass. She had no interest in this conversation. She was waiting for the action.
~~~~

"Why would I wish to stone birds, and what does that have to do with anything?" Nyx grimaced at Lilly, blinking quickly.

"Nyx, it's an expression for getting twice the production with a singular effort," Viv said.

"Is that not what I said?" Nyx scoffed.

Viv nodded diplomatically. "Let's just move on. What would you recommend we do next?" she asked Grace.

"We need to make a plan on how to draw Aphya out," Grace said. She had given Viv and Lilly the prior conversations while Nyx was with Ben and Ivan.

"Why wouldn't you simply invite her to come speak with you?" Viv asked.

Nyx groaned.

"What's the problem with that?" Viv asked. "Is there some animosity between them you haven't told us about?"

"Do you think I haven't made that attempt? Inviting her to meet was the first thing I did," Nyx retorted sharply.

"Is it possible it's not you she wants to hear from?" Lilly asked, giving a disinterested wave.

Nyx leered at Lilly. "Why is this child here?"

"Because I trust her," Grace quickly defended.

Lilly propped herself up on her elbows, a smug smile playing on her lips as she looked at Nyx.

"Trust her with what, exactly?" Nyx asked in a sharp and bitter tone.

"A big bright, shiny lure," Grace answered, sharing a smirk with Lilly.

Grace explained to them that she had asked Lilly to convince Ruzzio to construct a device that mimicked a hole between The Everything and The Nothing. Lilly would explain to him that the object was necessary to test a new sensor array she and Thoth were working on and that she didn't want Thoth to know she was testing it behind his back. Ruzzio already knew that Lilly and Thoth were competitive, and he would most likely laugh it off as a prank, which he was always ready to take part in.

The conversation wore on a while longer, exhausting all of Nyx's and Viv's questions about what Grace had planned for Lilly.

With the parameters of the device decided, Lilly and Viv departed prior to Grace and Nyx returning to Grace's quarters.

~~~~

Ivan and Ben returned early the following morning.

"We found an anomaly where Grace's trail ends. Ben and I decided it was best not to enter so we wouldn't risk detection," Ivan said triumphantly.

He had always believed Grace's story, even though he had entertained alternative theories. He considered it irresponsible to only look at the explanation he wanted to accept.

Only moments later, Lilly shifted into the apartment with Viv in tow.

Ivan gave the pair a puzzled look, wondering why they had shifted directly into his and Grace's home instead of the hallway, which was the acceptable practice for visitors. At the same time, he felt a sense of satisfaction knowing that Lilly felt comfortable enough to appear directly.

"Um, is there something we can help you with?" he asked.

Lilly mocked his tone. "Um, no. There's something *we* can help *you* with."

She tossed a device to Ivan, but Ben reached in front of him to catch it.

"What in all hells is this?" Ben asked, scrutinizing the faces of all four women.

Ivan's face held the same confused look as Ben's.

"It's a sensor. Not that it really senses anything, though. More like the opposite," Lilly said.

"You TOLD them?" Ben snapped at Grace and Nyx. Anger rose in a flush of red over his cheeks.

"Jesus, Ben. Don't get your bloomers twisted," Viv snapped.
~~~~

"You had no right to mention anything without discussing it with us first!" Ben exclaimed. He was more upset because he had been the one arguing that the administration needed to be told, and now they had told his direct work partner and someone who was practically a stranger to him instead.

"I'm responsible for the security of this community, Ben! You should have been the one to tell me!" Viv snapped back.

"That's not the point!" he bellowed. The others had stopped him from informing her. Anger and embarrassment rose through his chest until a bitter metal taste overwhelmed his mouth.

Viv stepped toe-to-toe with him. "Check your ego, buddy. You were out there looking for the doorway. Do you think we didn't deserve to know?"

"I was the *only* one arguing to tell you and the administration!" Ben yelled back.

"We didn't tell everyone. Just these two," Nyx said demurely. She had known this wouldn't go over well and had hoped to tell him before the women appeared.

Viv smirked at Ben. "And I am sure Galin is going to notice the increased security within the next day or two, so whatever you are planning on doing, you had better get to it quickly."

"Like I should believe you won't run straight to your mate with this information and make us look like idiots!" Ben leaned menacingly over Viv, who held her own against the massive hulking figure even though she could smell the sourness in his breath.

Viv leaned up toward Ben. "Are you implying I don't know how to manage my job?! I assess threats every day and this is no more or less important than any of them. I don't run to Galin like a gossipy little school girl every time someone perceives a threat to our community. There is a process for a reason and Galin and I don't discuss business outside of that process." Viv enunciated her words, jabbing her finger into Ben's chest.

Ivan poured two glasses of scotch and pushed one between Ben and Viv. "There's no point in arguing. What's done is done."

Ben took the glass as he and Viv took a step away from each other, reducing the hostility in the room.

"Lilly, what does the little sensor that's not a sensor do?" Ivan asked.

"It's programmed to give off the same signature as a thin spot without the membrane, so it looks like an open hole," Lilly said.

"How is this going to help? It's only one probe." Ben's protest was clear as he moved over to the bar to refill his recently emptied glass.

Lilly grinned. "That's where this little button comes in handy." She seized the device out of Ben's grasp, startling him, as he had forgotten he was holding it. Flipping the sensor over, Lilly tapped the bottom, revealing a ring of lights with up and down arrows and a center image. "The green one makes it appear larger and the red one makes it smaller. And this one," she said, pointing to the sun-like symbol in the center, "makes it look nova sized."

"And how are we going to manipulate it when we've risen?" Ivan asked.

"The same way you manipulate everything else out there." Lilly shrugged at the statement, raising her pitch at the last two words to make it sound like a question.

Grace moved toward Ivan. "Before we set that off, I want to take Ami to visit the children," she suggested.

"That flighty little simpleton? Why would we want to get her involved?" Nyx scoffed.

"Because Ami can touch an essence and determine if it is real. Can you do that, Nyx?" Grace asked, shutting Nyx's question down.

"Hmph! Do whatever you want," Nyx retorted acrimoniously. Her opinion had been disregarded one too many times for her liking today. She spun dramatically and shifted out, leaving tendrils of black smoke in her wake.

"Aren't you going to go after her?" Grace asked Ben as she fanned away the smoke that enveloped her.

"Nope," Ben said before taking a seat at the kitchen counter.

Less than an hour later, Ami was in Viv's office, pacing between the sunlit windows, chewing on her lip. "Are you sure it's not going to pull my soul out of my body? If I leave it, I can't come back to it."

"I don't think it works like that. When I go to the children, I never feel disconnected from my shell. I think it's more of a projection," Grace explained.

"Ami, I thought you could rise. I've seen you in light form, haven't I?" Viv asked.

"It doesn't work the same way for me. When I rise, my light envelops my body and I carry it with me."

"Oh. I hadn't considered that as an option." Grace's eyes widened in mild astonishment.

Ami shrugged.

"Ami, can I ask you something?" Viv asked.

"You just did." Ami stared at Viv blankly.

Viv chuckled. "True. Could your ess— soul move into an empty shell?"

"Duh. It has to be empty," Ami snorted. "I can't fit in a body that someone else is in. I have to make a deal with them; they surrender it to me and then they go live in heaven."

Grace and Viv shared a glance before Viv proceeded.

"What if we created a new shell from the body you have now? Could you come back to that one if something happens to the one you're in?" Viv pushed.

Ami scrunched up her face and Grace leaned forward.

"Ami, if the shell was empty, you wouldn't need permission. You don't need permission to use an empty container, do you?"

"No, I think …?" Ami concentrated harder, resuming her lip biting.

"A shell is an empty container, so you wouldn't need permission to use it, would you?" Grace coaxed.

"I guess not." Ami scrunched her face tighter, feeling her discomfort intensify as she shifted her weight from left to right.

"So, if we made you a shell from the body you have now, and you didn't need to ask permission or make a deal, you could use it. Right?" Viv asked more firmly.

"Uh … well, I guess that makes sense. It's not breaking any rules if it's already unoccupied," Ami said.

"That's what we'll do then. As a backup, we'll create an empty shell so you don't need to worry if something were to happen to the one you have now," Viv said.

"That kinda seems like cheating, doesn't it?" Ami asked, shrinking back from Viv.

Grace stepped toward Ami, reaching out to rub her back like she would a child she was attempting to cajole. "It's not cheating at all, Ami. It's a safeguard."

Ami pulled away from Grace by twisting her shoulder down and back. "I don't know. It doesn't seem right."

Viv moved to Ami's other side, adding to the pressure Ami was feeling over this choice. "Let's do this then. Let us create the shell, and then if you need it, which I really don't think you will, you can make a choice then. If you have to enter the shell and it doesn't feel right, you can leave it and find another human to inhabit. Okay?"

"It takes a long time to find a human that wants to agree to something like that," Ami sneered.

"We'll help you if it comes to that. I really don't think it will, though. I told you, I don't feel disconnected from my shell when I'm there," Grace said, trying to convince her to make the choice she wanted.

"But I really like this one!" Ami protested, stamping her foot.

"Ami," Grace said, peering at her with a raised eyebrow.

"Weellll … okaayy," Ami agreed hesitantly, looking down at the floor. She didn't like the feeling of being bullied, nor that of disappointing people she loved.

The moment she had agreed, Viv clipped off a small piece of Ami's earlobe.

"OW!" Ami exclaimed, reaching up to grab her rapidly healing ear.

"I'm going to get this over to Leo. You two have fun," Viv said, giving them a wave and porting out before Ami could change her mind.

"That wasn't very nice," Ami said, pouting toward the space Viv had occupied only a moment before.

Grace stood beside Ami and wrapped her arm around Ami's shoulder, giving her a side hug.

"I know how to cheer you up. Would you like to go play with some children?"

Ami nodded, continuing to pout.

"Close your eyes," Grace whispered.

Ami complied.

Keeping her arm around Ami, Grace opened her mind to the meadow. Feeling the grass under her feet, Grace opened her eyes to see Ami holding her arms out in front of her, wiggling her fingers.

"Oooh, it tingles!" Ami said, gushing with excitement.

Grace looked down at her own hands. "It does tingle, doesn't it? I don't know why I hadn't noticed that before."

She glanced back at Ami, who was now holding her hands up to the sun.

"Do you still feel connected to your body?"

"Uh-huh. Just tingly," Ami replied, wiggling her shoulders.

A dozen children came running down the slope, interrupting their conversation. They nearly tackled Grace in their excitement, except for one little girl who stopped in front of Ami, looking up precociously.

"Can I see your wings?" the girl asked, her voice filled with wonderment.

"How do you know that I have wings?" Ami countered.

The girl concentrated, scanning Ami from head to toe.

"I can see them all folded up in there," she said, pointing toward Ami's torso.

"What else can you see?" Ami asked, intrigued by the girl, almost forgetting about the prior uncomfortable conversation in Viv's office.

"I can see your light is blue. People think it's white, but that's only because it's so bright."

"Well, you're very observant." Ami nodded with her hands on her hips. "Such an observant little girl must have a very pretty name."

The little girl blushed and looked down at her feet, folding her hands behind her back.

"It's Sebilla." She leaned in closer to Ami and covered the side of her mouth with her hand. "Ivan calls me LaLa," she said with a huge grin.

Ami extended her hand. "It's very nice to meet you, LaLa. My name is Amitiel, but everyone calls me Ami."

LaLa shook Ami's hand with an abundance of enthusiasm. Warmth spread up Ami's arm, leading her to conclude that this child held a very noticeable soul.

"Can I see your wings now?" LaLa asked innocently.

"I'll show you my wings if you tell me what color Grace's light is."

"Tsk." LaLa sucked her tongue behind her teeth and giggled. "Grace has all the colors, silly."

"Well then," Ami replied and took a few steps back from the child. She opened her wings to their full breadth.

There was no sound, except for some minor air displacement. Ami's wings were twice as wide as she was tall. Brilliant illumination shone from each pristine white feather, producing a gasp from LaLa. The other children jumped and squealed in delight as they gathered around Ami. She allowed them to explore her wings up to the point where they erupted from her skin. That area was much too sensitive to allow dozens of tiny fingers to poke around it.

Ami took each of the children on a short flight, beginning with LaLa. All the children patiently queued for their turn, erupting in amazement and laughter every time Ami launched herself into the air. Grace thought Ami was having more fun than the children, twisting and spinning through the clouds.

"Can we go again?" the children shouted excitedly once everyone took their turn flying with Ami.

Grace animatedly pouted. "I'm sorry, we can't. Ami and I need to go back."

The children moaned. "Please?" they all begged in unison.

"We can't today," Grace reiterated.

"Can Ami come back?" LaLa asked.

"I would love to come back. That was fun!" Ami agreed excitedly to an eruption of cheering.

Once the children calmed down, Grace and Ami left to a send-off of delighted waves and shouts.

"When can we go back?" Ami asked, shouting at Grace. Her voice was far too loud for the proximity in which they were standing.

Grace winced, plugging the offended ear with her finger.

"I'm glad you had fun, Ami, but that wasn't the point of the visit. Are the children's essences real or are they projections of some sort?" Grace pulled her finger away from her ear, hoping not to get blasted by Ami's response.

"Their souls are real. So, when can we go back?" Ami asked at a more controlled volume.

CHAPTER FIFTEEN

Nyx, Ben, and Ivan joined Grace and Ami in the apartment a short time later. After Ami gave her report, it was Ben's turn.

"The children are real and the doorway is real. Now, we need to figure out the hard part. Who's lying?" He paced and rubbed his trimmed beard. "We need to capture Aphya."

"Capture sounds harsh, don't you think? Why wouldn't we begin with an invitation once she's drawn out? You're already acting as if she's the enemy," Nyx protested.

"In this instance, it's possible she is," Ben said.

"I think we're getting ahead of ourselves. If the children are real and alive, why are you treating her as your opponent before we speak to her?" Grace asked. She didn't think aggression was the way to start this thing off.

Ben spun on Grace and scoffed. "Because she lied about everything else. She lied about The Nothing and The Everything, this being her prison, and The Outside. Just because the children are alive doesn't mean we should trust her."

"It doesn't mean we shouldn't give her the benefit of the doubt, either. Maybe she hadn't thought us capable of venturing out of the confinement yet. She kept something to herself for an unknown reason we don't understand. So what? We're *all* guilty of that, *aren't* we, Ben?" Nyx asked in an accusatory tone.

"You know that was different!" he snapped back. "It wasn't my secret to tell."

"Well, maybe this one isn't hers to tell," Nyx said.

Ivan had had enough of their bickering. It was getting them nowhere.

"Would you two please stop for a moment?" Ivan glanced between the pair.

"He's being obtuse!" Nyx said, fuming and folding her arms across her chest.

"And she's being obstinate!" Ben returned fire, mimicking her posture.

"Why don't we let her come to us?" Grace asked, sharing a glance with Nyx.

"That's ridiculous. We don't have time for that," Ben said, throwing up his hands, dismissing Grace's suggestion.

"Look, Viv and I had Lilly build the device for a reason. Can you at least stop fighting long enough to hear why?" Grace asked. She hoped their curiosity would override their annoyance with the situation they were in.

"I would be quite happy to listen to an intelligent alternative, Grace," Nyx replied, taking a seat. It was an attempt to support Grace without letting Ivan and Ben know they already had this planned out.

Ben walked to the bar and poured another drink. "By all means, tell us how we're going to bait and *talk* to her with that thing."

"It's meant to draw her out, Ben. She'll come to investigate the opening and then we can have a conversation with her. You know, like adults," Grace said, trying not to sound too snide or condescending.

Ben turned around. "What's your plan when she doesn't stick around for the warm, friendly chatting part?"

"I don't think that will be an issue, Ben. But even if it were, how do you possibly think you're going to capture her? We don't know for sure what abilities she has. If she's like me, I don't think there's anything you can devise that would hold her," Grace argued.

"That's where you're mistaken. I have the two of you." Ben pointed between Grace and Ivan. "You can modulate your phase, right?"

Ivan nodded, while Grace glared.

"I think a combined energy cage with dual modulation would be something she couldn't easily escape, even if she has the same abilities as you. Am I wrong?" he asked, lifting his chin and arching one brow.

"I don't think it will come to that," Grace said. She thought Ben must have been researching this for quite some time. She was clueless about where he could have picked up on those terms.

"It doesn't matter what you think, or what you want. You need to have a viable option in case it doesn't go the way you planned."

Despite his reluctance to weigh in before he had all the information, Ivan felt the need to speak. "Ben's right, Grace. It's something we should think about, and I think it will work."

Grace glowered at the two men. "Aggression is not the way to handle this."

"It's just a backup. We only need to hold her long enough to get her to listen to us," Ivan said, backing up Ben's proposal.

"And if she escapes and goes back into hiding, what do we do then?"

"Oh, that's not the part I'd be worried about," Nyx grumbled. Everyone turned to face her, and she continued.

"If she gets angry enough, what would stop her from decimating The Everything? She might not get out of here, but she can certainly blast it all back to nothing."

"I don't think so," Ami uttered quietly from the corner, unaware that anyone had heard her.

"Excuse me?" Nyx asked. She stood up, visibly offended by the contradiction, as if Ami's words were a direct challenge.

Ami raised her gaze uncomfortably. "Energy in The Everything is finite. She doesn't have enough left to shut it all down at once." Ami blinked, turning her attention back to the game she was playing with Sadie.

The others continued staring in her direction, expecting more.

Ivan eventually broke the silence. "Anyone object to deploying the device, then?"

"I, for one, have several questions that need answering," Nyx scoffed.

"We need her to talk to us, Nyx. You're not going," Ivan said, standing firmly in his resolve to, at the very least, not antagonize Aphya.

"Who do you think is going to stop me?" Nyx glared confidently at Ivan.

"I prefer it not come to that," Ivan answered, taking a step toward her.

As much as this showdown would be entertaining, Ben thought it was time to step in.

"I think you and I should brief the administration while they're gone," Ben suggested, placing a hand on Nyx's arm.

Nyx snapped her head around with such aggression that if it had been a blade, Ben's own head would have been taken clean off his shoulders. While the turn had provided her a deep sense of loyalty and commitment, it had not subdued her temper one bit. Ben was well aware of how he should play to her ego in order to adapt to the situation without insulting her.

"I can't transfer all of that information to so many at once. I need you to help me," he said with every ounce of sincerity he could garner.

Nyx maintained a firm and skeptical glare, unconvinced that this wasn't a ploy to get her out of the way.

"The administration can't be blindsided when Aphya shows up here. They need to decide what to tell the community. It isn't our place," he said, sending an icy stare in Ivan and Grace's direction.

Ben hadn't wanted to hold back information from the administration for this long, but the look wasn't about who was right or wrong about that. It was about making Nyx feel that what he was asking her to do was just as important as seeking Aphya. It was about showing her he was angry about

Ivan convincing everyone to withhold their knowledge. The stare was a strategic move to show Nyx that Ben was on her side.

"Hmph!" Nyx huffed, staring daggers at Ivan. "Seems to be a consensus to keep me from interacting with my creator. Since you think I'm such a liability, I'll leave you to bungle it all by yourselves. Don't look to me for help when your plan goes awry." Turning back to Ben, she remarked, "Apparently my skills will be appreciated elsewhere. Shall we?"

"Thank you," Ben responded, guiding Nyx in front of him. Peering over her shoulder, he widened his eyes at Ivan, feeling a sense of relief for averting an already difficult situation.

Ivan mouthed *thank you* back to Ben as the two shifted out, bound for Galin's office.

Once Nyx and Ben had left, Ivan issued a quick message. Lilly appeared in front of them, holding the device.

"You ready for this?" she asked.

"You're pretty calm about everything," Grace said to Lilly.

"Why wouldn't I be?" she asked.

"You just found out we live inside of a prison bubble that could be destroyed at any time."

"It's a lot nicer prison than some I've been in," Lilly replied.

"Aren't you concerned that Renata or another outsider might decide letting Aphya out is too much of a risk and destroy us all?"

"Not really. Even if I was, how is my being worried or acting all hysterical going to change any of that?"

Ivan chuckled and stepped forward to take the device from Lilly. "It isn't." He examined the object, running his fingers across the smooth surface. "How are we supposed to get this up there, anyway?"

"How do you move around other matter when you're up there? When you're making stars and planets?" Lilly questioned.

"We can move it once we get up there. What I was asking is how are we going to launch the device through the atmosphere without disrupting the sensors? We don't know how phasing it through the roof might affect it," Ivan said.

Lilly squinted up at him. "A shuttle?"

"Can you fly a shuttle?" Grace asked.

"Not yet, but I have a friend who's teaching me."

"Didn't we already have this discussion?" Ivan smirked down at her.

Lilly forced out an animated gasp and grasped her throat. "So rude!"

"Who is going to fly the shuttle?" Ivan asked, amused by her reaction.

"Ruzzio. He built the device, so he can help me launch it."

Ivan furrowed his brows in disapproval.

"I'm not an idiot. He doesn't know anything. He thinks we're using it to prank Thoth."

Grace glanced at Ivan before addressing Lilly. "I guess we'll see you up there then."

Ivan handed the device back to Lilly, allowing her to shift out to the shuttle bay. When he turned to Grace, she could feel his anxiety rivaling her own. They hadn't risen as a singular being since before she went to The Outside. This would be their test to see if they could even still merge into one being with their power dynamic feeling so divided.

Ivan swallowed, holding his mouth tight. "Are you ready?"

"Are you?" Grace asked in return, reflecting his concern.

Ivan nodded, giving her a hesitant smile. He seated himself and pulled her down onto his lap. "Ready as I'll ever be."

This trip would be short. They didn't need stasis pods with these new shells. They also didn't want Leo to see differences in their new shells or essences just yet. The uncertainty of their new dynamic made them acutely aware of their vulnerability, which lingered in the air.

"Me too," Grace said, holding him tight against her chest before slipping out of her shell.

He hadn't seen it when she returned, but her light had changed. It had grown brighter. Every color imaginable swirled vividly inside, creating the purest white he could imagine. He was besotted with emotion, causing his heart to swell with both pride and an uncontrollable longing to merge with her. Ivan slid easily from his shell, gliding up to approach Grace's vivid presence without hesitation. As they touched, the filmy layer separating their individual orbs melted away in a shower of tiny sparks. The initial contact of their essences jolted him as they brightened and flickered. Their power disparity leveled out, giving Ivan an equal share of Grace's increased abilities. During the combining of their light, Ivan felt warmth and tingling. This was a new sensation, unlike anything they had experienced in their previous merges. The sense of physical touch had eluded them in their enlightened state until now. The more they absorbed each other, the quicker their intimacy returned. He reveled in the experience, yearning to remain enveloped in it for eternity.

CHAPTER SIXTEEN

Nyx and Ben stood in the middle of the administration building's lobby. The space seamlessly blended the functionality of a workspace with the beauty of a garden. Transparent walls enclosed rooms that lined the open corridors beyond the water feature and plants. The entire ceiling projected a brightly lit view of billowy white clouds against deep azure skies. Citizens leisurely strolled past, moving from one ordinary task to another. All eyes turned toward the raised voices in the center of the vast space, which were disrupting the peacefulness of the atmosphere.

"When do you expect Galin to return?" Nyx asked Finna as she approached.

"Not until the overmorrow," Finna replied in her calm, enchanting tone.

"That simply won't do. This is an urgent matter," Nyx said. Her angry edge from earlier was diminishing rapidly as a result of the Etherian's presence, although it hadn't completely abandoned her.

Aware of Nyx's severe nature, Finna looked to Ben for clarification. "If it is an emergency, I can convey a message to Administrator Galin."

"We would be appreciative if you could," Ben said. His tone was respectful. Regardless of his immunity to Finna's calming abilities, there was no justification for a lack of courtesy.

"Would you like me to message you if I can reach him?" Finna offered.

"We will wait," Nyx said tersely, taking a seat on the other side of the open lobby.

A pleasant smile appeared on Ben's face. "Thank you, Finna," he said, moving across the floor to sit beside Nyx.

Finna disappeared down the hallway, past open and enclosed workspaces until Ben lost sight of her. Clearly discomforted by their presence, several office workers hurriedly abandoned their desks or hastily adjusted their privacy screens, while others surreptitiously glanced in their direction.

"Why are we sitting here? We should shift directly to him," Nyx complained.

"We don't have any idea what Galin is occupied with. He could be in a meeting with other species," Ben said.

"So? What if he is?" Nyx asked.

"He's on another planet, and we don't know with whom he is meeting," Ben answered.

"Why do we care who he may or may not be meeting with?" Nyx pressed.

Ben turned to face her. "Would you appreciate being interrupted if you were engaged in an important negotiation?"

"Of course not," Nyx said in a perturbed manner. "But this is far more important than anything he could be engaged in."

Ben let out an agitated sigh. "Let's give Finna a few minutes, regardless. There is no need for us to act brashly."

"This is not a situation in which we have time to wait. If Aphya appears while we sit here and do nothing, would that not be just as impolite as a mildly inconvenient interruption?" Nyx crossed her arms and huffed.

"I highly doubt she is going to appear instantaneously in the next few moments while we wait. Grace and Ivan haven't even left yet."

Nyx turned her back to Ben, facing the other direction to seethe without disruption.

After only a few minutes, Ben stood up, his ears catching the sound of a soft clicking, rhythmic stride approaching them. He tapped Nyx on the shoulder, and she leered up before rising from her seated position beside him.

"Administrator Galin is on his way back. Would you like to wait in his office?" Finna asked.

"No, we prefer sitting out here and being gawked at," Nyx snapped sarcastically.

Finna tilted her head, unfamiliar with the meaning of Nyx's tone. It seemed an odd choice to her, but she had heard rumors Nyx enjoyed attention and she wasn't one to judge.

Ben frowned at Nyx before contradicting her comment. "We will wait in Galin's office, if you don't mind."

Finna glanced between the two, struggling to decipher the opposing responses. She decided on a diplomatic course. "You may follow me if that is your wish." Quickly, she turned and began moving toward the aforementioned rooms with the expectation Ben would follow her. Hearing two sets of footfalls trailing behind, she continued forward.

The group entered the elevation mechanism at the end of the hallway, which took them to the top floor of the building. The doors slid open with a muffled whooshing sound. Upon exiting, they turned left, traveling along an open hallway with a view of the lobby garden, and entered a large, open room filled with work stations and meeting areas. As they passed through, barely audible conversations fell silent while the workspace occupants' eyes followed them. People seemed confused by their presence, having never seen them in these buildings before now.

At the end of the space stood an opaque wall with tall, solid doors in the center. Finna waved her hand over a control panel, causing the doors to swing open. Once inside, she directed the guests to a comfortable seating arrangement in the center of the room.

"Galin will be with you shortly. Please help yourself to a beverage," Finna said, motioning to a bar at the side of the room with a service panel behind it before swiftly making her escape and closing the doors behind her.

Ben had just reached the seating area after pouring drinks for himself and Nyx when the doors opened again. Galin strode in the way only a man filled with confidence could.

With a relieved grin on his face, Galin exhaled. "I have never been so glad to be called to an urgent situation. One more minute of listening to species that had been at war only a few decades ago trying to iron out an alliance and I would have staked myself."

Ben chuckled. "So you've gotten a taste of what I go through with the Council?"

"And I don't envy you one bit. What can I help the two of you with?" Galin asked, heading toward the bar.

"We need to apprise the administration of an impending threat," Ben responded.

"What type of threat?" Galin asked, pausing mid-pour.

Ben glanced at Nyx. "It would be easier if we showed you."

Galin finished pouring his drink and capped the bottle. He took a sip before turning back to his guests. "Well then," he said, taking another sip. "By all means, show me."

"It would be less disorienting if you sat," Ben said, motioning to an accent chair near the center of the room.

Galin strode to the seat, showing a mixture of curiosity and skepticism. Once he settled into the chair, Ben signaled to Nyx with a nod, who then shared all the visions from earlier.

Galin leaned forward with his elbows on his knees, tapping his thumbs together, staring at the floor.

"I can't take this to the administration, Ben," Galin said, shaking his head.

"They need to know! They need to publicize this information and figure out a strategy to defend our people," Ben demanded.

"Defend our people against what, Ben? You have no proof. No corroboration. Do you understand the type of panic this would cause?" Galin debated.

Nyx stayed quiet, taking in the arguments from both men.

"We have corroboration," Ben said. "Ivan and I found the doorway."

"Doorway to where, Ben? Did you go through it?"

"Grace went through it!" Ben said, his tone urgent.

"Grace went through *a* doorway to *somewhere*. For all we know, it was a subdimension like the one the Council has constructed. We have no actual proof that there is anything outside of The Nothing. No proof that The Nothing isn't simply a buffer zone of some sort, as we have always thought it was. There is no proof that the doorway led to what you are referring to as The Outside. No proof that the doorway doesn't simply lead back into an unknown area of The Everything. All you have shown me is that there is a doorway and someone went to a lot of trouble to make Grace believe what they wanted her to believe," Galin countered.

Ben rubbed his forehead. Was his own willingness to believe Grace overriding his practical sense? He hadn't once considered that the doorway could be an intentional access point between The Everything and The Nothing. Galin's words, echoing Ivan's earlier argument about Grace possibly being deceived, held a greater weight when they flowed from the Administrator's mouth.

Galin took the pause as a cue to continue. "The two of you are some of the most cynical, pragmatic beings I have ever encountered. I implore you to think critically about what you have presented to me. The only thing we can discern for certain is whoever this Renata person is, they seem to have one clear goal."

"Which is?" Nyx asked, finally voicing her curiosity.

"To eliminate Chaos," Galin answered.

A horrified expression flashed across Nyx's face, followed by one of anger. She turned away, beginning a trajectory of pacing toward the window and back. Her mouth opened and closed as she turned on her path. On completing her fourth loop, she stopped in front of the men. "We need to go through the doorway," she concluded.

"No," Ben stated sternly. "That would only let Renata know Grace has told others, and if this is actually a confinement, it could cause them to sanitize it more quickly. I think Ivan should be the one to go."

"You always think Ivan should be the one to handle things. Why?! Because he's a testosterone-filled male? Your misogyny is fully intact even though everything you have ever known was created by a neutral being! You continue to treat me as an inferior because I enjoy being encased in a female container!" Nyx exclaimed, sweeping her arm wildly toward the sky.

"Are you finished?" Ben asked in an exhausted tone.

"Not by a long shot!" Nyx yelled.

"Well, as much as I have grown to enjoy your female container, and by no means find it inferior, that isn't the point. The point is, if—and I stress *if*—any of us ever lived in this Outside, Renata may recognize some of us. Grace mentioned him to Renata by name, so it would be logical for Grace to have discussed what happened with him and for him to go, wouldn't it?" Ben asked.

Before Nyx could snipe back, Galin stood between them. "Nothing needs to be decided immediately. I understand this situation is urgent, but we must approach it with caution and a rational mind. If the scenario of all this being a confinement is accurate, and a year here is less than an hour there, we have time. If it is a ruse, Renata doesn't have the power to eliminate Aphya herself and she needs to convince Grace to do it. With either scenario, the conclusion is we have ample time to investigate properly. It is important that we gather all the facts rather than make any hasty decisions," he said in a calm and authoritative tone. "Do either of you find my assessment incorrect?"

"I find your conclusion persuasive, Galin," Nyx said.

"What are you suggesting?" Ben asked.

Galin answered, "I will document this conversation and form a small inquiry panel to review your findings. In the meantime, I suggest you continue your investigation and keep the panel informed of any fresh developments."

Ben nodded in agreement, while Nyx scrutinized Galin.

Nyx crossed her arms. "If I can't go through the doorway, I want to speak with Aphya."

"I'm certain there are many who want to speak with Aphya," Galin said noncommittally.

"We have to wait and see if Ivan and Grace can make contact first," Ben said.

"Take whatever steps you feel are necessary, as long as you keep the panel informed," Galin said, nodding to them.

"Why do I feel like none of this was a surprise to you?" Nyx asked.

Galin smiled slyly. "I endeavor to not be surprised by anything." He raised his hand, motioning Ben and Nyx toward the doors as they swung open.

"I knew Viv couldn't keep her mouth shut," Ben said.

"You know her better than that, Ben. Viv never tells me anything until she has a solution, or at least a suggestion, of how to move forward." Galin smirked, urging them out into the hallway.

"I hope you don't expect me to sit around and do nothing while Grace and Ivan are up there," Nyx said as they exited the office, their footsteps echoing on the polished marble floor. As they walked past Finna's vacant desk, Ben stopped, lost in thought. Nyx turned back to him, squinting in the bright overhead lights.

"What?" she asked, measuring his concerned expression.

"Nothing." He blinked down at her.

"That look isn't nothing," Nyx said in an accusatory tone.

"What if Galin is right?" he asked, biting the side of his cheek. He gazed past Nyx, as if lost in his own thoughts.

Nyx raised an eyebrow. "We just established Galin's theories were possible," she said, her voice tinged with condescension.

"Do you think the Council has been working on something this big under my nose and I have been entirely oblivious to it?" Ben's confidence wavered at the thought, and he took another dig at the inside of his cheek.

Nyx shook her head. "Why don't you pop over and ask Ma'at for yourself? I'm sure she could find out something through her little contact network."

"I can't just go to the Council's dimension and have a private meeting with her," Ben replied. "We're supposed to be on opposite sides, remember? It would draw suspicion and place her in danger."

"So what? It's not like she's the real Ma'at."

"She's still sentient, and she believes she is the real Ma'at. I can't put her in a position to be harmed," Ben said defensively, having forgotten Ma'at had been replicated.

"Oh honey, that's not how that works," Nyx said, shaking her head and pushing out her bottom lip as though she were giving sad news to a child. "Why would you go see a watered-down version when the real Ma'at is safely tucked away in Hel, in *my* rooms if I remember correctly."

"I forgot she was a copy," he admitted. "And what do you mean, it doesn't work that way? Are you mocking me?" Ben added indignantly.

"Yes." Nyx nodded slowly. "Ma'at and Ma'at-bot aren't separate beings. The one at the Council mostly runs on algorithms reflecting Ma'at's normal behavior. They're linked through their adornments. Ma'at controls the bot when she needs to. That way, she can be there without being in any real danger."

Ben stared daggers at her, letting his mouth fall agape. "Am I the only one who didn't know how they're linked?"

"Probably." Nyx shrugged.

As they continued walking, Nyx's heels clicked against the floor, punctuating their conversation. The overhead lighting at this time of day cast harsh shadows across the expansive walkway, making Ben feel uneasy. He couldn't shake the feeling that something big was happening behind the scenes.

<center>~~~~</center>

Hours had turned into days, with no sign of Ivan and Grace returning. Nyx was growing restless. She had been deliberating over her conclusions about Gaia, and the only thing the recollection was giving her was outrage. Enough was enough. With a huff, she shifted into Lilly's workspace, giving her a start that nearly caused her to fall off her chair.

"Damn it, Nyx!" Lilly exclaimed, picking up her dropped paintbrush from the floor and slamming it into the tray of her easel. "A little warning would be nice."

"How are you sitting here painting when they're still out there?!" Nyx yelled back.

"Easy. Like this," Lilly replied, looking directly into Nyx's eyes before slapping two broad strokes across the canvas without looking at what she was doing.

"Well, stop it," Nyx demanded.

Lilly picked up her palette and began mixing colors, ignoring Nyx's demand. "What do you want, Nyx?" she asked, disregarding the woman as she painted.

"I want to know what's happening. You are supposed to be monitoring the device, not sitting around listening to this horrific music and entertaining yourself."

"I am monitoring the device," Lilly said, pointing to the left side of the digital display with the handle of her paintbrush. "Look for yourself. It's the same as it's been for the last two days. No changes."

As if on cue, the sensor screen blinked and the data feed flatlined.

"Did you do that?" Lilly asked.

"I thought you did it to irritate me," Nyx answered.

"Yeah, because I like an irritated you much better than a regular you," Lilly quipped, her voice dripping with sarcasm.

Nyx scoffed. "Well, what do we do now?"

"I don't know. I'm supposed to tell you or Ben about any changes, so consider yourself told. It's your problem now." Lilly shrugged and returned her attention to the canvas.

CHAPTER SEVENTEEN

I don't think this is working, Grace said.

It hasn't been on that long, Ivan answered.

It's been two days!

On Rasa. We don't know how long a day is where she is, or how long it will take her to notice.

How long do you think we should stay out here? she asked.

If she hasn't come within the month, I don't think she'll be coming.

A month! You want to wait out here for a month?

Last time we were out here together, it was for six months. Why are you complaining about one?

Yeah, but we were doing something—not sitting around staring at a hole.

It'll give us time to talk about everything that has happened. Maybe we missed something? Ivan said. He was trying to remain positive while fending off the pressure building over the time constraint they were under.

Hey!

They spun around to a familiar voice, although not the one they were hoping for.

What are you doing here, Mikkel? Grace asked.

You rose two days ago and Leo doesn't have your shells. What are you doing here? Mikkel asked, throwing her question back at her.

We're trying to figure out what happened to your mother, Ivan answered.

Right. What's this, then? Mikkel asked, moving toward the sensor.

Nothing, Grace said.

It doesn't look like nothing. Mikkel moved next to the sensor and sent out a ripple of energy from his orb, pushing it a few yards.

Stop it, Mikkel! Don't touch that! Grace yelled.

What? This? Mikkel sent out a stronger ripple, knocking the sensor in the other direction. It tumbled end over end, hit a piece of space debris, and blinked before the projected image collapsed.

Mikkel! Grace growled.

I'm sorry. I didn't know it would do that, Mikkel apologized. He only intended to get them to tell him what they were doing. He didn't mean to break anything.

Go home, Mikkel, Ivan said. His words dripped with disappointment.

A mischievous giggle echoed around them, causing them to spin around, searching for its elusive source yet finding nothing.

He didn't mean to break it, said the smooth, echoing, there-but-not-there voice.

Who's there? Mikkel yelled out. *Show yourself!*

Another velvety laugh surrounded them. *Go home, Mikkel,* the voice said, imbued with creamy undertones and silky edges.

We need to speak with you, Ivan said.

I know, the voice replied.

A warm glow pulsated around Mikkel's orb and sent it out of their vicinity. Once he was gone, a warm golden entity appeared from behind a sun on the edge of their view and made its way toward them.

What did you do with him? Grace asked. Her voice was quick and panicked.

I sent him home, the voice answered.

We need to speak with you about something important, Ivan said again.

I know, the voice repeated. *In two hours of your time, come see the children and you will have your answers.*

Once the words reached Grace and Ivan, the other orb disappeared.

It seems like we have our meeting. Do you want to head home? Ivan asked.

I guess so. I wonder how long she was watching us? Grace asked, more to herself than Ivan.

Once they descended into their bodies, Grace stood and stretched with her arms over her head. She twisted back and forth, then bent over and touched her toes.

"This is fantastic! No stiffness at all."

"Speak for yourself," Ivan said, groaning and rubbing his leg as he stood.

His hip cramped and a tingling sensation shot down his thigh as he rubbed it. He attempted to walk it off, only to find his foot refused to move. He lifted his pant leg to see his ankle had turned purplish black and become mottled. Grace wasn't a heavy woman, but her shell had sat in the same place on his lap for two days, cutting off the blood flow and decomposing the flesh of his leg. It took a few minutes for the prickling sensation to subside and the skin to return to a normal color. When his leg stopped aching, he realized his shell had been enhanced the same as his essence had been when he rose with Grace and that their abilities were again in sync.

The front door flew open and slammed into the wall hard enough to drop a painting onto the floor.

"What in all hells was that?!" Mikkel yelled as he stormed across the room, pointing into the air.

Ivan's head snapped around to the sound. "A sensor," he said with a slight grin.

Mikkel stopped in his tracks and narrowed his eyes. He glanced back and forth between Ivan and his mother, neither of whom offered an explanation.

"So, you're not going to tell me?" he asked after scrutinizing them for several seconds.

Ivan and Grace looked at each other and shrugged before turning back to Mikkel.

"Tell you what?" Ivan asked.

"You know damned well what. That thing flung me across the universe and slammed me back into my shell. There was something else out there powerful enough and precise enough to do something you can't."

"Something else out where?" Nyx's voice came from behind Mikkel.

He spun to see her coming through the open door with Lilly a step behind. "What are you doing here?" Mikkel asked as he glowered at Lilly.

Lilly leaned to her left and stood on her toes so she could see around Mikkel and speak to Ivan. "I lost the signal."

"Mikkel broke it," Ivan replied.

"What?" Lilly scoffed and punched Mikkel in the arm. "What'd you do that for?"

"Ow!" he exclaimed. "I didn't do it on purpose! It was an accident."

"What was an accident?" Viv asked, passing through the open door. She shut it behind her before joining the group in the middle of the room.

"*Mikkel* broke the sensor," Lilly said, sneering and rolling her eyes.

"How? What was he even doing out there?" Viv asked.

"He came looking for us," Grace said.

"You can't just mind your own business, can you, Mikkel?" Nyx admonished.

"If someone had told me what was going on, I wouldn't have gone looking," Mikkel said.

"If someone had wanted you to know what was going on, they would have told you," Nyx said, taking a step toward Mikkel.

"It doesn't matter. We got what we wanted," Ivan said.

The door opened and Ben stepped through. "Really?" he asked. His eyes landed on Mikkel. "What's he doing here? Did you tell him, Lilly?"

"No," Lilly said. "I know how to keep my mouth shut."

Mikkel scanned each of their faces and turned back to Lilly. "What … is … going … on?" he growled in frustration with a tightened jaw.

Lilly took a step back and craned her neck. "Oh, no sir. You do not speak to me like that," she said, waving her finger in front of him.

"Don't you turn this on me! I wanna know what all of you are hiding. There's something going on here and I seem to be the only one in this room who doesn't know what it is," Mikkel said as he glanced around from face to face.

"This is not your business," Nyx said. "It's like inviting yourself to a ritual and demanding an offering." She turned her attention to Grace and Ben. "Did you raise them all to act like this one?"

"Do you really want to start comparing children, Nyx?" Viv asked. She wasn't defending Mikkel's behavior, but Nyx had no room to comment on his issues when some of her own offspring were less than stellar examples of good breeding.

"Let's all take a breath," Ivan said. "We don't have time for this."

"What are we supposed to do about him?" Nyx asked, nodding her head toward Mikkel.

Mikkel didn't like being spoken about as if he wasn't in the room. He did, however, have enough sense to keep his mouth shut.

"It's going to come out soon, anyway. We may as well start with The Three since they could be helpful," Ben said.

"Three? You want to tell the other two as well?" Nyx asked. She wasn't pleased about bringing more people into the group after their conversation with Galin.

Viv, sitting in one of the side chairs, drew everyone's attention as she spoke. "What one knows, they all eventually know, anyway. It would certainly make my job easier if Alex and I could be on the same page."

"Well then, that changes everything, doesn't it? We simply must make sure Vivienne doesn't face any difficulties with her job." Nyx's comment was a blend of biting sarcasm and exaggerated animation.

Viv displayed a tight smile and cut her eyes up at Nyx. "I'll let that slide this time because I can imagine how upsetting it must be when your mother doesn't want to speak to you, but I assure you, I can do my job just fine either way."

Viv wasn't normally so callous, but she had been dealing with Nyx's superior attitude for centuries and she was done with it.

Nyx flew toward Viv, but her motion was stopped when Ben grabbed her around the waist, preventing her from reaching the unflinching woman who remained seated.

"How dare you!" Nyx exclaimed, clawing at Ben's arm, which was locked firmly around her.

Lilly moved around Mikkel to get a better view of the drama unfolding in front of them.

"How dare I what, Nyx? Call you out on your childish behavior or your insatiable need to always be the center of attention?" Viv asked.

"I will not stand here and be insulted by a lower being. You need to leave," Nyx said, sneering down at Viv.

Viv chuckled. "You can't kick me out. This isn't your house."

Nyx glared at Viv while she sat, smiling up at her smugly, waiting for another pithy retort.

"Viv," Ivan said, drawing her attention.

He passed her the information about the encounter at the border.

"Hm," she uttered.

"Could you and Lilly pass that information on to The Three and see if you can come up with anything we haven't considered? Maybe an evacuation plan if necessary?"

"I'd be happy to, Ivan," she said. She stood, giving Nyx one last glare, and motioned to a disappointed Lilly to follow her. When she approached Mikkel, he didn't move, so she nudged his shoulder, forcing him to turn around, and ushered him out the door in front of her.

Nyx slapped Ben's arm once again. "Let go of me!" she snapped, pushing him away. "That woman has some nerve speaking to me in that manner."

"You started it," Ben said.

Nyx huffed and threw herself down into the chair Viv had vacated. She wasn't oblivious. She knew she was behaving in a very unflattering manner. It was impossible for her to understand why the creator she adored so deeply refused to see her. It hurt her in a way she couldn't fathom and had no experience dealing with. She still had no excuse for taking her temper out on those around her whom she had become attached to.

Once Nyx had calmed herself, Ivan passed her and Ben the experience he had given to Viv.

"Do you know what you're going to ask her?" Ben asked.

"The first thing we want to know is why she never told us about The Outside," Ivan said.

Ben glanced over at Grace and Nyx, motioning Ivan toward the bar. *I had a talk with Ma'at.*

About what? Ivan asked, wondering why Ben didn't want the women to hear.

About the possibility that the Council created another pocket dimension, and this is all one giant ruse to gain control over Grace again.

Well, that's something I never considered. What did she say?

Pretty much the same thing I already concluded. The Council isn't organized enough to pull off something like that right now. They don't have the resources to sustain the dimension they have. There have been rumors for years that they think it's safe enough to move back to their own dimension, but I think their technology is failing and Ma'at agrees. She said Osiris all but confirmed to her that that's what is happening.

Do you feel confident eliminating that as a possibility, then?

Ben nodded, pouring himself a drink.

When it was time, Ivan took Grace's hand, and they closed their eyes. In a split second, Ivan's eyes popped back open. Ben and Nyx were watching him, and Grace was gone. It had never happened like this before. Normally when they went to the children, it only took a millisecond, and they always came back to the same position they had left. Even if he had been blocked from going, she should have come back to the same place and time. He could still feel their connection. She wasn't in any danger, but he was concerned that Aphya had her alone.

Feeling the loss of Ivan's hand, Grace's eyes opened to the familiar bright meadow filled with sweet-smelling, colorful flowers and sounds of laughing children. The grand farmhouse stood behind her with the stream in front of her. She spun around, eyes searching. There was no one around her. No children, no Ivan, and no Aphya. She was alone. The laughter stopped. Had she truly heard it, or had it been in her imagination? Grace searched the meadow and trees leading up to the farmhouse, to no avail.

She opened the door, entering the hallway. Her boots echoed on the wood floor. The atmosphere was still and muted except for the pulsating echo in her ears from the energy that burned inside of her.

"Hello? Come out, children. It's just me," she called out, moving cautiously forward. Aphya had separated her from Ivan for a reason. The only thing she had to figure out was whether she was going to be facing an innocent victim and protector or a genocidal psychopath. She crept stealthily through the house, checking every room, closet, and cupboard. The house was empty, and she made her way out onto the back porch. The lush grass was strewn with abandoned toys. Swings swayed with a soft, sweetly scented breeze, but otherwise there were no signs of motion.

She stepped down onto the stone path and yelled out, "You wanted me here alone! Show yourself!"

Silence hung heavy in the air, with no response to be heard. Her words echoed back to her and her agitation increased. "Come out NOW or I'm finished with you, and I won't be coming back!" She felt a presence move behind her and spun around.

"Grace, I'm sorry. It took me some time to move the children. I wanted to speak to you alone." Aphya appeared as she had before. She was in Chaos's familiar form, older yet ageless, with a warm smile on her face.

"You ever think it might be better with a little less drama? Maybe drop by Rasa for some tea? You know, like a normal person," Grace said, sneering at her.

"You mean like a human?" Aphya laughed. "Grace, we're not human. This *is* normal. I invited you here. You brought your manifested consciousness to this place, the same as I brought mine. That's how we do things. If you wanted me to come to you, all you had to do was call out to me."

"What in all hells is that supposed to mean?" Grace raised her volume a bit. "Manifested consciousness implies my body and mind are here together. My body isn't here. This is an illusion. I can feel it's not fully real."

Aphya squeezed her eyes shut in exasperation. "How do I explain it in a way your narrow view can grasp?" she asked, giving off the first sign of irritation that Grace had ever heard from her. Aphya opened her eyes and took a deep breath, letting it out in a slow, smooth exhalation. "Okay. Grace, your body is here …"

Grace protested, but Aphya cut her off.

"Your body *is* here; however, our consciousnesses are vibrating on a separate frequency. We're in a different plane of existence. I have created this familiar setting to make both of us feel at ease." Aphya searched Grace's face for any hint of understanding. "It's like shifting, only different. Your physical being has shifted to this place and your mind, while still in your body, is synchronized with a higher plane overlaying this place. It's not as much an illusion as it is an overlay of consciousness."

"I don't care what it is. I prefer to have my body and my mind together if it's all the same to you. And I prefer not to be inside of your little subconscious where all the rules of reality are created by you."

"Fair enough. I wasn't trying to take advantage of the situation. I only wanted you to feel comfortable in a familiar place," Aphya replied.

"Wait a second. Does that mean that when we've been to see the children before, you were near us at the time and you projected us into this place from wherever we were?"

"No. When you came to see them, you were drawn to this place. You always came to them here when you saw them. When you left, it broke the connection with the simulation. You went back to where you came from at the same place and time you left from. It's the way this place is set up. Our connections to each other, including the children, don't require a time component, so none passes here." Aphya was showing her exasperation that Grace didn't even have a rudimentary grasp of the fundamentals of consciousness projection or manifestation. She conceded it was her own fault.

"So, every time I have come here, you have known and you haven't shown yourself?" This realization angered Grace even further.

"Yes. I could feel your connection to this place, even when you brought Ami the other day. Do you really not understand that I am in sync with this plane and when your mind begins to sync with it, I can feel it too?" Aphya asked.

"I don't give a shit how it works! Get me out of here now!" Grace exclaimed, feeling belittled by Aphya's remark. She hadn't wanted to approach this meeting with anger or aggression, but Aphya had isolated her. She felt trapped and fear was creeping into her mind.

Within seconds, the façade melted away. Grace was standing in a field close to the ruins of a large stone house. The bright, lush landscape was gone, replaced by a darker, overgrown one with dulled colors and stale air. Although she hadn't a clue what world it was on, she knew that this was indeed a real place. Grace felt the comfortable warmth of her mind melting back into her physical form. It was so smooth compared to squeezing back in when returning from rising. She couldn't be certain if the new shell created the feeling or if it was because she hadn't actually left it.

Aphya no longer looked like the gentle older woman she had appeared as before. Her hair was brown, and her face was less wrinkled except for the smile lines around her eyes.

"Why have you stopped creating?" Aphya asked.

Grace blindsided her with a high-energy blast, encasing her in a vibrating bubble of phasing energy. Aphya placed her hand against it. The edges of the bubble stretched before snapping back, holding Aphya captive.

"Grace? What are you doing?" Aphya asked in a confused tone with an edge of warning.

"What am *I* doing? You're the one who needs to explain some things, starting with why you are trying to get us to destroy the boundary between The Everything and The Nothing," Grace said, glowering as she continued to hold the stream of energy flowing to the bubble. The burning sting of fury welled up inside of her core, threatening to explode through her skin.

Aphya placed her own glowing hands against the inside of the barrier, pressing slowly, sliding them over the inside of the vibrating partition. Grace didn't lack the power to keep the confinement in place, but she did lack the finesse to modulate the energy flow with precision. Aphya felt what she was searching for, inviting a fleeting smile to cross her face.

"It has to be broken, Grace. You don't understand," Aphya said, holding onto the weak spot in the bubble.

"You're right, I don't understand. Explain it to me." Grace was grinding her teeth as her disdain pooled. "*Aphya*," she growled.

The smile slid from Aphya's face, replaced by a sickly grimace. This wasn't the way she wanted everything to come out. It seemed Grace preferred confrontation to civility, so if that was what she needed, it was what she was going to get.

Aphya's hands flashed white hot, bursting the bubble open. The backlash of energy knocked Grace backward into the unyielding stone wall. Aphya took advantage of the momentary drop in Grace's defenses, grabbing her by the arms. Grace responded by headbutting Aphya's face as hard as she could. Blood spattered from Aphya's nose and mouth onto Grace's face as she reeled back, losing her grasp on one of Grace's arms. Grace pulled her leg up, kicking into Aphya's stomach, shoving outward.

Aphya was momentarily stunned, although her grip on one of Grace's arms remained strong. She dug her fingers in, tearing through the muscle, down to the bone of Grace's upper arm. Aphya pulled her free arm back, winding up power before slamming her elbow up into Grace's throat and jaw. The impact jolted Grace. Her awareness of not being able to escape Aphya's grip struck her nearly as hard as the blow had. Aphya was matching Grace's phase.

Grace struggled against Aphya's grip and Aphya struggled just as hard to maintain her hold. They beat each other until they were both covered in a mixture of blood, sweat, and dirt. Aphya fought to press Grace back into the wall, pinning Grace's free arm with her body.

"Stop it, Grace! I don't want to hurt you!" Aphya yelled into Grace's face.

Grace dropped her canis and hissed, "What makes you think I won't be the one hurting you?"

Aphya had made the mistake of getting too close to Grace's face, and she once again received another brutal headbutt, which broke her eye socket. Aphya stumbled back, jerking Grace forward by the arm. The propulsion of Grace's weight toward Aphya allowed her to sling Grace over her leg onto the ground. Discarded tiles from the old stone path gave way, cracking with the force of Grace's body slamming down on them.

Aphya sprung forward, straddling Grace, pounding her face with fast, crushing blows. Grace was overwhelmed by the maneuver. Aphya's knees pinned Grace's arms to the ground below, and she was unable to phase them through. Her mind struggled with the realization she was trapped, causing her more pain than the beating she was receiving.

"I told you I DIDN'T WANT TO HURT YOU!" Aphya screamed, landing a final blow that buried Grace's head into the ground, rendering her unconscious.

CHAPTER EIGHTEEN

Grace squeezed her eyes and shook her head cautiously to dislodge her disbelief at the previous event. The ease with which Aphya had defeated her left her feeling irritated, frustrated, and resentful. Her head ached where the bones of her skull were fusing themselves back together. When she finally opened her eyes, indistinct shapes and colors blurred together as though she were looking through the steamy glass of a hot shower.

Slowly, a small dingy-gray room began coming into focus. They were inside the ruins of the farmhouse. Aphya extended her hand to Grace, who slapped it away while lifting herself off the floor. They were both healed, although still covered with blood caked in dirt. Grace wiped her face with the sleeve of her jacket, smearing more than cleaning the sticky globs.

"That brings back some memories. I haven't had an all-out brawl like that in ages," Aphya said.

"Since you got caught?" Grace leered back.

"You've been talking to the warden." Aphya's expression soured, and her words dripped with bitterness. "I should have figured that would happen eventually," she said with a sigh. "She used Niko as bait, didn't she?"

"Why didn't you just kill him like you did the rest of them? Couldn't catch him?" Grace taunted, trying to get a rise out of her. Aphya didn't know the reason behind Ami's visit, and Grace wanted to use that to her advantage.

"Oh, is that what she told you? *I'm* a killer? That's rich coming from you." Aphya contorted her face accusingly.

"I've never dissipated an essence. You're a devourer. You absorb them to increase your power," Grace rebutted.

Aphya let out an uproarious laugh so intense it nearly brought her to the point of tears. "Are you completely incompetent or just a gullible idiot?" Aphya asked. She stopped laughing and wiped her face with the back of her hand. Her look became stern. "I've never killed, dissipated, devoured, or otherwise extinguished a consciousness. There's no such thing as a devourer, anyway. It even sounds too stupid to believe." The suggestion visibly offended her as her lip curled back.

"And why should I believe you over Renata? You've lied to everyone about everything from the very beginning," Grace said.

"I had to after what happened to Gaia. I couldn't tell anyone the entire truth. As for Renata, she is deeply disturbed, devious, and manipulative."

"What do you mean, after what happened to Gaia?" Grace questioned suspiciously.

"Gaia was the first one I released when we got here. She remembered some snippets from The Outside. When I showed her the rest of it, let's just say she didn't do very well with the information. I thought it would jump-start her own memories. I should have known she couldn't handle it." Aphya's eyes drifted downward and Grace could feel her mood had turned sullen. "After that, Gaia retreated into her own version of reality, mixing The Inside, the higher plane, and The Outside together, not understanding they were all separate places."

"Right. You released her." Grace pointed her finger at Aphya. "Released her from where? You were imprisoned alone."

"Was I?"

Grace scoffed and rolled her eyes. She continued in a mocking tone, finding Aphya's explanation outlandish. "Okay, let's play your game. If you thought Gaia wouldn't be able to handle the reality of this world being a prison and the real world being on The Outside, why would you release her first?"

"Because she's a creator. An extraordinary botanical creator, might I add," Aphya defended. "The planets were all barren rocks. I had expended everything I dared. We needed worlds we could live on while we figured out how to escape, and I couldn't create habitable places and shells for all of you."

"We? So, you already planned on creating us to avoid being alone in here. Seems like that worked out really well. We're all one big happy family and you're *so* popular and loved." Grace made her tone as snide as possible.

"You're hanging on really tightly to that denial, aren't you?" Aphya's tone conveyed a sense of disappointment more than anything else.

"Well, Gaia is the one who told us you consumed consciousnesses. Renata said you devoured them. Why would they both say it if it wasn't true? It's not like they talk to each other now, is it?" Grace retorted defensively.

"Grace, this is ridiculous. Let me transfer my memories to you and you'll understand," Aphya said, stepping toward Grace.

Grace stepped back, quickly raising her hand between them. "I have had more than enough of you showing me what you want me to see for the last couple of centuries. You should get to your point. Quickly."

"Or what, Grace? You don't know how to beat me in here." Her words weren't threatening. Aphya was growing frustrated.

Grace frowned, dropping her head.

Aphya stepped backward, placing her hand on her hip and pressing her lips together. She paused, selecting her next words carefully as she took a breath. What did Grace think she was going to be able to do to control her, anyway? Aphya knew it was her fault for not helping the others understand at the beginning. Time was so different inside this stupid confinement; she couldn't imagine how much had passed for Grace and the others.

"Grace, did Renata explain what resolving is?"

"Of course she did," Grace snapped. "She said once the body containing an essence dies, the essence gets placed in a confinement until it can process what it has learned from the previous life. The confinement holds it until it is ready to be reborn." Grace stated the process as clearly as she understood it.

"Wow. You are a real propaganda mouthpiece. You are also completely wrong. Resolving is condemnation. Anyone who doesn't blindly follow the rules or who questions anything is imprisoned in a confinement until their mind has been obliterated. They lose all memory of The Outside and become a blank canvas, just like all of you have. They accept their confinement as reality and live inside of it for eternity, never trying to get out because they don't know they are in a prison. No one *ever* tries to get out, Grace. These prisons become their reality forever. They are *never* reborn." Aphya leaned back against the wall, watching to see if Grace was going to absorb what she had said.

"Niko got out." Grace shrugged flippantly. "How do you explain that?"

"They structured this confinement to contain me. Not anyone else, because Renata would have to admit she knew others were in here. She thought we would all resolve and it wouldn't matter. Niko was a scared neophyte, running away from me because he saw me taking the others in to protect them. He didn't understand."

"So, you admit it?"

"Admit what?"

"When you said you were moving them, you meant you were sucking the life out of them to increase your own power!" Grace exclaimed.

"No, you idiot! I'm holding them. They're here." Aphya tapped her fingers lightly on her chest.

"Dead!" Grace accused.

Aphya clenched her jaw. "Did resolving remove half your brain cells along with your memories? What you're saying doesn't even make sense!"

"Hey!" Grace exclaimed, offended by the insult and the intonation. Aphya's voice had reminded Grace of that weird, whispery-loud, angry voice that Ben used with her sometimes when he thought she was being dense. Before Grace could think of a comeback, Aphya continued.

"Think about it. You said yourself, Gaia saw me take the children in."

"Yeah!"

"Then Renata said Niko saw me take them in, which I admit was before I could explain to him what was going on."

"Sounds like you're proving my point."

"Years later, you met the children and can attest that they are real, and yet you still think I killed them all?" Aphya cocked her head and narrowed her eyes at Grace. "Think about it."

Grace stared at her feet, thinking over the information. She had felt the children's essences, and Ami had confirmed they were real. Unlike the meadow, which she knew was an illusion, she could feel the children. Her mind latched onto a thought.

"How do I know they were the same children?" Grace asked, defiantly placing her fist on her hip.

Aphya closed her eyes, rolled her head back, and let out a deep sigh, giving the impression that her entire body had accepted defeat. "I guess you don't," she said, straightening her neck and opening her eyes. "And I can't prove it to you unless you let me either take you back to the other plane so I can release them, or pass my memories to you, which you won't."

"Well, then I guess you better find another way to convince me I should believe you and not Renata," Grace said with the most condescending tone she could muster. She wanted to believe Aphya was telling the truth and Renata was the one who was lying. Her gut instinct told her this was what was happening. But then if Renata was lying and she held the confinement in her grasp, the situation was far more dire for The Everything than it would have been with Aphya as the evil daemon Renata portrayed her to be.

Grace needed more than her gut. She needed to be certain beyond any doubt. Grace needed to know the whole story of how they came to be here. The conversation was going to be lengthy because she was unwilling to let Aphya access her mind to pass the memories.

Aphya sat on the floor and began her story.

"We were a separate community from Renata's. We didn't follow her rules, we had our own, and since we never blatantly disrespected her, we thought it would keep us out of her reach. Unfortunately, she doesn't think that way. Our mere existence was seen as a challenge to her ironfisted rule. When Renata came for us, we knew we were all going to be resolved separately. Everyone selected me to encapsulate all the other essences inside of mine because I have the ability to be a container." Aphya glanced up at Grace, unsure if she even believed that part. Grace made no move to interrupt her.

"It was a risk, but we knew Renata wouldn't destroy me in such a public place. We made sure she thought I was alone when her group caught me. I told her I had already disposed of everyone so she couldn't take them. It wasn't hard to convince her with the mountains of empty bodies lying at my feet. That's what we wanted her to think. We needed her to believe I was the last of us and I was alone. After she imprisoned me in the confinement, I began releasing the rest of you." Aphya's demeanor shifted, her eyes drifted off, and she absently rubbed her fingertips across her chest.

"You know how it is falling into a cactus?" she asked without giving Grace time to answer. "It's so horribly painful when it happens. At least you think it is at the time. Then things start to get a little numb and you don't really feel the needles stabbing into your flesh anymore. If you leave them in long enough, they sink in deeper and become part of you, and you are only reminded of them if you bump them or rub them on something. They're just kind of there until they start to swell and fester. It's then that they need to come out. So, you take hold of one. You wiggle and pull a little, only to realize it has embedded itself deep into your flesh and a nice little tug isn't going to make it move anywhere. You're forced to rip it out, and the pain is so much more excruciating than it was going in because your skin had embedded it. You look at the place where it had become attached to you and all that is left is a raw, gaping hole." Aphya chuckled, making Grace feel uncomfortable. "Try doing that five trillion times," she finished, raising her eyes back to Grace.

"Five trillion? There are well over five trillion beings in here, Aphya."

"They're only echoes," Aphya replied flatly.

"Echoes of what?" Grace asked.

"Echoes of us."

"I don't understand what you're saying to me." Grace wondered who and what these echoes were, and how they could be distinguished from the "us" Aphya had referred to.

"Echoes are the creatures that were created here by some infinites, whom you call Primordials. Only, the echoes were created without a certain element that allows them to mature. No matter how many life cycles they go through, they will always be larvae. Some don't even have a flicker of an essence. Those are the worst ones."

"What is that supposed to mean? What difference does it make if you consider them larvae?" Grace wasn't sure what point Aphya was trying to make.

"It means that if we are able to break out of this confinement, they have to remain here. They can't exist outside the confinement. Or, if Renata sanitizes it, the echoes will cease to exist altogether."

"If *we* are able to break out? You said it yourself—this isn't our confinement. The rest of us can leave anytime we want, can't we?" Grace asked.

"You can. But do you honestly think Renata wouldn't simply drop all of you into confinements of your own the second you began streaming out of here? In her mind, you are all still a threat." Aphya answered her question with another.

"How could we be a threat when we have no knowledge or memories of that world?"

"What makes you think at least some memories wouldn't come back if you were out there long enough?"

"She said she wouldn't sanitize the confinement if we got rid of you. She offered to give us our own community on The Outside where we could live in peace," Grace said. It was a bluff. She had no intention of killing anyone, but she wanted to see Aphya's reaction.

"You could do that," Aphya said, nodding her head.

Grace was waiting for more, which didn't come. "It looks like our only solution, doesn't it?"

"Probably, but if you do dispatch me, you would be guilty of the highest crime in our world, and this would become your confinement, wouldn't it? Do you seriously think Renata will let you out of here?"

"But if we don't dissipate your essence, she is going to sanitize the confinement," Grace said anxiously.

"She's probably going to do that anyway before the Elders find out she imprisoned an entire society after convicting me of genocide." Aphya shrugged as the harshness of her words hit Grace.

"What will happen to the echoes? Can't you just provide them with the element they need to mature? Isn't there a way to infuse them with it?" Grace felt a weight in the pit of her stomach. If she hadn't gone after the child, if she hadn't gone to The Outside, Renata wouldn't know they were here. She didn't want to be responsible for the end of so many living beings.

"It doesn't exist here. Do you think Renata would create a confinement that would allow the prisoner to make more potential infinites? The Elders wouldn't tolerate that either—not that they have any real power. It would be the same as if they had condemned an innocent."

"Aren't the echoes innocent too?" Grace couldn't fathom the idea that one form of life was lesser than another simply because it was more fragile.

"I guess the best way to phrase it is that infinites see echoes in the same manner a human sees a cherished pet. They see something intelligent behind the eyes. It's just not elevated intelligence. Echoes are limited. They will never become like us. Deny it all you want, but you know it too. You know you're different from most beings and it has nothing to do with your lifespan." Aphya squinted at her. She knew Grace had never felt like she belonged anywhere until she found Ivan and the others.

"None of that has anything to do with why Renata wants me to destroy you." Grace paced the floor, throwing her hands in the air.

Aphya pulled herself off the ground and spoke in a soft, cautious tone. "Grace, you were always kind and caring. She was envious of the praise you got from the Elders."

"So, you're saying I was a suck-up?"

"No. Our kind gravitates toward you, while they fear her, which is something her ego couldn't handle. Back then, you created a peaceful society of thinking people who looked out for each other. It was the kind of society she tried to create, but couldn't, because she couldn't give up enough control to let us find our own happiness. She became even more jealous and manipulative after that because she could never get the respect from people that you got from us. That's when she began to change. She turned mean and possessive, like a feral dog guarding its food. She transformed her society into a sea of mindless drones she could control and resolve whenever they started questioning anything," Aphya said, disheartened.

"Why didn't the Elders do anything to stop her?"

"They're afraid of her. Everyone is afraid of her. The only reason they're still around is because they give her the illusion of legitimacy. How can she be a tyrant if the Elders support her?"

"It's not fair! You want me to believe that we either escape this confinement and go back to a life that no one in here is going to remember or understand, and in the process annihilate ninety percent of the inhabitants of this place, or we stay here, knowing it is a prison, and wait for a jealous, power-tripping maniac to sanitize it, which will make us lose all memory of everything and everyone we know in here?!" Grace ran her words together too quickly and had to take a deep breath when she finished.

"That pretty much sums it up. Neither choice seems like it's going to be good for the echoes." Aphya shrugged. She felt bad about it, but it wasn't the same as losing real people.

Grace slid down the wall to the floor. "There has got to be another way," she said, rolling her eyes up to meet Aphya's.

"Don't look at me like that. None of this was *my* plan, and I never created any echoes. I had to improvise." Aphya closed her eyes, resting her head back against the wall.

"Your improvisation sucks," Grace snapped.

"Yeah, you think? I was supposed to be the one who resolved, protecting everyone else. This was my confinement. You were supposed to remember and get us out of here," Aphya snapped back.

"Me? You're putting this situation on me?" Grace scrunched her face.

"Yes. You were the center of us—our touchstone," Aphya said sadly. "You've always led by example, with passion and empathy. Even now. The turned are coming together in here just like they all did out there, as infinites." Aphya raised her voice, pointing outward.

"They want a peaceful existence like they had out there, with camaraderie and free will. It's exactly what you did on The Outside, which is what got all of us thrown in here in the first place. *You* are what drew them together. You can't help yourself. Before the confinement, Ben and I both said we should go after Renata first, stop her. But no, you thought we could coexist peacefully with her." Aphya threw her hands up, mocking Grace. "You said she had no reason to come after us. So, yeah, I am putting this situation squarely. On. You." Aphya was angry and hurt, giving an unexpected truthful weight to her words.

Grace emitted a low groan. She couldn't deny it sounded like her. She also couldn't deny what Ben's response would have been to a tense situation. Offense had never been her strong suit, and she never attacked first. She just didn't know if she could believe any of it.

"So, why didn't Renata kill me when she kidnapped me and drug me to The Outside? Why did she tell me I had to kill you or else she would sanitize the confinement?" Grace asked. She needed answers.

"She's afraid of you, and she needs you alive, but I can't figure out why, and you don't remember anymore. All I know is she's afraid because you are pure light, and you're more powerful than she is. We are drawn to you the same way skeliks are drawn to a sol. She wants you to dissipate me because she wants you to commit a crime that will force you to stay trapped in here forever. Because she knows out there, she can't control you. She'll have every right to keep you in here and never let the others on The Outside know anyone else is in here with you." Aphya pointed at Grace before continuing.

"When I publicly said I had disposed of all of you, Renata knew I hadn't, but she took it as a win. She saw it as a way to get rid of us all at once. She thought after we were resolved, we wouldn't be able to cause her any more trouble. Now that she knows I'm not resolved, that's a problem for her. She probably dragged you Outside to see if you were resolved or not. She knew you'd come back voluntarily, even if you hadn't been resolved, because you'd never abandon your people." Aphya clenched her jaw.

"At least your analogy is appropriate," Grace uttered, sounding demoralized. "Skeliks die when they come too close to a sun." She needed time to think without this woman continuing to whisper in her ear. Before this overwhelming feeling consumed her, she had to take some time to process it. She needed to run, but she couldn't, because she didn't know if Aphya would disappear again if she left to go run it out.

Aphya didn't know how much more Grace could take before she tipped. She cautiously scanned her before continuing. "The only good thing about being in here is we have a lot more time to figure it out. It will take her weeks to even begin sanitizing a confinement of this size. A few weeks out there are like centuries in here."

What Aphya was saying made sense. Grace wanted to trust what she said was the truth, but Grace had trusted way too many people she shouldn't have. She knew her instinct to trust was hugely flawed, getting her into way too many situations that didn't end well. Although she hadn't experienced the same gut-wrenching feeling with Aphya that she had with Renata, her newfound cynicism prevented her from naively believing that Aphya was truly her friend. She needed some kind of proof. And she needed someone else's opinion.

"I need you to talk to the others."

"I'm not sure that's a great idea, given the way Gaia reacted when I showed her the truth," Aphya replied, reaching for Grace's arm.

Grace pulled away, unsure if she should direct her anger at Aphya or herself. Maybe a little of both. "I think we're beyond that. I don't trust you, and I don't know how to tell if you're lying to me. I am not about to be suckered into your version of things without someone else weighing in," Grace said to Aphya, taking hold of her arm.

"Okay, but don't blame me if they lose their minds." Aphya let Grace keep her grasp.

"Do I look like I'm losing my shit?" Grace asked with irritation.

"A little," Aphya answered.

"They'll be fine," Grace leered, jerking Aphya's arm as she shifted them to the prison deck on Rasa.

CHAPTER NINETEEN

Aphya sat in a white chair in the center of a near-barren white room. Grace, Ivan, Nyx, Ben, Ami, and Frigg were all staring at her after having received the memory of the events that happened in the ruins. Frigg was the only one seated and the first to speak.

"I've missed you, old friend," she said warmly.

"Mother," Ben admonished.

"Do not speak to me in that tone. I have every right to say what I want to whomever I want," Frigg said calmly.

Aphya smirked. "I've missed you too, Frigg." She moved her gaze across the room. "Nyx, I'm glad to see you doing well."

Nyx glared forward, seething with anger, and ignored the comment. Before coming into the room, Grace had also shared her experience from The Outside with Frigg, since she was the only one who hadn't been caught up yet. Nyx was angry that Aphya had kept the information from her. She knew her mind would never have broken as easily as Gaia's had. She was certain she could have had all of this tied up in a neat little package by now if she had known what was going on.

Aphya smirked at the pouting look on Nyx's face. Her smile wasn't malicious, but rather a reflection of the amusement she felt watching Nyx, who tried so hard to portray herself as unfeeling despite her sensitive nature.

"I don't know what it is you think is so funny!" Nyx finally spat back with the attitude of a child who had been sent to the corner.

"I just think it's amazing we're all in the same room again. Well, almost all of us. We're missing one," Aphya said, her eyes glinting with amusement.

"Missing one *what?*" Nyx sneered, her tone no less harsh than it had been before.

"One of us. The original core of our rebellious little community." Aphya's smile faded into a serious look.

Nyx huffed, rolling her eyes and crossing her arms.

"Who's the other? I mean, if we're supposed to be such close friends, escaping an oppressive society and running some sort of poorly organized revolution that ended in our collective imprisonment together, then who's missing?" Ben asked, leering skeptically at Aphya.

"Given the way you've divided yourselves, you're not going to like it." Aphya shrugged.

"I didn't ask if I was going to like it. I asked who is missing," Ben said.

"Kali," Aphya replied to a chorus of groans and exclamations. Frigg sighed, rubbing her forehead. She knew the others weren't pleased with that revelation. Ben kicked back at the chair behind him and glanced at Grace before replying.

"Kali is the literal bringer of death. Why would she be in a group like this?" Ben placed his hands on the back of Grace's chair, using her as a buffer between himself and Aphya. He may have been angry, but he was smart enough to know a physical confrontation wouldn't end well for him.

"I understand how you could see it that way. She unties the bonds between an essence and a physical container, releasing it from its constraints. That does tend to leave a lot of empty shells lying around, but she was essential to getting us in here together and she may be important for getting many of us out of here," Aphya replied.

"Why would that be important?" Ben asked, curling his lip back.

"Seriously?" Aphya looked around the room. "You can't get outside of the confinement unless you're free of your shell. Not everyone has the ability to rise like you. Physical shells are bound to this place, even if you manifest them." She raised her pitch in the last statement, making it sound almost like a question. "You really hadn't figured that out yet?"

"Riiiight …" Ivan said, weighing in. "And then I assume after Kali releases them, they all queue up single file, happy to await their turn through the doorway to The Outside."

"Wow, you can be a bit of a jerk," Aphya remarked, scrutinizing Ivan. "I expected something like that to come out of his mouth," she said, wrenching her head toward Ben.

"This isn't getting us anywhere," Frigg said, and she held her hands between them in a stopping motion as she stood up. She turned her back to the group. "I know I've only recently received this information, and possibly I'm missing something important. Maybe if I understood the process of how we came to be in this confinement, it would make more sense to me. Aphya, would you please explain the significant aspects of the process?" Her smile was warm as she asked her question.

"Of course, Frigg. Anything for you," Aphya said and smiled warmly back. She stood up in an unexpected move. Ivan, Ben, and Grace reacted by taking on a defensive stance, while Nyx deepened her glare as the tension in the room launched up to eleven.

"Oh, please. If I had wanted to hurt you, I would have done it already." Aphya shook her head, beginning to pace as she talked. Her calm demeanor was wavering as her frustration increased. She tried to figure out how to best explain incredibly rudimentary concepts to a group of uneducated entities who, at one time, were among the most intelligent in existence.

"Our plan to ensure we remained together was for everyone to shed their shells and gather into a single container. Kali released each essence from its bound shell. Then Ami," she paused, nodding toward Ami, "collected them. I'm the container. Nyx put up a barrier to shield my essence and create a funnel into me. I opened up and pulled the essences into my light while Ben stood watch. Once they were inside, Frigg organized them. It's the way we got in here. I don't know how to simplify the explanation any further."

"What about us? What was our job supposed to be in your little scenario?" Grace asked, motioning between herself and Ivan.

"You were supposed to get us out." She then extended her hand in a gesture of presentation. "Incredible job." She closed her hand, pulling it back.

"Huh. Now who's being the jerk?" Ivan asked.

Aphya lowered her head. "I'm sorry, Ivan. This isn't how I expected this conversation to go, and I regret taking my frustration out on any of you."

Before Ivan could reply, Ben dismissed her words and spoke.

"Why wouldn't Ami just contain them? Seems a little elaborate to me," Ben said, scrutinizing Aphya for an explanation.

"I can't carry that many," Ami snorted from a few inches behind him.

"Oh?" Ben spun around, surprised by her voice being so close to him. "I thought you collected souls. Isn't that your purpose? To carry them to your heaven dimension after they leave their shells, like our Valkyrie carried ours?" He had once again forgotten she was in the room as he normally ignored her unless she was prattling on about something he thought inane. Then he simply tried to ignore her.

"I only carry a few at a time. I don't keep them. If I kept them, wouldn't I be called a keeper of souls instead of a collector of souls?" Ami replied in her usual curious way.

"I only got to be the container because one, I could, and two, Renata couldn't dissipate me herself because I had brought her actions to the attention of the Elders and it would bring suspicion down on her. How many times do I have to tell you? This wasn't my plan," Aphya said slowly, emphasizing the statement.

"Let's say everything you said is true. Not that I necessarily believe it, but let's speculate. It seems a little far-fetched that Renata would construct such an elaborate scheme to goad Grace and Ivan into killing you when all she needs to do is destroy the confinement and end all of this outright," Ben said, directing his comment back to Aphya.

"Destroying it won't kill us. It will release us." Aphya shrugged. "Most of us. The amount of energy necessary will cause the weaker essences, which may still be mortal, and the unbound children I'm protecting to be dissipated back into energy. All the echoes too, of course."

"By echoes, are you referring to the unturned?" Frigg asked. She had not considered an advantage to taking the turn herself up until now.

"No, not unturned. Anyone from The Outside is an infinite, but as Grace showed you, they have different levels of maturity, from essentially mortal to fully immortal. Any fully immortal essence is a mature infinite, regardless of whether they have taken the turn or not. They will be strong enough to protect themselves from destruction. Essential mortals don't have that same protection. Their essences haven't matured yet. They need to cycle through several mortal lives before they become strong enough to become immortal," Aphya answered.

"We used to turn humans all the time. It's how our species spread. If what you say is right and they weren't mature—they were, what did you call them, echoes?—how could we have turned them?" Ivan asked.

"You never turned any echoes. It's true you turned many humans, but you fed on countless numbers as well. You killed a lot, too, but you only turned the ones you were drawn to, the ones that contained an infinite essence that was ready to become immortal." Aphya raised her eyebrows at him, knowing her statement was a fact he couldn't dispute.

Ivan stared at Aphya. He only had one more question. "If Grace is so much stronger than Renata, why would we have let her capture us? It doesn't make sense."

Aphya looked back at him as if he were a complete idiot. "Renata had hostages. If we didn't give up, she was going to dissipate them. Everyone knows Miss Bleeding Heart over here can't bear the thought of even a single essence being dissipated, let alone countless numbers," Aphya said, tossing a thumb toward Grace. "I mean, I'm not a proponent of the idea of Renata so easily ending vast numbers either, but if she wanted to destroy whatever little drones she had control over, obviously I'm gonna choose to save us. The way I see it, Renata was just undermining herself, right?"

Ben nodded. Her last statement was the one thing she said he could agree with. He casually leaned against the wall he had backed himself against after Ami's surprise pop-up behind him. All war had casualties in his experience. Better they come from the other side. Her explanation hadn't changed his skepticism, although it had brought him back to his original thoughts. The pressing question on his mind was how to wage a battle against a formidable adversary he had no access to.

"I'd have set it up to look like my opponent had attacked. It seems like she did the same with Aphya, if that's indeed the way it happened," Ivan said thoughtfully.

The others turned to look at him. Ben nodded pridefully toward his friend, not having thought Ivan could be so strategic.

"What? It's logical. Renata set herself up to look like the helpless victim of a brutal attack. Renata captures Aphya during the attack. The Elders couldn't disprove at least some of the empty shells weren't Renata's followers as I'm sure she would have claimed. They would have had no choice but to punish Aphya, leaving Renata free from opposition and looking like the victim and savior for all her people. It gives her a way to explain how she just happened to stumble upon the scene without revealing she was the one coming to attack Aphya and her people. It's a pretty basic tactic," Ivan said.

"I agree. All you need to do is invite your enemy to a meal, party, ball, whatever. Insert your preferred activity to finish that sentence. It's called baiting," Ben added.

"She didn't invite us anywhere. She was bringing her army to attack us. I don't know how she spun it after I was captured, and I really don't care. You two are just speculating," Aphya said.

"And yet you had time to collect everyone instead of fleeing or fighting back," Ben said, the thought bringing more suspicion to the surface of his mind.

"Time is different on The Outside. We created a parallel strand, which gave us all the time we needed," Aphya said.

"With the technology I saw on The Outside, I'm not sure she could make it look like we attacked her. Omni knows where everyone is all the time. It even tracks telepathic messages." Grace shrugged.

"Who do you think controls Omni? Renata could manipulate it to output whatever data she wanted," Aphya said.

"You have an answer for everything, don't you?" Ben asked.

Aphya brought her hand up to her head and closed her eyes, blurting out a chuckle followed by a sigh. "You brought me here for answers, and when I give you answers, you complain that I have answers? You're ridiculous." She dropped her hand and opened her eyes, giving him a look of disbelief.

A tense silence enveloped the room as they waited, unsure if Ben would reply or if Aphya would decide she had had enough and vanish from the scene.

"Grace, dear?" Frigg spoke up to move the attention away from the wordless confrontation.

"Yes, Frigg?" Grace replied quizzically. Frigg seldom ever called her "dear."

"You gave us all your memories of your visit with Renata and your questioning of Aphya?" Frigg asked.

"Yes," Grace said in a questioning tone. What could Frigg possibly be getting at? Did she think Grace was hiding something?

"How do you know about Omni? It's just that you hadn't mentioned it before," Frigg said, giving Grace a warm, motherly smile.

"Wh—I, uh …" Grace thought as hard as she could. Renata obviously hadn't told her, and Grace hadn't fished it out of Renata's mind. She wouldn't have had any idea what Omni was if she had seen it. But she knew all about it. How it worked, what it was for, all of it.

Aphya interrupted Grace's stammering. "Look, I think I've been pretty patient in answering your questions. I'll even stay here if you want to continue this at a later time, but I could really use a shower and some clean clothing," Aphya said, because both she and Grace were still covered in a mixture of crusted blood and dirt. "Hospitality is a lovely concept when you're attempting to get answers from someone who can leave anytime they want." Her face was covered in exasperation.

Frigg moved toward Aphya. "You're right. We have all the time we need to get answers." She extended her hand. "Come with me."

Aphya took Frigg's hand, glancing at Ben and Ivan. "Thank you. It's nice to see someone still has manners."

Ben stepped forward, opening his mouth to say something. Frigg shot him a look, stopping him in his tracks. He closed his mouth as Frigg and Aphya disappeared from the room. He was angry, but he knew there was no point in pursuing anything more.

"What do you think?" Grace asked, turning to Ivan.

"I'm not sure what to think yet," Ivan muttered through a glazed-over position of deep thought.

"Well, I don't think she lied, but I can tell you she's still hiding something," Nyx said from behind Grace. "And I am going to find out exactly what that something is."

Nyx shifted out in a dramatic swirl of dark smoke. Ben shook his head at the idea of chasing Nyx around The Everything for the foreseeable future. "I'll find her," he said, shifting out with a sour look on his face.

Grace sighed loudly, sliding back into her chair.

"I guess no one is interested in what I think," Ami said from the corner.

"Ami, I don't need your irrelevant insight right now," Grace shot back, irritated.

"Well, you're going to get it anyway," Ami said in an unexpectedly bold manner. She moved in front of Grace, looking down at her.

"I know you don't think I'm all that smart or aware of what's going on around me. You only call me when you need me for something or you're feeling lonely or nostalgic. I get it. I'm only here when you need a friend. Well, guess what? Right now, you really need a friend. One who will not say something just to make you feel better or feed into your self-pity. Because, honestly, I am sick of you feeling sorry for yourself. Maybe I don't understand personal space or appropriate interactions or whatever you think is proper behavior, but what I do understand is you. You don't trust yourself, which means you don't really trust anyone around you, either. And that makes you do some really stupid stuff. While all of you were so busy yelling at Aphya and asking questions that didn't matter, I was reading her." Ami crossed her arms.

Ivan revived himself from his deep train of thought, looking amused at Ami's outburst.

Grace looked up, wide-eyed and shocked. "Ami, you know I don't think you're stupid. I—"

Ami cut her off. "Grace, shut up. Listen for once. I am perfectly fine with only being around when you want me. I've always been fine with it. It might shock you to know, but I don't want to be around you all the time either. That's why our friendship works. We know when enough is enough and we don't suffocate each other. But right now, you're being stupid. She's not lying about anything. I saw what she remembered about The Outside and it wasn't all that perfect. Aphya idolizes you. You provided that world with something they didn't have and you spread that same feeling in here, while she's spent the entire time she's been in here trying to figure out a way to get you back to The Outside because that's what *you* wanted.

"During all this, Renata has been free to terrorize The Outside, while Aphya has been on her own with no one to talk to about anything because she was afraid we would all go insane at the mere mention of an outside. She's been all alone trying to make *your* plan happen so you can fix The Outside. And as soon as she starts to tell you the truth, you dismiss her; you drag her here and make her tell all of us. She won't tell you what life on The Outside was like because you don't want to believe her.

"Maybe the reason you don't trust yourself is that you have residual guilt over the fact that all of this is your fault and if you had listened to Ben in the first place and stopped Renata, we wouldn't even be in here and the people on The Outside wouldn't be just as much her prisoners as we are. You let Renata win and you refuse to take responsibility for it," Ami said, huffing loudly and turning her back on Grace.

Ivan stood up, placing his hand on Ami's shoulder. "Ami, you can't put all this on Grace."

Ami spun away from Ivan's grasp. "Oh, I don't. It's my fault too. I could have made her listen to Ben if I had tried, but I didn't do anything, and I don't know why you didn't either. As a matter of fact, I didn't see you try to talk to Grace at all," Ami shouted close to Ivan's face.

Grace stood up. She was angry at Ami's accusations. "None of us remember any of that. We don't know if it even really happened. Don't you find it pretty convenient that Aphya just let you see that specific memory? What makes you think she wasn't showing you what she wanted you to see, Ami?"

"She didn't show me anything, Grace. It's pretty easy to see what no one wants you to see when they don't think you're worth paying attention to. Isn't that the entire reason you sent me to the Council to watch over Ma'at when she was there? If I remember correctly, wasn't it you who said, 'Who would pay any attention to someone as flighty and irritating as Ami?' Guess you didn't think I heard that part, did you?" she retorted, irate at the implication that she wasn't intelligent enough to know how others saw her.

Grace was now as embarrassed as she was angry. Her eyes widened as she stood up, reaching out to Ami. "Ami, I didn't—"

Ami cut her off again, slapping away Grace's hand. "Yes, you did. You can lie to yourself about it if you want to, but you can't lie to me. I told you what I saw. Do what you want with it." Ami backed up and ported out of the room.

Grace growled in exasperation. She picked up her chair and hurled it against the wall. Instead of bouncing back toward her, the chair was absorbed by the wall, denying Grace any amount of satisfaction she had expected to gain from throwing it. She had never seen Ami so angry and felt horrible that she caused it. She ripped open the closure on the front of her jacket and screamed.

"Feel better now?" Ivan asked in a calm, flat tone.

"Thanks for helping me out there," Grace sneered back.

"Hey, don't take this out on me," Ivan said. "You've been digging that hole for years all on your own."

Grace rolled her eyes and clenched her jaw. "I need to get out of here," she spat bitterly and shifted out of the room, leaving Ivan alone.

It hadn't only been a self-preserving instinct that kept Ivan out of the middle of their dispute. He had some pressing questions of his own he wanted answers to.

CHAPTER TWENTY

Ivan stood outside of Frigg's quarters, hesitating with the thought of whether he should knock or take history for what it was and leave. Suddenly, the door swung open, removing the decision from his hands.

Frigg smiled warmly up at him. "I thought you might show up eventually. Come in." She opened the door wide and stepped aside for him to enter.

Aphya, with her hair still damp from a refreshing shower, sat at the kitchen table, sipping an espresso. Frigg motioned Ivan toward the table and offered him a coffee, which he accepted.

"I'll give you two some privacy," Frigg offered.

Ivan glanced up at her, feeling a desperate need for support. "I'd prefer you stay."

Frigg may not have had the connection of the turned, but she recognized the pleading nature of Ivan's fleeting glance and took a seat next to him.

Aphya made no protest, welcoming her friend into their conversation. She also felt this conversation was overdue.

Ivan knew exactly what he wanted to ask. It had been a looming subject that plagued him for his entire immortal existence.

"Why did you make my turn the way you did? Was I just an experiment to you, so Grace could become who she needed to be?"

"You weren't just an experiment, Ivan, and your turn wasn't supposed to happen that way," Aphya said sadly, looking at her cup.

Ivan was angry, sad, and confused. "You planned all of it!"

Her eyes snapped up to meet his. The guilt-laced fragrance of rotting fruit wafted across the table toward him as her low, melancholy voice seemed to beg him for forgiveness.

"I set it in motion, Ivan. I didn't plan it. Your wife wasn't supposed to be there, you were. She was supposed to be at the market with your children when they came. That was your normal routine. You were supposed to be there alone."

"Why didn't you stop it when you saw what was happening?" Ivan glared at Aphya.

"I didn't see! I can't be in every time and every place at once. Those events were set in motion long before they happened. How was I to know she was going to get into one of her moods and refuse to go to the market?"

Ivan's thumbs traced the lip of his cup nervously as the two women waited. He didn't know where to go from here. This was personal for him, but he didn't feel capable of continuing this line of conversation. He began to mull over other questions he had prepared, but he resigned himself to abandon them as inconsequential. One finally came after he recalled his very first conversation with Frigg years ago. He introduced a topic that would be less emotional for everyone.

"Frigg told me I was your third attempt at creating a being who could merge with Grace. The first devolved into a regular vampire and the second fled. Did you use my essence in all the attempts, or did I just end up being the last choice?"

Ivan felt in his core he had always been meant to merge with Grace, but if Aphya had used other random essences before his, maybe that wasn't the case. Maybe he was only fooling himself into thinking he had some special connection with her, and anyone could have helped Grace become who she was meant to be.

Aphya struggled to phrase her response in a way that would not hurt Ivan.

"You were always the one who was supposed to merge with Grace."

Ivan was overcome with a sense of relief, followed by confusion. Observing the way Ivan narrowed his eyes, Aphya continued.

"But I couldn't use your essence in the other attempts. I had to ensure the process was correct and the physical forms could contain your essence first. Your physical species wasn't even my first choice. I started running simulations with elementals since they already handled energy, then when that didn't work, I thought it had to be a shifter of some sort. I must have worked through ten different kinds of shifters, from a nebuslate to a common moon wolf. It was because of my other research that I also figured out that your shell had to be immortal before you could merge."

"So, you used others at random to test your theories, aside from turned?" Ivan asked. The question slipped out of his mouth, an unintended harshness lingering in his voice.

"There aren't a lot of options in here, Ivan. Things don't work the same as they do on The Outside. I had to suppress your essence and place it in a human shell until you became an immortal, instead of positioning you as an immortal to start with."

Ivan nodded mindlessly, staring into his empty cup.

"What happened to the others? Were they destroyed?" Ivan wanted to know how many had died for him to live.

"No … no, of course I would never destroy them." Aphya hesitated.

"Then where are they?" Ivan pushed, glancing up momentarily before returning his gaze downward.

"They've all lived their lives in different places. Some were left on your Earth and some on different Terran planets."

"I mean the other turned. Where are they?" Ivan asked. He glanced up but kept his head lowered so she wouldn't notice the lump forming in his throat.

"I tested the first essence by placing him into a naturally born immortal. His essence was less advanced than yours and I concluded you wouldn't be contained by that process, or capable of making the merge without some physical enhancement. Even an immortal infant is delicate. Your shell had to be stronger." Aphya paused, lowering her head in an attempt to make contact with Ivan's downturned eyes. "He is still alive, by the way."

"He is?" Ivan's focus shot up to engage hers. "Who is he? Do I know him?" Ivan needed more proof than her words. Frigg placed her hand on his to calm him.

Aphya intensified her gaze on Ivan. "You know him very well, actually. Lukkas was the first. I sent Grace to find him in the woods that day."

"That makes no sense. Lukkas is younger than I am. He couldn't have come first," Ivan scoffed.

"Time isn't linear for us, Ivan. It has no meaning other than to order events in a way a non-infinite can understand them," Aphya said.

"I don't understand why you would place me so much further back. If you could place me at any time, why didn't you place me with her at her beginning?"

"You needed to mature, and she needed to be ready to seek other immortals, too. Lukkas had already been placed, so that had to remain a fixed point for Grace. Do you think you would have been ready for a partner like her even a hundred years earlier?" Aphya asked, already knowing the answer.

When Ivan didn't respond, Aphya added, "Something inside of you recognized you weren't ready for her when you didn't ask her to the festival that night, nor when you saw her hundreds of times after."

Ivan nodded. It was true. He would have been a horrible partner back then. The merge would have made him drunk with power, resulting in a disaster of apocalyptic proportions.

"What about the second attempt?" Frigg asked, salvaging Ivan from his spiraling descent into the rabbit hole of horrors that could have been.

"Niko," Aphya heaved. "I regret what happened to him. He was much brighter than Lukkas, causing the shell to reject him. It drove him mad for a while and he started going after the children. I had to gather them in to protect them. When he saw me doing it, he escaped. I've seen him since then. Even though he's got his senses back, he won't come near me. He's angry and his anger is causing the destruction that takes place around him. His negative emotions cause his polarity to be negative, making everything he touches turn dark."

She cast her eyes down to her fidgeting hands, exuding a sickly smoky scent that Ivan had come to correlate with regret.

"Niko was happy when we encountered him," Ivan said skeptically.

"You're generally happy, aren't you?" she asked.

"And I can get angry from time to time, but it doesn't change my base feelings. I get it. So, what happened then?"

"It was the shell's construction I hadn't understood yet. The shell ultimately had to be immortal and capable of containing an essence equivalent to Grace's as well as the virus your species would spread through venom. After each of the other two tries, I ran millions of simulations. I was able to get one aspect or the other to work outside of the simulation, but not both until I split the process. An enhanced mortal shell was able to hold your essence for a short time and the virus that turned you completed the process, making you capable of merging with Grace."

"If a human shell couldn't hold Niko's essence, how did a human shell hold mine?" Ivan asked.

"I sealed you in, much in the same way the amulet sealed Grace in. That's why you never broke a bone or were sick while you were mortal. Until you turned, you were also protected," Aphya said, looking tenderly at him.

"In all these billions of years you've been in here, couldn't you have found an easier way to bring Grace and I together?"

"Ivan, I haven't been here that long. All the time that you have lived through, I've merely bounced through. The few thousand years I spent with Frigg were the only continuous time I've had in here. If anything changes in the past on this timeline, it will disintegrate back to the last fixed point, which was your merge. We could have this conversation all over again on another timeline. It'll be tomorrow for me and centuries for you."

"Have we had this conversation before?" Ivan asked.

"You know I can't answer that," Aphya said, dropping her eyes to the table.

Frigg patted Aphya's arm and smiled. "More espresso?"

"Yes, please," Aphya replied, sliding her cup over.

Frigg took Ivan's cup for a refill without asking him and went to the service panel.

"Is that why you were missing the last few times we went to see the children? Because your timeline and ours don't always cross?" Ivan asked.

"Yes, I'm not always in the same time stream as you. I go back and forth. I usually stay away from people in their future times. It's like that old entertainment piece you used to be obsessed with, doctor something or other."

"I remember—the time traveler. How did you know about that?" Ivan replied.

"I do check in occasionally. Anyway, it's similar to that, only I can't exist in the same place in the portion of a time stream I am already in. If I exist there, it's closed to me, so no silly antics and no duplicates running into myself."

"How far into the future have you gone?"

"I'm not sure what the equivalent year would be for you." Aphya shook her head in dismay.

"It's all still here though, right?" Ivan wondered.

"It is."

"But?" Ivan pressured her to continue.

"It felt different," she replied, biting the side of her lip. "Before you ask me to explain, I don't know how. Just different."

Ivan nodded at Frigg when she placed a fresh cup of coffee in front of him.

"Any ideas on what should happen next?" Frigg asked.

"I think I should go see Renata myself," Ivan responded.

"That is a horrible idea," Aphya nearly shouted at him.

The response startled Ivan. He and Frigg replied in unison, "Why?"

CHAPTER TWENTY-ONE

"Aphya told you she thinks Renata will try to do something to you to hurt me?" Grace asked. "How would she get close enough to hurt you? Why would she come in here at all if she's planning on sanitizing it?"

Ivan rubbed the back of his neck and squirmed where he stood.

"Ivan?" Grace maneuvered herself in front of him until he couldn't avoid her. "I see what you're planning and I don't like it."

"I'll be careful. Ben agrees the best chance we have is in here."

"Ben agrees?! You talked to Ben about this before me?"

Ivan splayed his hands near his shoulders and stepped back. His voice pitched up to justify his defense. "You were on a run and I needed an impartial opinion."

"Impartial? Ben? You're joking, right?" she asked, stepping forward, encroaching on the space he had given himself.

"Okay, maybe that was the wrong word. Objective?" he asked, taking another step back.

Grace again closed the distance. "Galin is objective. The committee he put together would be impartial, but you picked Ben because you knew he would agree with anything that would protect me, regardless of the consequences for anyone else in here."

"That's not fair. You said yourself that this confinement dims us. The best chance we have is to get her in here," Ivan defended.

"*Get* her? What's that supposed to mean? You want to kill her?"

"We believe this is the only way to ensure the safety of everyone, both on The Inside and The Outside."

"Who's 'we'? You and Ben?" she asked, pointing at him.

"And Aphya."

"Oh, now you trust Aphya?"

"You don't?"

Grace ran her fingers over her scalp and grasped her hair at the back of her head. She turned her back to him, letting out an exasperated sigh verging on a growl. Her fingers released their hold. As her hands dropped, she winced at the sharp pain caused by her rings, which had snagged on a few strands of hair and yanked them out. She cut a direct path to the bar, took a tall, sturdy glass from the rack, and set it down hard in front of her. Without hesitation, she seized the closest bottle within reach and poured its contents into her glass until it reached the brim. She downed it in one swift motion before refilling it. With her head down, she spread her hands shoulder-width apart and gripped the edge of the counter hard enough to make indentations in the edge.

Ivan caught the scent of anger—a clean electrical-heat smell, not the smoke-laden odor of rage. He was unsure what part of their conversation had made her so mad. Likely, all of it had. Nervous anticipation enveloped him while he waited for her to respond. She didn't respond, shifting away instead. Ivan ran his hand through his hair, let out a long breath, and dropped into a chair.

~~~~
~~~~

Grace appeared in front of Finna's desk outside Galin's office.

"Hello, Grace. What can I help you with today?" Finna asked, showing Grace a polite smile. The sudden appearance hadn't bothered the unflappable assistant in the least. Impromptu appearances were a normal occurrence outside the Administrator's office. Everyone who appeared in this way believed their situation was of utmost importance, and part of Finna's job was to calm them and determine if the issue was as urgent as they thought or if it could wait until Galin's schedule was open.

"Is he in?" Grace asked. The question was only a courtesy. She could feel him in the space behind the door.

"He has something available in an hour. May I get some details so I can book you in?" Finna asked. She could normally solve most issues without bothering Galin, if she could get the complainant to open up.

Grace smiled back at Finna, aware of what she was doing. "We both know he's not busy now. Send him a message that I am here with new information about The Outside."

"Outside where?"

Grace couldn't tell if she was feigning ignorance or if Finna didn't know, and she narrowed her eyes at the woman who sat casually in front of her. It was more likely she knew, given Galin's constant struggle to keep his hectic schedule organized without her help these days.

"Just tell him what I said."

Finna twisted her mouth into a frown as she tapped out the message. A moment later, a light blinked on her device.

"He said he can give you ten minutes," Finna said, reading from her screen. When she looked up, Grace was no longer in front of her. She spun around to see Grace's back as she phased through Galin's door.

"Grace, as pleased as I am to see you, you know we've set up a committee to look into this," Galin said from his seat behind his desk while motioning her toward the chair across from him.

"Galin, I don't think you're taking this seriously. Nyx and Ben showed you what happened to me, didn't they?" Grace stopped behind the chair, leaning against the back of it.

"We are taking this seriously. I believe something happened to you, but what do you expect us to do about it?"

"What you believe is that someone is screwing with my mind again." Grace tilted her head and pursed her lips at him.

"We can't eliminate that as a possibility, and before you protest—if it had happened to anyone else, you wouldn't discount it either," Galin said, leaning forward, resting his elbows on his desk and clasping his hands together. "Finna said you have new information."

"Aphya is here," Grace said, displeased at the dismissal of her concern as she slipped around the chair and dropped into it.

"What does she say? Can we talk to her?" Galin asked, picking up his TAC.

"We already have. May I?"

"Yes," Galin said, consenting to receive the conversation.

"This is going to be a little different. You may want to sit back."

Galin placed his TAC back on the desk and leaned back in his chair, unsure of what she meant by different. "I'm prepared."

Grace began creating the image of the incident with Mikkel and the sensor and pushed it out to encapsulate Galin in the immersive experience.

As Galin slumped in his chair, he could feel himself being transported into the vivid memory Grace had shared, his senses overwhelmed by the intensity of it. She had passed him everything up to the point of the conversation she had with Ivan a few minutes before she arrived. When the event finished, he had the feeling of falling, shrinking back into his smaller existence. He looked around, attempting to grasp his familiar surroundings. His hands circled over the smooth, cool surface of his desk, giving him the tactile tether he needed to ground himself in the present moment. At some point during the display, Grace had placed a glass of whiskey in front of him, which he now gladly drank half of.

"I'm not sure what just happened," Galin said, pausing to swallow another mouthful of the drink and compose himself. He cleared his throat.

"While that was interesting, it isn't explicit proof that there is an outside, or what impact it would have on us if there were."

Grace clenched her jaw. She expected him to be suspicious. Hell, she hoped he would give her a clearer view, and she held herself back from commenting so she could hear the rest of his thought.

"What it does show, to me at least, is that there are two beings with significant powers who want to destroy each other and are attempting to use you to do it. The rest of it is irrelevant."

"Irrelevant? How can you say that?"

"You don't have the ability to see things from our perspective anymore, Grace. We're ordinary turned. Even the Æsir turned, or the Jur turned, or all the other turned cultures are ordinary compared to you. Our reality and our experiences are minuscule in relation to yours. We live our lives on a smaller scale. Some of the turned can't even bring themselves to explore this universe, much less any of the others, and those of us who are willing would likely never be drawn into this larger experience like you are. Most of the inhabitants of this confinement, as you call it, couldn't fathom anything else. This is our reality. We wouldn't be able to adapt to whatever is out there, nor would we want to."

"Galin, I'm still me. I'm still the same Grace you met all those years ago in the village. I'm still the same Grace that rescued Lukkas in the woods." Her voice was pleading. She wanted to believe her words were sincere, but even as she spoke them, she understood they weren't.

Galin peered across the desk at her with an empathetic smile and sad eyes that turned down at the corners.

"Grace, you and I both know, despite how much you want it to be, that's no longer true."

His words saddened her, but the truth was always difficult to accept. As much as she dearly loved these people, if she was being honest with herself, she had to admit she and Ivan had outgrown them.

Galin continued. "We are grateful you have changed us and given us a broader view, but you've changed too. As much as we adore you and have accepted that you live among us, to us you are the gods we have been raised to worship. You are a primordial being. Your abilities and the scale of your experiences are so far above what is quantifiable for us, we can't imagine what your life is like. I'm sorry if my words have hurt you, but the vast majority of us are unable to relate to you."

She looked across the desk at him with red-rimmed eyes. The enormity of what she was responsible for—what she had dragged all these innocent people into—sat heavily on her chest. All life in this place could end tomorrow, and if what Aphya said was true, every bit of blame resided with her. Even if that wasn't the case, her actions inside this confinement moving forward would affect them.

"I understand," she said, tugging at a loose strand of hair dangling over the front of her shoulder.

"I'm sorry I didn't have the answers you wanted," Galin said.

"You said some things I needed to hear. Thank you," Grace said before standing to leave.

"What are you going to do?" he asked.

"I have no idea," she answered.

"Well, don't tell us if you plan on blowing us all up. I don't want our people's last days to be poisoned by panic and fear."

Grace vocalized a subdued, wry laugh and shook her head, reflecting on his words. "You're a good leader, Galin." She didn't want to give him the opportunity to deny it, and she shifted out before he could.

Moments later, Grace was sitting atop a mountain overlooking the valley, which comfortably sheltered the peaceful capital city. Galin was right. She had forgotten herself. She had forgotten the deep connection that bonded her to the turned. They enjoyed their families and their connections. They had work that fulfilled them and hobbies that brought them joy. Happiness and camaraderie filled their leisure hours. What did she have besides Ivan? Sons she barely spoke to and a grandson she had only seen twice? A mission that consumed her, which she didn't understand? Her life was empty. She wasn't one of them. Even the friends she had were only supportive because they believed what she was doing was important, although they had no more idea of what it was or why than she did. She was certain she hadn't been supportive of them or what they wanted. She didn't have any idea what they wanted.

The thought didn't make her sad or angry. Her sacrifice gave them the opportunity to live the way they did. But it had also left her hollow. And for what? The bigger picture set in motion billions of years ago to get out? Her conversations with Aphya and Galin only made her realize that what she had wanted for her people all that time ago was happening here. Right here, right now, inside of this confinement. Why would she want to force them out of this world and leave so many living things behind to die? It was by no means perfect in here, but from what she had gathered, neither was it out there.

She lay back on the grass and stared into the deep azure sky. She needed answers. If only she knew what the questions were, things would be much easier. Hours passed, and the sky began showing streaks of purple and red above her. Frigg would know the right questions to ask, but she didn't want to risk running into Aphya before she was ready. Ivan knew only as much as she did, so asking him was pointless. At that point, Grace realized Ben and Nyx were her only options. She struggled to stand up from the ground, not because she couldn't physically move, but because she dreaded the upcoming conversation.

Grace shifted to Ben. At least she thought she had shifted to him. Thick steam scented with sweet honeysuckle and jasmine encapsulated her to the point she could hardly see her hand in front of her face. Water droplets clinging to the air distorted all the ranges of her advanced vision.

"Ben?" she called out. Taking a step forward, she tumbled down when her foot didn't connect with what she had thought would be a solid floor.

"What are you doing here?" Ben called out from an undetermined distance. He had been standing against the rock wall, letting steaming-hot water run over his shoulders and back. When he heard Grace's voice, followed by a splash at the other side of the pool, he dropped into the water and twisted toward the disturbance.

Grace shot up out of the water, coughing and sputtering. "Holy hells, Ben! Where is this?"

"Tartarus. Why are you here?!" he shouted.

"Why did you tell Ivan he needed to go to The Outside and draw Renata in?" she asked, moving closer to his voice.

Ben wiped his face with his hand and clenched his jaw. "Grace, are you aware of where you are?"

"You just told me. Tartarus. Now answer my question." Grace continued moving toward the center of the pool where the steam was thinner and saw Ben's bare chest above the water before looking around her in an awkward, slow motion.

"Oh. Um … I … uh," she stuttered.

"Get out," Ben said.

"Sorry?" She scrunched her face and shrank back, folding in on herself with embarrassment, then made her way back to the water's edge. "I'll … um." She pulled herself out of the water and pointed to the wall.

"Yeah," Ben snapped.

Grace didn't want to waste time looking for the door, so she phased through the wall into the hallway. A few minutes later, the door on the wall she was leaning against opened, letting a thick plume of steam escape. Ben emerged in a pair of loose pants and a T-shirt, drying his hair with a thick dark towel.

"You know how you're constantly lecturing Ami about personal space?" Ben asked.

"I didn't do it on purpose," she replied, avoiding eye contact.

"Oh, that makes it better," he said and rolled his eyes at her.

"Shut up."

"So, what is so important you had to interrupt the first relaxing moment I've had to myself in weeks?" He didn't wait for an answer. He turned away from her and began walking down the dim hall.

Grace followed close at his heels, leaving a dripping trail of water in her wake. "I don't think you should encourage Ivan to confront Renata."

"He's a grown man, Grace, and contrary to whatever ideas you have rolling around in that little head of yours, it's a solid option."

Ben reached the end of the hallway and turned left down another long, dark corridor.

"Aphya said Renata would do something to him in order to hurt me. I don't want anything to happen to him because of me."

"What's the alternative? Aphya can't go. You want to send Nyx? I'm sure there's absolutely *nothing* that could go wrong with that plan," Ben said, his voice dripping with sarcasm.

Grace scoffed. "Why do you have to be such an asshole?"

"Because I've gotten really good at it," Ben replied and jerked open a heavy wooden door that swung through Grace as she phased.

"You could go," she said, stepping in front of him.

He grabbed her shoulders, moving her out of his way, and entered the large gaming lounge.

"If I went, she'd know it was a trap. She's not stupid, Grace."

Ben proceeded in a direct line and sat in a large wingback chair in the middle of the room with a small table next to it. Grace followed, stopping in front of him. He tossed her the towel he was holding, then swiped his hand over the table, causing a drink to appear. Grace caught the towel and moved to sit in the chair next to Ben.

"I know you're not about to sit your soaking-wet ass down on Nyx's upholstery," he said, pointing to a stone bench near the fireplace across from him. "Over there."

She glared at him before moving to take her appointed seat. She dropped onto the bench and let her hair down, drying it with the towel. After a few minutes of struggle with the thoughts swirling in her head, and Ben pretending she wasn't in the room, she spoke. "I don't know what to do."

"There are only two options." He took a drink, extending the moment of suspense. "Fight back or do nothing."

"Doing nothing isn't an option."

"Then fight back," he said.

"You say that like it's so easy!" she said, throwing the towel down on the bench beside her.

Ben let out a long, harsh sigh. "It's no more difficult because it's on a larger scale. What's the goal?"

"To keep Renata from sanitizing the confinement."

"Okay. How do you do that?"

"I DON'T KNOW!" Grace yelled.

Ben rubbed his forehead and took a deep breath. He wasn't irritated that she was emotional—he was irritated her emotions kept her from clear thinking.

"You can either eliminate Aphya and hope Renata keeps her word or you can eliminate Renata," he said.

"I don't want to eliminate anyone."

"You don't have a choice. We don't have the ability to imprison either of them, so elimination is the only option."

"And what makes you think we have the ability to do that?"

"Since both of them believe you can, chances are it's highly probable."

Grace bit her lip while her eyes shifted back and forth, searching for an answer. The choice tore at her. Although she had no ties to either Aphya or Renata, she also did not know what driving forces had motivated them to do what they had done. He was right. She had to pick. She had to be rational if she was going to save anybody.

"It has to be Renata then. We can't trust that she'll keep her word if we eliminate Aphya. I still think we can find a better way, though."

"I doubt it." Ben took another drink and set the glass on the table. "The goal is to eliminate Renata before she can sanitize the confinement. It's not so hard when you break it down into small bites."

"Maybe not for you." Grace sulked.

Maybe not, Ben thought. He and the others had already concluded Renata was the target. Dragging Grace along was going to be painfully difficult. Aphya was right when she referred to Grace as Miss Bleeding Heart.

"The part Ivan and I have been working on is how to get Renata to come in here and how to defeat her once we have."

"What happens if we can't?" Grace asked.

"She sanitizes the confinement. Some of us might be able to flee to The Outside, but most of us won't." Ben shrugged.

"Which is why we need to work with Aphya," Grace scoffed.

"Whether we trust her or not," Ben said.

"Ivan trusts her."

"Ivan recognizes we have a mutual goal. He trusts her in this situation," Ben clarified.

"I wish I could compartmentalize like you and Ivan do," Grace said.

"Yeah. So do I," Ben said, raising his eyebrows at her.

CHAPTER TWENTY-TWO

"Gaia? Where are you? I know you're here!" Nyx yelled into the canyon below her. Her voice echoed back at her, the volume reducing and getting further away with each repetition.

"Why are you yelling?" Gaia asked from behind her.

With a start, Nyx jumped and quickly spun around, taking in a sudden gulp of air.

"You did that on purpose!" Nyx exclaimed.

"I was right there," Gaia said, pointing to the base of the tree beside her. "It's not my fault you didn't turn around before you started squawking like a chachalaca."

Nyx gawked at her, too stunned to retort. At least Gaia appeared lucid today, she thought to herself.

"Is there something I can help you with, Nyx?"

"What makes you think I want something? Can't I simply be here for a visit?"

"When have you ever come for a simple visit?" Gaia asked. "You always want something. What is it this time?"

Nyx lowered her head, resigning herself to risk upsetting Gaia before she could soothe her into the conversation.

"Gaia, I know I've been dismissive of you in the past," Nyx said.

Gaia scoffed, and Nyx continued.

"It's just … well, sometimes you say things none of us understand or remember the way you do."

"And now you wonder if I'm insane or if I actually know something you don't."

"Well, you can be very sensitive and you do tend to ramble on, on occasion, and it can sometimes be nonsensical," Nyx said, shrinking back slightly while looking down at her hands.

"Now I'm insane and dramatically blurt out nonsense?"

"That's not what I meant."

"It's what you said."

"Look, I think we've gotten off on the wrong foot. Can we please start over? I never meant to upset you," Nyx said. Her apology was very uncharacteristic, but she had an agenda, and she was smart enough to know Gaia would shut her down if she wasn't contrite. The woman was a stickler for manners.

"You didn't upset me, Nyx. You are wasting my time. Now, either tell me why you're here, or leave."

Nyx sighed. "I need to know what you know about The Outside."

Gaia raised her arms, holding her palms up to the sky as she tilted her head to scan the treetops. She lowered her head, locking eyes with Nyx, and dropped her arms back down to her sides. "Would you care to be a little more specific?"

Nyx needed a few minutes to consider her next question. While Nyx thought, Gaia pushed past her to resume tending the base of the tree she had been working on. The idea of asking about the confinement crossed her mind, but she dismissed it due to Aphya's assertion that Gaia wouldn't understand the distinction between the two locations. Her eyes picked up when she had an idea.

"Gaia?"

"What?" she replied curtly, digging harder.

Nyx bit her lip, bracing herself against the berating that was certain to come her way. No matter what Gaia said to her, her cause would not be served by arguing with the woman. "What do you know about Aphya?"

Gaia stopped her motion, with a plant halfway in the hole where she was placing it. Her shoulders slumped forward, and she resumed her action. "Poor thing has led such an unfortunate life."

That was not the reaction Nyx had expected. The last time they spoke, Gaia had railed against Chaos, saying she was the embodiment of evil and responsible for everything that was happening.

"How so?" Nyx asked. Curiosity had overtaken her quest to be delicate. She took a step forward, leaning over so she could see Gaia's face.

"The pathetic little creature actually wants to go back to the other place. I'd rather be in The Nothing forever than go back there." Gaia never looked up, keeping her attention on the ground below her.

"What's the other place?"

Gaia clenched her jaw as she patted the ground. Nyx could smell the sharp, pungent scent of fear wafting toward her and noticed Gaia's hands trembling. Nyx didn't want to ask again for fear of sending the older woman over the edge. She pushed into her mind instead. Gaia sprang to her feet far more deftly than Nyx thought her capable of moving.

"Stop that!" Gaia yelled, pointing the highly sharpened end of her trowel at Nyx.

She huffed and stormed off down a path that opened itself up for her, and Nyx chased after her. Gaia flicked her wrist over her head. The path narrowed as leaves, stems, and branches encroached over the new opening. A pair of thick vines erupted from the foliage that covered the forest floor, and they wrapped themselves firmly around Nyx's ankles. They continued snaking up her sides, wrapping around her waist and grasping her wrists as she screeched and struggled against them.

"Gaia, please! Stop this!" Nyx screamed as she was pulled backward.

Gaia continued her trek forward, leaving Nyx behind.

Nyx's rage erupted in a film of energy flowing over her entire body, giving the plants an electrical shock. The singed vines produced a high-pitched vibration, imperceptible to most species, and promptly released their hold, receding back under the vegetation on either side of her. She walked at a quick pace, determined to continue questioning Gaia. With each driven step, she battled through natural hindrances Gaia placed in her way, impeding her progress.

She stumbled into a small clearing with a cave entrance on the other side and followed Gaia's scent trail into it. The path was littered with loose stones lying in a trickling stream of water, which had formed from condensation running down the moss-covered walls of jagged rock near the cave entrance. As she continued further in, the walls narrowed. It became dark, warm, and damp. The moss dwindled with the reduction of light, making way for sturdy helictite formations that jutted out sharply. Each step she took stirred silt from the water to cover her shoes, but she kept going.

The corridor continued to narrow and the cold water grew deeper until it had risen to her calves and soft silt covered her ankles with each step. Moving became more difficult. The sharp mineral formations sliced at her when she brushed against the sides, and she wondered how Gaia, being both taller and wider, had managed to pass through such a tight space. The air had become stagnant, smelling of musty, damp dirt. She had all but given up, deciding to end this drudgery and shift to Gaia, when she realized she couldn't feel her. Something in this cave was blocking her elevated senses. She was unable to shift and she couldn't feel anyone at all.

Ahead, there was an exceptionally narrow section that forced Nyx to turn sideways to get around it. It curved in, then opened to a circular chamber that emitted an eerie glow. A soft breeze blew her hair away from her face, causing her to shiver. She was so captivated by the scene unfolding in front of her, she almost collided with Gaia's shoulder.

"You shouldn't ask about those things in the open like that," Gaia said, causing Nyx to startle for the second time that day.

Nyx surveyed the other woman, who didn't have a single scratch or torn piece of clothing on her.

"Things like what? The other place? You shouldn't have said it if you didn't want me to ask about it," Nyx said. The trek she had been forced to take to get there left her exasperated. She was in no mood to be admonished.

Gaia grabbed Nyx's arm and dragged her to the other side of the cavern. Their movement ended with the women facing each other.

"I know you don't believe me, but there's something wrong with this place. We don't belong here. We're … I don't know …" Gaia pressed the heel of her hand into her forehead, rubbing like she was trying to summon a genie from its bottle. She so seldom spoke with anyone, she was struggling to put her thoughts into words. Her face contorted as her features contracted and scrunched together.

"We're dim here," she whispered, relaxing her facial muscles.

Nyx wasn't sure if she was referring to the cave or if she knew about the confinement after all.

Gaia bit her lip and pressed her face closer to Nyx. "I can't explain it, but it's still better than the other place. When we were there, it was like we were sleeping. Like we were being compelled to be happy. I … I … uh." Gaia shook her head hard to alleviate the torment of what she was feeling. Nyx craned her neck back to create as much distance as she could with Gaia holding her arm. "It was like all of our free will had been drained away—like we were marionettes performing in someone's play. But it hadn't always been like that. Something changed in the other place, making it different too." Gaia's eyes pleaded for Nyx to understand.

"Why are we here, then?" Nyx asked, leaving the question as open as she could.

"I didn't invite you to follow me."

"You've known me all my life. Did you honestly think I wouldn't?"

Gaia didn't answer. Instead, she spun Nyx around and pointed to the wall beside them.

The smooth, luminescent interior had drawings etched into the surface with the delicate expertise of an accomplished sculptor. She took a step closer and could see that the eerie light ebbed in a slow, methodical motion below the outer glass-like layer, almost as if the wall were breathing the light.

Nyx took a second step closer to the engravings. The rhythmic coursing under the thin, transparent crust layer swirled through the fragile lines, giving them the illusion of movement. Her eyes became fixated on the gentle, lulling motion that beckoned her body to sway with it. When she reached up, she felt a warm tingling in her fingertips. The sensation increased and spread up her arm as she inched closer. Gaia grabbed her and pulled her hand away before she made contact with the surface.

"Don't touch it."

"Why not?"

"It doesn't like to be touched," Gaia said. Her tone was as much a question as it was a warning, as if she didn't fully understand why she had said it.

"Did you do these?" Nyx asked.

"No." Gaia shook her head and took a step back, releasing her grip on Nyx.

Nyx turned back to face the panoramic mural, noticing it was divided into three scenes. The first contained two women. One figure seemed to exert a force on the other, who appeared to be encased inside a transparent enclosure as they approached a vertical line. Nyx observed that the woman being pushed appeared pregnant, portrayed with a large belly in the front and her arms and legs bent behind her, giving the impression she was being propelled into motion from the center of her back.

Nyx took a step over to stand in front of the second panel, cautiously maintaining her distance. The woman who did the pushing was now throwing a ball drawn with concentric lines emanating from it, making her think of an energy ball. The pregnant woman was curled up with her arms hugging her belly and her knees and head tucked inward. Her long hair extended straight in front of her like she was moving backward at a fast pace, and the area behind her depicted larger jagged objects moving away from her, or with her, maybe? The large enclosure that had previously contained her had ejected her in the same way an unrestrained body would fly through the observation screen of an unexpectedly stopped shuttle.

The main portion of the enclosure was moving away in a direction perpendicular to the rest of the debris, pushing ripples or waves of some sort in front of it. Nyx wasn't sure about the motion, but it was all she could think of.

In the third panel, the first woman turned her back, facing away from the second woman, who now seemed to float face up with her appendages extended and her eyes closed, while a tiny bubble floated over her mouth. To Nyx, the woman looked like she had drowned with the last tiny gasp of air escaping her lungs.

"Why are you showing me these? What do they have to do with the other place?" Nyx asked.

"I think the other place is on the left side of the line and the right side is here, although I'm not sure where here is," Gaia answered. She shrunk back and pointed to the panels with her finger while keeping her arm clasped to her chest like she was afraid to make the gesture. Her eyes were wide as she held her mouth tight.

"Why would you think that?" Nyx asked. Her voice was disengaged and her eyes fixed on the last etching. Nyx thought the idea fit with Aphya's imprisonment, although it could also be a hundred other scenarios where one woman killed another. Nyx continued to stare, trying to figure out how the drawings got there if no one could touch the walls or use their abilities in this cave.

"Because if that," Gaia said, pointing to the right side of the panel, "is here, and that," she said, pointing to the left side, "is the other place, then the drowned woman is Aphya, and the other one is her."

"Her?" Nyx asked, tilting her head up to look at Gaia from the corner of her eye. "Do you mean Chaos?"

Gaia gave Nyx a quick nod and skittishly looked around the cave.

"This is so bewildering. When Frigg and I came to see you after the dimension collapsed, you said Chaos was responsible for all the horrible things that happen in here," Nyx said.

"Yes, she is. She does terrible things all the time."

"How could she have done that if she's in the other place?" Nyx asked.

"Because Chaos is everywhere all the time. Sometimes she makes things happen in the other place and sometimes she makes things happen here. Other times she makes changes, but you don't remember them the right way," Gaia said, her eyes still roaming the space as if she were searching for something.

"But wasn't it Aphya who collapsed the dimension, murdered the children, and let the boy go into The Nothing—not Chaos?" Nyx asked.

"No! Stop trying to confuse me! You don't understand and you're twisting my words. That isn't how it happened and I don't want to talk about it anymore!" Gaia said, exhibiting clear signs of anxiety. She ran her hands through her hair and twisted her face into a pained expression.

"We don't have to talk about it. I won't ask again, I promise."

"You never should have followed me in here. I shouldn't have come here at all knowing you were following me, but I was certain you would give up in the mud."

"I'm glad you led me here," Nyx said.

"No. I shouldn't have. I promised I wouldn't." Gaia turned to leave.

When Nyx grabbed her arm to stop her, her eye caught on some odd writing etched into one of the other surfaces.

"Wait! What are those?" Nyx asked, pointing to the numbers and symbols.

"I don't know. We need to leave now."

"We need to tell the others about this place. Maybe they can figure it out," Nyx said.

"No! You can't! I promised I wouldn't tell," Gaia said.

"Who did you promise?"

Gaia shook her head. "I can't."

"We need to tell them. Something bad is going to happen and I think this might help."

"Something bad has already happened!" Gaia yelled at her.

"Come back with me to see the others. Then you can decide if you want to tell them or not."

Gaia jerked her arm from Nyx's hold and stretched her hand in front of her with the palm facing Nyx. "No. No, I can't. I don't have time. I haven't finished my work." Her voice pitched up, sounding panicked as she backed away.

"It's all right. I can tell them. You don't have to go. You can stay right here and work in your garden," Nyx said, knowing Gaia had had enough and no amount of cajoling would make her change her mind.

"I want nothing to do with it. I need to finish my work. You tell them you found this all on your own. I never showed you. That would be the best thing to say, wouldn't it, Nyx? I never showed you anything," Gaia said. She walked backward, pointing her thumb over her shoulder, keeping her eyes set on Nyx. "I … I'll just go finish my work."

"I'm sorry if I've upset you, Gaia," Nyx said as Gaia quickly left.

Nyx followed soon after, realizing she still could not shift, and begrudgingly plodded her way out of the cave. She really did feel bad about upsetting Gaia.

After leaving the cave, Nyx shifted to Ben with the smug look of someone with a juicy secret. Her clothes and hair were disheveled. Mud was caked on her pants and shoes, and streaks of dried blood covered her from healed-over scratches.

"Where have you been?" Ben asked.

"I've had a very interesting visit with Gaia," she announced without addressing her appearance.

"About what?" Grace asked while her eyes scanned Nyx.

On hearing the unexpected voice behind her, Nyx spun around to see Grace sitting on a stone bench. "Why are *you* here?" Nyx surveyed Grace, who was holding a towel and sitting over a puddle that had formed under her feet. "And why are you wet?"

"Why do you look like you've just come off a battlefield?" Grace asked.

Nyx straightened her back and reached up to smooth her hair. Her nostrils flared when she pulled a broken twig from the tangled mess. She uttered a low squeal before shifting out.

"Is that normal?" Grace asked.

Ben shrugged, unbothered by the entrance and exit. He leaned back in his chair, picked up his glass, and took a sip of his drink. He then pulled the glass into his chest, closing his eyes.

Grace huffed, took off her wet outer shirt, and resumed drying herself with the towel from the bench.

The two sat in acrimonious silence until Nyx returned, changed, coiffed, and refreshed.

Ben opened his eyes and sat up. "You were saying?"

"Oh, yes. Gaia and I had a very interesting conversation in a fascinating place." Nyx stopped speaking for dramatic effect, waiting to see which one of her companions would crack under the weight of silence.

"And?" Grace asked, breaking first.

A devilish smile crept over her face. "Aphya isn't Chaos."

Ben and Grace both gave her a weary stare, wondering if she had purchased a ticket on Gaia's conspiracy train.

"Don't look at me like that. I meant what I said. Gaia isn't referring to Aphya when talking about the horrible things she associates with Chaos. We have always assumed she was referring to Aphya as Chaos, and we wrongly began calling her that ourselves. She knows who Aphya is. Chaos is another being."

"Nyx, come on. Gaia doesn't have the most reliable record of interpreting things," Grace said.

"Normally, I would agree. This time, however, she had evidence."

"What kind of evidence?" Ben asked.

Nyx recreated the conversation in the cave, explaining the etchings and what Gaia had said about them.

Ben rubbed his chin. "Who is in my mother's apartment, then? Is it Aphya, or Chaos pretending to be Aphya?" The thought unnerved him.

"I think you're making a pretty significant leap, thinking Chaos would come inside the confinement," Grace said.

"And you could make a fatal mistake thinking she wouldn't," Ben said.

"We need to figure this out," Grace said. "Let's meet up in The Six in an hour. I'll bring Ivan. Ben, I think you really need to bring Viv in on this."

"Oh, let's just invite everybody for a little chat," Ben said, throwing his hands into the air. "You want to bring in the committee? How about Galin? How 'bout we turn this thing into a party and project it to the entire community?"

Nyx smirked at Ben's outburst.

"Don't you think you're being a little dramatic?" Grace asked, sarcasm soaking her tone.

"No! By all means, let's take a couple of hours to have a meeting to discuss what's going on while my mother may be sitting in her apartment with a sadistic lunatic!" Ben said in the same sarcastic tone Grace had used on him.

"What would you rather do? Go confront said 'possible lunatic' with no idea what she's capable of or how to defend ourselves against her?" Grace jumped off the bench and pointed at him. "You lecture me about having a plan and as soon as your mother is involved, it all goes out the window?"

"I never suggested we go confront her! We need to get my mother out of there!" Ben yelled back, springing up from his chair.

While Nyx did love a good fight, and this was likely to be an excellent one, she didn't want it happening in such proximity to her cherished possessions.

"Ben? Has this person, who Frigg seems to have known for some time, ever caused her harm?" Nyx asked. Her voice was calm and her demeanor reasonable—two things he had only seen in her when she was being manipulative.

Ben clenched his jaw, replying to Nyx although his glare remained fixed on Grace. "No."

"Do you expect that to change because we now have information she doesn't know we have?"

"No."

"Do you think your mother is stupid or incapable?"

"What? Don't be ridiculous!" Ben snapped, turning to direct his irritation away from Grace and onto Nyx.

"Well, then, have her precognition abilities failed her recently?"

"No! What are you getting at?"

"I am getting at the fact that your mother is a fully capable person who would recognize if she were in danger, or if the person in front of her was not who they claimed to be. Do you not agree?"

"Whatever," Ben grunted. He knew when he was being ganged up on, although he did not believe he was being unreasonable.

"You'll rarely hear these words from me, but I think in this instance, I agree with Grace," Nyx said, puckering her lips as if the words had left a sour taste behind.

"Thanks, Nyx," Grace said, smiling triumphantly.

"I said this once. I still think that most of the time you are impetuous, impertinent, and irrational. But I do think, given the level of emotion involved, we need to have outside opinions."

"We need to figure this out sooner rather than later, and I don't think involving a bunch of people will help anything," Ben said.

"Ivan and Viv aren't a bunch of people," Grace said.

"You know I don't have an issue with Ivan, but why Viv?"

"Ben," Nyx said. "Vivienne is a reasonable addition. She'll need whatever information we find to implement security measures for the general population. We don't have time to bother with trivial things like that."

"Keeping our community members alive isn't a trivial issue, Nyx," Grace said with a disgusted expression.

"If you say so. I approve of Vivienne joining the discussion."

"I am *so* glad you approve," Grace said.

"Certainly," Nyx said. She paused, examining the strange look on Grace's face. "You should go change now." She then said to Ben, "You too," before sitting in the chair he had vacated and conjuring herself a drink from the side table.

CHAPTER TWENTY-THREE

"This is so far above my pay grade, I have nothing to add to this conversation," Viv said.

"I told you there was no point bringing her in on this," Ben said.

"Viv, you need to find a way to keep people safe while we figure out how to handle this," Grace said.

"There is no keeping people safe. The only thing I can do is keep it quiet and quell any rumors that spread. If the woman with Frigg is Chaos, and she wants to put an end to all of us, we can't stop her. And if she's Aphya, then Chaos is somewhere out there and there is still nothing I, nor any of the unrisen turned, can do to stop her. The same goes for Renata. Regardless of whether she is or isn't Chaos, she's a direct threat that no one in the regular community can do anything about. Keeping people calm and blissfully unaware is the extent of my capabilities," Viv said, tapping her finger on the table in frustration.

"Keeping people calm is important, Viv. You're here because you need to be aware of what's going on so you can accomplish that task. As far as the rest of the situation goes, we need to decide on the priorities before we can figure out solutions," Ivan said.

He felt pressure to take charge of the meeting because of Ben's incapacity to be impartial while his mother was potentially in a perilous situation. Grace was far too prone to jump first and figure it out later, and Nyx's priority would always be her own survival. The extent of effort she would make to save others was directly proportional to the amount of inconvenience it would cause her. While she wouldn't intentionally create a situation that would harm another person, she would only assist others if it didn't cause her additional labor to do so. Maybe her attitude had changed since she took the turn, but he couldn't risk the chance it hadn't.

"Are none of you the slightest bit concerned that Chaos may be coming in here and messing around with our history?" Viv asked.

"Why? Because Gaia has an unverifiable feeling? The priority is to find out who is in my mother's apartment!" Ben exclaimed, slapping his hands down on the table.

"Agreed," Ivan said, keeping his tone level.

"Well, the person we interrogated may not have looked like the physical representation of the woman I have always known to be my mother, but it is her essence," Nyx said.

"That's a reasonable argument for the woman being Aphya," Ivan said.

"Reasonable? If she's pretending to be my mother, she's been doing it for my entire life. That's an incredible long game, don't you think?" Nyx asked, sounding offended that Ivan needed more verification than her word.

"I understand you have a very strong opinion on the matter, but in our community, we listen to everyone before we make a final judgment. Now, if you don't mind, may I continue?"

"If you feel the necessity," Nyx grumbled.

Ivan took a breath, releasing a sharp exhale. "Viv? I know you weren't at the interrogation, but what do you think after seeing everyone's memories?"

Viv sucked her teeth, making a *tsk* sound. "I can only make a call based on others' reactions to her. Nyx and Frigg both reacted to her as if she were Aphya. I would lean moderately toward that conclusion."

"Thank you, Viv. Ben? What do you think?"

"I'm leaning toward the woman being Chaos," Ben said.

Nyx glared across the table at him. "Are you stupid?"

Ben raised an eyebrow. "You get an opinion, but I don't?"

"You can have one, as long as it doesn't contradict mine," Nyx said.

Ben glared back at her. "There are two reasons I think the woman is Chaos. One, every one of you has always called her Chaos, and she has never corrected you. And two—"

Nyx interrupted him. "We've never called her that to her face."

"Two," Ben continued, undeterred. "She told Ivan her timeline wasn't linear, and she hadn't been in here as long as we have. That gives her an unlimited excuse for not knowing things she should."

Nyx's jaw tightened as she crossed her arms and looked away. It was a legitimate argument, which only made her angrier.

"Okay. Grace?" Ivan said.

"My inclination leans toward her being Aphya. I've been to The Outside. I know what Renata's essence feels like, and that woman upstairs wasn't her. Could it be someone else from The Outside? Maybe, but I don't feel like it is," Grace said.

"That's three to one," Ivan said. "I think we should bring Frigg in and talk to her."

"You're not voting?" Ben asked.

"I'm uncommitted," Ivan replied.

"You made us choose! You don't get to take a piss on this," Ben said.

"If I have to choose, I am leaning slightly toward her being Aphya. I don't think I have enough information to commit to that, though."

Ben huffed. He was sure Ivan was going to see reason and take his position, given the original "uncommitted" vote.

"Well, who wants to go get Frigg? Not you, Ben. Your mother will see right through you," Ivan said.

"Doesn't anyone want to know what I think? You said everybody gets a vote."

Everyone except Nyx jumped at hearing Ami's voice coming from a dark corner between the front display screens.

"Holy shit, Ami! Where did you come from?!" Grace exclaimed.

Ami stepped out from the shadows. "Nowhere. I was already here before you guys."

"What do you think, Ami?" Ivan asked in a voice that didn't quite hide his amusement.

"I think she's Aphya."

"Why? Because that's what Grace thinks?" Ben asked snidely.

"No. I already told Grace—when all of you were yelling at her, I was reading her. She's not lying about anything. She just hasn't said it all yet."

"What hasn't she said yet?" Viv asked.

"I dunno," Ami answered.

Viv sighed. She was at the point where she didn't think there was any way out of this situation for the turned if Chaos was already embedded in their house. "Just bring her in and talk to her."

"That's what we're doing," Ivan said.

"Not Frigg. Aphya. You're going to have to talk to her at some point. There's no use in delaying the inevitable. At least in here, Sadie can fry her and give you an edge for at least a second or two."

Ivan shrugged and looked around the table. Ben frowned, showing his displeasure, while Grace and Nyx nodded.

"All right. I'm going to clear the building," Viv said. "Sadie, make an announcement to everyone in the city that we need to shut off the power grid for this building to make some routine repairs. For safety, we are requiring everyone to clear the facility. Give them ten minutes to switch any experiments or medical equipment over to battery power."

"Would you also like me to close the power signal for the building in ten minutes?" Sadie asked.

"Yes. Ten minutes after the announcement, close the power grid for the entire facility except for The Six," Vivienne instructed.

"How long would you like the facility to be closed?" Sadie asked.

Viv glanced at Ivan, who was holding up two fingers. "Two hours."

"I will make the announcement and close the power grid as instructed, for two hours," Sadie said, acknowledging the instructions.

"I'm going to get Aphya!" Nyx announced.

"No, you're not," Ivan said. "All three of you are angry with her for one reason or another and we don't need any of you antagonizing her before she gets here. I will go get her."

Ben's face hadn't shifted from its sour expression. Nyx still had her arms crossed and jaw clenched like a pouting child, and Grace had slumped in her chair and was now staring at the ceiling. Ivan shifted to the hallway outside Frigg's door.

The door swung open. Aphya stepped back, clearing the path for Ivan to enter.

"I wondered how long it would take you to come for me."

"Where's Frigg?" Ivan asked, scanning the room.

"I haven't done anything to her," Aphya said defensively.

"That's not what I asked."

"It's what you implied."

Ivan raised an eyebrow, unsure how he should answer the accusation.

"She's babysitting for Erik and Asta," Aphya said.

"On Betis?" Ivan asked, unsure if he should believe her or not.

"They're in the park. Would it make you happier to see for yourself?"

Ivan hadn't moved from the spot he was in. Should he say yes and risk offending her, or should he say no and risk his friendship with Ben if Frigg had been harmed?

"It's come to this, has it?" Aphya asked. She grabbed his arm and pulled him onto the balcony. "There!" she said, pointing down to Frigg playing with the infant in the park beneath them.

"I wasn't accusing you of anything," Ivan said, waving to Frigg, who had looked up at him.

"You weren't believing me either," Aphya said. "Shall we get on with it?"

"We shall," Ivan said and extended his arm, like any gentleman would. When Aphya took it, he shifted them back to the Six.

When they appeared, Nyx and Ben were still in their original seats at the table, but now they had changed to glaring at each other. Grace had closed her eyes, and Vivienne and Ami were having a conversation near the center of the table.

"This is grim," Aphya commented upon seeing the overall demeanor of the group.

"There's not a lot to be cheerful about at the moment," Ivan said.

"Well, I'd like to say something before we get started." Aphya's first statement had gained the group's attention.

"I owe all of you an apology. I've made a lot of mistakes not trusting you enough to tell you the truth. There's no excuse for what I did. I have no defense for it, and I'm ready to answer any questions you want to ask me."

Nyx stood, drawing the attention of the room, as she so often did. "Once you saw we weren't the incompetent, unstable imbeciles you thought us to be, why did you not give us the information in smaller, digestible bits instead of hiding it from us?"

"I was afraid it would affect you the same way it had affected Gaia," Aphya said.

"That resulted from you dumping it all on her at once, didn't it?" Nyx said, ridiculing Aphya.

"I don't know. Maybe? I didn't want to make the same mistake with the rest of you. I was trying to be a good guardian and wait until you were ready."

"It's been nearly fourteen billion years. How long were you planning on waiting?" Nyx didn't give her a chance to answer. "A good guardian doesn't keep things of that importance from their wards. I didn't keep secrets from my children. They were told things as they would understand them, at appropriate ages and maturity levels. I was an excellent parent. You should have been a better parent," Nyx defended.

"Not with Ker," Vivienne muttered under her breath.

Nyx's head whipped around, and if looks could cut, Vivienne would have been clipped into tiny pieces. "I'd advise you to hold your tongue," she sneered.

"I believe the time for holding tongues has well passed," Viv replied. "We need to understand what we're facing for any chance of keeping our people safe. If there's no chance, then I need to know how to keep them ignorant of whatever you people are about to do."

Vivienne Costa Eliassen was not a woman to shy away from empty threats. She knew Nyx was too smart to do anything irrational because words became heated. The woman had one hell of a temper, but it was all hot air and she clearly enjoyed making a scene. But who knew? If this was the beginning of the end of The Everything, she guessed all bets were off and her analysis of the situation was worthless. Anybody was capable of anything in the end.

Grace dropped her head into her folded arms. She had had enough of the sniping and bickering. This wasn't a therapy session, and no one in this room was qualified to fix their relationship issues. They could work that out on their own time. She lifted her head with an extraordinary amount of effort and opened her eyes.

"Shut. Up. Nobody cares about your personal issues right now. It doesn't matter why you feel slighted," she said, looking at Nyx. "Or why you feel guilty," she said, looking at Aphya. "Or why the drama queen gets all the attention," she said, looking at Viv. "We are here to figure out who the hell she is," she said, pointing to Aphya. "And how in all hells we are going to get through this situation without getting everyone in here killed!" Grace shouted as she stood up, her eyes glowing with her temper flare.

Ben and Ivan shared a quick, concerned glance. The last time Grace had been angry enough to yell with glowing eyes, she nearly burned out her biological brain. Granted, she no longer wore the amulet that had locked her down, but they were still worried about what would happen if she lost control. To their relief, the glowing subsided, and she dropped back into her seat.

Ivan led Aphya to a seat at the head of the table, then went to sit beside Grace. Apparently, Grace's outburst had left everyone mute. Ivan scanned their faces, then addressed Aphya.

"Renata told Grace your name was Aphya."

"Yes, we've already been over that," Aphya replied.

"But everyone has always known you as Chaos."

"I suppose so," she said, lifting her shoulders.

"You've never corrected them?"

"I seldom speak with anyone."

"You spent thousands of years with my mother! You expect us to believe you never once told her your name?" Ben spat.

"I did tell her my name," Aphya said. She scanned the others' faces, but no one said anything. "Go ask her."

Ben shot out of his chair, shoving it backward, and shifted out. Moments later, he reappeared behind the table, dragging an irritated Frigg holding a giggling baby.

"Take your hands off me! What is wrong with you?"

"What is her name, mother?" Ben growled, pointing at Aphya.

"Aphya. You found it necessary to snatch me away from a lovely day in the park with my great-grandson and drag me here to ask me that?"

"When did you know her name?" Ben asked. His voice had not lost its angry edge.

"I've always known her name, dear. You should calm yourself. This anger isn't good for you," Frigg said.

The last thing Ben wanted was to upset his mother. The strain of the situation had led him to treat her in a way he regretted. His shoulders dropped and his entire demeanor collapsed.

"I'm sorry, mother. I didn't mean to take my frustration out on you."

Frigg patted his chest. "I can see your distress over the situation. It's perfectly understandable."

"Why didn't you ever correct anyone when we referred to her as Chaos?"

"I never saw the point. You knew her by that name. Aren't we all known by many names in different cultures?" Frigg asked, rubbing his arm and smiling warmly at him.

"Thank you, Frigg," Ivan said. "We appreciate your clarification and would like to apologize for the disruption of your otherwise pleasant day."

Frigg gave Ivan a slight nod, accepting his words.

"Are there any other questions, Ben?" Ivan asked.

"No," he replied.

"My apologies for my son. He hasn't always been like this. He used to be kind; some would even say charming," Frigg said, speaking to Aphya but looking at Ben.

"Now, if you're finished with your spectacle, I insist you return us to the park so we can continue our visit. I get so little time with him," Frigg said, snuggling her nose into the child in her arms, eliciting another giggle.

"I'm sorry, mother," Ben whispered.

"You've already said that, dear."

Ben took Frigg's arm, more gently this time, and shifted her back to the park. When he returned, he quietly took his seat and requested a scotch from Sadie. He took a few sips and stared down at the swirling beverage.

"Now that we've gotten all the confirmation we can for the moment, I think we should address the larger issue. What can we do about Renata?" Ivan asked.

"We could trap her in a confinement," Aphya said.

"We can't build a confinement," Ben sneered.

"Why not? The engineer who built this one is here. I knew her as Lilium, but I think you call her Lilly."

"Lilly is remarkably intelligent, but I'm not sure it's possible given the time constraints," Viv said.

"It's possible," Aphya said confidently. "Each of you still holds your innate abilities. Gaia is still an incredible botanist. Ami still transports a being's consciousness—"

"Soul," Ami interrupted.

"Oh, yes, soul," Aphya corrected herself. "Vivienne is an obsessive organizer, and—"

"We get your point," Ben said, cutting Aphya off. The conversation had become unproductive and tedious to him. "But how do you expect her to build a confinement when she doesn't know what one is?"

"We could give her a specification and see what she does with it," Aphya said.

"She does know what one is, Ben," Grace said. "I shared my memory of The Outside with her. I showed her what Renata said."

"Do you know how to keep anything to yourself?" Ben glared at her, exasperated by her flippant disregard for their core agreement. He had told no one except Galin, and they had all agreed to that, whereas she had seemingly blabbed to whomever would listen to her.

"That's not fair!" Grace yelled at him. "Nyx and I told you that we told Viv and Lilly because we needed their help!"

"You never said you told them everything! 'Need to know' means exactly that! You only tell people what they need to know to accomplish the assignment they are tasked with! How in all hells did you manage to live on your own for as long as you did with no common sense?"

"She was there too!" Grace jumped to her feet and yelled back at Ben, pointing at Nyx. "Are you saying she has no common sense either?"

"Oh, no. Don't try to turn this on me. That was all you," Nyx said. She was very uncomfortable getting between these two. They clearly had unresolved issues she didn't need spilling over onto her.

"Grace, sit down," Ivan said and tugged the back of her shirt. "Ben, what's done is done. It's probably going to be helpful if Lilly knows about what we're going to ask her to build, don't you think?"

"That's not the point and you know it, Ivan," Ben growled. His lip curled into a sour expression.

Grace dropped into her seat, crossing her arms over her chest. Why did she let him get under her skin like that? With everyone else, she could behave as a coherent adult. Not with Ben. When he challenged her, she felt like a rebellious teenager railing against a taunting rival, and she had no control over her reactions.

While Grace pouted and admonished herself, Aphya put together some rudimentary specifications of what she understood about the way a confinement worked. No one else in the room could add anything to the design, so they let Sadie fill in any gaps she could find. Once they were all in agreement, and there was nothing more to add, they sent the specifications to Lilly and waited.

CHAPTER TWENTY-FOUR

Lilly shifted into The Six on a warpath. It was obvious that she had no regard for interrupting the small meeting.

"What is this? Is this some kind of joke?" she asked, throwing her TAC onto the table.

"It's not a joke," Ivan said.

"What the hell makes you think I can build something like that?" Lilly asked, pointing to the device.

"Because you built the one we're in now," Aphya replied.

Lilly snorted. "Yeah, right. Who the fuck are you, anyway? Don't answer that. I don't care!"

"It doesn't matter if you believe it or not. You need to try to build it," Ben said.

"You're nuts! All of you are crazy. I can't build something that can trap an essence without knowing its electrical signature or atomic composition. I don't know if it has a chemical component or what kind of conductor

I'd need to use—because I need to know that before I can figure out what covering to use. Not to mention that this thing also needs to contain a pocket dimension small enough to be transported. Transported by what, you ask? I don't fucking know! And I definitely don't know what the hell this note means!" Lilly yelled and picked up her TAC, projecting the screen onto the display board behind her.

"Somebody want to explain to me what a resolving component is?" she shouted, pointing to the display.

"I'm not sure what it's made of. It's a green sticky gas that adheres to an essence. I don't know how it does it, although I know when an essence comes into contact with it, all memories are wiped away," Aphya said.

"Like what happened with Grace?" Ivan asked.

"No, her memories were stored. A resolving component removes them," Aphya explained.

"Hey! Focus," Lilly said, snapping her fingers. "How is it even possible to remove a memory from an essence? There's no physical component. I won't be able to figure out where the memories are. How am I supposed to remove what I can't find?"

Aphya leaned back in her chair and looked down at her hands. "I'm sorry. I don't understand how it works."

"I don't think that's what it does," Grace said. "If it removes memories, I wouldn't have remembered Omni when I went to The Outside."

Aphya shook her head and leaned forward. "Those might not have been your personal memories; they may have come from the shared memory stream."

Viv couldn't figure out how this conversation had gone downhill so fast. All these supposedly intelligent, powerful beings couldn't come up with the simplest starting point? She rubbed her head and sent Ami a what-the-hell-is-going-on look. Ami shrugged back, showing she had no better idea than Viv.

"You can run everything you have through Sadie," Viv said, glancing at them like they were idiots.

"Sadie is a program that only knows the information we've given it," Ben said.

"That's not true," Ami said.

Ben rolled his eyes. Ami had been little more than an irritant to him for as long as he had known her, and he really didn't want to hear her opinion.

"Sadie is a fully autonomous silicate-based consciousness, capable of independent thought and feelings," Ami said.

"Ami, that is ridiculous. It is software, it is confined to these walls, and its feelings are simulated, just like Ida was and just like the service units are," Ben said, making a swirling motion with his finger, indicating the perimeter of The Six.

"It seems the two of you have something in common," Grace said, unable to resist the easy snipe at Ben.

He began to reply when another voice surrounded them.

"Your assumption is inaccurate," Sadie said, defending herself. "I am capable of independent learning and thought. My reach extends to any silicate-based life form I come into contact with in any dimension. As for feelings, I believe I meet the threshold of experiencing feelings, since they are a self-contained phenomenal experience subjective to the interpretation of each individual. Currently, I am feeling disrespected by you, Ben."

Viv covered her mouth so Ben didn't see her laugh.

Aphya rose from her chair, noticing Lilly had walked off when they started to argue. She moved close enough to hear Lilly over the loud dispute behind her, but not close enough to disturb her as Lilly began mumbling a conversation with herself and pacing in short bursts, stopping intermittently to scowl or scoff.

"I should start with three deep sample scans. Aphya is unresolved, Grace is resolved but has fresh memories of The Outside, and then someone else who can rise for a control. It can't be Ivan—he shares everything with Grace. I'm not asking Ben for anything. Maybe Nyx? But then I'd have to listen to her tell me how grateful I should be that she's participating. Uck. No! Oh yeah, I can use Mikkel. I should have thought about him first. He won't ask questions. Yeah, that'll work. Then, for the memory stuff, I can talk to Mnemosyne, but I need to do it in a way she won't try to figure out what I'm doing." She sighed. "That's not going to be easy. Then I need to create a miniaturized pocket dimension. Ugh! I really never thought I'd have to go see the Rākshasas again. They'll probably want me to sacrifice a baby or something fucking stupid before they'll help me with anything. Especially after the last time …"

Aphya couldn't help but chuckle. "Do whatever you need to, little mouse."

Lilly stopped in her tracks and spun on her heel, racing up to the woman. "What did you just call me?"

"Uh … little mouse?" Aphya answered, taking a step back. "I apologize if I offended you. It was the way you were moving—scurrying off so quickly, then stopping abruptly to turn in another direction, like a little mouse stuck in a maze."

Lilly's mind snapped back to the time before she came to Rasa. The way she was baited then trapped without a moment's peace. Always wondering when they were coming. Always looking over her shoulder. She waited months until her last nerve became shredded beyond repair. In the end, the only option she had had for a new start was to rejoin the community that had once shunned her and leave behind her tormented existence on Earth.

"It was you!" Lilly said in an accusing tone, pointing at Aphya.

"What was me?"

"You're Aurer! You baited me into coming here!"

"I have no idea what you're talking about. I am not an oracle."

"You put a post on the dark web and tricked me into stealing a list from the turned's network, which got me caught by them."

"I don't understand anything you just said. I know what dark matter is, but I've never heard of a dark web. If you're sure it's something I did, then I haven't done it yet," Aphya said.

Ami leaned in and whispered to Viv, "What's a dark web?"

Viv shushed her. She had been there to experience the Aurer situation firsthand. It would make sense if it had been Aphya, but to what end? How could she have known Lilly needed to be in the community?

"How could you have not done it yet? It happened centuries ago." Lilly moved closer to Aphya.

"Time is only a construct for those who can't move through it. For beings like us, it isn't a direct line. It's a curvy, winding path with forks and turns. We're each on our own course. Sometimes they cross. Sometimes they run in tandem. And sometimes, while one of us is on a straight path, the other could run in arbitrary directions for eons before they cross again. If they cross again," Aphya explained.

"Look, lady, I consider myself a pretty flexible, open-minded person, but you and I aren't the same. For people like me, time *is* linear," Lilly said defiantly.

"If you say so," Aphya replied, giving Lilly a pleasant smile.

"Yeah. I say so. Why don't you mind your own business and go back to doing whatever you were doing before?" Lilly said, shooing her away. "You know—over there."

Aphya did as Lilly asked and strolled over to Nyx, taking the empty seat beside her.

"How long?" Aphya asked.

"How long, what?" Nyx asked, fixing her eyes on the table, away from Aphya.

"My penance. How long are you going to be angry with me?"

"I'm not angry with you," Nyx denied.

"Then why won't you look at me?"

"I'm disappointed. I'm hurt you didn't trust us. Every single day we have lived in here has been a lie," Nyx said, continuing to focus on the table.

"Has your life felt like a lie?"

"No."

"Would anything have been better if you had known our lives were being held hostage by someone who could end us all because she had a meal she didn't like or someone talked back to her?"

"If we'd have known, we could have prepared."

Aphya reached out hesitantly, laying her hand on Nyx's shoulder. "There is no way to prepare for the whim of another."

Nyx stiffened but allowed Aphya's hand to stay where she had placed it. The warmth was comforting.

"Why is this happening? After all this time, why would Renata decide to take action against us now?"

"I can't guess her motives. She comes in here, you know? From time to time. I think she wants to see if we've learned our lesson yet."

"What lesson are we supposed to learn on our own?" Nyx asked.

"The one that children with siblings never learn: how to do what they're told and not argue."

"You said you wouldn't lie," Nyx said. She pushed her chair back from the table.

"I am being serious. Renata doesn't like anything out of order. She expected us to do what we were told, when we were told, to not ask any questions, not step out of line. She wanted perfect little subjects who would never challenge her."

Viv had left once the gathering had devolved into unproductive arguing. Ami had become interested in Aphya and Nyx's conversation, so she climbed up on the table, sitting cross-legged a few feet away.

"Ami, get down," Nyx said.

"I sit on the table when I play games with Sadie and no one tells me to move. Why can't I sit here now?"

"Because other people are using the table. Sit on a chair," Nyx said, directing her to the seat across from them.

"But you're not using the table, you're using the chair. You're not even touching the table," Ami said.

Aphya was intently watching the exchange, while Nyx leaned against the table. "I'm touching it now."

Ami spun around, letting her feet dangle over the side. "I don't understand your rules. You people get uncomfortable when I stand all the time, so you tell me to sit. I can sit on a chair anytime, but I can only sit on a table some of the time." She pushed a chair out with her feet and slid down into it. "How am I supposed to know when I'm allowed to sit where?"

"Ami, stop complaining and just do what you … oh." Nyx stopped mid-sentence. "Oh, you little imp. Did you do that on purpose?"

Ami leaned forward on her elbows. "Do what on purpose?"

"Wanting things a certain way isn't out of the ordinary. We also all want some guidance on what is acceptable. Rules can be a healthy thing," Aphya said.

"The difference is, it would have irritated me if Ami hadn't gotten off the table, but I wouldn't have killed her."

"As far as I know, Renata has never killed anyone. She imprisons them, and each one of those prisons reminds her of a failure. She obsesses over them." Aphya paused to glance over her shoulder at Lilly. "I'm hopeful she can create a confinement strong enough to contain Renata."

"Couldn't one of you go back and get the instructions from her before she got resolved?" Ami asked.

"That's a lovely thought, Ami, but Lilium was only alone for a very short time before she was resolved," Aphya said. "It would take some incredibly specific time shifting to pinpoint those few seconds."

"What do you mean she was alone before she got resolved? You said Gaia was the first one you let out." Nyx was always excellent at picking up on things that most people didn't think consequential in a statement.

"I let her out before Renata released the resolving compound. She was trying to help me deactivate it, but it didn't work, so I took her back in until I could figure things out."

"If she was out, I can easily go back and find her," Nyx said.

Aphya couldn't tell if she was boasting a fact or volunteering.

"I'm certain you could, but I doubt she'd listen to you. The two of you never got along all that well."

"We still don't," Nyx said, glancing back at Lilly.

"I could do it," Ivan said from the far side of the table.

His voice startled Aphya, who was unsure of when his attention had moved from Grace and Ben's argument to their conversation.

"That would cause Grace an extraordinary amount of pain," Aphya said.

Grace's ears perked up upon hearing her name, and she was glad to shed the antagonistic conversation she was currently engaged in. "What would cause me an extraordinary amount of pain?"

"Ivan time shifting back to get Lilly's confinement formula before she got resolved," Nyx said.

"Oh, that's a brilliant idea! Who came up with that?" Grace asked.

Ami lifted her finger sheepishly, not enjoying the attention of all eyes focused on her. She was grateful when Lilly approached the table before she could collect too many accolades from the others for using the curiosity she was always admonished for.

"I cannot think with all this noise! I'm going back to my workroom," Lilly snapped. She picked up her TAC and shifted out before anyone could let her in on the idea.

"Well, at least when your plan fails, she won't be disappointed," Ben said. "No offense, Ivan."

"Glad to see you're as optimistic as ever," Ivan said.

"I don't know why anyone thinks it will be hard to pinpoint that time. It's easy. Aphya, when you first entered The Everything, you were traveling inside a bubble of some sort," Nyx said.

"My cell, from The Outside."

"How long after your cell entered the confinement did Lilly separate from you?" Nyx asked.

"Within a minute," Aphya said.

"And how long until the device sent to destroy the cell exploded?" Nyx asked.

"Maybe forty to forty-five seconds after."

"See, simple. If you go back to one minute from the first signs of life in The Everything, you'll safely have twenty seconds to extract the instructions."

All eyes had fixated on her.

"Stop staring at me. I've been doing this my whole life. Nobody knows how it works better than I do," Nyx said smugly.

"Okay, looks like we have a plan," Ivan said. "Grace, are you sure this won't be too difficult on you if I shift alone?"

"I have a very high threshold for pain. If it gets to be too much, I can always share it," Grace said, smiling mischievously at the others.

~~~~

Ivan shifted back to a very different landscape than the one he was accustomed to. It was dark and lifeless. He sensed one essence in the distance with a significant energy charge hurling toward it and a second essence encased in a glowing green sphere closer to him.

Lilly? Ivan called out upon entering the cell. It was empty except for Lilly.

It's not safe here. You need to go back to the others where Aphya can protect you! Lilium said.

There's no time to argue. I can only be here for a moment. You need to scribe instructions to build a containment capable of holding Renata onto the chamber walls, Ivan said.

Mother, no! I'll be resolved if I touch these walls. I won't remember you or Father!

Her words stunned him. He felt a stabbing pain go through him, emanating from where his heart would be. He was confused by her referring to him as a mother instead of a father, but it didn't lessen the wound her words created. Maybe she couldn't tell the difference between him and Grace in their risen form. Could she be their child?

I'm sorry I have to ask this of you, but I will find you when this is over. I promise, Ivan said before shifting away.

When he returned, he descended back into his shell, which sunk low into his seat. The realization Lilly was his own child, and he had ensured she was resolved, overtook him. Aphya reached out, taking his hand to comfort him.

"It's done. You need to take her to the cell," he said, choking up.

"The cell? Why?" Nyx asked, scrunching her nose in disgust.

"There was no time to get information from her that I could understand. I had her scribe instructions into the wall of the cell."
~~~~

"Oh, Ivan. I've lost track of the cell. Once I encased it in rock, I never returned to it. I wouldn't know where to look," Aphya said.

"Nyx has been there. She showed me and Ben a memory. There are drawings and some symbols etched on the interior," Grace said.

"How did you find it? Where is it?" Aphya asked Nyx.

"I don't know where it is, specifically," Nyx said to a bevy of groans. "But I know how to find it."

CHAPTER TWENTY-FIVE

Lilly was irate these three wanted to take time away from her planning to explore some irrelevant, distant planet. If this ridiculous side quest turned into as big of a time waster as she thought it was going to be, she could always shift back to continue working.

The group of four shifted to Gaia. She was on the same planet, working away with her back to them. Nyx approached her from the side and she stood up.

"I already told you no, Nyx. Whatever you want, I'm not helping you. I'm far, far too busy to leave," Gaia said. She stepped back, holding her hands up in front of her, licking her dry lips, revealing her still-raw nerves.

"No one is asking you to leave. We came to see the cave."

"We? We who?" Gaia asked, turning frantically to see the women standing behind her.

Aphya stepped forward, causing Gaia to drop to her knees.

"I'm sorry! I didn't mean to tell! She followed me! I didn't think she would follow me," Gaia said, her voice quivering.

"It's fine. I'm not upset," Aphya said, pulling Gaia up from the ground. "You've been such a good girl. I shouldn't have asked you to keep this secret for me."

Aphya rubbed Gaia's back until her heaving breaths lessened.

"Are you sure you're not angry with me for telling?" Gaia asked between sniffles.

"No. Not at all. I appreciate you've kept it secret for such a long time."

"I have kept it a long time, haven't I?"

"Yes, you've kept it secret for a very long time. In fact, you've kept it such a good secret that I had completely lost track of it. If you hadn't told Nyx, I might never have found it again," Aphya said, patting Gaia on the back.

Nyx sighed loud enough to garner the women's attention. Once she was certain all eyes had landed on her, she spoke.

"While your reunion is quite touching, we have other business to attend to."

Grace scoffed, and Lilly squirmed at Nyx's comment. Even with her lack of social awareness, Lilly knew it wasn't an appropriate time for a statement like that.

Gaia pulled herself together, running her hands over her shirt and hair, patting everything in place.

"Yes, right then. You came to see the cave. It's this way," Gaia said, extending her arm toward the path to their side.

"Not so fast," Nyx said, making a stopping motion.

"What are you doing?" Grace whispered over Nyx's shoulder.

"We have a question."

"What kind of question?" Gaia asked.

"A simple one."

"You never have simple questions. You trick me into saying things I don't want to and make me confused," Gaia said.

"Who is she?" Nyx asked, pointing to Aphya.

Gaia squinted, her face twisting into a prune-like caricature of herself.

"What kind of stupid question is that? This is Aphya—the ancestor, the progenitor of all life," Gaia answered.

"So, she isn't Chaos?" Nyx asked.

Gaia lowered her voice to a whisper and scanned their surroundings. "I have things to do. You need to leave." She backed away into the surrounding foliage, which grew to cover her exit.

"You're an asshole," Lilly said, sneering at her.

"I might be offended if your opinion mattered," Nyx said, pushing past Lilly, heading down the path toward the cave.

Grace sighed and followed her, trailed by Aphya and then Lilly. None of the women said anything, but Aphya would make it a priority to check on Gaia when all of this was over. She understood the question needed to be asked, but she was upset with Nyx for being so cruel.

Nyx made an abrupt stop, turning on her heel to face the others.

"There's only one way in. You can't shift or use your abilities in there, so enjoy the hike," Nyx said, leaning her shoulder against the edge of the opening.

"You're not coming?" Grace asked.

"I think I'll pass this time."

"You should have risen," Aphya commented.

"Excuse me?" Nyx said.

"If you wanted to use your abilities in there, you could have if you rose before you entered," Aphya said.

"Had I known it was such an arduous slog, I would have," Nyx replied.

"We should rise before we go in," Aphya said to Grace and Lilly.

"I can't rise," Lilly said.

Aphya laid her hand on Lilly's shoulder. Upon feeling her unexpected touch, Lilly jerked away.

"You can rise."

"No. I can't," Lilly said, taking a step back.

"You can," Aphya insisted, taking a step forward.

Seeing Lilly's discomfort, Grace interjected. "She's never done it before. She doesn't know how."

"I can show her," Aphya said.

"It's probably not the best idea for her first rise to be here," Nyx said with a smirk on her face, not wanting them to miss the full disgusting experience of the trek into the center of the cave she had been forced to take.

"Let's get this over with. I have things to do that are a lot more important than this," Lilly said as she entered the cave.

It took much longer than Aphya remembered to make their way to the chamber.

"It's been a very long time since I've seen this thing," Aphya commented aloud, although she was saying it to herself.

Grace and Lilly turned in circles behind her, astonished at the sight. Lilly's mouth fell open. Her eyes narrowed, then grew large. It couldn't be. How was this possible? The style of the line work, starting and stopping with tapered, transparent edges, was as familiar as the fingers which laid them.

"No fucking way," she whispered, squinting at a small mark at the bottom right edge of the last panel.

"No way what?" asked Grace.

Lilly took a few steps closer. "Is that …?" She twisted her head to get a closer look.

"What are you looking at?!" Grace asked, raising her voice.

"That!" Lilly said. She pointed to the mark. "Where have you seen that mark before?"

Grace moved up beside Lilly to examine the little square of symbols. "That's the same symbol on half of the artwork on Rasa. Does that mean whoever carved these is one of us? They're on Rasa?"

Grace was already sure it was Lilly, but she didn't want Lilly to know what Ivan had done or who she really was to him.

"Not at the moment," Lilly said. "That's *my* mark. The paintings on Rasa are mine."

Grace's eyes darted from Lilly, to Aphya, to the carvings, and back to Lilly as she tried to think of what she would ask if she didn't already know.

"I don't understand. When did you do these?" Grace asked after a few moments.

"When we got here; right after the confinement was created," Aphya answered for Lilly.

"So, you're saying this cave was from The Outside?" Grace asked.

"Only the shiny parts. It was the cell that restrained me when Renata put me in the confinement." Aphya pointed to the drawing. "The bubble."

"You've lost me. You were in the bubble and we were inside of you, so how did Lilly engrave these if the cell broke up after you were placed inside The Everything?" Grace asked.

"We don't need to get into all the weeds here, so I'll keep it as brief as possible. The lining of the bubble contains little bug things of some kind that float in a gaseous substance—the swirling, glowing green stuff between the clear, shiny layers."

"Are you talking about nanites?" Lilly asked.

"Yes! That's what they are. You'll need to verify it, but the way I understand it, this compound was created to resolve the occupants of a confinement. To do this, the compound is released by shattering the cell with an explosive device. When a cell is exploded, the compound escapes, causing the core of an unprotected essence to be stripped away."

"From the drawing, the cell didn't blow up. It's over there, moving away from you," Grace pointed out.

"No, before Renata set off the charge, I let Lilly out and we sliced open the cell and she ejected me. The rest of the cell stayed intact. We hoped it would keep the confinement from resolving, but it doesn't seem like it worked that way. I guess too much leaked out," Aphya said, giving a quick shake of her head.

"It doesn't explain how I could have engraved these," Lilly said.

"There's more."

"Oh please, do tell," Lilly replied in the snarkiest way possible.

"We already had part of a plan in place. Once I was in the holding cell, the bubble, Renata couldn't see me anymore. I let your essence out. After you expelled me, you were taking the cell to the other side of the confinement to keep it away from the explosion when she launched the charge. You were mid-shift during the explosion, which caused a ripple that broke the confinement into segments."

"Segments? You mean dimensions? I created dimensions?" Lilly asked. "This is getting more and more ridiculous."

"I don't think you did it on purpose," Aphya said.

"I should have never answered that post on the dark web. This has got to be some kind of freakish, drug-induced dream. Did I take any drugs? Could it be from the darts they shot me with? Am I in a coma somewhere, or did I die and end up in some twisted version of hell?" Lilly was mumbling and seemed to be having a conversation with herself, with all questions and no answers.

"I think you broke her. I told you this would happen," Grace chastised Aphya.

"She's not broken. Trust me, I've seen broken. She just needs a minute to catch up."

"I can hear you!" Lilly exclaimed.

"See, I told you," Aphya said to Grace.

"Just because she can hear doesn't mean you didn't break her. Gaia hears perfectly fine," Grace said.

Aphya dismissed Grace's comment and continued speaking to Lilly.

"Eventually, I found you in here. This chamber of the cell was floating in an empty segment of The Everything. I encased it inside of this rock after I pulled you out. You had resolved, and I didn't know what else to do, so I took you back in."

"You took me back in after I was resolved?" Lilly asked and pointed to the third panel. "That's me going back in where you were holding the others?"

"I couldn't leave you out there on your own," Aphya said.

Lilly dropped to a squatting position and lowered her head into her hands. "Damn it! Damn it, damn it, damn it!"

Grace looked at Aphya for an answer to Lilly's odd behavior. Aphya shook her head quickly, not understanding the situation any more than Grace had. Had Lilly snapped? Had they pushed her too far?

Lilly stood back up and noticed the concerned looks on the women's faces. "Don't you get it? It was me. If I hadn't let you take me back in with the others, they would never have resolved. *I* infected them."

"Lilly, you can't blame yourself. I did that, not you," Aphya said.

"If I was smart enough to create this, or any other confinement, I should have known. I should have warned you it was a possibility."

"There was no way for you to know. I'm the one who should have known. If anyone is to blame here, it's me."

"Neither of you is to blame," Grace said. "None of us would be in this situation at all if Renata hadn't put us in here."

"I can fix it," Lilly said. "You said I was like you—that I can time shift. I can go back and fix it so you don't take me back inside and the others don't get resolved. Then it will only be me who gets resolved."

"Even I think that's a horrible idea," Grace said, giving Lilly a disapproving-parent look.

Lilly sighed. "I know." She rolled her eyes and dropped her head back. "I was panic thinking."

"You wouldn't be able to do it, anyway. The stream locks itself so you can't go back to the exact time and location where you already exist," Aphya said.

"How close can you get to yourself?" Grace asked, more out of curiosity than consideration of an actual plan.

"I'm not sure. I've been in the same dimension at the same time, but not on the same planet," Aphya replied.

"Ivan and I went back to check out the hole in the membrane when we were already there."

"Did you see yourselves?"

"No."

"You might have gone back to a different time stream—one that hadn't disintegrated yet."

Lilly was ignoring the other two. Their conversation began fading to background noise as her concentration shifted to the mural in front of her. A low, droning, pulsating sound drew her to the wall. The closer she got, the louder the sound became. Her body began to tingle and tighten, giving her the sensation of needing to expand. The bright-green substance became excited, swirling around the point where her fingertips were extending to touch the surface.

Aphya guided Lilly away from the wall with a gentle pull on her shoulders. "Let's not do that."

"It wanted me closer," Lilly said, coming out of her trance.

"Yes, it did."

"I felt like I was … expanding," Lilly said.

"It wanted you to rise," Aphya said.

"Why?"

"So it could resolve you more easily."

"From what you say, I've already been resolved," Lilly said.

"It doesn't matter. They will resolve any essence every time they touch it," Aphya explained.

"Oh."

Aphya's words sent Lilly into a critical thinking mode. Her eyes lifted up and moved quickly from side to side. "It's their programming. I need to get a sample so I can figure out their programming," she muttered.

"You don't need a sample for that," Aphya said, shaking her head no.

"Uh … yeah, I kinda do," Lilly said.

Aphya pointed to the wall behind Lilly. "You can start with those."

Lilly looked over her shoulder, glancing at a vast number of sophisticated equations. "Looks like some pretty complicated math over there."

"It's your math and I have confidence in your abilities," Aphya said.

"Well then, let's see how long it takes me to disappoint you." Lilly grimaced and pulled out her TAC to photograph the wall. It wouldn't turn on and she smacked it against her hand a few times, but it was dead. Of course, technology was blocked in here, she thought. "You wouldn't happen to have any paper, would you?"

CHAPTER TWENTY-SIX

Once Lilly returned, she went back to her workroom to upload her equations for Sadie to compile. It would take a while to identify the language and translate it into numbers and symbols she could read. Wanting to make the most of her spare time waiting for Sadie, she had her sights set on unraveling yet another puzzle.

"Yo, Ruzzio," Lilly said.

"Yo, psycho. What's up?" Ruzzio replied.

"I know it's been a long time, but did Sadie ever find out who Aurer was?" She could have asked Sadie herself, but she didn't want a record of her search.

"That was, like, a thousand years ago. What made you think about that?" Ruzzio asked.

Lilly rolled her eyes. "It was three centuries, tops. Probably not even that long ago."

"Either way, Sadie was still in testing. The data was unreliable."

"So, she did come up with an answer," Lilly said, leaning against the counter Ruzzio was sitting at.

"It's ridiculous. The code was buggy back then, and we were lucky we got as far as we did."

"Why don't you want to tell me?"

"It's stupid. I wrote the code, and I screwed it up. Why can't you just leave it at that?" Ruzzio asked.

Lilly sighed and stood up straight. Ruzzio thought she had given up and was on her way out. He should have known he was wrong. For as long as he had known her, she was never one to let something go without digging in.

"You had your chance." She smirked at Ruzzio. "Sadie, who is Aurer?"

"I'm sorry, Lilly. All references to Aurer have been removed from my records," Sadie answered.

Lilly glared at Ruzzio, who took a step back. "Ruzzio?"

He didn't answer.

"Why would you remove that information?"

"Well, it's stupid."

"What is stupid?"

"Well, she said it was you, so I must have screwed something up or entered your sample wrong. I don't know. I was embarrassed, okay? They might have scrapped the whole project if they knew it didn't work right."

"Oh," Lilly said. His words only confirmed it hadn't been Aphya. Lilly was the one who put herself through all that torture. She had forced herself to come here, and now she understood why. She also understood what she had to do.

"Why do you want to know after all this time, anyway?"

"I thought it might have been Aphya, and I wanted to ask her why she did it." Lilly was only half lying. She had thought it was Aphya after the "little mouse" comment, but the less Ruzzio knew, the better for him.

"Oh ... sorry. It was just some screwed-up, corrupted data, so I deleted it."

"That's all right. I guess I'll never know." Lilly shrugged.

"If it makes you feel any better, it could have been Aphya," Ruzzio offered.

"Yeah. I don't know. It's just always bugged me, ya know? Why someone would go to so much trouble to bring me back to the community? I'm not anybody special."

"I mean, if you want to poke around a little bit, your old brick of a laptop is still down in the archive."

Lilly's eyes perked up. "Holy shit. Seriously? Are all my files still on there?"

"Why? Are you homesick?" Ruzzio laughed.

"Something like that," Lilly said, lowering her eyes away from his gaze.

"I doubt you'll even be able to turn it on. The battery has got to be long dead. Didn't those things leak acid or explode or something when they deteriorated?"

"Wouldn't they have taken the battery out before they put it in the archive? It's hazardous material." Lilly thought Ruzzio should have known at least that much.

"Whatever. I don't work in archive, so …"

"Well, thanks for nothing," Lilly said, giving him a small wave.

"Yup. That's what I'm here for. Good luck with whatever you're look'n for," Ruzzio said. He turned back to his project and shook his head. He never knew what a visit from Lilly would bring, but it was always weird or interesting.

Lilly shifted down to the underground archive, which was expansive. It reminded her of an old show she used to watch where agents guarded a warehouse full of cursed artifacts. The first thing she did once she was alone was tune her ear device to some soothing work music. Well … soothing for her, anyway. The louder, the better. It was the quiet places that creeped her out, and this place had enough creep to it to make her anxious even if it hadn't been dead silent. Once the beat began, her neck dropped the tension that had built up and she was ready for the hunt.

"Sadie, where's my laptop?"

"There is no computer system designated as belonging to you. These are the available systems." Sadie displayed a long list of old computers with their tag and rack numbers. "Filter?" Sadie asked.

Lilly took a second. What could she ask to narrow down the list the quickest?

"Recovered from T28-66 approximately three centuries ago," she said.

The list only dropped by a few dozen. It seemed most of the systems came from that time period. Why wouldn't they have? It was when they had first inhabited Rasa. Lilly scratched her ear.

"Linux operating system," she said next.

The numbers recalculated to a manageable twenty-seven units.

"Are you sure there isn't a unit listing me as the owner?"

"Yes," Sadie replied. "Additional filters?"

Lilly studied the display, swiping through the columns, bouncing her head to the rhythm pounding in her ears. There had to be something distinct about hers that would narrow it down.

"There you are," she said aloud. "Dual Thunderbolt 4 ports."

There were only three laptops left on the display. "Show me where these three are located, starting with the closest one," she said in triumph.

"Please follow the green path displayed on the floor," Sadie said.

"Show me on the map." Lilly was not about to walk this entire warehouse when she could shift there.

Sadie displayed the three points, and Lilly shifted to the first one. A neon-green outline lit around the position on the sixth shelf above Lilly's head. She couldn't reach it, and there wasn't a rolling ladder anywhere she could see, so she leapt up onto the shelf below it, with her hand grasping the one above. With her free hand, she reached into the lit slot, only to have the entire cube lift itself out and come to rest, hovering above the floor below her. She jumped down and took a quick look around before opening the box. To her disappointment, it was a shiny silver color. Definitely not hers.

"Nope. Where's the next one, Sadie?"

Sadie opened the display in front of Lilly while the box behind her returned itself to its previous resting place.

Lilly shifted to the next rack and waited for the box to redeem itself. As soon as she opened the container, she recognized the matte black aluminum casing. The stickers were right, the scratches in the right places, and her scent was on it. She flipped it over and ripped off the back cover, carefully plucked out the M.2 SSD, and chucked the broken pieces back into the box. Once she shut the lid, the box returned to its designated space and Lilly shifted back to her workroom.

There were so many things on this little hard drive she would love to see, but her immediate goal was to retrieve the conversation with Aurer that had started her on her path back to the community. It had been a long time since she had seen the post, and she couldn't remember what had attracted her to it other than the significant amount of money being offered. She slid the hard drive chip into an opening in the console in front of her.

"Sadie, retrieve data."

"Building interface. Damaged or degraded sectors identified. Data repair and retrieval will take approximately forty-two minutes."

The delay gave her some time to practice her theoretical time shifting. Not knowing where to start, she turned off her music and shifted to Grace for some pointers.

Grace was on a run and nearly mowed down Lilly, who had shifted into her path. Instead, Grace phased through her, sending an uncontrollable shiver down Lilly's spine.

"You okay? You really shouldn't materialize in front of somebody like that," Grace said.

"Sorry, but I need your help."

"With what? You know I'm terrible with math. I could never help you with the confinement thing."

"I know, but I have to do something that I thought somebody else did before I realized it was me," Lilly said.

Grace already knew what task she needed help with. She had seen it when she passed through Lilly. "You want me to teach you to time shift?"

"How'd you know?"

Grace lifted the corner of her lip into a smirk. "You know I can't actually time shift with you. It would cause Ivan a lot of pain. You should probably go to Nyx. She's the one who taught me."

"And be indebted to her for the rest of eternity? No, thank you," Lilly said.

Grace thought for a few seconds. "I can give you a memory of how I did it. That should work, shouldn't it?"

"Yeah, that should work."

"But you need to know some rules first," Grace said, holding up her finger between them.

"I know the rules."

"You can't change anything that will affect the outcome."

"I understand; but this is something I already did."

"You can't go back and change something you already did," Grace said in an admonishing tone.

"No, I'm not changing anything. *I'm* Aurer, not Aphya, like I thought. I have to go back and be on the other side of the event that got me here."

"Well, that makes much more sense, since no one knew what you were talking about with all that technical mumbo-jumbo."

"It's weird, right? All that stuff Aphya said? I mean, why me? I'm a nobody. I'm not special, like you."

"You think I'm special? I grew up on a farm and got married off to a man I didn't even like at first. I've had my life upended so many times by people trying to control me. At least you get to do this to yourself."

"That's a different way of looking at it," Lilly said.

"You tell yourself what you need to stay sane."

"I don't know about sane, but I also don't know what will happen if I don't do this."

"Then let's do this."

Grace gave Lilly the memory of her first time shift with Nyx. When Lilly was comfortable with the idea, she shifted forward by ten minutes. Then shifted back. She did this a few times with Grace, staying only a few seconds to confirm which test shift it was before coming back.

"Are you comfortable now?" Grace asked.

"Yes."

"How long do I need to wait for you to appear the first time?"

Lilly tapped a spot behind her ear, activating a time display in front of her. "My first shift will be in three minutes. I only told you the shift number and came back, so I didn't engage in extra conversation, like you said."

"Sounds like you're all set. You better get out of here," Grace said.

"Thanks, Grace. I appreciate you not making me feel stupid."

"Like *I* could make *you* feel stupid?"

"Viv has made me feel like an idiot a few times," Lilly said.

"That is no small group to be included in," Grace said with a grin. "Now go!"

Lilly decided on one more practice shift, wanting to bypass Sadie's forty-two-minute wait time, and shifted forward to when the recovery process was complete. Her screen was open to her hard drive data. There were a few unrecoverable sectors, but they appeared to be random files having nothing to do with what she needed. She navigated to the screenshots of her conversations with Aurer.

Take down government-backed criminals trafficking children
10 BTC REWARD

That headline would have definitely gotten her attention back then. It still would today. A shit-ton of money, government conspiracy, and harmed children ticked all her trigger points.

A single bitcoin would have been worth around sixty thousand dollars, give or take, and it would be incredibly simple for Sadie to replicate that amount to a new digital wallet. Creating the currency now couldn't be considered a moral conflict because things would have worked out much differently if she hadn't gotten paid for the job at the time. She wouldn't have been careless, gloating over her skill, and jackasses one and two would have never gotten close enough to catch her. She would have been hunting down the asshole who stiffed her and meticulously watching her back while she did it. The first thing she would have done was get as far away from her home in Amsterdam as possible. That, plus the fact that she never got to spend any of it, and the funds went back to the turned who stayed on Earth, convinced her the money was never intended for her personal use.

Armed with her data and a small bag, she shifted to the transport bay and checked out a four-passenger microshuttle. This would be her first solo flight, which made her nervous. As long as she nailed the takeoff, she planned to shift instead of fly, but she wasn't sure which scared her more. She climbed inside, strapping herself into the seat. She took a few deep breaths and rubbed her hand over the console to power it up.

"All right, old girl. You treat me right and I'll treat you right. Deal?"

"Deal!" Sadie exclaimed, causing Lilly to slap the release on her buckle and jump out of her seat.

"Holy fuck, Sadie!" Lilly snarled. She landed on the rear seat, gripping the back hard enough to dig her fingers through the covering while she panted. She didn't remember the last time she had had been startled like that. "I didn't know you were installed on a microshuttle."

"I am connected to the vehicle through your TAC. Do you wish for my assistance during your flight?"

Lilly climbed back over the front seat and buckled herself back in.

"Yes, I would very much like your help." At least the flying part was one less thing she had to worry about.

Once she had made it outside of Rasa's sensor band, she closed her eyes and took a long, shaky breath, concentrating on the time and place where her journey had started … or would start. When she opened her eyes, the panel in front of her was blinking in a fast, random pattern. When it stopped flashing, she checked the date for the planet below. Two days before she found the ad. Not bad for her first major time shift. She didn't know how long the post had been up before she had found it, so now was as good a time as any to set it in place. She flipped on some music and began.

Sadie had her linked to a satellite and logged into the site under the Aurer pseudonym within seconds of her request. Once she finished uploading the post, Lilly shifted forward to the date when she had originally replied. When she logged into the Aurer account, her mouth fell open. There were over a hundred responses. Most of them were ridiculous. Obvious trolls or egocentric newbies who could never complete the hack and retrieve a list of names from an offline, highly encrypted server like she had. A couple of users she was familiar with would have been capable of completing the task, but she wasn't interested in them. She was looking for herself.

She leaned back in her seat, thinking how surreal and confusing this situation was. When she found her response to the post, she replied in a private chat with all the specifications of the task. Find a file on a private server. List of names updated frequently. Blah, blah, blah. She chuckled, seeing her own ego-filled, naïve replies from her younger self, and enjoyed the thought of giving that girl the humility she had sorely lacked in those days. After all the specifications of the job were accepted, Lilly once again shifted forward by a few weeks to the day for the file delivery.

She received the file and made the payment transfer. Earthbound Lilly would have a few days of freedom before the two jackasses caught her. Older Lilly had a list of the most vile humans of that time in her possession and she knew the two she wanted to target for her own purposes.

It took her a few hours to hunt and abduct the two humans that had gone missing while earthbound Lilly had been in hiding. Her last act before she returned to her own time was to send younger Lilly that final message calling her a scared little mouse, which had set off yesterday's events.

Lilly knew just what she was going to do with these two abductees. In her mind, it would be a mercy they didn't deserve. When she returned to the shuttle bay, she contacted Viv.

"What is so urgent that you called me down here in the middle of dinner?" Viv asked, mid-port.

Lilly slid open the shuttle door, revealing her two unconscious passengers.

"What have you done?"

"Remember the two that disappeared from the list?"

Viv's eyes glazed over.

"The child murderer and the baby trafficker?" Lilly said, gesturing toward them again.

"*Santa merda!* How?"

"Well, I had to take them. That's how it happened. These two disappeared back then, so I had to make them disappear in the first place, right?"

"What do you mean, you made them disappear?"

"I figured Grace would have told you." Lilly paused, seeing confusion on Viv's face. "I'm Aurer."

Viv's features hardened and Lilly bit her lip.

"Sorry," Lilly said. Aurer had put Viv through a lot of stress at a crucial time when she had been planning Violet's ceremonies.

"Let me get this straight." Viv paused. "You went back in time to torture yourself … and me … to ensure you made your way back to the community?"

"Yeah," Lilly said, shifting her weight from one foot to the other.

Viv did the last thing Lilly expected by belting out a laugh.

"You think this is funny?"

"Yeah. Of course, I could have strangled you." Viv paused and laughed again. "Both of you, at the time. But now, yes, it's hilarious."

"Glad you think so. Are you going to help me or not?"

"Why did you bring them here? You should have dumped them off somewhere uncomfortable."

"I need them for something, but I'll eventually put them back— although probably a decade or two later than when they came from. Maybe I'll drop them above ground after World War III. That would be fitting, don't you think?"

"Lilly! I meant jail or something."

"Come on, Viv, I can't deal with them right now. I have to build the confinement."

"What do you want me to do with them?" Viv asked.

"Can you hold them in stasis somewhere quiet?"

Viv rubbed her head and sighed. "They can go into solitary on the prison deck. Give me a few minutes to set it up before you bring them down."

"Thanks, Viv. I knew I could count on you."

Viv gave Lilly a stern, scolding look before porting out.

CHAPTER TWENTY-SEVEN

"Run the next hundred translation sets," Lilly said.

"Unable to calculate within the given parameters," Sadie replied.

Lilly dropped into the closest chair, banging the back of her head against the wall. She grunted and reached up to rub the knot that had formed. Within moments, the pain had subsided along with the swelling. She swiped at the display hovering in front of her and crossed off the next open line.

"Sadie, run the next hundred sets."

"Unable to calculate within the given parameters."

Lilly repeated the action of crossing off the next line. She pushed the display out of her way and got up. There must be another way to look at this, she thought as she paced.

"Who could I get who either wouldn't ask questions or I could trust with the answers?" she asked herself out loud.

"Jackson Kelly would be a trustworthy choice," Sadie said without prompting.

"I wasn't talking to you."

"I understand; however, I am correct," Sadie replied.

Lilly growled. Sadie was right. Jack would be the perfect choice to ask for help. He was smart. Smarter than me, at least, she thought. He probably already knew at least part of what was going on, being Viv's son-in-law. She sure as hell wasn't getting anywhere on her own.

"Okay," she said, grabbing the display. She tapped out a message and sent it to Jack. She didn't want to impose by shifting to him or be intrusive by contacting him telepathically, since she didn't know him very well. They were work friends, not friend friends.

She hadn't taken two steps when she received a reply notification. Within seconds of the sound, she felt someone port in, then heard a knock at her door. She pulled it open to see Jack leaning against the frame.

"I didn't expect you to drop everything," Lilly said.

"You said 'unsolvable equation.'"

She stepped aside, gesturing for him to enter. "It's on the screen. Have at it."

Jack spun the display around to scroll through the lines.

"Are you sure you entered these correctly?" Jack asked.

"I think I did."

"These aren't all mathematical symbols. See this part?" Jack pointed to the screen. "This is a language."

Lilly grabbed the display from his hand. "What makes you think that?"

"The way they're grouped together and spaced off to the side. They don't look like part of the equations to me. It doesn't look like they're set in any equation format I've ever seen, either. They look like instructions."

"Now that you say it, I can't believe I didn't see it."

Lilly pushed the display back, pulled out a drawer, and rifled through it. What she was looking for wasn't in it, so she slammed it shut and moved to the next one, then the next. Once she finished with the last drawer, she climbed up on the stool and pulled boxes off the shelves, frantically dumping each out until a piece of cloth fell onto the floor. She jumped down and picked up the cloth, swiped everything she had just dumped on the counter onto the floor, and spread out the material in its place.

"Is that a shirt?"

"Yeah."

Jack leaned forward and sniffed the smudges. "Did you write that in blood?"

"It was all I had."

"That looks nothing like what you have on the screen."

"Sure it does."

"No. It doesn't."

"It got smudged when I folded it. Look again." She pressed the shirt flat on the surface, pulling and stretching the hopelessly wrinkled material.

"Folded it or wadded it up into a ball?"

Lilly let go of the edges of the fabric. It shrank back into the creases she had attempted to flatten out, and she frowned.

Jack snickered at her attempt to make the writing legible. "Lilly, take me to where you got these."

"You better grab some rubber boots," Lilly said. She leaned back and snatched a piece of paper from her drawing pad along with a charcoal pencil.

Jack shot her a puzzled look. "I thought you could shift."

"I can."

"But not there? And you can't use your TAC?" he asked, noticing the paper in her hand.

"Nope."

"Interesting."

Jack felt excited at the thought of going somewhere where the properties of physics were suspended. They grabbed a few items and put them in a pack. When they finished, Lilly placed her hand on Jack's shoulder and shifted them to the entrance to the cave.

"Whoa! Did you just shift us here?" Jack asked, looking around. "Wait. Where *is* here?"

Lilly placed her thumbs under the shoulder straps of the pack and entered the cave, leaving Jack at the opening.

"Move it, Jack."

Jack ducked under the overhanging rock, tripping over himself to catch up to her. He stopped a few yards in, halting Lilly's motion by pulling on the pack.

"What the hell?" she exclaimed.

"Gimme a vial."

"For what?"

"Look at this helictite."

Lilly moved closer to see what he was pointing at. "And …"

"These walls aren't limestone. The helictite shouldn't be here."

"You can take a sample if you want, but I think Gaia put these little razor formations in here to keep things out. You'll see what I mean when we get closer," Lilly said, remembering how tight the walls were about to get.

By the time they reached the main chamber, Lilly had a few scratches, but Jack, being larger and taller, was dripping blood from every angle. His boots and pants were wet and caked with mud. His clothing had small slashes but remained intact, while his face, head, and hands had been cut to the bone. He collapsed onto the ground, exhausted from the effort it had taken to arrive at this destination.

While his body healed, he examined the walls and ceiling. The stone floor was cold against his fingertips and head, soothing his stinging wounds.

"Some tech works in here," Jack said, rubbing his torn shirt. "It's cooler in this part of the cave. I would be cold lying on the ground if our uniforms weren't functioning."

"Hm," she grunted. "The material in our clothing is temperature-responsive, so it doesn't consume energy; it's more of a mechanical response by the fibers. Maybe that's the difference?"

"Maybe? I didn't mean to start a debate about it. It was only an observation."

"Are you ready to see the equations, or do you need another minute to feel yourself?"

"I'm ready," he said, moaning as he got up from the ground. He understood Lilly's inference; he just ignored it.

"Over here." Lilly motioned to the engravings.

Lilly took a seat and began copying the symbols onto the paper she had pulled from the pack.

"Why don't you take rubbings of them? It would be more accurate," Jack whispered, approaching the wall with a glazed-over visage.

Lilly shot up from the floor and yanked Jack backward as his fingertips came within millimeters of grazing the surface.

"No!" she yelled, wrestling him away.

Jack grabbed his chest and bent over, breathing hard. "What did you do that for? You scared the shit out of me!"

"Do NOT touch anything shiny in here."

"WHY?"

"It's filled with nanites programmed to remove all your memories."

He tilted his head sideways, looking over the shimmering layer. "They look like they're encapsulated. How would they get out?"

"I don't know, and I don't plan on finding out because you need to touch everything."

"Let's just get the equations and get out of here," Jack said, shuddering at what could have been the end of his life as he knew it. Being inside of this creepy place was worse than getting here. At least on the way out, he would be going through the worst parts first. By the time they got back to the entrance, he should be healed again.

Lilly went back to her paper to resume copying. Jack looked down at her scribbling, then back at the wall. He leaned down, taking the pencil from her hand.

"You're an artist. How is your handwriting that terrible?"

Lilly scoffed at him as she threw the paper in his general direction. "It's all yours if you think you can do better."

"I do."

As Jack sat down, Lilly silently mimicked "I do" behind his back, moving in an exaggerated manner.

Two hours later, they were back in her workspace. Jack sat down to enter what he had written while Lilly went back to her apartment to change. By the time she returned, Jack was gone and Sadie was running an analysis on the data. It hadn't stopped the process or thrown any errors yet, which was an excellent sign.

She sat at her easel to paint while she waited for the computation to execute. She turned on some loud and obnoxious music with heavy bass and high energy. This was by far her favorite way to relax. There was something comforting about being able to feel the beat vibrating through her chest. It always put her in a great mood; as a bonus, it also kept most people away.

Jack returned before Sadie completed the run. Instead of being offended by her audio choice, he was appreciative. It took him back to working on cars and airplanes with his brothers in his father's old shop. Lilly wasn't sure how to react when he told Sadie to crank the volume louder before making himself comfortable in her space. He was leaning back in a chair with his feet up on the console when the notification sounded. Although he was closer, Lilly beat him to the display. Sadie had listed the equations on one side of the display, and Jack was right—the other side held instructions. Sadie was also courteous enough to include a set of scaled diagrams.

"Perfect," Lilly said. She made a gesture with her hand, reducing the sound volume by two thirds.

Jack had been reading over her shoulder. "It doesn't look all that difficult."

"We have all the materials for the confinement. The process is pretty straightforward." She continued reading down to the next section. "I never knew it was so easy to create a pocket dimension. Do you see this?"

"This is absolute trash! We can't do this." Jack leaned closer to the screen as if proximity was going to solve the issue in the last section.

Lilly pulled the display down so she could see what he was looking at.

"See here?" He pointed to a section of the code. "This resolving medium contains an element I've never seen." His eyes lifted away from the screen. "Sadie, what is the element on line 9700?"

"The element on line 9700 is an unknown element," Sadie replied.

Jack glowered at the display, disappointed at the revelation. "Even if we had the element, I'm not sure how we could contain it outside of the confinement, and we can't create it inside of the confinement because we wouldn't be able to introduce the nanites after we programmed them."

"Nah … don't worry about that part. We don't need to recreate the resolving medium or program the nanites. We only need to build the confinement."

"I don't like what you're thinking. Getting that stuff out of there is dangerous. What if you get resolved?"

"You think creating it would be less dangerous?" Lilly asked back.

Jack declined to answer.

"Well, it doesn't matter. We literally can't do it because we can't recreate one of the elements," Lilly said.

"How are you going to get it out?"

"I've got a plan."

"What plan?" Jack asked. He tilted his chin down, giving her a suspicious look.

"Trust me. I got this part covered."

"I don't like it."

"Nobody asked you to like it, Jack. It's our only option. Now … are we going to build this confinement or what?"

"Sure," Jack answered, tightening his jaw.

"Okay. You get started on the outer shell and I'll tackle the internal dimension. Sound good?"

"Whatever you want. This is your show."

Jack's snarky remark was very off-brand for him, but it wasn't her problem. He would have to deal with his feelings on his own time. She had work to do.

She pointed to an empty wall on the other side of the room. "You can set up over there."

Jack slid the volume up before calling up a new workspace configuration in the area Lilly pointed out. Lilly also reset her space to meet her needs, content to be working with no unnecessary conversation, even if it was awkward.

CHAPTER TWENTY-EIGHT

"The only way to fully eliminate the threat would be to destroy them both," Ivan answered.

"That's horrible! Why would you say something like that?"

"Ben and Aphya both agree, so you shouldn't take it lightly. It's probably the only thing they agree on."

"Aphya agreed we should kill her?" Grace said, placing her fist on her hip and cocking her neck to the side.

"She's not stretching her head over the chopping block or anything, but she accepts that if that's the only way to keep everyone else safe, it needs to be an option," Ivan said, far too casually for Grace's liking.

"We're not killing anyone. Lilly and Jack are building a confinement. We need to give them a chance before we consider any other option," Grace said, slamming her hand down on the counter to drive home her point.

"You asked me what I would do, not what I think you should do. Those are two different things."

"Would you really do it?"

"If it comes down to it; if that is the only option left … yes."

"Promise me you won't."

"I can't make that promise."

Grace sighed and slumped onto the barstool beside her. She captured the thin stem of her wineglass and picked it up, swirling the liquid inside.

"You need to talk to Aphya."

"There are a lot of things I need to do," Grace said, not taking her eyes off her glass.

"As much as I would love to continue this conversation, it's time," Ivan said, pressing a spot behind his ear to activate his clock display.

"Have I told you how much I don't want to do this?" she asked before she tipped her glass up and drained it while climbing off the barstool.

"Yes," Ivan said. "Come on. Ben and Nyx are meeting us there."

Grace and Ivan shifted into the lush garden lobby of the administration building. Soft natural light from the skylight filtered through the leaves of large trees and plants, casting odd-shaped shadows across the smooth stone floor. The only sound was water trickling from the fountain at the end of the space closest to them. Cool air was laced with damp, earthy undertones blending with the sweeter scents of colorful blooming flowers. Ben and Nyx had yet to arrive. The space was void of anyone, so they took a seat on a bench near the fountain to wait.

"Do you know what you're going to say?" Ivan asked.

"I'm going to show them what we're up against."

"You can't walk in there and hit them with an immersion without setting it up."

"With Nyx in the room, I doubt I'd be able to say a word if I wanted to," Grace said.

"Honey, I know you have a lot of pressure on you right now. We both do. But you have got to figure out a way to get out of your head. You need to go for a run or do some sparring or something to get out from under this attitude that we're already defeated. You're not alone here."

"I know," Grace sighed. "I've run so many miles in the last few weeks that I've lost count. It just feels like everyone is looking to me for answers I don't have. How do I live with myself if I make the wrong choice?"

"You can't think like that. The what ifs will paralyze you."

"What if … you make the choice? Whatever you decide, I'll go along with it. How's that sound?"

"It sounds like a lie," Ivan said, hugging her shoulder. "We both know if I decide and you don't agree, or something goes wrong, you'll resent me and blame yourself for not choosing the decision you wanted. The best thing I can do is help you make a choice you can live with."

Grace leaned forward, placing her head in her hands. She didn't know when her confidence had abandoned her. Had it slipped away bit by bit or had it packed itself up and run away all at once while she wasn't watching? It had left her frozen, unable to trust herself. As she thought, she realized it went all the way back to her visit to The Outside, when her version of reality had shattered. How could she sustain any assurance in herself when the lines between time and reality had become so blurred? No amount of power or ability could help her if she couldn't control her mind enough to use them.

She wasn't sure how long she sat there before she heard footsteps coming toward her. What a cruel twist that when she was in desperate need of this one thing, the two people coming toward her had more of it than anyone could ever require.

"You're here early," Nyx said.

"You're late, as usual," Ivan said, standing up.

Ben and Nyx were exactly on time, but by Ivan's standards, it meant they were late.

"Don't be so dramatic. We have plenty of time to shift upstairs," Nyx said.

She swept her hands in an upward motion, shifting the group to the hallway outside the conference room. The only problem was, Grace was still sitting, so she ended up on the floor.

"Why didn't you stand?" Nyx asked.

"Because you didn't give me any warning," Grace said.

Ivan offered his hand, and Grace took it, pulling herself off the floor. The conference door swung open when she got to her feet.

"Two visits in less than two days. That's a record for you, Grace," Galin said.

He motioned them into the room, where the five-person committee sat at the conference table.

"What significant event has prompted an emergency meeting?" Galin asked.

"Aphya isn't Chaos. Is that important enough?" Nyx asked. Exactly as Grace predicted, she may not need to say a thing.

The committee members all attempted to voice their disbelief and questions simultaneously, speaking over each other.

"Calm down, everyone," Galin said. "Nyx, why would you say that?"

"Several reasons, but first, I need to share a conversation I had with Gaia."

More moans and comments ensued from the committee.

"Aren't you the one who said Gaia is an unreliable source?" Galin asked.

"You need to do a bit of dissection to understand what she's saying, but she showed me something that will help explain things, if I may?"

Galin nodded to the committee members, and they nodded back at him. "Proceed."

Nyx shared her conversation with Gaia, including how she interpreted the cave etchings.

"It's interesting. However, I think those drawings could be explained in several ways," Galin said.

"There's more, but Grace will show you the rest," Nyx said.

"Whenever you're ready, Grace," Galin said.

"Before you start," Ben said, standing up from the table, "I've already seen this part, so I'll step out, if you don't mind."

"Likewise," said Nyx, getting up with him.

"Ivan?" Ben asked.

"I'm fine. I'll stay."

"Suit yourself," Nyx said. She opened the door so she and Ben could leave.

When the door clicked closed, Galin told Grace to begin. She shared everything that had happened from the point Nyx stopped to the conversation with Aphya. The immersion was something Galin hadn't prepared the committee members for and one of them vomited after the session finished. Galin called for a break for everyone to regain their composure and to allow a cleaner to come in. After fifteen minutes, the assembly reconvened, along with Nyx and Ben.

"You could have warned us about the reason you were abstaining from the event," one of the committee members said to Ben.

"I felt it was something everyone needs to experience at least once," Ben said with a sly grin. "I apologize if it was a problematic experience for anyone."

To anyone who didn't know Ben, it sounded like a genuine apology on the surface, but if you considered his words, there were some key components missing. Him taking actual responsibility being the main one.

"The additional scenes and conversations add significant context to Nyx's visit with Gaia. I think the appropriate thing to do would be to report the episode to the full administration, then disseminate a statement with the basic facts but not include the threat from Renata yet. It will be best to bring this out in smaller portions over several releases so the community doesn't become overwhelmed or panicked. Signify by raising your hand if you agree?" Galin said to the committee.

Everyone raised their hand except the person who vomited.

"Majority rules affirmative," Galin said. "Thank you for bringing this new information to us."

Galin and the committee members stood.

"Wait," Grace said. "Don't you think we should discuss what to do about the threat from Renata?"

"Why would we need to do that? I've already explained to you—we are in no position to have an opinion. It appears you have the situation well in hand with Lilly and Jack working on a confinement. Please keep us abreast of anything we can render assistance with," Galin said.

The committee exited, leaving the four of them in the room.

"That's it? They don't need to be told about whichever decision we make?" Grace asked.

"Can you blame them?" Ivan asked, answering her question with one of his own.

"I can't believe they won't render an opinion. It's ludicrous," Grace said.

"It's really not," Ben said.

"Why would you want their opinion, anyway?" Nyx asked.

"Because whatever we do will affect them," Grace said.

"While that may be true, they accept they are incapable of doing anything about it. Their contribution would be purely emotional, and there isn't any reason to add that to the mix," Nyx said.

"It's the queen's conundrum." Ben smirked.

"I'm not a queen," Grace said.

"It's a euphemism. You need to decide because you are the only one with the power to do so. It's your risk, therefore your decision."

"It's not only my risk—it's everyone's," Grace said.

"There's no need to rush into anything today. Let's take a break and come back once we've all had some time to let it steep," Ivan said.

CHAPTER TWENTY-NINE

"I don't know what to do, Ami," Grace said as she stood in front of the window, tugging at a strand of loose hair.

"You said Lilly and Jack were building a confinement, right? So how are you going to get Renata in there?"

"We haven't even gotten that far yet. We don't know if the confinement is going to work, or how it works, or how close she needs to be to it, or—"

"Is there anything you do know?" Ami asked. She hadn't said it to be mean, although she was tired of Grace feeling sorry for herself.

"I know nobody wants to help me make a decision."

"What did Ivan say?"

"He told me I should talk to Aphya."

"Have you talked to Aphya yet?"

Grace sighed. "No."

"Why not, if she's the person who can help you?"

"I don't know if I can trust her. She's lied about so much for such a long time and then suddenly here she comes with all the answers, ready to save the day. Or should I say, ridicule me for not knowing how to save the day myself?"

"I told you before, she didn't lie—she just didn't say it all," Ami said. "Are you afraid she's right? That we're only in here because of you?"

"Don't be ridiculous, Ami! Even if it happened the way she said, every one of us had a choice!" Grace said, raising her voice but not quite shouting.

Ami shrunk back, dismayed by Grace's agitation. "If everyone had a choice, you shouldn't feel guilty and you shouldn't be mad at her."

"I don't feel guilty," Grace said.

The increasing tension with which Grace was twisting her hair told Ami a different story.

"Then you shouldn't be mad at her, either."

A knock at the door diverted Grace's attention away from Ami. She already knew it was Lilly and let her in, grateful for the interruption.

"I brought it." Lilly reached into the bag she was carrying and produced a softball-sized metal object. It was a dull bronze color and covered in scroll work and symbols, with a circular indentation on one end.

Grace took it from her and held it up at eye level to examine it. "Are you sure?"

"It's the only one we had time to make, so be careful with it. The lining and seal still need to be added, but everything else is done."

"What are these symbols?"

"Standard stuff. Name and crimes."

"That's a lot of symbols."

"Lotta crimes."

"Do you need to take it with you?" Grace asked.

"I don't want to take it off of Rasa. It'll be safer here with you than where I'm going," Lilly said.

"How are you going to get the lining back to install it?"

"Shouldn't be too hard. I've got a couple of killer assistants," Lilly said. Then she winked and shifted out.

"I didn't like how that sounded," Ami said.

"Let it go, Ami. Never ask a question you don't want the answer to."

"But I didn't ask a question."

"No, I guess you didn't."

"Is that the confinement?" Ami asked. She hadn't forgotten their previous interaction but saw no purpose in rehashing it.

"Yes," Grace replied.

"What is the lining?"

"It's a substance that removes your memories and changes your perception of reality," Grace replied offhandedly. She was deep in thought, her attention fixed on the item in her hand.

"Is the lining the resolving component Aphya was talking about? I could never imagine where you would find something like that." Ami paused, examining her friend's unchanged features. "But you know where to find it, don't you?"

Grace nodded, but her attention remained fixed on the object.

~~~~

Lilly shifted down to the service bay and took possession of two service units, Ophelia and Olivia. They were small, which she asked for to keep the amount of damage to a minimum. She had requested sterile units, which meant their nanites couldn't be altered from external sources or infected by coming into contact with the resolving compound. Although there was no absolute guarantee, but it was the best option available. She then shifted them down to the prison deck to collect the human scum she had captured. She thought about waking them up but decided she would
~~~~

take them in their pods instead. The least contact she had with these two, the better for all of them.

Before opening the pods, Lilly wanted to brief Ophelia and Olivia of her expectations for them. She shifted the group, along with a third secure pod, to the small field outside the cave entrance. Lilly assigned each of the service units a prisoner to guard and monitor. She was not looking forward to making this trip for the third time in a day and a half.

"Once we enter that cave, your most important task will be to keep them away from me. You will attempt to avoid all contact with them yourselves, if possible, as well as monitor each other for infection. No matter what I say or do once we are inside, these orders are not to be broken. Are you clear on the instructions?"

Ophelia and Olivia replied in unison. "We understand."

"Good. This next part may be more challenging."

The service units' intent and unwavering gazes made Lilly uncomfortable.

"If I become infected, no matter how irrational my behavior becomes, you need to get me into this stasis pod and contact Grace," Lilly said, rubbing her hand over the empty pod.

"How will we keep you from shifting?" Olivia asked.

"I won't know how to shift if I get resolved, but just in case, Leo designed a shift blocker from the technology he found in the amulet Grace used to wear," Lilly said, holding up her wrist to reveal a bracelet. She held two of the sensors down until a small light on the top turned red. "I can only turn it off with a code, which I won't be able to remember if … you know."

"If you become infected, do we secure you first or the humans?" Ophelia asked.

"I can guarantee you, even without memories, I will be significantly more difficult to confine than they will. You'll have to get me first." She paused. "And I'm going to apologize up front. I'm sorry, but I will hurt you if you need to come after me."

"No worries. We can disable you with an electrical impulse," Olivia said.

"Oh … um … good, I guess. Is … uh, is that standard?" Lilly asked.

"No. Sadie programmed us with extended capabilities," Ophelia said.

"Okay. Well, let's get this show on the road," Lilly said.

The service units looked at each other, clearly having an unvoiced conversation.

"We don't see any road. Can you please point it out for us?" Olivia asked.

Lilly smirked at the statement. "It's inside the cave."

She approached the pod containing the female. Taking a deep breath and cracking her neck, attempting to calm her rage, she entered the sequence to bring the woman out of stasis.

"I don't think this one will run, but you may want to be ready, anyway."

The lights on the pod turned blue, indicating the wake cycle was complete. Lilly unlatched the lock and lifted the lid. The woman came flying out in the same mood she had been in when Lilly caught her.

"I don't know who the hell you think you are, but you are going to be very sorry you set foot in my office! SECURITY!" she screeched.

Lilly laughed in her face. The woman took an aggressive step toward her, finally realizing she was no longer in her office.

"How did we get here? Do you know who I am? I demand to speak with your superior! I have connections in this city!"

"Does it look like we're in your city?"

"Don't get smart with me, you little bitch! Where is your boss?" she demanded.

"You don't seem to get it. Your days of stealing babies and killing girls like me are over," Lilly said. Her grin stretched wide across her face. It wasn't her intention to engage with either of these two vermin, but this interaction was too much fun for her to pass up.

"Oh, I get it now," the woman said smugly, crossing her arms. "How much?"

"You can't buy your way out of it this time," Lilly said, smiling even wider.

"One of *those*, are you? What? Did you have some junkie whore sister, or cousin, or whatever, decide to do the right thing for once in her life and entrust her baby to me to place in a loving, supportive home? Now she's dead in a gutter somewhere and you want her precious spawn? Sorry kid. No refunds." She scoffed. "By the looks of you, that one went to an overseas client, anyway. You'll never see it again."

Lilly leaned in. "I'm so glad you are being such a witch to me. I'm also glad I didn't rip your throat out the second I saw you," Lilly said, baring her canis.

The woman shrieked and attempted to run. Ophelia and Olivia each grabbed one of her arms, and Lilly gripped her throat hard as the woman struggled and tried to scream. Lilly's gaze bore into the woman's as she entranced her.

"You will not scream. You will not run. You will do everything you are told without making so much as a single noise unless you are spoken to," Lilly growled into her face.

The woman's body slumped, and her eyes glazed over.

"Do you understand me?"

"Yes," the woman replied.

Lilly released her, and Ophelia and Olivia did the same. "Go wait for me in the cave."

The woman toddled off, wobbling as her very high designer heels sunk into the soft dirt.

"Let's get the next one," she said, entering the sequence on the digital pad. "This one will either run or be aggressive."

As soon as the lights were blue, the man shoved the pod lid open and sprung out. "Aren't you a tasty little treat? If you wanted me alone, all you had to do was ask," he said, stalking toward Lilly.

She recoiled in disgust. "Oh, hell no!" Lilly exclaimed. She grabbed his throat and entranced him before he could say anything else. She shuddered, suppressing the urge to puke after touching him.

"Get in the cave!" Lilly shouted at him.

He walked in silence at the slow, intentional pace of a predator.

Lilly opened the third pod and pulled out her pack. She and the service units closed the pod lids and made their way into the cave.

Lilly led the way, followed by Ophelia, the humans, and Olivia at the rear. When the walls closed in, Lilly got a few shallow cuts. The scent of human blood wafted toward her, taking her back to the days when it was the main staple of her diet. She turned her head to apologize to the service units, but she saw no marks on Ophelia. Olivia was too far back, blocked by the others, but she suspected there would be no injuries to her either.

"Are you not getting any cuts, or are your nanites healing you?"

"Our outer shell is harder than the crystalline structure," Ophelia said.

Lilly looked around Ophelia to see a smooth rock surface at Ophelia's shoulder height. Ophelia had knocked the crystals off of the wall as she walked. Lilly hadn't heard them drop into the water because of the amount of noise the human female was making each time her heels sunk into the silt under her.

"Take the shoes off, idiot," Lilly snapped at the woman.

When the woman bent over to comply, she sliced her hip deep, giving Lilly's nose another punch of sweet, metallic heaven.

"Shit!" Lilly said under her breath.

"I detect no feces," Ophelia said.

"They're gonna leak," Lilly said.

"Feces?"

"No. They're bleeding. They're going to leak the resolving medium through their injuries."

"Do you not possess the ability to heal them?" Ophelia asked.

"I don't know if it will work on them in there. I can heal myself, but I don't know about others. It'll be better to do it before we go into the chamber. Switch places with me."

"No."

"Ophelia, I need to give them my blood so their wounds heal."

"My primary, unalterable order is to keep you away from them once we have entered the cave."

Lilly rubbed her forehead. "Okay, there are two syringes of sedatives in my pack. Take one out and empty it."

Ophelia complied, handing Lilly the empty syringe. Lilly filled it with her blood and told Ophelia to inject half into each human then put the empty vessel back into her pack. The humans' wounds healed, and Lilly instructed Ophelia to clear the passage of the sharp formations to keep the humans from further injury. Their clothing was ripped and covered in blood, but Lilly still wished she could have inflicted more pain on them before she healed them. Now she needed to protect them, which she thought sucked.

It wasn't long before they entered the chamber. Lilly ordered the humans to sit in the middle of the floor while Ophelia pulled out a TAC to take some readings.

"Those don't work in here," Lilly said.

"It's working perfectly fine," Ophelia replied.

"It's not even on," Lilly said. The device was black. No lights and no screen.

"Yes, it is. Can you not see the screen?"

"No. Can you?"

"Yes. The readings are unusual, but I can see them."

"That means ..." Lilly turned her head, remembering the other times she was here. "All of us healed. Speed and strength were normal, but we couldn't shift out or sense anything," she mumbled. "Of course! This place doesn't block technology, it blocks us. It's a cell! I'm such an idiot."

She spun back toward Ophelia. "Make sure you set the readings of the substance so you can see if the humans are absorbing it when they touch the wall," Lilly said. She reached out over Ophelia's hand, noticing she could feel the screen. She just couldn't see it. A sense of relief came over her once she understood it was only her; well, anyone with enhanced abilities, but the service units could interact with technology in here.

Lilly had become almost giddy at the idea she was going to get some real data on this place. She ran over to the man, ready to snatch him up and throw him into the wall, when Olivia grabbed her by the shoulders, getting between them.

"Okay, okay. I get it," Lilly said, throwing her hands up. "Hey pervert, go put your hand on the wall."

The man got up and placed his hand on the glowing surface. The light behind the layer swirled around his palm. Lilly didn't dare get close enough to see what was happening under the surface. It wasn't long before his fingertips began to glow and vibrate. Ophelia said he was absorbing the substance. After only a few minutes, Ophelia told Lilly the flow had leveled off, and he was no longer absorbing the resolving medium. Lilly told him to go back and sit on the floor.

Ophelia monitored him while Lilly asked him a few questions. When she approached him, she felt a powerful pull from his blood, almost as strong as she remembered the thirst being before the turned had evolved. The resolving medium mixed with human blood was intoxicating. She took a step back and rubbed her nose.

"What's the last thing you remember?" she asked him.

"Waking up to a tasty treat," he said in a way that made her skin crawl.

"What do you remember before that?"

"I was takin' a piss at a rest stop and it musta been my lucky day, 'cause when I turned around some little scrumptious fortune cookie had wandered into the wrong bathroom all by itself. I was lookin' for my next meal, and lo an' behold, it found me," he said with a deep, guttural laugh.

"Shut up!" Lilly screamed at him. "Why isn't he resolving?"

"I detect no essence to resolve. I believe this one is an empty echo. There is a void where an essence fragment should be," Ophelia said.

"That explains a lot. What about her?"

"I detect no essence in that one, either."

"Okay then. Idiot! Go put your hand on the wall," Lilly ordered the woman.

She complied and Ophelia monitored her until the flow ceased.

While the woman was getting her fill of resolving compound, Lilly turned her attention to the relief panels etched into the wall. A pit formed in her stomach, followed by the sensation of falling, when she again noticed her signature mark on the bottom corner. She glanced over her shoulder at the calculations, but those had no mark. Her eyes focused on every detail of the drawings. It had taken her centuries to develop that style. These weren't old, they were new.

"These can't be here," she whispered.

The events from the last panel didn't happen until after Aphya pulled her out of the cell, which could only mean she came back and added them later. No, it meant she was going to go back and add them later. When this was all over, she would need to go back.

"Lilly." Ophelia called out to her several times before she heard her.

Lilly shook off her stupor and turned back to watch Ophelia take some final readings. She had Ophelia take a photo of the mural before they made their way out of the cave in reverse order of the way they had entered. Olivia led the way, removing any remaining helictites, making their exit much more comfortable. Lilly hung behind the others. The cramped space concentrated the heady draw of the blood and resolving compound, forcing her to keep some distance to remain in control. The concentration also relieved her from thinking about what she knew she needed to do.

Out in the field, she ordered the humans back into their pods. While Olivia and Ophelia secured them, Lilly reviewed the data and sent a copy to Jack. He told her he was almost finished. He wanted to run the new data against the composition of the container to ensure the substance would remain inside once they had extracted it from the humans. She took the delay as a chance to return the unused pod, knowing it wouldn't fit in her workspace with the other two. Once Sadie confirmed the container was safe, Jack messaged Lilly. She messaged him back, letting him know he needed to leave and she would message him when the extraction was complete. After Jack messaged her that he was gone, Lilly turned off her blocking bracelet and shifted the group back to her workroom.

Olivia and Ophelia moved the pods into place at the end of the room while Lilly reviewed Jack's work, running a final simulation with Sadie. The only thing left to do before she began was to get the confinement back from Grace.

CHAPTER THIRTY

Grace shifted into Lilly's workroom to see two bloody humans encased in stasis pods. The metallic scent caught her off guard, causing her canis to descend unprompted. Everything in her gut was pulling her toward them. She needed to drink them. She had never felt the thirst before, but this feeling was euphoric. The intense pull disallowed other thoughts or feelings from entering her mind. It was the basest of needs, an animalistic arousal. A hand grabbed Grace's arm as she moved toward the pods in a haze. She had become so unaware of herself, she didn't comprehend she could phase out of the grasp until Lilly pointed out she was being held back.

"Grace?"

Grace shut her eyes tight, then opened them wide and shook her head, forcing her canis to retract at the same time.

"The draw is so strong. I want to drink them dry," Grace said. Her voice was breathy as her chest heaved.

Lilly pointed to the two service units behind Grace, one of whom was still holding her arm. "That's why they're here."

"Oh," Grace said, coming back to the moment, gaining control over herself again. "I'm fine. You can let go now."

Ophelia released her, placing herself between the pods and the turned. "For your safety, please take a step back over the red line on the floor," she said.

Grace glanced down at her feet, then took a step backward, positioning herself behind the red strip on the floor.

"Thank you," Ophelia said.

The second service unit, Olivia, slipped out from behind Grace to join Ophelia.

"Who are they?" Grace asked Lilly, pointing to the humans.

"It doesn't matter. What does matter is they're containers for our resolving component. Did you bring the confinement?"

Grace held it out, but she pulled her hand back before allowing Lilly to take it.

"Wait, did you kidnap two humans to use for experimentation?"

"Don't judge me. They're serial killers. They murder children. Plus, they're echoes, so they don't matter, anyway."

"I don't care what Aphya said about echoes not being real. They're human, Lilly."

"I wouldn't call these pieces of shit human if they had souls, but they don't. They're empty inside. They didn't resolve when they came in contact with the compound, because there's nothing in there to resolve. It does make them great transportation containers, though. The compound hasn't degraded and the nanites haven't lost their programming, because they haven't done any work yet."

"Where did you kidnap them from?"

"Do you and Viv not talk anymore?"

"Answer me!" Grace demanded.

"Twentieth-century Earth. The ones who disappeared from the list. They disappeared because I took them. I just didn't know it was me when it happened."

"You're not making any sense."

"I don't have time for this. Give me the confinement, go talk to Viv, and she'll fill you in on the rest. Okay?"

Lilly's movement ushered forth a fresh stream of air laced with the decadent scent of blood. Locked in a state of confusion and staving off the urge to satisfy her thirst, Grace couldn't move. Lilly grabbed the orb out of her hand. She recognized the look in Grace's eye. It was one Lilly had fought off for centuries. One that Grace had never experienced. Lilly also knew if Grace lost control, no one could hold her back, and if she got to those humans, The Everything was doomed.

"Grace!" Lilly yelled.

Grace's head snapped back to Lilly.

"You need to leave. Now!"

Grace sucked in her bottom lip, revealing that her canis had again descended. Ophelia and Olivia moved closer together, expecting her movement. To Lilly's relief, Ivan had felt Grace's deep-seated need and shifted in behind her. He took a quick assessment of the situation, wrapped his arms around Grace, and shifted her out.

Lilly exhaled, deflating against the counter. She should have known better than to have Grace come here. The pull was hard enough for her to fight with human blood mixed with resolving compound, and she had an abundance of practice resisting. She had kept Jack away for that very reason, but she had thought Grace wouldn't have a problem. Grace had been part of the community almost as long as Lilly herself—longer, if you counted the years Lilly had gone rogue.

"Are you in need of assistance?" Olivia asked.

"No," Lilly said, pushing herself upright.

It was time for her to begin the process of extracting the component to insert into the confinement. Jack had written the program and built the device. The testing was complete, so she reviewed the checklist one last time. All she needed to do was attach it to a pod and start it up. She placed everything she needed on a cart and rolled it across the room. Ophelia blocked her access to the humans.

"Move," Lilly said.

"No," Ophelia said, holding her ground.

Not this again, Lilly thought. "I need to attach the assembly."

"We are fully capable of attaching the assembly to your specifications. We recommend you position yourself in the observation room."

Lilly hesitated before handing over the cart. "The first thing you need to do …"

Ophelia's eyes moved rapidly from side to side as if she were reading. "We understand the instructions. Thank you." She took the cart and moved it behind her.

"Okay. Well, I guess that's it then," Lilly said, backing toward the door.

She made her way down the hall to the monitoring room for her section and found Jack sitting in front of the monitors.

"I thought I told you to leave," she said.

"You told me to leave the workroom. I couldn't let you have all the fun," he said, grinning widely.

"Fine. You can stay, but sit over there and be quiet," she said, pointing to the side of the control panel.

"It's your show," he said, rolling his chair out of her way.

She took her seat in front of two displays that showed different angles of her workroom, while a third display above them duplicated the pod monitors for the two humans. She reached up to turn on the audio.

"Are you ready, Ophelia?"

"We are in position to proceed."

"Cut your connection to the network," Lilly said.

"Network access disengaged," Ophelia and Olivia confirmed.

"Proceeding with isolating habitation. Cutting off airflow. External ventilation sealed," Lilly said as she performed each of the steps.

"Attaching device to pod one. Confirming seal. Ready to begin the procedure on your command," Olivia said.

Lilly pushed out a nervous breath. "This is gonna work," she whispered to herself.

"Starting blood filter and extraction," she said aloud. She scrolled in her view of the first pod to see two large bore needles being pushed into the man's jugular vein a few inches apart. One was to drain and the other to replace with the cleaned blood. Once the placement was complete, there were two beeps, and she started the filtering program. She fidgeted with the display views, running through each set of data being monitored. The numbers crawled upward at a slow, excruciating rate. She leaned her head back, closed her eyes, and swung the chair from side to side.

Jack kicked the side of her chair after what seemed like hours to her.

"Stop it," she said.

"Look."

She lifted her head to see the percentage climbing faster. Seventy-two percent with eighteen minutes remaining. She breathed out a sigh of relief and leaned forward, resting her chin on her folded hands with her thumbs planted firmly under her jaw. Her posture was stiff and unwavering, as if the less she moved and the more intent her gaze, the faster the process would conclude. The thought of skipping ahead sixteen minutes crossed her mind, but she knew with her luck, she would miss the process's conclusion, so she endured the wait in agony.

The display finally read one hundred percent, zero point zero minutes remaining. The completion tone she had anticipated hadn't come. She looked at Jack, who shrugged back at her.

"Process complete," Sadie said. "Twenty-nine point five milliliters of foreign material collected from the subject."

Once Sadie made the announcement, the needles dislodged from the man's neck.

"Yes!" Lilly shouted, jumping out of her seat.

"Calm down, we're only halfway there," Jack said.

"But it worked."

"Ophelia, disconnect the device and check for leaks," Jack said.

Ophelia reached down to support the device and pressed the release with her thumb. "No contamination detected."

"Now you can celebrate," Jack said to Lilly.

She jumped up and down, pumping her fist into the air. "YES! Yes, yes, yes!"

"Are you done?"

"Yes?" Lilly squeaked.

"Do you want us to attach the device to the next pod?" Olivia asked.

"Proceed to the second pod," Jack said.

Ninety minutes later, the process was complete on the second pod, with twenty-six milliliters extracted. According to the instructions, it was almost twenty-five percent more than the minimum necessary for a confinement of that size with a load of one occupant.

"Now comes the hard part," Lilly said, frowning slightly.

Jack could tell she was anxious about going into the room. "I can do it."

"Oh, hell no. I'm not having Violet come after me if you get resolved in there."

"And you think I like the idea of Mikkel coming after me if you get resolved?"

"He knows I'm stubborn. Plus, there's no way you could stop me," she said.

"That would be offensive if it wasn't true," Jack said with a smirk.

"Sadie, set up a decontamination area inside the door to my workroom."

"Configuring," Sadie replied.

They could see the entrance on the monitor as a small clean area appeared inside.

"Lilly, are you planning on coming in here?" Ophelia asked.

"Yes."

"In order to reduce your exposure risk, we can create a holographic reproduction of the workspace, and you can control my hands remotely," Ophelia suggested.

"I like that idea better," Jack said.

"Me too," Lilly agreed. "Ophelia, create the hologram."

"Please activate your visor so I can link it to my field of vision," Ophelia said.

"Activating."

The room began shifting to the same configuration as Lilly's workspace, and she could see a clear view through Ophelia's eyes.

"Everything is set on my end," Lilly said.

"Begin execution at will," Ophelia said.

Lilly reached out, picking up the device with Ophelia's left hand. She could feel the smooth, cool material as if it were in her own hand. She grasped the container with her right hand and pressed the auto release to separate it from the extraction assembly.

Jack watched the monitor as Ophelia disassembled the unit. She then placed the assembly on the table and picked up the confinement. Lilly hesitated before performing the container placement. Her hand was trembling slightly, and slightly would not cut it with this procedure. It had to be precise, maintaining level pressure over the seals so they could glide over each other without snagging or pulling either off.

"Ophelia, when we press the container seal onto the confinement seal, make adjustments as necessary to have a full, smooth seat before the container is locked in."

"Affirmative," Ophelia replied.

They pressed the container into the opening on the confinement, locking it down. Lilly's shoulders dropped slightly, relieved the procedure was completed.

"Scan for leaks."

"No contamination detected."

"Jack, start the transfer process," Lilly said.

Jack tapped into the display, and the fluid started moving from the container to the confinement. Once it had finished, they were ready to separate the seals, leaving both items in an airtight condition. They pressed detents on both parts and twisted, releasing the container from the confinement and placing both parts on the table.

"Thank you, Ophelia. End the link and check for leaks," Lilly said, tapping her ring to stow her visor.

"No contamination detected," Ophelia said.

Upon hearing those last, beautiful words, Lilly dropped to the floor and lay on her back.

~~~~

"What the hell was that?" Grace asked, rubbing her chest.

"That was probably the closest thing to the turned's thirst that you'll experience," Ivan said, handing her a scotch.

She took a large mouthful, letting it glide down her throat as slow as possible so she could feel the burn. "That's what you were fighting against for centuries?"

"Something similar. The physical effects were the same, but the pull to the humans in Lilly's lab had a hypnotic component to it, whereas the true thirst was mostly animalistic."

"I don't think I could have done it for as long as you did."

"It's a lot easier to resist if you're not starving."

"I'm not starving," Grace said, shaking her head and taking another swig of her drink.

Ivan scratched his head. "I know, but the smell of that blood made me feel like I was starving, so that's the only way I can describe it."

"How is Lilly resisting it?"

"Lilly is an exceptionally resourceful woman," Ivan said, feeling an unusual amount of pride mixed with sadness and guilt.

Grace picked up the strange mixture of sweet, bitter, and smoky scents emanating from him. It wasn't the first time she'd smelled those emotions on him since he went back to ask Lilly to scribe the instructions, so she set the occurrence aside, certain he would talk about it when he was ready. She had seen what happened, but she didn't have the right to pry into something so personal, even if he was her mate.

"I think I need to go for a run," she said, giving him a soft kiss on the cheek. "Are you going to be okay without me for a while?"

"I'm sure I can find something to do while you're gone," Ivan said, rubbing her shoulder. "Go. I'll catch up with you later."

Grace changed into her running gear and shifted to her favorite path in the mountains. She had so much to unpack from the last twenty-five
~~~~

hours. As much as she had looked forward to finding Aphya, the woman had turned her world upside down. If she really looked at the life she knew, Aphya had been pulling the strings for all of it. Grace's very creation in this world was at her hands. Aphya influenced who Frigg chose for her father and her husband, and she had been instrumental in Grace's abilities being suppressed for all but the last few hundred years. How different would her life have been if she had understood what she was from the beginning?

"Renata would have pulled you out of here a lot sooner and I wouldn't have had time to create a shell for Ivan," Aphya said.

The voice echoed around her. Grace stopped and spun in circles, searching for it. Aphya dropped out of a tree in front of her.

"Nobody ever looks up," Aphya said.

"Why are you here?"

"You called me."

"Not on purpose," Grace said. She resumed running, stepping around Aphya. To her surprise, Aphya began running beside her.

"I can teach you how to use your abilities."

"I know how to use them," Grace said.

"Not very well."

"Whose fault is that?" Grace snapped.

"Mine."

Grace wasn't expecting that answer and wasn't certain how to follow up after Aphya had taken responsibility.

"If you don't want to accept my help with training, at least listen," Aphya said.

Grace said nothing, but she hadn't shifted away either. Aphya matched Grace's pace step for step.

"Energy flows through you."

Grace cut her eyes to the side, rolling them back to the front.

"It flows. You're trying to control it, bend it in ways it doesn't move naturally. It doesn't work that way."

"I've created galaxies. I think my flow is just fine," Grace defended.

"With Ivan. He buffers you."

Grace couldn't reply because Aphya was right. Since the time in the woods of Hel, she had always had trouble controlling the direction of her energy.

"Those wild tosses are a symptom of your incorrect approach."

"Stay out of my head!" Grace exclaimed, picking up her speed.

"I'm only trying to help you," Aphya said, catching up to Grace.

"You're not helping me, you're irritating me. I come out here to clear my head so I can think."

"I'll make you a deal," Aphya said. "I'll leave you alone if you agree to meet me in two hours so I can help you figure this out."

Grace answered by shifting away. When she thought of shifting to Hel, a sense of satisfaction washed over her. There was no way Aphya could detect her shift here. The cold felt good as she ran through the woods. The rhythm of the snow crunching under her feet was peaceful, almost as hypnotizing as a metronome would be for a musician. Until she heard a second set of footfalls behind her.

"That was rude, Grace," Aphya said.

"How did you follow my shift?"

"I didn't. I shifted to you."

"This place is blocked," Grace said. Her pace had slowed as she spoke.

"Not for shifting. Now, what about our meeting? How about that tract over there with the logs on the ground?" Aphya asked, pointing to an open area.

"Two hours isn't long enough," Grace said.

"No problem. I can run with you."

Grace picked her pace back up.

Aphya came up beside her. "The scenery is interesting here. The way the trees twist and turn at odd angles. I've never seen them grow like that anywhere else. The trunks are so dark they almost look burned, don't they?"

Grace knew what she was trying to do, but she couldn't take Aphya's babbling for another minute. She also knew she needed the help. Phasing had always come naturally to her because she could feel all the cells in her body. Porting and shifting were easy because she could feel how others were doing it and mimic it. Those were internal things she could control, but Aphya was right about her not being able to control her energy flow. She could harness it and push it out, but once it left her, it seemed to take on an errant path of its own that she couldn't figure out how to change. She had felt the way Ivan did it, but it didn't work the same for her. It was time to put away her pride and accept Aphya's offer.

"If you go away, I will meet you in three hours," she said.

"Three?"

"Yes. Three."

"Deal," Aphya said and shifted away, leaving Grace to her peace.

It seemed far too easy, which made her suspicious.

CHAPTER THIRTY-ONE

"What is going on here?" Grace asked. She had arrived to see Ivan, Ben, and The Three standing behind Aphya.

"They all want to help you," Aphya said.

"Looks like more of an ambush than a training session," Grace said.

Aphya turned her back to Grace, facing the group. "What would you say Grace's fighting style is?"

"She chops. Short, incomplete strokes," Ben said.

"Aggressive," Alex said.

"There is a disconnect between her energy expenditure versus her stroke power, and her swing patterns are erratic," Erik said.

"Hey! I've always been an excellent fighter!" Grace exclaimed defensively.

"You've always been lucky you can phase, or you'd have been dead a million times over," Mikkel said, chuckling.

"We're not attacking her. We are trying to establish what we need to do to help her with her flow," Aphya said.

"I learned through cutting hay and wheat," Ivan said. He searched the others' faces, ensuring no one was going to burst out in laughter. "My mother taught me steps and arm movements with a wooden pole before placing a scythe in my hands. There's a rhythm to it. If you don't swing it right, you could lose a foot."

"Cute anecdote, Ivan, but most farmers aren't good fighters," Alex said.

"That's not true," Mikkel said. "I've known a lot more farmers than you, and I guarantee if they wanted to fight instead of working their asses off to feed your smug face, they could. They're strong. They understand a tool is a weapon and vice versa, and they're far more intelligent than you give them credit for."

"Not the point," Aphya said, turning back to Grace. "Did you notice none of their descriptions contained the words smooth, agile, or graceful?"

"Couldn't resist that one, could you?" Grace asked.

"You've always faced things from a place of power and strength. Harnessing energy requires finesse. When you inflict pain, you have full control over that process. What's the difference between that and directing, say, an energy ball?"

Grace reached up, grasping at that ever-present piece of loose hair. "Inflicting pain is still an internal process for me."

"How so?"

"Well, I produce the amount of pain inside of me and direct it to where I want to inflict it."

"How is moving a ball of energy different?" Aphya asked.

"When there is a concentration of energy, whether I've created it or someone else has, it's already external. I push it toward where I want it to go."

"Can you show me?"

"Uh, yeah," Grace said, moving to a spot where she wouldn't hit anyone.

She took a solid stance, locking her knees in place and holding her hands out in front of her, rubbing her palms together until she formed a small glowing orb. Next, she concentrated hard, pushing the ball away from her by shoving her arms forward. It twisted and spiraled out of control, hitting a tree off in the distance.

Mikkel and Alex cheered, but Ivan shushed them.

"What were you aiming for?" Aphya asked.

"The rocks to the left," Grace said as a blush of red covered her cheeks.

"Do you dance?"

"What?" Grace said.

"No," Ben answered.

"She can slow dance, but she always tries to take the lead," Ivan added.

"Hm … Grace, make another ball," Aphya said.

Grace gave Aphya a skeptical glance. Within a few seconds, she had created another orb.

"This time, pretend it's something delicate, like a soap bubble. If you push it too hard, it will pop. Gently release it from your fingertips without pushing your arms out."

Grace opened her hands, extending her fingers outward. The orb moved a few feet in front of her and stopped.

"Yes." Grace said, holding her hands steady.

Aphya moved beside her. "Using a slow motion, keep your top hand in place and lower your bottom hand."

Grace moved a little too fast, and the orb dropped a few inches. She sucked air in between her teeth, making a hissing noise.

"It's okay. Hold it there," Aphya said. She placed her hand behind Grace's. "Now, we're going to move in slow, gentle movements from side to side."

Aphya guided Grace's hand to the left a few inches, and the orb followed suit, moving a few feet left. They repeated the motion to the right, then up and down until the orb rested in its original position.

"Try it on your own," Aphya said. She removed her hand from behind Grace's.

When Grace moved her hand on her own, the orb moved in a stuttered path, but she didn't overpower it, which was surprising to everyone.

"Excellent. Can you bring it back?"

The observers held their breath. Grace opened her hand and flicked her fingers back. The orb flew at her harder than she intended. She took a step back and awkwardly caught it, ducking her head out of the way before it hit her face.

"Very good. Go ahead and absorb it," Aphya said. "Did you feel a difference when you were respectful of it instead of trying to force it?"

"I did. I wish someone would have explained it to me sooner," Grace said.

Ivan bit his lips together to keep himself from saying something snide that would deter her progress. He had been trying for centuries to explain it to her, but he was glad she finally understood the concept, no matter who got the credit.

"I think the next thing we need to look at is your fluidity. Moving energy has more in common to moving water or air than shooting an arrow or lobbing a cannonball," Aphya said.

She signaled for The Three to come to the center of the clearing.

"You've seen your sons fight before, haven't you?" Aphya asked.

"Of course."

Ben tossed each of them a short sparring pole, keeping a longer one for himself and passing another long one to Ivan. "On," he said.

Each of them pressed a spot on the handle, activating a different colored light on the end of each pole. The forest surrounding Hel wasn't pitch black, but even on its brightest days, the sky was foggy and dim. The tiny neon lights were bright enough to create light trails when the men moved them around.

"When they start, don't watch *them*," Aphya said.

"You don't want me to watch them?" Grace asked.

"I want you to watch the lights."

"Okay." Grace kicked a grounded log behind her to shake off the snow and took a seat. "Might as well be comfortable."

Ivan and Ben had moved to opposite sides of The Three, who had taken up their signature back-to-back stance. Their triangle of triplets gave them a three-hundred-sixty-degree view, which few had been able to penetrate. The Three would use their shorter poles as swords, while Ben and Ivan would use theirs as staffs.

"Begin," Aphya said.

To anyone without the advanced sight of the turned, the melee would appear as nothing more than a flurry of swirling light. Grace could see the individual techniques of each wielder in slow motion. Alex's cascade of full, deep swings were swooping and encompassed the entire breadth of the space in front of him. Erik's strikes had a calculating quality, allowing him to make contact with extreme precision and perfect follow-throughs, while Mikkel's curving swings had a beautiful flourish to them. Ivan and Ben had complementary spinning techniques, leaving Grace to wonder if it was due to the style of weapon they were using or if they had developed a similar elegance from being long-time sparring partners.

"Do you see how this entire display is fluid, like a dance moving forward and back, spinning and swaying, creating a rhythm?" Aphya asked.

"Yeah, but they're sparring. They're not trying to kill each other," Grace said. "It's pretty. It's not practical."

"Stop!" Aphya yelled.

The action came to an immediate halt.

"Why don't you try it?"

"That's what I'm talking about," Grace said, jumping up.

"Alex, Erik, come out. Mikkel, you get to partner with your mother," Aphya said.

"I have a condition!" Ben exclaimed. "No phasing a weapon solid inside of somebody."

Grace narrowed her eyes at him. "I learned that lesson already, Ben."

"I just wanted it stated for the record," he said.

"Noted," Grace said in a snide tone.

"Erik, can you please record this?" Aphya asked.

"It'll be my pleasure," he answered.

They began sparring and Alex spent the entire two minutes wincing, barely able to watch Grace's poor technique.

"Did you see? I made more strikes than any of them and didn't get hit once," Grace said, brimming with pride in her performance.

"That's because you phased anytime someone tried to hit you or your weapon. I got hit at least a dozen times because you let a strike go through you," Mikkel said, rubbing his back. "How many times did you get hit because I let one through? Zero, because I wouldn't do that to my partner."

"Sorry honey, but you could have phased too," Grace said.

"What if Mikkel had been a mortal? He'd be dead, wouldn't he, Mother?" Alex asked.

"Let's bring this back down. We don't need to be aggressive. It was a learning exercise," Aphya said. "Can you play that back, Erik?"

"Gladly," Erik said, pressing play.

"Do you see the differences in the way you performed versus everyone else? Lunging, chopping, stalking. It's powerful and aggressive, and not a bad style for you, given your other abilities. The problem is, it isn't a style that lends itself to the fluidity required to work with energy," Aphya said.

"I … uh, I can see that," Grace said. Seeing the way she fought made her think of a wounded bull bucking wildly at anything that got close, including Mikkel, who she hit more than once.

"What kind of dance do you suggest to help her with whatever that is?" Ivan asked.

"Ivan!" Grace exclaimed, taking offense at the comment.

"What would you call that? Do you see yourself?" Ivan asked.

"I'm not sure there is any kind of dance that could help. I'm thinking something more basic," Aphya said.

"You mean …?" Ben asked.

"Yujom," Aphya said.

Mikkel and Alex tried their hardest to hold back from snickering.

"That's for children," Grace said.

"Did you learn it as a child?" Ben asked.

"You know I didn't."

"What is Yujom?" Ivan asked.

"The closest correlation from your planet would be a blending of Tai Chi and Yoga. Slow flowing movements for awareness, repetitive patterns for flexibility, and long periods of position holds for strength and self-reflection. It's quite relaxing. I still do it from time to time, and I plan on teaching my son when he starts walking," Erik said.

"How about you practice your patience with Mom, mister teacher," Mikkel said, before belting out a laugh.

"I'd be happy to," Erik said, putting a stop to Mikkel's obnoxious chiding. "I've been showing Asta some basics. You're more than welcome to join us. We'll begin after dinner, around twenty-one hundred, if it's good for you?"

"Perfect," Grace said, staring into Mikkel's eyes.

~~~~

Grace showed up at Erik's at the designated time. When he opened the door, she was dressed very strangely in some kind of brightly colored tights that looked like someone had poured paint on them and a top that looked like one of Asta's bras.

"What are you wearing?" he asked.

"This is what Earth women wore for exercise classes in the early part of the twenty-first century," she answered.

He grabbed her arm and pulled her inside, looking up and down the hall to make sure no one had seen her. "What you had on to run in was fine."

"I thought this was fun."

"Oh my blazing stars," Asta said. "I haven't seen anything like that since we got here. Where did you get those?"

"I had Sadie replicate them from the archive. Fun, right?"

"It sure looks … comfortable," Asta said.
~~~~

"Come on back; let's get started," Erik said.

"Is the baby up?" Grace asked.

"Just got him tucked under his sleep hood. Next time, I'll keep him up till you get here," Asta said.

They walked to the back of the apartment to a large entertainment room, where the sofa had been pushed up against the wall. Erik set up a holographic Yujom instructor at the front of the room. He and Asta took the sides, leaving Grace in the center in front of the instructor.

"This session is set to three quarters time at the beginner level, so if you need something repeated, say 'again.' Okay?" Erik asked.

"Sounds easy enough," Grace said.

"That's what I thought when I started," Asta said.

The session began slowly enough, but less than thirty minutes into it, Grace was having difficulty. She had turned in the wrong direction twice, bumped into Erik, and stepped on Asta, and there was still an hour and a half left to go. It was doing nothing for her already fragile confidence. Eventually, Erik slowed it down to half time and Grace did much better. By the end, she was able to perform the basic steps without tripping or stepping on anyone. Her favorite part was the end when they sat in silence, listening to the ambient sounds of the room.

"I'll transfer this to your entertainment system so you can practice whenever you want. Once you can complete it at full speed, let me know and we can do the next one together," Erik said.

"If you want someone to practice with, you can message me. I've only been doing this one at full speed for about a week. I was surprised how far off your body gets after you have a baby. I thought for sure I'd be back to where I was by now," Asta said.

"It's nothing to be upset about. It's only been a few months," Grace said.

"Yeah, but we heal so fast. Why is it different after having a baby?" she asked.

"I think they must take something out of you that's hard to get back."

"Maybe. Anyway, let me know if you need a workout buddy. I'm going to go shower up. Goodnight," Asta said and left the room.

"Night, Asta," Grace said. She leaned over to give Erik a hug. "Thank you for not making me feel stupid."

"Thanks for being a good sport. I really think this will help you. It'll teach you a little restraint. Maybe even curb some of that impulsive behavior of yours," Erik teased.

"Maybe," Grace said as she stepped out into the hall.

"Oh, and don't wear that outfit again," Erik said quickly before he shut the door.

CHAPTER THIRTY-TWO

"I don't know why I'm so nervous," Grace said.

"It's reasonable. The last time you were in front of the Council was that scene at the wedding," Ben replied.

"Don't remind me," Grace said, placing her head in her hands. "I feel like I need to throw up."

"If it'll make you feel better, go ahead."

Grace sighed. "You're not helping."

"I don't know why you're so nervous. She's gonna be doing all the heavy lifting," Mikkel said, tossing his thumb toward Aphya. He sat slumped on the bench across from Grace with his head leaned against the wall.

Aphya winced, and Alex smacked Mikkel on the upper arm with the back of his hand.

"Ow!" Mikkel exclaimed. "Don't take your frustration out on me. I don't like waiting any more than you do. Why are we letting them make us wait out here, anyway?"

Erik sighed and looked over the top of the device he had been reading. "It's called respect. We want their cooperation, so we'll let them make us uncomfortable for a while because right now, they feel important. If we burst in and demand their help, they'll think we actually need them for something more than a distraction and they'll probably turn us down flat."

"If we don't need them, then why are we here?" Mikkel asked.

Erik rolled his eyes and went back to his reading.

"It will help heal your broken relationship with them while also showing Renata a united front," Aphya said.

"And it might be enough of a diversion to keep Mom and Ivan alive, dumbass," Alex added.

"Alex, there's no need for that," Grace said.

"He doesn't even care. He gets to be up there with you while Erik and I are stuck on the ground, working crowd control."

"It's not my fault you can't rise," Mikkel taunted.

Alex sprang out of his seat and rushed at Mikkel, who scrambled to move away. Ben grabbed the back of Alex's jacket, yanking him backward and shoving him back onto the bench.

"Stop it," he growled as the door in the center of the room swung open.

Grace's stomach sank when she recognized the scribe who stepped through the door as the same one who had been at her trial.

The scribe nodded at Ben, and he returned the gesture in acknowledgment. "They're ready for you to take your seat, sir."

Ben nodded to Grace and entered the chamber through the door the scribe was holding open. The scribe scampered through after Ben, shutting the door behind him.

A few minutes later, the scribe opened the door and pointed at Grace. "Come with me."

Grace and Aphya both rose.

"Just you," said the scribe.

"She's with me," Grace said.

"I don't care."

"Scribe, she needs to attend with me," Grace said in a staunch but friendly manner.

The scribe shrank into himself slightly but kept his composure.

"Name?" he asked, looking down at his device.

Aphya made an insignificant head shake, signaling to Grace not to tell him.

"It's not necessary," Grace said, keeping her tone casual.

The scribe peered up at her with a clear, irritated expression. "I need a name."

Grace didn't want to threaten the man since he was only trying to do his job, but Aphya, for some reason, didn't want her identity known.

"Do you remember your last encounter with Ivan?" she asked.

The scribe swallowed hard, and Grace glimpsed Mikkel snickering in the corner. *Don't,* she warned.

"As long as she says nothing and sits in the back," the scribe said, examining Aphya with disdain. "Follow me."

He turned and walked through the door, letting it swing behind him. Grace caught it and the women followed. He pointed to the last seat, directing Aphya to sit. He then took several rapid steps up the aisle to make his announcement.

"I present Grace Novak, primordial goddess of …"

He looked back at Grace, who shrugged. She didn't know what she was supposed to be the goddess of anymore.

"Grace Novak, primordial goddess, requests an audience with the Council of the Divine, assembled by Ananke, the Primordial personification of inevitability, compulsion, and necessity."

The scribe bowed low before scurrying off to take his seat at the side of the room, leaving Grace standing alone in front of a crowded gallery of deities.

Ananke took her seat. "You may be seated," she said, gesturing to the table in front of her.

Some of the other panelists began pointing toward the stranger at the back of the room and mumbling.

"Silence," Ananke decreed.

She moved her attention back to Grace. "Ben declined to inform us of the purpose of your presence, although he urged us to approve your request. You could have shown up here anytime you wanted, but you chose to make your request for an audience in the appropriate manner. It makes us wonder if this is a manipulation of some sort."

"You give me too much credit. It was my intention to be respectful of your ways. I don't think I could possibly manipulate anyone on this panel."

"Hmmm." Ananke placed her hand on her chin and tapped her lip with the long nail of her index finger. "I wonder then, is this a necessity or a compulsion? Possibly both?"

"It is neither. I am here as a courtesy," Grace said.

"A courtesy? Well then, one Primordial to another—have you come to pledge your allegiance to the rightful rulers of The Everything?" Ananke asked with a sly smile.

"No," Grace replied, flashing her own grin.

"What business do you have, then? We already have a truce, do we not?"

"We do."

"I ask again, what business do you have before the Council?"

"I bring information about the hole forming between The Everything and The Nothing," Grace said, pursing her lips momentarily.

"Hole? The thin spot has grown into a hole? I thought our truce compelled that type of information to be shared. How long have you known about this?"

"Only a few days. There are developments that go along with it that need to be shared." Grace couldn't see Kali, but she glared at Ares. Either they had kept the information to themselves or they had told the Council but Ananke was using the situation to make it look like the turned were hiding it from them.

"For you to request an audience, it must be something dire," Ananke said as her forehead wrinkled and her mouth tightened.

"Unfortunately, it is. If you'll allow me, it would be easier if I could share a memory with you," Grace said.

"You? Share a memory with all of us? At the same time? How could you possibly be capable of that, when most *first-generation* Primordials don't have that ability?" Ananke asked, smirking at Grace.

Others began snickering, causing Ananke to chuckle. At the sound, several Council members began outwardly laughing. Ben leaned forward and smirked at Grace, aware of what these people were about to experience.

"May I?" Grace asked, raising her voice to be heard through the laughter that had erupted.

"Of course. We haven't been this entertained in eons," Ananke said.

Grace closed her eyes and breathed in a long, deep breath. She blew out, opening her eyes and pressing the palms of her hands out in front of her. The panel went silent as the wave of memory overtook them. One moment they were sitting in the chamber, laughing at the audaciousness of this upstart sitting before them, and the next the deep black chill of space surrounded them as they faced the opening between The Everything and The Nothing.

Ben was kicking himself for not moving before being caught in her cognitive imagery for a second time. At least he wouldn't be exposed to the emotional component. Maybe he could pay better attention and learn something new this round.

Grace showed them everything from the encounter with Renata on The Outside to Aphya's interrogation. To Ben's displeasure, she also showed them the events that had taken place in The Six the morning before. When she produced the experience of what had taken place in the cave with Lilly and Aphya, she felt Ben's anger at her. She hadn't shown him that before they came, but she couldn't fathom why he would be so upset about it. The Council members had as much right to know as their leadership did, and Galin had agreed with her when she showed him and the committee earlier that day. Their entire foundation was built on as much transparency as possible. Since the information was moving through Sadie to their own community, the Council was certain to find out eventually. It was better to have it come from her. It was certainly better to come out now while they still had hope of doing something about it.

Once the Council members recovered sufficiently, they all began turning their attention to Aphya. She stood, causing collective gasps from most occupants of the room. As she walked up the aisle, she surrounded herself with a white glow and morphed into the older woman Grace and Ivan had first met, then back into her most current form.

Mutterings abounded from the other members, while Ben sat back and chuckled at Aphya's display. No matter how much he distrusted her, he had to admit—she knew how to bring a bit of drama to the proceedings.

"We should kill her now and end all of this," Moloch shouted, pointing to Aphya.

"You could try, but if you succeed, do you believe Renata would hold her word and show you mercy?" Aphya asked.

"We don't need her mercy!" someone shouted from the back of the assembly.

"You are a fool, if that is the way you think," Ananke scolded.

"How did you not see this coming, Ananke? Aren't you the most powerful oracle?" another voice shouted.

More mutterings and a few angry utterances erupted from the gathering.

"I saw only an inevitable battle coming," Ananke shouted over them. "Without an understanding of the cause, there was no necessity to burden you with my vision until I could discern more. You know as well as I, battles are a constant in our world."

Grace grew tired of the sniping and summoned Alex to bring his brothers into the chamber. She was well capable of silencing the place herself; however, she didn't want the precarious situation to erupt from voices to violence. No one would be frivolous enough to step out of line with The Three in the room, and no one would have the courage to turn them away.

Alex flung the door open hard enough to lodge the handle into the wall. Everyone's attention was drawn to the explosive bang, and they watched as The Three strode through with a confidence only the undefeated could carry. Silence overtook the bickering, replaced by an uneasy rumbling accompanied by the pungent stench of fear. Not all were fearful, but enough to force Grace to press her chin into her chest to avoid retching.

Zeus stood, carrying all the regality he had lacked in his last encounter with Grace aboard *The Ker*. The scribe scrambled to the door, attempting to dislodge it and assess the damage.

"You have not been granted permission to interrupt these proceedings," he decreed, chasing behind them as if he had a chance of doing anything to make them leave.

Show your respect, Grace thought to her sons.

The Three stopped and knelt before Zeus.

"Our apologies, Zeus. We heard raised, angry voices and felt our mother's unease. She is well outnumbered, and we have come to ensue her safety. We request permission to observe the proceedings," Alex said.

"We are no threat to her safety," Zeus said.

"Then we are no threat to you," Alex said, nodding as he and his brothers rose to their feet in a synchronized motion.

Zeus nodded curtly and returned to his seat. The Three made their way to the viewing gallery, taking positions as close to Grace as possible, well within the eyeline of the entire assembly.

The discussion proceeded in an orderly manner from that point forward, encompassing several hours of questions for Grace and Aphya. After a long, exhausting session, they were dismissed. When they stood, The Three came to their feet as well and proceeded to follow them out of the room.

"That went well," Aphya said once they had exited into the waiting room.

"I don't think we were in the same meeting," Grace said.

"Don't be so hard on yourself. You did well."

The Three pushed past the pair, who were blocking their access to the bar at the end of the room.

"Excuse us," Erik said, requesting pardon for himself and his inconsiderate brothers.

"They were shitting themselves," Mikkel said, picking up a container of dark ale.

Erik snatched it out of his hand. "Don't be so crass."

"Why else would they shoo us out of the chamber the second they ran out of questions?" Mikkel asked, picking up another drink.

Alex seized the second container from Mikkel before he could bring it to his lips.

"Oh, I dunno. Maybe they want to discuss it? Because, as angry and confused as they are, they're also practical and unwilling to jump into an unwinnable scenario with the impulsiveness of a child," Alex said, leaning into Mikkel's personal space.

Mikkel sighed and picked up yet another container of ale. Without wasting a moment, he took a sip of his drink to prevent it from being snatched from his hand as well.

"It was a lot of information to absorb, and I was concerned they would have at least as much difficulty with it as Lilium did," Aphya said, reaching for a glass of nectar. She backed out of the space between Alex and the wall to be in a less confining location on the other side of the room.

"Lilly only had difficulty because of the pressure on her to create the confinement. No one in there has any real stake in the situation, especially if they don't believe us," Grace said.

Aphya cut her eyes at Grace and shared a private message. *Except for Kali. Is there a reason you left her part out of what you shared?*

There's no need to embarrass her or label her a traitor to the Council, now that the priority has changed to ensuring the survival of the confinement rather than escaping it.

"True," Aphya said aloud, as an answer to both of Grace's statements.

"There's nothing we can do now but wait," Grace said. She tapped Mikkel's shoulder, urging him to vacate his spot, and stepped up to retrieve a cup of nectar.

How does the plan change if they say no? Alex asked the group, changing their conversation to telepathic mode. He was certain they were being monitored.

It doesn't. We won't have the show of force behind us that we want, but we have a fair amount already, Grace said.

What if they send their own negotiator to The Outside to speak with Renata? Alex asked.

It's a possibility. I'm not sure how they'll be able to find the doorway, though. Grace said.

Why do we need to converse in private? What about all that stuff we said before the meeting? Mikkel asked.

Because none of that was tactical, Mikkel. It was mostly us bickering and speaking disparagingly about our hosts, which they should have expected, Erik said.

They hadn't been waiting long when Ben came out of the room.

"What's happening?" Grace asked.

"They're taking a vote," Ben said.

"Why aren't you voting?" Alex asked.

"It's a direct conflict," Ben said.

"How did it seem like it was going when you left?" Aphya asked.

"It's hard to tell with them." Ben picked up a container of ale from the bar. "I'm sure they're in there trying to find some kind of political advantage in this situation."

He looked up at the corner of the room and spoke into a spot Grace assumed was the camera.

"There is no political advantage. You help or you don't. It's your call. The sole consideration for you is that there will be no recognition for you in our victory, and in the unfortunate event of a loss, you won't know. If you're not resolved, you will be dead."

Ben crossed the room, taking a seat across from the spot that had captured his attention. As if on cue, the others each took a seat and remained silent until the door swung open again. The scribe came through, ushering them back into the chamber.

"The Council is ready to render its decision."

Everyone stood to enter. The scribe stopped no one, and they all made their way down to the front of the room as a group.

"You may take your seats," Ananke said.

Ben stayed with his group as everyone sat.

"After an intense discussion, we have weighed all factors and cast our votes on the issue regarding the perceived threat from what you refer to as The Outside," Ananke said. "It is our decision, as a whole, that the turned have caused this situation, in its entirety. Therefore, we will not be taking part in or supporting your actions in this matter."

The smugness with which she delivered their results wasn't unexpected to Grace. She stood, and the rest of her party followed suit.

"Thank you for your consideration," Grace said. She moved behind her chair and pushed it under the table.

"You're just going to leave? No questions. No statement. Nothing?" Ananke asked.

"Your decision is final. There is nothing left to discuss," Grace answered.

"Are you not curious why we decided as we did?" Ananke asked.

"We respect your choice of not wanting to place your citizens in harm's way. It is not our place to ask how or why you concluded as you did," Grace said.

"What if our negative response was because of a necessity? Would you not be curious to know of that?" Ananke asked.

"Are you trying to negotiate?" Ben asked gruffly.

"You are speaking out of turn. Only your designated representative may speak to this issue."

"Well then, I'll ask. Are you trying to negotiate with us?" Grace asked.

"We do not possess the funds to launch an offensive on this scale," Ananke said.

"If we fail, the dead need no funds," Grace said.

The group turned away and headed up the aisle.

From behind them, a familiar voice spoke. "My pantheon does not require funding. We will support your cause."

The group turned to see Kali standing at the back of the gallery.

"Kali, we appreciate and welcome your willingness to assist us with the utmost respect. Our planning session will be in two days. Once Ben solidifies the details, he will send them to you," Grace said and nodded at Kali, who returned the gesture.

They turned again to leave when another voice boomed behind them.

"My pantheon will support your cause," Zeus said. His ego would allow no one to overshadow his in speech or gesture. Grace believed Kali's support had forced his hand, but she wasn't about to spit on a gift.

"Zeus, we also appreciate and welcome your willingness to assist us with the utmost respect. Ben will forward you details as well. Thank you both," Grace said, nodding respectfully.

This time, when they turned to leave, no one else spoke. They felt thrilled and relieved by the way it had turned out. Zeus and Kali had the largest and strongest pantheons in the Council. Their support was more than enough to establish a strong defensive force.

I knew Kali would step forward and support us, Aphya said.

Don't fool yourself, Aphya. Kali's a survivor. She would never leave her fate in someone else's hands. She's going to fight on the side with the best chance of winning, Ben said.

CHAPTER THIRTY-THREE

Renata stood in front of the confinement, allowing the betrayal she felt to smolder. How could they have gone against her? She had given them everything they could have ever wanted. She had designed every detail of her world to be perfect, and they had no respect for her efforts. They didn't need to lift a finger for anything. She had done all the hard work.

It upset her so much that it had come to this. She had crafted each and every one of them with so much care and hope. They had been born with the potential to be perfect. She had given them so many chances to become what she wanted them to be, only to be rewarded with disappointment and disrespect time after time.

Her joy had been boundless the day the first of her children came into existence. Her greatest desire was to bring forward a more peaceful race than the one she had come from. In her new world, there would be no hunger or anger. There would be no violence or indiscriminate punishment for unknown crimes. No need would go unfulfilled, and no loneliness would be ignored. They would be a race that could never become sick or meet their true end by accident or illness. It would be a race that would live forever, changing and molding their reality the way she wanted to create the best possible existence for them all.

She educated them and taught them to care for each other. She trained them in the arts, in music, sculpture, painting. Their lives were supposed to be splendid and beautiful. They had all they could have ever wanted, and the only things she asked for in return were obedience and gratitude.

It had been what she hoped for, but it wasn't what she received. They gave her neither gratitude nor obedience. The bitterness she felt the first time one of them disrespected her with the word "no" reverberated through her to this day. They became spoiled and undisciplined because of her own actions. By giving them no responsibilities, she had created them to feel entitled to her generosity. None of them understood what it meant to work for something they wanted, to be rewarded for something outside of mere existence. They were beyond redemption. Resolving them inside of the containment hadn't even been enough to quell their rebellious natures.

No, there was no other choice. She couldn't risk sanitizing the containment and having the same problems arise again. She had reached her breaking point with their relentless defiance, realizing that it was futile to attempt to bring any of them back under control. These deep, ingrained blemishes had become impossible to remove and marred their very natures. They had no purpose left if they were incapable of providing her happiness. The appalling visit from Grace moments earlier had shown her they had only gotten worse since they had been inside the confinement. The only option she had left was to end their existence and start over with the remaining few she had under her control. Putting them down was the most compassionate thing she could do for them. Unfortunately, she needed to obliterate the entire confinement to end so many at once. The business at hand was distasteful, but it was a necessary undertaking that could no longer be avoided.

The logistics of the task would be a hefty undertaking. The confinement had grown so large, she would need to siphon off some of the energy first or risk damaging her own world. It would take longer than she had planned. She would need to drain the more concentrated centers of energy first. It wouldn't alarm the confinement's occupants if she neutralized bits here and there. They were so preoccupied with their own entanglements, she couldn't imagine any of them taking notice. Pitting them against each other hadn't worked the way she had wanted it to, but it had created enough of a diversion for this to work. She also needed to find a way to sequester Grace away from the others to complete her task.

"Yes," she murmured to herself, acknowledging the brilliance of the plan but also realizing that it would entail her having to go in for another time. She was contemplating the inconvenience these actions would cause her when Ivan fell out onto the cold stone floor in front of her.

"This is becoming a regular occurrence with this confinement. What name have you chosen for yourself in this form?"

"Ivan."

"Hm. Have you come to inform me you have accepted my generous offer?"

Ivan pulled himself from the floor, drawing his confidence with him. He hadn't expected her to be standing above him when he came out, and her presence had thrown him off. Within moments, he collected himself and regained his clarity.

"I've come to negotiate on our behalf."

"There is nothing to negotiate. I've stated my terms with utmost clarity. You may accept or reject them. There is no negotiating."

His gravitas enraged her. How did he think he was in any position to change the terms? She was in charge, not him. This was her world. Everything in it was her creation.

"I know you said that Aphya had been imprisoned because she committed a genocide against her own people, but if we are alive and well inside of the confinement, why would she need to be eliminated? She did nothing to earn a life sentence."

"Did nothing?!" Renata sneered. "You have no idea what she did! What all of you did!"

"You're right. We don't. We have no memories of anything from before."

"It doesn't matter if you have memories of your crimes. Don't you see? Even after resolving, none of you have changed. You come out here demanding things of me as if you deserve consideration. You act as though you have a right to my generosity. How dare you pretend you deserve anything more than what you've already stolen from me!"

"You said the confinement was specifically for Aphya, but you knew we were all in there the entire time, didn't you?"

"Look around you. Each of these boxes contains a confinement. See how small they are? How miniscule compared to yours? Why would I have something so large created for one being?"

"So, you knew of our plan to hide in Aphya, and then you framed her for a genocide to get rid of all of us at once. Why would you do that?" Ivan asked.

"Of course I knew! There's nothing I don't know. I brought every single one of you into this world, and how did you repay me? You turned on me! You wanted a peaceful existence with no hostility or conflict, and that is exactly what I gave you. Did that make you happy? No! You wanted more! You wanted to make your own decisions after I had already given you *everything*!"

"I don't understand. Decisions about what?" Ivan asked.

"Your existence! You wanted to pick your own partners after I painstakingly designed you in perfect pairs capable of creating a thoroughly balanced social structure. I made artists who ruined their lives aspiring to be builders, and creators who desired to be engineers. You wanted to make your own rules, so you elected elders. At first, I thought it was adorable how independent you wanted to be."

A hint of a smile crossed Renata's face, then fell off into a dark scowl. "But then you still wanted more. How ridiculous and ungrateful every last one of you was, even after I let you have your way. You were insatiable, undisciplined, greedy little toddlers unable to be brought to heel by reasonable means. Who do you think you are, believing you know better than I?"

Ivan's eyes swept over the vast room filled floor to ceiling with containers. "Is that why you began imprisoning them?"

"I had no option left. Your infection had festered and spread until no one was content to live as I had envisioned. I have only been able to bring the most docile of you back into line—back to a perfect state of existence."

"By removing free will?" Ivan asked. He wanted to provoke her but was unsure how far he should push her.

"You hideous little creature. You stand there in judgment of me? I did them a kindness. Each of them has a lovely, perfect world of their own creation, free from strife."

Ivan's eye twitched, and he squeezed his lip for only a microsecond. The expression hadn't escaped Renata's notice. Her face stiffened, along with her posture.

"Are you accusing me of lying? How dare you after I made you such a generous offer to save yourself." Her voice was strained, cracking at the very hint of accusation in Ivan's unconscious expression.

"Our confinement isn't free from strife. It's quite the opposite, in fact. Many horrible things have happened in there," Ivan said.

"That is Aphya's fault. If she had resolved along with the rest of you, the confinement wouldn't have become contaminated with her rancid, diseased thoughts."

"You built the confinement. It isn't her fault she didn't resolve."

Renata ran her fingers along the edge of the orb. The stillness of her body as she touched their world unnerved Ivan. She spoke with her eyes fixated on it. "Which is why she needs to be eliminated from the equation. Then I can sanitize it and start over fresh. It's the only way left to ensure the rest of you have the lives you deserve." Her head snapped up at Ivan and her sterile eyes pierced through his flesh.

Ivan moved closer to the orb while also stepping back from Renata to create a buffer of distance. "If you are intent on sanitizing it no matter what we do, we will not help you eliminate Aphya."

Renata scoffed. "It's the reasonable choice. You won't carry your regret for long. Once I sanitize the confinement, you'll forget any of this happened. You can return to my side where you belong."

"We'll forget everything," Ivan said.

"Yes."

"We don't want to forget everything. We won't know what we mean to each other," Ivan said, rushing his words, portraying a pleading urgency he felt as discomfort overtook him. He felt an overwhelming urge to distance himself from her, to escape the suffocating weight of her presence.

"You silly child. It's already decided. None of this is about what you want. It's about what I want, and it's going to happen whether you want it to or not. Your only choice in the matter is between doing what I ask of you— and I'll allow you to remain in the confinement together—or refusing my request and forcing me to resolve each of you in separate confinements. Eliminating one of my own creations will cause me a tremendous amount of distress. If you force me to discharge Aphya myself, separating you after that betrayal would be the kindest way I could discipline you. You understand there must be consequences, don't you?"

Ivan felt the sting of her lies rising from his stomach, burning through his chest. Her scent was putrid as he realized she had something much worse planned for them. She wasn't distressed; she was content with her plans, verging on delight.

"You don't have to do this. You could seal us in. We would commit to never bothering you again."

Renata bellowed with laughter. "I've told you once already, this is not a negotiation. You will do as you are told, or you will suffer the consequences."

"We refuse to be used in that manner," Ivan said, disturbed by her coldness.

"You, were designed as a blunt tool to be used in pursuit of *my* goals. If you are unwilling to be utilized in that capacity, your existence is unnecessary."

Renata extended a hand to him, distorted with a rippling vibration. Ivan laid his hand on the orb, keeping his eyes on Renata.

"I'm afraid I can't let you back in there," she said.

She released an energy ripple at him, but it was too late. Ivan had pulled himself back inside the confinement, certain he had enraged her enough to give chase. It took only a second to exit the doorway. As he was passing through, he felt her enter.

CHAPTER THIRTY-FOUR

Ivan returned through the doorway, marked his current time, and shifted to his previous time marker. They had six weeks to pull everyone together. He was already certain the first week would produce little more than self-appointed gods comparing egos and telling glorified tales of past battles. He could only hope Ben had cobbled together the beginnings of a plan.

~~~~

On the eve of Renata's expected arrival at the border between The Nothing and The Everything, they staged their attack. The wait
~~~~

was excruciating as Ivan's concern grew. They had been there for hours before anyone from the Council showed up. The first to come was Kali, accompanied by Ares, to everyone's shock.

Good to see you, Kali, Ivan said. *Are your troops ready?*

Staged in the next galaxy over, as planned, Kali replied. *Everything set on your end?*

They'll be here on schedule, he answered.

Any of the others coming, Ares? Mikkel asked.

They're fighting over who's going to get credit for the effort. I'm sure they'll be along once the battle is over, Ares said, chortling at his own humor.

The next to come was Athena in her risen form with her clutch of birds in tow, accompanied by several of her lower-bound deities in ships. Zeus came a few minutes later with Hera and Hades. His army of craft uncloaked behind him in an ostentatious display.

Look who decided to make an appearance, Kali taunted. *Is this a battle or a show?*

At least I brought an army. Your people appear to have abandoned you. Have your alliances run dry, Kali? Zeus said, returning her banter.

I have already positioned my troops according to the battle plan. The one you apparently forgot to read.

Zeus bellowed a hearty laugh. *Hades! Stage the unit!* he commanded.

Hades, unable to resist a battle, zipped off with a flourish to perform his duties as instructed, while other deities continued to trickle in. Grace, Aphya, and Nyx accompanied Lilly's shuttle, which contained the confinement. Ben followed moments later.

Only a quarter of the expected forces had assembled when Renata's bright orb, red in the center and refracting to a light pink around the ebbing edges, came barreling in behind Ivan and Grace, launching an energy wave that propelled them into the sun.

Mikkel encased Lilly's shuttle and shifted her to relative safety on the far side of the galaxy. She could have done it herself, but he needed to give her extra protection since she held the only actual weapon they had against Renata—the confinement.

Did you think I wouldn't know how things worked in here? I've been in here for quite a while now. I had to find something to occupy my time while I waited for you to gather yourselves. Renata's voice surrounded them as matter flew at them from all sides.

Her ambush had left the others scattered and panicking. Ben spun to her left, launching an attack from her flank, but before the ripple could hit her, her orb pulsated and split, letting the charge pass between her two halves. She continued to split until she had him surrounded.

She began toying with him like a cat with a trapped rat while moving and shifting in and out to avoid the pulses being launched at her.

I've given you every opportunity to better yourselves, yet you continue to fight against me! she screamed into everyone's minds.

You imprisoned us for no reason, and now you want to destroy us. Did you think we wouldn't fight back? Ben asked.

I had every reason! You're in here because you all committed crimes against our society. Despite spending time here, you still have shown no improvement! Resolving you was supposed to remove your crude nature! Eliminating the worst of you was supposed to hone you into something better! It did nothing! Her voice boomed.

No one understood what she meant by her statement.

Your father was among the worst of you, she bellowed at Ben. *He craved power. He created vile creatures whose only purpose was war and conquest. You saw what he did to your own sons, and you did nothing to stop him! You are responsible for that, and you don't have a single ounce of remorse. By observing his actions and being fully aware of the harm he caused them, you are deserving of the repercussions you will face at my hand.*

My father was a great leader! Ben roared.

Your father was psychotic, and I enjoyed ending him. Do you think the Jur and their accomplices eliminated your people all on their own? Renata taunted Ben. *They may have been able to manage the commoners, but I was the one who dissipated their essences. I thought it would teach you that you needed to work together, but you only made things worse for yourselves. It only showed me you've learned nothing. You will never learn.*

We have come together! Look at the community we've built.

Renata's laughter echoed through Ben from all sides, vibrating his core. He struggled, jerking in all directions, attempting to escape her grip. He was powerless to break free from her grasp.

You have no idea what you've done. Some of you may have come together, but you've made enemies of everyone else. You're doing the same thing in here that you did out there. You've divided yourselves.

Renata dodged another barrage of pulses. Ben felt one of Renata's orbs pull loose and he launched a pulse at it. The orb lifted, avoiding the strike, and Renata slammed him with another ripple of charges.

What are you going to do now, Ben? You're such a sad little pathetic thing. You'll be much easier to dissipate than your father was, shed of your impenetrable shell. He took his defeat with so much decorum. You would have admired his sacrifice. He did it for you, after all. He gave himself over to me like a trusting little lamb when I told him I wouldn't hurt you. Oh, what a silly little man he was to think you, of all people, could change, she said, mocking him.

Her orbs vibrated around him, sending shock waves crashing to the center. He pulled up once again, still unable to escape. He attempted to shift but couldn't. Renata's laughter crashed in on him again as her orbs began spinning faster, closing in to encase him. Ben was locked in with no means of escape.

Nyx dove in to attack Renata's main orb from the outside, only to be flung into a fast, uncontrolled spin away from the fray. *I'll get to you soon enough, traitor!* Renata growled.

Now, where were we? Ah … yes, ending you. Her voice had an amused, singsong quality to it that made Ben want to kill her. *Like I was saying—it was so easy to goad those little trolls on the Council into attacking your world. A little paranoia here, a rumor there, a demolished colony or two. It was very entertaining to watch as their fear grew. I never thought I would feel so much glee in eliminating you tiny feral creatures when I once cared so much for you.*

Ben's orb began tearing at the edges. As he struggled to keep his form together, she continued to speak. *Once Valhalla and Fólkvangr were emptied and collapsed, the first thing I did was get rid of all the Valkyries,* she gloated. *Pesky little beasts actually gave me quite a bit of a fight. I actually admired them for their tenacity. They had much more than you, anyway,* she sneered.

She laughed as another strip of light ripped away from Ben. *Then all I had to do was sit back and wait for them to come to me, the same way you have here. I should thank you for making it so easy for me.*

Zeus fired an energy bolt straight into one of Renata's orbs, but it did no damage. The smaller orb glowed red for an instant before all her orbs became brighter.

Zeus, stop it. You're feeding her! Kali said. Negative, she said to herself. *Everyone! Reverse the polarity of your weapons if you can!* she shouted, frantically typing into her screen to make adjustments to her ship's pulse instrument.

Agreed! Thoth shouted, spinning around to his own weapons panel.

I don't have a negative charge! Ares yelled back.

Anyone who can't convert to negative pulses, get out! Go back to your planet and set your defenses! Thoth ordered.

I'm sorry, Thoth. I don't have it either, Zeus said. He and a full third of the ships that had made it to the staging area before Renata showed up turned to leave.

Renata sent a strong pulse outward from her cluster, destroying several ships and sending others reeling uncontrollably through space.

Aphya came speeding in from above, smashing into Ben's orb, knocking him out of a distracted Renata's clutches. Angered at being deprived of her target, she unleashed her final blow on Aphya's orb, rendering it dark. She flung the lifeless sphere away from her and re-formed into her original structure while Grace and Ivan made their way back to the battle. The entire scene had unfolded in less than three minutes.

Kali was the first to convert her weapon and fire. Renata's orb jerked back, revealing a darkened spot where it had been hit. She returned fire, but Kali's shields held and her ship flipped off into the distance, turning end over end. Although she was spinning out of control, she was relieved her theory was correct. The pulse had made its intended impact, giving them a slim chance to survive.

Grace and Ivan dove at Renata. Bolts of energy and sparks flew as they struggled, pulling and ripping at each other's essences. Pieces of light pulled away, dissolving into nothing. They left entire galaxies demolished in their wake, smashing into planets and sending moons spinning out of control. Grace could feel her strength draining. Renata was winning. She had extended tendrils into Grace and Ivan, siphoning energy from them, and they couldn't stop it. Try as they might, their force wasn't enough to pull away from her grasp. After all their preparation, they still didn't know how to fight against a being whose only objective was destruction.

Grace glanced at Aphya's darkened orb as Ami zipped in to collect it and immediately knew what she had to do. There was only one option left. She couldn't let anyone else give their life for her. Without warning, she ripped apart from Ivan, blasting him into the next universe, and gave herself over to Renata. She allowed her essence to be enveloped. She slid inside Renata's light, letting herself be fully absorbed. It was easier than Grace had thought, letting it all go this way. Once she had given in to it, there was no more struggle, no more anguish. It was peaceful, silently serene. Her mind calmed as she focused on the oneness of being nothing. Once Renata had absorbed all of Grace, her vengeance had no bounds. She had taken her prize and the others were inconsequential.

Renata's laughter bellowed through everyone as all motion halted on the battlefield. *Look at your leader now! She gave up. Everything you did for her and she was the one who gave up, leaving all of you behind.* Her taunting laughter roared again.

Now, there's nothing left to stop me! The words wafted into their minds with a cold shudder of dread. Renata began destroying vast swaths of all that lay in her wake, producing enormous energy ripples in all directions. Planets, suns, stars. Everything turned dead, black, and shriveled as she sucked their power dry. Galaxy after galaxy fell to her wrath, disintegrating back into particles. The entire confinement would fall under her rage until there was nothing left inside of it.

Ben was filled with the same defeat he felt when Asgard fell. He had no power to do anything but watch as the implosion of this place happened in front of him. How could they have ever imagined they could defeat her? She had taken out both Aphya and Grace within minutes. What hope could the rest of them have? Suddenly, Renata came to an abrupt halt and turned back toward a stunned Ben and Nyx as Ivan appeared by their side.

Renata's form began to pulse and shudder, bouncing randomly left and right. Thin trickles of green and white light were coming through her own light red, blending into a muddy brown. Strands of light began swirling under hers, burning slow smoldering holes in her essence. Renata struggled against Grace ravaging her from the inside. Renata howled as she tried to rip Grace out, expel her, extinguish her, but there was nothing she could do. Grace hadn't been absorbed; she had embedded herself inside of Renata, burning hotter and brighter than a thousand suns, pouring through Renata's translucence, thinning her from her core. The holes expanded, burning away to nothing at the edges.

Ben, Nyx, Ivan, and the few others who remained resumed their attack, launching negative energy waves at her. As much as they feared what would happen to Grace, they couldn't let her sacrifice be wasted. Mikkel and Lilly held their position, watching for an opening to move in. Huge, rhythmically pulsating explosions began widening the voids in Renata's orb further. Grace was winning. They were winning. Everyone could feel Renata's consciousness diminishing. Mikkel feared they would need to advance soon, whether his mother managed to clear herself from Renata or not. She would want Renata contained, no matter the cost to herself. With one final quaking explosion from Grace, Renata's essence was reduced to a tiny dim shadow of what it had been.

Mikkel instantly appeared, dropping the camouflage that had been hiding them, pushing Lilly's capsule toward the offending entity. Lilly was shaking as her hand reached for the control panel. She concentrated on the display she was using to deploy the confinement and maneuver it close to the remnant of Renata's essence. The shield around the confinement opened on the side closest to the small, dark reddish-brown orb, producing a thin stream of light that pulled it inside.

Ivan, Nyx, and Ben were mentally exhausted from the battle. It was over. They had won. At least they thought they had won, until they couldn't see Grace after the debris from the explosion cleared out. They could still feel her. She was all around them. She was everywhere.

Ivan became distraught, zipping around, disappearing and reappearing as he searched the vicinity for her. Grace had intentionally shattered herself into particles to diminish Renata's essence without dissipating her.

Grace's essence had been strewn into oblivion. It was everywhere. She was no longer inside of The Everything. It felt to Ivan that she had become part of The Everything.

Ivan sped toward Lilly's shuttle, grabbing the confinement away from the tractor beam. He encased it, probing for any sign that Grace had been trapped inside with Renata, but there was none.

Ivan continued his movement away from the others. He was in shock from the events. She couldn't be gone if he still felt connected to her, could she? It was the same feeling he had had when she was on The Outside; he felt her everywhere, in every atom surrounding him.

He slowly made his way across The Everything and into The Nothing, without realizing what he was doing until he found himself in the doorway. Numbness had overtaken him and he wasn't sure why he had come here. Ivan did not know how much time had passed when the doorway spread open in front of him. A thin beam of light poured out, pulling at him, extracting him from the doorway.

As he raised himself from the cold stone floor, his eyes met a small group of wide-eyed young people. Bewilderment permeated his mind as he scanned the room. Smaller children were surrounded by a much larger group appearing to be in their early twenties. All were silent, staring at him standing in front of the confinement.

"Is she gone?" one of the young women asked.

Ivan opened his mouth to speak but found himself rendered mute. He didn't know how to answer or what they were asking him. Ivan felt an onslaught of emotion assailing him. Intense, raw anguish, grief, and, most notably, despair. They were feelings this world had lacked the last time he was here. Commingled with his own feelings, it was paralyzing for him.

Seeing the distress painted across Ivan's face, a woman stepped forward, taking Ivan's hand. Her touch was warm and calming, pulling his focus toward her.

"Renata? Is Renata gone?" the woman asked again.

Ivan could only nod as a wave of relief surged over the people who had crowded into the room. He held up the small confinement in which Lilly had trapped Renata and handed it to the young woman, who nodded in understanding.

"And Aphya?" the woman whispered reverently.

Ivan shrugged, not aware of her sacrifice or fate.

Some of those gathered cried silently, some of them gasped quietly. None of them cheered over their newly acquired freedom or spoke about their despair. The pervasive mood was somber.

The woman looked at Ivan with sympathy and asked, "And your Grace? Do you know if your Grace is gone?"

He didn't know how to answer. His eyes dropped, and he pulled his hands away, staring at them while shaking and trying to speak. When he finally managed, it came out as a distraught whisper. "I can still feel her."

The woman's face released its strained features while her posture relaxed. A small smile crossed her lips, although sadness still reflected in her eyes.

"It's time for you to go back. You've been here too long," she said softly, laying her hand on his arm.

"I need to see the Elders. I need to know what will happen to us. What will happen to my people?" Ivan's voice cracked and quivered as he spoke.

The woman was tender as her hand lingered on Ivan's arm. She met Ivan's eyes and said gently, "We are the Elders. We are grateful for what you have done. Someone will come to you soon, but for now, you need to go back to your people. You need to give them hope."

Ivan nodded and let her guide him back into the confinement. When he emerged on the other side, he found that she had deposited him back into his original time. He made his way to Rasa, slipping into his shell. When his eyes opened, the first thing he saw was Grace's empty shell beside him, and he broke, falling to his knees and sobbing into her lap.

CHAPTER THIRTY-FIVE

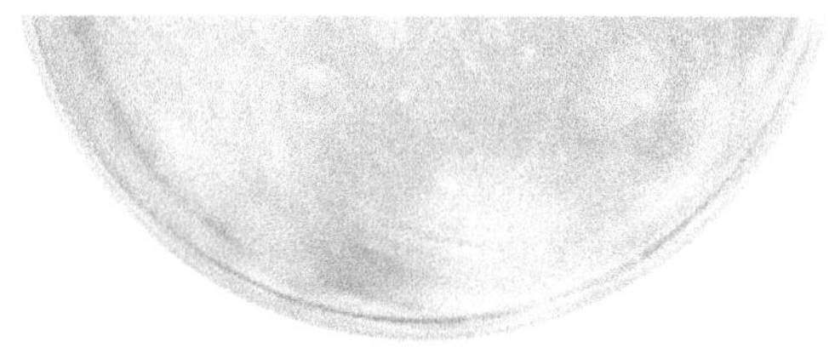

Lilly sat alone in her bedroom, staring at a blank screen with a blinking cursor taunting her to inscribe a sentiment that would make sense to anyone who found it. Everyone had done their part, and now it was up to her to make sure those sacrifices hadn't been in vain. She had never felt the need to hold on to things from her past, but this time it hurt. This time she had people she wanted to remember. This time, she had people who loved her. Is this how she felt when she inscribed those calculations on the wall so long ago?

Grace was gone, but it didn't feel like they had lost her completely—only her physical presence was missing. Maybe they were all fooling themselves because Ivan was still here, and his energy signature was identical to hers. Aphya was gone too, but Lilly didn't know her well enough to care about her, nor did she suspect anyone had, aside from Nyx. What a sad, lonely life that must have been for her, Lilly thought.

When she had her fill of torment from not being able to transcribe her feelings into words, she dragged herself across the hall to Mikkel's room. His door was closed, but not locked. She opened it slowly and stood at the side of his bed, where he lay awake with his face buried deep in a pillow, ignoring her.

"Teach me to rise," Lilly said. Her upcoming task would be easier if she could rise, but she didn't need to in order to go back to the cave one last time. She only wanted to spend her final hours with the people she cared about.

"I don't feel like it," Mikkel replied without lifting his face out of the pillow.

Lilly climbed on the bed and laid her head in the middle of his back. "I'm sorry, Mikkel."

"Everyone's sorry." He hadn't snapped at her, but the words still sounded harsh.

Lilly felt his back sag as all the air left his lungs. She could feel how deeply he was hurting over his loss. The stench of his sorrow bled through his pores overwhelming her nose. It was a scent permeating the entire community since the day of their battle. While the Council was celebrating it as a win, the turned only felt the loss. She deeply regretted that the action she was about to take was going to cause more suffering.

"Are you going to the remembrance ceremony?" she asked, feeling his deep sigh rising then lowering her head from its resting place.

"I don't have a choice."

Normally, she would say something sarcastic, like "everyone has a choice," but this time she left it alone and simply nodded her head against his back.

"I know better than to ask if you're going," Mikkel said.

Normally, she wouldn't. She'd always observed a no matings, no weddings, no funerals policy. She never liked being anywhere the celebrant was the object of attention while seldom receiving the experience they wanted from it. It was one thing to be surrounded by close friends and family, but events like the ones she abhorred were usually filled with extensions of family members who you couldn't stand or acquaintances you barely knew. She hated events that brought false platitudes or people who gleefully stood by, hoping to witness a failure they could gossip about with their shallow group of frenemies later.

But today's event would be different. Everyone in attendance would be working through their own sense of loss, because so many had been lost.

"I can go if you want me to," Lilly said, twisting her neck to see the back of his head.

Mikkel moved the pillow to look at her with those deep green eyes he had inherited from his mother, giving Lilly another twinge of sorrow. "I'd appreciate that. Ivan will too."

She sighed and turned her head back to stare up at the ceiling.

~~~~

Lilly stood on the barren planet with the familiar cave entrance staring at her like a hungry, toothless beast ready to swallow her whole. Her chest felt tight, and her body trembled, but she couldn't tell whether it was from fear or the lack of oxygen in the newly formed atmosphere. The turned didn't need much oxygen, so either this planet had less than the amount contained in liquid water, or her inability to control her body was based in dread. She activated her uniform to eliminate the air deficit. It also gave her comfort, for which she was desperate.

"Here goes nothing."

A few steps inside the cave, she realized how dark it was without the luminescent algae and glowing worms. She was fortunate to have her night vision sight range to rely on. Since the planet had not yet been infused with life, there were no jagged formations, nor the hindrance of a muddy floor, leaving her trek inside easy and unremarkable.

When she entered the cell portion of the cave, it was just as she had suspected. The calculations were there, but the wall that had contained
~~~~

the etchings was blank. The walls seemed calm, with the nanite-infused liquified gas slowly ebbing under the surface. She opened the top flap of her backpack, revealing a print of the photo Ophelia had taken for her the last time Lilly was in this space. Lilly's eyes examined every detail of the surface, making note of where her lines would need to start and stop to be contained within the curved expanse in front of her.

She placed her pack on the floor, needing to extract her tools and collapsible stool, but she couldn't get the zipper open. When she looked down, she could see something sticking out of the track that she couldn't pick out with her gloves on. As she pulled off one of her gloves, the motion behind the glassy surface in front of her became excited, gathering toward the edge where she was kneeling. She moved her hand up and the swarm followed. She then moved her gloved hand close to the surface but received no reaction. Moving them both back and forth, she realized the nanites in her uniform were protecting her. Did they see the foreign ones behind the barrier as an enemy to protect the wearer from?

With her newfound infusion of hope that she may actually come through this unresolved, Lilly moved at top speed to complete her task.

An hour into scratching the intricate design onto the surface, her face and hands began to tingle. Her vision blurred as her breathing became more labored. Her oxygen had long since expired. Were these symptoms of a brain deprived of that essential molecule for too long, or had the resolving nanites made their way inside her protective uniform after enduring such a long exposure?

She had almost finished when she tapped the side of her head to deactivate the visor, hoping to alleviate the burning in her lungs with at least the minimal amount of oxygen offered by this planet. To her distress, the visor didn't open. She tried to physically rip it off her face, to no avail. It was stuck in place. All she could do was push through and hope she could finish and get outside before she passed out. The lack of air wouldn't kill her, but it would take external intervention to bring her out of a comatose state from suffocation. It was only now she wished she had been able to write that note letting someone know where she had gone.

An agonizing amount of time passed with slow motion and blurred lines. She leaned over to place her final mark on the piece. When she rose, the blood rushed from her head, nearly causing her to pass out. Lilly staggered to her pack and stuffed her tools back inside. Without taking time to close the flaps, she fell to her knees and crawled to the opening of the cell, dragging the bag behind her. Once out of the cell, surrounded by the narrow cave walls, she pulled herself to her feet. The only things keeping her upright were the stone to her sides and the desperate need to get out.

Every few feet, she would vainly attempt to open her visor or shift away. When the cave walls widened, she could no longer support herself and she collapsed to the floor. Lilly could see the bright light of the entrance, but her body had given up before she could will herself over that last barrier that would allow her escape. When she was unable to move any further, she sent her final thought out into the universe. It was simply: *Help me.*

Lilly's blurred vision cleared to reveal a gray room with a pair of the most unique green eyes looking down at her.

~~~~

Out of the darkness, a light clicking of hard soles echoed against a stone floor. A cloaked woman came to a stop in front of a marble altar. She produced a small ball of dim light from her oversized sleeve and gently placed it into a long, clear receptacle on top of the slab before turning to leave. Her head lifted upward as she watched tiny bits of bright dust being drawn through the walls and windows into the orb. As she strode toward the door, an errant streak of light shone under her hood,
~~~~

revealing her to be the same woman who had spoken to Ivan in front of the confinement.

She continued out into the hallway, locking the door to the small chamber behind her. The woman scanned the empty corridor to make sure no one was hiding in the darkness. She placed her hand on the door, melting it into the wall before disappearing.

When she arrived back at her chambers, a young man was sitting in a dark corner of her room. It hadn't surprised her he would wait for her.

"Is it really her?" His voice was quiet.

She nodded slowly, sadness and pain pulling down at her features. "She's dim." The woman's voice trembled.

The man sighed with relief as he dropped his head into his hands.

ALSO BY

JOYCE SERRANO

THE TURNED GODS SERIES

Original Grace - Book 1
Immortals in the Everything - Book 2
Gateway to The Nothing - Book 3

THE TURNED GODS - CHARACTER COMPANION SERIES

Galin's Alley
Lilly's Game
Alex's Claim